Scared Stiff

Annelise Ryan

KENSINGTON BOOKS
http://www.kensingtonbooks.com

KENSINGTON BOOKS are published by

Kensington Publishing Corp.
119 West 40th Street
New York, NY 10018

All Kensington titles, imprints and distributed lines are available at special quantity discounts for bulk purchases for sales promotion, premiums, fund-raising, educational or institutional use.

Special book excerpts or customized printings can also be created to fit specific needs. For details, write or phone the office of the Kensington Special Sales Manager: Kensington Publishing Corp., 119 West 40th Street, New York, NY 10018. Attn. Special Sales Department. Phone: 1-800-221-2647.

Kensington and the K logo Reg. U.S. Pat. & TM Off.

Library of Congress Control Number: 2010927977
ISBN-13: 978-0-7582-3454-4
ISBN-10: 0-7582-3454-6

First Hardcover Printing: September 2010
10 9 8 7 6 5 4 3 2 1

Printed in the United States of America

This one is for Mom.

Acknowledgments

I have been truly blessed with both the best agent in the world, Jamie Brenner, and the best editor in the world, Peter Senftleben. You guys keep me focused and encouraged, and make this journey so much fun. Here's to a long and exciting road ahead.

And once again I want to extend a hearty thanks to all the family, friends, and coworkers who make me laugh with such regularity because it's what keeps me going. I strive every day to return the favor and hope this book will be some small part of that.

Chapter
I

Despite the fact that I hang around dead bodies a lot these days, I find the scene before me very disturbing. The backdrop is ordinary enough: a well-maintained, ranch-style suburban home set on a generous plot of land near the edge of town. But any sense of normalcy ends with the front yard, which is littered with dead bodies. Fortunately, only one of the bodies is real, though I suppose it's not so fortunate for the victim in question, who I've been told has been murdered.

As if the body farm isn't surreal enough, my clothing adds to the absurdity, I'm wearing a full-skirted, white ballroom dress with puffy sleeves that make my shoulders look wider than a linebacker's. Clipped to the bodice is my ID badge, which bears my name, Mattie Winston, and my title, Deputy Coroner. Though I'm still kind of new at this dead body stuff, I'm pretty sure my outfit isn't the sort of couture one would normally wear to a crime scene. But then, who knows? I don't think there's a designer who has tackled this particular niche. I can see possibilities though: shirts and pants with chalk outlines drawn on them, sexy, peek-a-boo blouses with strategically placed bullet holes and knife tears, and, of course, lots of bloodred colored material.

In spite of the macabre scene and thoughts, in a perverse sort of way I'm happy to be here. Five minutes ago I was at a Halloween costume party being bored to tears by "William-not-Bill," an obsessive-compulsive, germaphobic accountant in a Dracula costume. He is a date my friend Izzy fixed me up with, making me wonder what horrible thing I've done to Izzy to earn such retribution. After less than an hour in William-not-Bill's company, listening to him give me a paranoid's primer on how many infectious ways there are to die, I was trying desperately to come up with a plausible plan of escape. Fortunately my beeper chirped and saved me. My relief was countered by a smidgen of guilt when I remembered that work for me meant someone else was dead, but probably not as dead as the date I was on. It was stone-cold, bones-only, well-beyond-the-putrid-stage dead.

I tried not to look too relieved at my reprieve as I snatched my beeper up from the table and gave William-not-Bill an apologetic smile. "Duty calls," I said, feigning disappointment. "I'm afraid we'll have to make it an early night."

William-not-Bill frowned and said, "Darn it. Are you sure you need to go?"

I'd never been so sure of anything in my entire life. "I'm afraid so," I told him.

"I'd really like to see you again. Can I give you a call sometime?"

I would have rather stabbed myself blind with a dull fork and was tempted to say so when Izzy, who is only five feet tall and dressed tonight as the Keebler elf, tapped me on the shoulder.

Aside from being my date rescue, Izzy is my neighbor, my landlord, and my boss. He is also the anti-me: dark where I'm light, short where I'm tall, and male to my female. We do have three things in common however: fat-hoarding metabolisms, fondness for men, and jobs that require the removal of human organs. Izzy removes organs because he's the county's medical examiner. I used to remove organs, or at least assist in the process, inside a hospital operating room, which is where my soon-to-be ex-husband, David, works as a surgeon. But after catching a coworker named Karen Owenby playing with a certain private organ on David, I ditched both him and the job. Now I work with

Izzy in the ME's office, and while I still assist with organ removal, the goods aren't as fresh as they used to be.

"Mattie? You ready?" Izzy asked as William-not-Bill pouted like a child.

"Absolutely." I got up from the table and beat a hasty exit—not an easy task given the wide girth of my gown, the two-foot wand I was carrying, and the crown that kept sliding off my head. I left Izzy, whose legs are only a third the length of mine, behind in my wake, along with several broken drink glasses my skirt knocked from tables as I passed. By the time Izzy caught up to me I was standing next to his car in the parking lot, tapping my foot impatiently.

"What's the rush?" he asked. "Afraid a house might drop on you?"

"I'm Glinda, the *good* witch," I reminded him. "Houses don't fall on Glinda."

"Then why the big hurry? I haven't seen you run that fast for anything other than ice cream in a long time."

"Very funny," I said, giving him a dirty look. "I didn't want to give Dracula a chance to ask for my number again. Though I have to admit his costume was perfect. He spent our time together sucking the life out of me." I shook my head woefully. "I can't believe I let you talk me into dating that bozo. He has a comb-over, for Christ's sake. His only saving grace is that he's tall." This is actually an important asset for me. I hit the six-foot mark at the age of sixteen, which made me a good foot taller than all of the boys for most of my high school years. That, combined with my ample bosom, made me very popular during the slow songs at school dances.

Izzy opened his door, got in the car, and reached over to unlock my side. The car is a fully restored Impala from the sixties. No such thing as automatic locks. Unfortunately, there are no bucket seats either, which means I have to pretzel six feet of me into the same amount of space Izzy uses.

I ripped the crown from my head and threw it and my wand into the back seat. Then I tried unsuccessfully to stuff the skirt of my gown down around me. As we pulled out of the parking lot, I imagined it must look like a giant puff ball was sitting in the passenger seat.

"Give William a break," Izzy said as I spat taffeta. "So he's got a touch of OCD. What's the big deal? It's his attention to detail that makes him such an ace accountant."

"A *touch* of OCD? I'll have you know he shot his cuffs at least fifty times, straightened the tablecloth a dozen times, and counted how many people were at the party every ten minutes. I can't guess how many times he cleaned all the silverware at the table. And don't even get me started on the fangs."

Izzy conceded with a sigh. "Okay, maybe he's a little anal retentive."

"Doubt it," I snapped back. "He's got his head so far up his ass there isn't room there for anything else. And just how old is he, anyway?"

"Late forties, maybe early fifties."

"That's a bit of a spread, don't you think? He's got to be at least fifteen years older than me."

"I'm twelve years older than Dom."

"That's different. You're gay."

"What's that got to do with it?" Izzy laughed. "Besides, it's not like you were looking for a serious date. You just wanted someone to tote along to make Hurley jealous."

This was true. Steve Hurley is a tall, dark, and blissfully blue-eyed homicide detective that I've known for all of three weeks, ever since I became Izzy's assistant. For me it was lust at first sight, which unfortunately occurred over Karen Owenby's freshly murdered body. Things kind of went downhill from there, particularly after I became a suspect in the case.

"Clearly it was a wasted effort," I pouted.

"Hey, it's not my fault Hurley didn't show up at the party."

With that one sentence, Izzy shot straight to the heart of my misery. I sulked for the remainder of the journey, which was all of three minutes since Sorenson isn't a very big town. When we arrived at our destination, I unfolded myself from Izzy's car like a performer in Cirque du Soleil and stood a moment to let the blood flow back into my legs. Then I reached into the back seat and took out my processing kit.

That's how I ended up here on the edges of suburbia, surrounded by bodies on a Saturday night, dressed like a white witch carrying a large tackle box.

Chapter
2

Izzy and I pause long enough to don gloves and shoe covers. With that done, he grabs his camera while I take out the digital recorder he gave me a couple of weeks ago for documenting scene observations. I turn the recorder on and put it in voice activation mode. After trying to find a place on my outfit to clip it, I settle for sticking it down inside my cleavage, or what a boy in my high school geography class once dubbed the "hot-and-gentle divide."

Despite the darkness outside, the yard is brightly lit thanks to Halloween spotlights and the flashing bars atop the cop cars parked in the driveway. At the foot of a huge oak tree off to my right, a man sits strapped into a large wooden chair. On his head is something that looks like an old-fashioned electrocution helmet. Nailed to the tree a foot above his head is a large board that has the words ON and OFF painted on it with a fork-shaped lever clearly placed in the ON position. Wires are running from the lever to the helmet and the clothes on the man appear to be singed.

On closer inspection I see that the helmet is actually a metal mixing bowl turned upside down and the handle on the board is made out of tin foil, but the effect is realistic enough to make me shiver.

On the opposite side of the tree is another body, this one hanging from a thick rope, its face painted a ghastly blue, the body swinging slightly in the night breeze. A third body is half buried in a makeshift grave, its hands and feet protruding from the freshly turned soil. At its head is a gravestone that bears the inscription: WHO TURNED OUT THE LIGHTS?

Four more bodies are strewn about, all of them wearing blood-soaked clothes. One has a large butcher knife protruding from its chest; another has its head lying a conspicuous distance from its body. The third one is missing its arms and legs, though they are lying nearby, and the fourth one is splayed halfway down the steps of the front porch, a glistening trail of blood marking its journey from the front door.

This last body is the one I zero in on since there is a trio of police officers—two in uniform, one in plainclothes—grouped around it. I know most of the cops in town either because they're Sorenson lifers like me, or because we became acquainted years ago when I worked in the ER. I even dated one of them briefly, a sweet guy named Larry Johnson who is the plainclothes officer in tonight's group. I never felt any reciprocal attraction to Larry, but if I had it would have died some time ago when he came into the hospital for hemorrhoid surgery. I was the scrub nurse on the case, and the sight of Larry's jingleberries hanging above his dingleberries would have put a definite damper on future intimacies.

One of the uniforms in tonight's group is a guy named Al who I've known for a decade or so, but the second uniform is new to me, and he looks like he's twelve. The one face conspicuously absent from the group is Steve Hurley's.

"Hey, where are Sleepy, Sneezy, and Dopey?" Larry yells as Izzy and I approach. Al and the new guy snigger. I realize they have misinterpreted our costumes, mistaking me for Snow White and Izzy for one of my dwarfs.

"I don't know," I say, setting down my scene kit and glancing around the yard. "Where are the real cops?"

"Ouch," says Larry as the other two groan. "Okay, truce."

I turn my attention to the body on the stairs and wrinkle my nose. There is a faint odor in the air, one that tells me this body has been here a while. The weather over the past week or so has been uncharacteristically warm for late October in Wisconsin, with temperatures in the high seventies during the day and the low sixties at night. Normally we'd expect highs in the fifties with frost or snow warnings at night, but this year October decided to go out on a high note. This last gasp of summer proved a delightful treat here in a state where snowblowers are considered a necessity five months out of the year, but it also allowed putrefaction to set in a little sooner than it otherwise would have.

"Do you know who she is?" Izzy asks, using his camera to shoot pictures and video of both the body and our immediate surroundings.

"We're pretty certain it's Shannon Tolliver," Larry says.

One of the advantages of living in a small town is that eventually you get to know almost everyone, if not by name, then at least by face. Here the six degrees of separation are often narrowed down to one or two. I'm at a slight disadvantage because of my last job. Even though working as a nurse in the operating room of the town's hospital allowed me to cross paths with a lot of people, most of them were draped, gowned, bonneted, and drugged into oblivion. As a result, I'm quicker to recognize some people by their navels or knees as opposed to their faces.

Tonight's victim is someone I do know by face, though it's hard to be sure it's her. The body is lying on its back with the feet at the top of the stairs and the head at the bottom. Gravity has done its job. What little blood is left in the body has settled in the head and face, causing gross discoloration and swelling.

"Who found her?" I ask.

Al says, "A couple of trick-or-treaters who got the scare of their life when their parents drove them to this house. The parents rounded the kids up and then called it in on a cell phone."

I grimace. Kids traipsing near our corpse and running hell-bent through the yard means contamination of our scene.

I note two holes in Shannon's torso that appear to be bullet entry wounds, both of them surrounded by the blood-soaked cloth of her blouse. Years of working as a nurse have gifted me with the rather dubious talent of being able to estimate blood loss with a reasonable degree of accuracy. A quick estimate of the dried pool beneath Shannon's body and the trail leading back from it to the house tells me there's a good chance she bled to death.

Squealing wheels sound behind us and, as I turn to see a familiar black car pull up, my heart quickens and a different kind of shiver goes through me.

Hurley.

He parks right behind one of the spotlights, forcing me to squint as I search eagerly for his long-legged stride. But something is wrong. The silhouette I see has two heads and way too many arms. For a second I think it must be Hurley's Halloween costume, but it turns out to be something much scarier. It's Hurley walking side by side with Alison Miller.

I feel a pang of jealousy and mutter a curse under my breath. Alison Miller, a photographer and reporter for the biweekly *Sorenson Journal,* used to be my friend. We went to high school together, and while we never hung out much, we maintained a cordial, if distant, relationship. Our current status is a bit more strained, thanks to her attempts to print a picture of me barechested on the front page of the paper a couple weeks ago, and the fact that she has suddenly become the main obstacle between me and Detective Hurley, assuming, of course, that Hurley has forgotten about that unfortunate incident when I barfed on his shoes.

It isn't just the sight of them together that bothers me. I knew they had plans to attend a Halloween party tonight—the same party Izzy and I just left—because I was there a week ago when Alison all but threw herself at Hurley and demanded that he take her. What bothers me is the fact that they never made it to the party but are still together. What were they doing while I sat letting Dracula turn me into one of the undead?

Both of them are in costume: Alison looks disturbingly cute dressed as a genie, and Hurley, rather unimaginatively, is dressed like an Eliot Ness–era FBI agent, though the hat does give him a sexy, debonair, I-want-to-bite-your-lip quality. I give their outfits a quick once-over searching for signs of disarray or a fresh-out-of-the-sack look, but don't find any. It's a mild reassurance at best, and any relief I might feel vanishes when I see the smug expression on Alison's face.

Her camera is slung around her neck and she is holding it with one hand, prepared to take a quick snap if something worthy should present itself. Even in high school Alison always had her camera close by and ready. It earned her the nickname Snapper, a moniker that always made all the boys snigger. Nowadays she's a freelance reporter/photographer and the primary photo source for our local paper, so a camera is still as ubiquitous an accessory as ever. I briefly wonder if she sleeps with it, but as soon as the thought hits my mind, I flash on an image of Hurley naked in bed with her, and my face grows uncomfortably hot.

"Hi, everyone," Alison says with a perky little wave of her hand. She eyes me and Izzy and says, "How cute. Snow White and Doc. What a clever idea."

Before I can correct her she has raised her camera, snapped a shot, and blinded me with her flash.

"No pictures unless I say so," Hurley grumbles, and I am instantly grateful for his reprimand. I smile in his general direction and blink hard several times, trying to get my vision back. Then I realize I probably look like I'm batting my eyes at him and stop.

"Not to worry," Alison says. "That was just a fun picture for Mattie and Izzy. Nothing official."

I can see the vague outlines of everyone as my eyes struggle to adjust to the dark, and it seems they are all looking at Shannon again. So I focus my own gaze in the same direction.

"What do we have?" Hurley asks.

Izzy says, "Mattie, do you want to take this one?"

Oh, goody, a chance to impress Hurley! I nod solemnly to hide my delight. Since I can't see very clearly, I try to remember what I'd noted earlier as I start to speak.

"The victim's tentative ID is Shannon Tolliver, a thirty-something female and the resident of this house. It appears she was shot at least twice, once in the chest and once in the upper abdominal area. Given the location of the wounds and the amount of blood beneath the body, I'd guess one or both of the bullets pierced the liver or aorta and she quickly bled out."

"Any guess as to time of death?" Hurley asks.

I'm still half-blind so as I move closer to the body to check for the presence of livor mortis and rigor mortis, I fail to see the bottommost step to the porch. My toe rams into the riser and my upper body continues its forward motion as my feet stop dead in their tracks. I feel myself falling and pinwheel my arms in a desperate effort to regain some balance, but the laws of physics are against me. I'm bracing for a collision with the hard wooden stairs when a strong arm wraps around my waist and pulls me back.

"Careful there," Hurley says, his breath warm in my ear.

I'm momentarily in heaven as I feel the length of my backside come into contact with Hurley's front side, but my rapture evaporates with his next words.

"Christ, you're like a bull in a china shop."

Hurley's arm uncoils itself from my waist and I miss its warmth immediately even though my face is burning hot enough to start a fire. My vision is almost back to normal and I can see Izzy shaking his head. He steps up and takes over the examination, leaving me to stand where I am, trying not to look as stupid as I feel.

A few seconds later I step forward more carefully and kneel on the other side of the body, taking care to shove the bulk of my gown between my legs so I don't contaminate the blood pools.

Together we begin our examination, looking for any gross trace evidence on the surface of the body before we touch or move anything. There are several stray hairs stuck in the congealed blood surrounding her wounds but their long length and blond color makes me suspect they are Shannon's own. I pick them up one at a time and place each in its own evidence envelope, sealing and labeling the specimens as I go.

Shannon's left arm is beneath her body, hiding that hand from view, so examination of that will have to wait until we move her. But on her right hand, which is flung out in front of her, I notice that the knuckles appear raw and abraded. I wonder if she incurred this injury in her crawl and fall down the stairs, or if she managed to deliver a blow to her attacker during a struggle. If the latter, I know there might be valuable evidence there so I carefully place a paper bag over the hand, securing it with evidence tape. In doing so, I notice her arm is stiff. Izzy notes the same thing in both of her legs.

"None of the lividity blanches and it appears she is in full rigor," he announces.

Eager to redeem myself in front of everybody, I jump in and say, "Given the outside temperatures we've had, that means she's likely been dead for somewhere between twelve and thirty-six hours."

Izzy nods approvingly and says, "That is correct."

I hear Alison mutter a little *hmph* behind me and can't help but smile. But then she says, "Twelve to thirty-six? Is that the best you can do? That's a twenty-four-hour window of time."

My initial impulse is to leap across Shannon's body, grab Alison by the throat, and throttle her. But before I can, Izzy jumps in.

"It appears there is the start of some putrefaction here," he says, pointing to a faint greenish patch of skin on the lower right side of Shannon's swollen abdomen, just above the waistband of her pants. "That helps us narrow things down a little more. Odds are she's been dead for around twenty-four hours, give or take a few. Here in the field, that's the closest prediction I can make, but once we get the body to the morgue and do some further analyses, we might be able to pinpoint the time of death more precisely."

I glance at my watch, see that it's just past eight-thirty in the evening, and do a quick mental calculation. "So time of death for now is likely sometime yesterday evening." I pause and glance around, suppressing a shiver when I realize Shannon's body lay out here all day long with no one noticing. It saddens me to think how hard she worked to decorate her lawn for Halloween, not knowing she would soon become a part of her own gruesome diorama.

After unfolding a white plastic sheet and carefully placing it over the body to preserve any surface evidence we might have missed, Izzy and I turn Shannon's body on its side to examine her back. There is a slight sucking sound as her body separates from the large pool of congealed blood beneath her and that, combined with the wafting scent of rot and decay, makes my stomach lurch.

Izzy examines Shannon's back and announces, "It's hard to be sure with all the blood but I don't see any exit wounds. So hopefully we'll have some ballistic evidence once I do her post."

Hurley is scratching down notes in a small spiral-bound notebook as we ease the body back into its original position, first making sure to tuck the plastic wrap sheet in place. With that done, Izzy and I secure the wrap, completely enclosing the body. Then we stand, remove our bloodied gloves, don new ones, and start taking in the rest of the murder scene.

I study the blood trail leading from the body to the porch and from there into the house. "It doesn't make much sense for the killer to have dragged her outside where she might be found sooner," I surmise. "And the amount of blood in this trail suggests she was alive until she got to the stairs. So I'm guessing she was shot somewhere inside the house and managed to drag herself out here."

Izzy says, "I agree."

"But why?" I pose. "Why come out here rather than phone for help from the house?"

Hurley rewards me with a smile that makes Alison's pout deepen. "Excellent question," he says. "Let's go inside and find out."

Chapter
3

It turns out a white ball gown isn't the best thing to wear to the scene of a bloody homicide. Despite my efforts, the hem of my skirt is spotted with blood and dirt. That means incurring a hefty dry cleaning bill before I can return it to our office receptionist, Cass Zigler, who let me borrow it from the wardrobe cache her thespian group owns. In order to avoid any further contamination of either the dress—which is actually two pieces, a skirt and a bodice—or the evidence, I slip on a pair of scrub pants from the stash Izzy maintains in the trunk of his car and remove my skirt.

Izzy, Larry, Alison, and I follow Hurley along the edges of the blood trail into the house, Izzy marking our progress with his camera. Alison really has no business being with us but I suspect Hurley is letting her come along because he doesn't trust her not to sneak a few pictures if left outside with the body.

We're only a few feet down the hallway when Izzy asks me, "How well did you know Shannon?"

The question makes Hurley stop and turn to look at me, bringing our human train to a halt. No doubt he's wondering if I will need to be recused from this investigation the way I was from Karen Owenby's. In the latter case I had to step aside not only because I knew the victim, but because she'd been having an affair with my husband, a fact that put me high on the list of suspects. This time I should be in the clear.

"Only casually," I assure everyone.

Larry pipes up. "A lot of people know Shannon. She's a waitress over at Dairy Airs."

Dairy Airs is an ironically named restaurant in town run by a family who owns a dairy farm. The menu is filled with fattening and delicious foods like fried cheese curds, cream puffs, cheesecakes, and my personal favorite, ice cream. The name, though cute, is an apt one since the place has made significant contributions to many of the derrieres in town, my own included. With all the wonderfully fattening delights the place has to offer, it's amazing to me that Shannon is so slender. If I worked there, I'd be big as a house in no time.

"To be honest," I say, "I know Shannon's husband, Erik, better than her. He's a radiology tech at the hospital."

Hurley frowns. "She's married? Where's the husband? Did he call this in?"

Larry repeats the trick-or-treater story, stating that the kids who found Shannon's body have since gone home with their parents. "We talked to them and they were pretty traumatized but I don't think they saw anything of consequence. She'd been dead a while by the time they found her. As for the husband, we're not sure where he is."

"He doesn't live here anymore," I tell Hurley. "He and Shannon split up three or four months ago. Did you try the hospital?" I ask Larry.

"We did. He's not there."

"Any scuttlebutt on why they split?" Hurley asks me.

I shrug. "I don't know. Erik never said anything other than that he'd moved out, but there were lots of rumors flying around the hospital when it first happened."

"What sorts of rumors?" Hurley asks, his blue eyes narrowing.

"The usual suspects," I tell him. "That Erik is gay, that one of them wanted kids and the other didn't, that he had an affair, that she had an affair."

Hurley stares at me a moment and his gaze is so intense it feels as if he's looking through my clothes to the skin beneath.

Heat surges through me and I have to resist the urge to start fanning myself. Finally he says, "So what do you believe was behind the separation?"

I think I detect some subtle innuendo in the question and I blush. I'm hot on the heels of my own separation, a fact Hurley knows all too well, and he also knows all the sordid reasons why.

"I have no idea why Erik and Shannon split," I say honestly.

"Are they just separated or have they filed for divorce?" Hurley asks.

Again I pick up a hint of subtext and I can't help but wonder if Hurley is somehow alluding to my own situation. The fact that everyone else in the room is watching and listening intently makes me realize they have picked up on it, too.

"I'm guessing they were only separated, given the relatively short time since their breakup and the fact that Erik never said anything about a divorce, but I don't know for sure."

Hurley stares at me a moment longer, then his gaze drifts down my body. Alison sees it and seizes an opportunity to jump into the conversation, stepping away from me to force Hurley's gaze in her direction.

"Shannon was dating someone," she tosses out, looking proud. And rightly so. Gossip is a hot commodity in small towns like ours, and having the latest info elevates one's standing in all social circles, especially one involving a homicide investigation. "She's been seeing that new psychologist who came to town six months ago."

Hurley poises his pen over his notebook and says, "Name?"

"Luke Nelson."

As Hurley scribbles down the name I add my own two cents' worth, just to show I'm not totally ignorant. "He's a psychiatrist, not a psychologist."

"What's the difference?" Hurley asks.

"A psychiatrist is a medical doctor and a psychologist isn't. Psychiatrists provide counseling and psychotherapy the same way psychologists do, but a psychiatrist can also prescribe medications and perform treatments, like electroshock therapy."

There is a moment of silence and I wonder if anyone besides me is picturing the grim electric chair scene out front.

"Has anyone canvassed the neighbors yet?" Hurley asks, shifting the topic of conversation and continuing deeper into the house along the blood trail. We all step in behind him.

Larry says, "One of the houses across the road is for sale and has been vacant for several months. There's no one home at the other, and based on the mail flowing out of the box, I'm guessing they're out of town. The closest house to the east is a quarter of a mile away and the one next door to the west is home to a ninety-seven-year-old woman who is nearly deaf, close to blind, and hasn't had her hearing aids in all week."

We arrive in the kitchen—the end, or technically the start of the blood trail—and everyone stops to gape at the scene. There is blood everywhere: on the walls, the table, the counters, and the floor. It looks like a blender full of catsup ran amok. And there are obvious signs of a struggle. One of the chairs is knocked on its side and the others are positioned at odd angles. Shards of broken glass, some with blood on them, are scattered at our feet, and there are puddles of milk on the table and floor. Still on the table are two plates bearing untouched pieces of cheesecake and a second glass of milk. Clearly this is where Shannon was shot and it looks like she didn't go down easily.

Izzy takes out his camera and begins a running commentary on the blood splatter evidence. "Based on the spray on the far wall over there it appears the perpetrator shot her from the doorway leading to the hall behind us." He pauses, snaps a few pictures, and then continues. "The first shot hit her when she was standing in front of the sink. It looks like she threw a glass of milk at the perpetrator, and it shattered all over the floor here. Based on the blood trail from the sink and the splatter on the wall to our right, I'm guessing Shannon was staggering her way around the table when the second shot hit." He snaps a few more pictures of the walls, and then he bends down to snap several shots of the broken glass and the floor under the table. "Well, what do we have here?" he says, gingerly picking his way across the floor toward the table. He reaches under the table, picks up a blood-covered cell phone, and hands it to Hurley.

"Looks like it's broken," Hurley says. He looks around the kitchen and adds, "I don't see any land lines here. That would explain why Shannon dragged herself down the hallway and out the front door."

I open an evidence bag and hold it out to Hurley, who places the phone inside. As I'm sealing the bag, he makes his way across the room to the back door. "This dead bolt is locked so I'm guessing the shooter left along the same path Shannon took."

Alison is holding her camera tightly at her side, her knuckles white from the strength of her grip. I can tell it's killing her that she can't snap any photos in here.

Hurley says to Izzy, "There're no signs of a struggle, but you never know. We need to swab all this blood evidence and make sure it belongs to Shannon. Who knows? Maybe we'll get lucky and discover she managed to injure her killer. Maybe some of his DNA is in this mess."

"Even if we don't get any DNA evidence here," I say, "we might be able to get some from her hand. She had some abrasions on her knuckles."

Izzy says, "I'll get a crew working on the blood evidence straightaway." I sigh as he takes out his cell phone and dials a number, knowing that the "crew" he's referring to will consist of him, me, and Arnie Toffer, our primary lab tech. It's going to be a long, bloody night.

I take a moment to look around, trying to see past all the gore to the kitchen beneath. I can tell the room would be a bright, sunny spot during the light of day, thanks to the pale yellow walls, white cabinets, and two large windows on the eastern and southern sides of the room. It saddens me to think of Shannon sitting here in the morning sunshine, sipping her coffee, reading the day's paper, and readying herself for the day ahead, not knowing it would be her last.

Who would want to kill her? And why? I flash on her husband, Erik, who I've known since grade school. He's always been a kind, gentle, and well-humored soul so it's hard for me to imagine him doing this, no matter how acrimonious his and Shannon's separation has been. Then I remember all the hideous tortures I imagined inflicting on my own husband in months past and rethink things. Of course, imagining them is one thing, doing them another.

I consider myself a fair judge of character—ex-husband aside—and decide I want to be there when Erik is notified of Shannon's death so I can judge his potential guilt for myself. Plus, if Hurley lets me go along it will give me time with him and might get me out of the blood-gathering duties. I am about to suggest this scenario when things take an unexpected turn.

From the front of the house, where Al and the baby-faced uniform cop are standing guard over Shannon's body, we hear loud voices and the sounds of a scuffle. Careful not to tromp on any of the blood evidence, Hurley turns tail and heads back to the porch. I fall into step behind him, managing to nudge Alison out of the way just long enough to take over the lead.

Out front we find Al and his partner restraining a man who is staring at Shannon's wrapped body with an expression of disbelief and horror. His face is the color of my dress.

"Oh my God," the man mutters, his voice cracking. "What the hell happened to my wife?"

Chapter
4

"Erik?" I say gently. I work my way around the blood pool and move to his side. He allows me to take his arm and turn him around so his back is to the horrific scene on the stairs. He blinks hard several times and then looks at me as if he has no idea who I am.

"Erik, it's me. Mattie."

He nods slowly before stealing a glance over his shoulder. I feel a shudder rip through his body as he quickly looks away, moaning.

Hurley steps up in front of us. "Mr. Tolliver?"

Erik nods.

"Let's talk," Hurley says. He takes Erik's other arm and steers him across the yard toward one of the police cars. I follow along, not only because I want to hear what is said, but because I'm not sure Erik will make the trip without collapsing if there isn't someone on either side of him. Plus, there's the whole being-with-Hurley thing.

Hurley opens the front door to a cop car and between the two of us we manage to ease Erik down onto the passenger seat. He glances about the yard and the look of horror on his face deepens so I step in front of him to block his view.

"Mr. Tolliver!" Hurley barks sternly, and it works. Erik shifts his focus back to us. "I understand you and Mrs. Tolliver are separated. Is that right?"

Erik, looking as miserable as any human being can, nods. He leans forward and buries his face in his hands. "Why?" he groans. "Why did it happen?"

At first I'm not sure if he's referring to his and Shannon's separation, or her death. But then he adds, "Why would anyone want to kill her?"

Hurley ignores the question and asks one of his own. "When is the last time you saw your wife?"

Erik looks up at him and his face screws up in thought for a moment. "The day before yesterday," he says, "around three in the afternoon. I went to Dairy Airs to talk to her about . . ." He hesitates, looking sheepish. "About some personal stuff," he concludes.

Hurley isn't about to let him off the hook that easy. "Such as?"

A cloud passes over Erik's face and he sighs. "She sent me some separation papers to sign and I wanted to talk to her about them."

I see Hurley's eyebrows shoot up and can tell he has picked up a scent. "How did the meeting go?" he asks.

"I tried to talk her out of it. The separation was her idea, not mine."

"Did you sign the papers?" Hurley asks.

Erik shakes his head and looks away for a second. "No. I . . . um . . . left them there."

I sense he is hiding something and can tell Hurley thinks so, too.

Erik leans back and braces himself with his hands on his knees. "Do I need a lawyer?" he asks.

Hurley shrugs. "I don't know. Do you?"

Erik stares at him for a couple of beats as a long, uncomfortable silence fills the void. Then Erik looks away and asks, "What happened to her?"

"She was shot," I tell him, and from the corner of my eye I see Hurley give me an irritated look.

Erik winces and says, "Is this someone's idea of a Halloween prank? Ring the doorbell and then shoot whoever answers? What kind of sick, depraved bastard would do something like that?"

I start to explain that Shannon wasn't shot on the porch but Hurley shuts me up with another look. Then he asks Erik, "Can you give me an overview of your whereabouts yesterday?"

Erik, who was an honor roll student throughout high school, is smart enough to understand the implication behind the question. His expression turns angry and he glares at Hurley. "I was at work at the hospital during the day, from seven in the morning until three-thirty in the afternoon. After work I went to the bank, then I stopped in at Duke's for dinner with a friend."

"Can I have the name of this friend, please?" Hurley asks.

Erik's cheek muscles twitch and I can tell he's on the verge of blowing but he manages to contain his ire and provide the name. "Jacob Darner."

"Continue," Hurley says once he has the information written down.

Erik sucks in a deep breath and blows it out very slowly before going on. "I left there around six and went home."

"Alone?" Hurley asks.

"Yes," Erik snaps. "Alone."

"And where might home be these days?" Hurley asks, scribbling away in his notebook.

Erik rattles off the address, an apartment on the other side of town.

"Did you go anywhere else?"

"Not until this morning when I went to work," Erik says tightly, his hands coiled into fists at his side. "Same hours as yesterday."

"Is there anyone who can verify that you were at home yesterday evening?"

"No."

"Nobody? No phone calls in or out, no visitors, no deliveries?"

"No," Erik repeats, his voice even tighter. Then he rises and steps out of the car so abruptly that Hurley and I both take an involuntary step back. "I'm done answering questions until I talk to a lawyer."

The two men indulge in a ten-second stare-down until Hurley says, "Fine. You're free to go for now but don't go far."

The muscles in Erik's cheeks twitch violently; his face is suffused with anger and indignation. I can tell he wants to say something more but after a few seconds he simply turns away and heads for his car.

"One other quick question, if you don't mind?" Hurley yells after him.

Erik pauses but doesn't look back.

"Do you own a gun?" Hurley asks.

I see the muscles in Erik's back tighten before he answers. "I've got nothing more to say until I talk to a lawyer." He continues to his car, gets in, starts it up, and peels out.

As we eat his dust, Hurley looks over at me with a thoughtful expression and says, "I'll take that as a yes."

Chapter
5

I can hardly bring myself to consider the possibility of Erik doing such a brutal thing to his wife, but I know people often hide their true selves from the rest of us. How much can we really know about any one person? Even those closest to us, the ones we live with and love, are capable of amazing dishonesty and dark, desperate secrets. That's a lesson I've learned the hard way of late, after being on the fool's end of my husband's deception and learning that others in the community were not who I thought they were. What terrible secrets might Erik be hiding? What secrets had Shannon been hiding? And had those secrets ultimately led to her demise?

I know the answers lie in the evidence. With my curiosity roused, I follow Hurley back to the house. As he heads for the kitchen again, I take a slight detour and find the room I think is most likely to hold evidence of secrets: Shannon's bedroom.

The décor is a bit shocking. Either Shannon wasted no time in erasing all evidence of Erik from her life or Erik had quietly tolerated Shannon's extreme feminine tastes. The bed is neatly made and covered with a white comforter fringed with lacy tatting, echoing the frilly lace trim on the curtains. The walls are rosy pink, a shade that is repeated in the striped cushions of a wicker chair, the accent pillows on the bed, and the giant rose pattern in the rug. I feel like I'm trapped inside a bottle of Pepto-Bismol.

I move to the closet and pull open the bifold doors. Every square inch of the space is filled with clothes, all of them feminine. If Erik ever had a corner to call his own, there is no trace of it left now. Dozens of pairs of shoes are neatly arranged on the floor. I take a moment to envy the variety of styles and imagine what it must be like to be a woman of normal size. I wear a size-twelve shoe and choices are pretty limited when you get into this Sasquatch range, so there's no Imelda Marcos thing going on in my closet. Plus there's the whole height thing, which makes me reluctant to wear any kind of heel. I've been told I should embrace my height and wear it proudly. But I'm a bit self-conscious thanks to years of being asked how the weather is "up there," and dodging "green" jokes (as in jolly giants, not environmental issues).

With one last, longing look at the shoes, I shift the focus of my pity party to the upper parts of the closet. Two overhead shelves hold purses, jeans, T-shirts, and a couple of basic granny nightgowns. These I can relate to. But the stuff hanging on the rack is another story.

I finger through the assortment, marveling at the petite styles and fashionable lines. Given that I'm six feet tall and weigh anywhere from one-seventy to none-of-your-freaking business, the clothes in Shannon's closet are utterly foreign to me. I remember that she had a small side career as a local model and wonder if any of these clothes were acquired as perks of the job.

As I work my way down the rack, I notice all the clothes at the right end are loose-fitting styles in sizes ten and twelve. The ones in the center are size eights and of a more form-fitting style, and to the far left are some sexy sixes. This variety of sizes doesn't surprise me. I have my own collections, though my sizes tend to range from not-so-fat, to Rubenesque, to Hindenburg. Apparently Shannon has had similar struggles with her weight, though on a much smaller scale . . . in every sense of the word.

I leave the closet and head for the dressers, taking care when I open the drawers in case there might be valuable fingerprint evidence there. One drawer is filled with pieces of sexy lingerie, some with the price tags still attached. No doubt these are for the new boyfriend. I did a similar upgrade myself a few weeks ago. It was easy to embrace the comfort of plain cotton, stretched-out elastic, and flannel granny gowns when I was seven years into my marriage, but now that I've been thrust back into the singles market, I need better window dressing.

Next I move to the bedside stands. The one on the right is empty and I guess that's the side of the bed that used to be Erik's. The bottom drawer of the stand on the left holds some body lotions and a night mask, but the top drawer is crammed full of letters. A quick sampling shows me that most of them are from Erik and bear postmarks dating back no more than three months ago.

I grab one of the envelopes and carefully remove the letter inside. It's a single sheet of paper with a tidy scrawl on it, two paragraphs of writing. A quick scan of the contents reveals that Erik was utterly blindsided by Shannon's request for a separation and still very much in love with her. His note pleads with her to reconsider and not waste all the years they've spent together and reminds her of how happy they'd once been. The next to the last sentence reads: "Remember the vows we took ten years ago." The closing is sweet and desperate in its simplicity, but also chilling given the night's events: "'Til death do us part. Love, Erik."

"What are you doing?"

The sound of Hurley's voice behind me makes me jump. I spin around, knowing I look guilty but trying not to. "I was curious about Shannon's life and thought I might find something in here that could offer up some clues."

"And did you?"

"Maybe." I'm none too eager to show the letter to Hurley, knowing it will only convince him more of Erik's guilt. But I have no choice so I hand it over. He reads it, looks at the stack still in the drawer, and says, "Interesting. Did you read any of the others?"

I shake my head. He looks at me with his eyes narrowed and I'm expecting him to chastise me for snooping but he surprises me by instead asking, "So what's your take on Erik? Do you think he did it?"

I want to blurt out an immediate denial but hold it back. "I don't know," I say finally, truthfully. "But I'm leaning toward no."

"Why is that?"

"He just doesn't strike me as the type. He's always been a very sweet, kind, gentle guy."

Hurley considers this a moment, then nods. "I guess we'll see."

"You think he's guilty."

"I'm leaning that way."

"Why?"

He shrugs. "Just a gut feeling."

"But you're not sure."

"Not yet."

"You'll keep an open mind?"

He looks miffed. "I always follow the evidence. Let's see what it turns up." He moves closer to the stand and scoops up all the letters from the drawer. Then he turns to me and says, "In order to follow the evidence, we have to collect it." He arches an eyebrow at me and I get the hint along with a hot body flush.

"All right," I say with a melodramatic sigh. "I'll go collect blood samples. But I have to tell you, snooping and reading letters is way more fun."

"Well, if you're nice to me," he says, a hint of suggestion in his voice, "I'll let you read the rest of them."

While I'm generally a pretty straightforward person, I'm not against using my feminine wiles if I think it will get me what I want. Plus, Hurley tends to bring out the vamp in me. So I flash my best coquettish smile at him and say, "Nice? I can do nice."

"Yes," Hurley says, his voice huskier. The blue in his eyes darkens and I'm suddenly very aware of the bed beside us. "I'll bet you can."

Chapter
6

All of the cops on site help with the evidence collection, so it takes just over two hours to swab, seal, and label what we need. Arnie offers to stay with the body to await transport—a service provided by one of two local funeral homes—and I'm more than happy to help Izzy take the evidence packs back to the office, where I keep a change of clothes.

By the time we finish loading everything into Izzy's car, I note there is a growing crowd of bystanders lurking on the edges of the property and cars parked down the side of the road as far as I can see. Despite the fact that there is police tape strung up around the perimeter of Shannon's yard, the onlookers have been difficult to keep out. Because it's Halloween, everyone seems to think the goings-on are some kind of holiday performance art. As a result, three extra police officers have been called in to help patrol the yard and keep the lookie-loos out. The cops performing this duty don't appear very happy; no doubt they've been called in on their day off. Not that that's unusual. In a town this small there are only two or three cops on duty at any given time, and whenever reinforcements are needed, it generally means calling in the off-duty crew. Normally they don't mind, but I know most of them would feel better about giving up their free time if they could at least get close to the crime scene instead of being forced to play sheepdog to the nosy herd.

Hurley gives Alison permission to shoot a few pictures of the nosy brigade, knowing it's possible the killer might be in the crowd, but caveats it by saying that he wants to see all the shots she takes and approve any that might be used in the paper. A couple of times I catch her aiming her camera at stuff other than what Hurley instructed but I can't tell if she's shooting surreptitious shots of the scene or not. I do know that if any unauthorized photos appear in the paper, Hurley will be royally pissed off. It's almost enough to make me encourage Alison to misbehave.

As we are about to leave, Hurley walks over to Izzy and me and says, "You're not going to post her tonight, are you?"

Izzy glances at his watch—it's going on eleven o'clock—and shakes his head. "How does noon tomorrow sound? Sunday is my one day to sleep in if I can."

"That works for me," Hurley says. "That will give me some time to do a little legwork to see what I can turn up."

"What kind of legwork?" I ask.

Hurley smiles and eyes me with a look that makes me imagine a very specific type of legwork—in bed and intertwined. "Why?" he asks. "Are you looking for a date?"

"No, thanks, I've already had one of those tonight."

His smile fades. "You were on a date?" His voice goes all huffy as he zips back into detective mode. "You didn't tell me you had a date tonight."

"I didn't know I was supposed to. Do I need an alibi or something?"

"It's hard to know with you, given past experience."

As comebacks go, it's a pretty good one. Better than I expected.

"So just in case," he goes on, taking out his little notebook and his pen, "why don't you tell me who it was."

"William," I say, being purposefully evasive. I glance at my watch, then turn to Izzy and add, "And if we hurry and get this stuff back to the office I might be able to join him for a late-night drink to salvage some of our evening."

Izzy blinks hard several times and stares at me. I can tell he's confused so I take his arm and steer him toward the car, effectively dismissing Hurley's nosy inquiry and escaping before Izzy can blow my story.

As we pull away from the house, I see Hurley standing there watching us, a scowl on his face, notebook and pen in hand. I can't help but grin.

"A late-night drink?" Izzy says as we turn the corner. "You're not really going to—"

"Of course not," I shoot back. "But Hurley doesn't have to know the guy is as exciting as a blank wall. That's what he gets for agreeing to go out with Alison."

"Whose clutches you left him in," Izzy points out.

I frown, realizing I haven't thought things through all the way. "You don't think they'll actually stay together, do you? It sounded to me like Hurley planned to spend the rest of the night doing investigative work."

"And Alison is an investigative reporter."

"Damn," I mutter.

Izzy shakes his head and sighs. "You really are rusty when it comes to this flirting stuff."

"Well, what do you expect? I spent the last seven years married to David, and while *he* may have been honing his flirting skills, I sure as hell wasn't."

"Well, if Hurley is truly interested, and I think he is," Izzy adds, making me flush with delight, "he's going to spend some of his time tonight investigating you. That means you should try to hook up with William again for real. Otherwise it undermines your whole ploy. Hurley will know you were just yanking his chain."

I look over at Izzy, hoping to see a sly grin on his face, but he looks deadly serious. "Are you kidding me? I'd rather have leech therapy than spend another minute with that loser."

"Hey, don't blame me," Izzy says with a shrug. "You got yourself into this mess."

"Besides, I couldn't hook back up with William-not-Bill even if I wanted to. I don't have his number."

"I do."

Crap. I sulk for a minute, then say, "Do you really think Hurley's going to try to watch me?"

"I've got ten bucks says he does. In fact, just to guard my bet, how about if Dom and I go with you? We can make it a foursome."

I consider what he suggests and realize that Izzy and Dom can provide a good buffer zone between me and Mr. OCD. What the heck. I can use a drink and it will be interesting to see if Hurley does show up.

"Okay, you're on," I tell him, secretly hoping I'm going to lose. "But I have to warn you. If William-not-Bill starts counting the swizzle sticks, I'm either going to kill him or bail."

Chapter
7

Once we arrive at the office and secure all of our evidence, I take a quick shower in the unisex bathroom and put on the change of clothes I have in my office: a pair of jeans and a blue cowl-neck sweater.

Beneath it all is my brand-spanking new underwear, much sexier than my old stuff. During the Karen Owenby case, a slight dressing mishap led to a pair of my old undies getting mistakenly tagged as evidence, but not before Hurley held them up before a crowd of cops and likened them to a schooner sail. There isn't much I can do about the size, but at least my elastic is now intact and there are enough frilly enhancements to hopefully distract one from the quantity of cloth involved.

I look in the mirror and decide I'll pass muster. The blue in the clothes sets off the blue of my eyes, and my hair—thanks to the miraculous ministrations of my new hairdresser, Barbara—looks passable. As a final touch, I throw on a minimum of make-up and a tiny spritz of perfume to cover up any lingering smells of blood, formaldehyde, and death.

By the time I'm done, Izzy's life partner, Dom, has arrived at the office and Izzy is cleaned up and changed. Izzy looks under-stated in a simple white shirt with the sleeves rolled up and a pair of black pants. In contrast, Dom, who is reed thin, fair-skinned, auburn haired, and not afraid to advertise his lifestyle, is dressed in a pair of skintight leather pants and a glossy shirt that looks like the lights on a disco ball. Dom's flamboyance is a definite detriment to his and Izzy's social life. While Izzy hasn't ever tried to hide his sexual orientation, he is a government official and has a reputation and appearance to uphold. As a result, he and Dom rarely appear together within the town limits, more often hitting up spots outside Sorenson whenever they feel the need to trip the light fantastic.

Dom, who is standing with one hip cocked to the side and his arms crossed over his chest, eyes me as I emerge from the ladies' room. "You look fabulous," he coos. "That Barbara truly is a miracle worker."

"Thanks, I think." The flattery is nice, but Dom's declaration of what a miracle worker my hairdresser is makes me wonder just how awful he thought I looked before. Barbara's full-time job is doing make-up and hair for corpses at the Keller Funeral Home. She also does side work on live people in the basement of the place, and Izzy took me to her a few weeks ago after declaring me in need of a major overhaul. The whole thing was a bit creepy at first but I eventually grew comfortable with lying down—the only position Barbara is able to work in—to have my hair done. And the woman is truly a genius. Not only did she give my hair the best color, cut, and style it's had in years while also helping me plan the perfect funeral, she introduced me to a whole new make-up regimen that, according to her, no longer makes me look like one of the undead.

Thoughts of the undead remind me of my pending date. "I guess you can go ahead and call William-not-Bill," I tell Izzy.

He shakes his head. "I'll get the number for you but you're going to do the talking."

I frown at him but realize he's right; the invitation needs to come from me. "What if he says no?" I ask as Izzy searches for the number in his Rolodex, wondering if my ego can handle being rejected by one of the dating world's bottom feeders. "What do I do then?"

"He won't say no. You're the first date he's had in over two years that didn't run screaming from the room after half an hour. Trust me; he's desperate for female company. He'll go out at anytime with anyone."

As Dom gives me an *ouch* look and mimes an arrow piercing his chest, Izzy hands me his cell phone and a card with William's number on it.

I dial the number on the card and wait as the call goes through. William-not-Bill answers on the third ring with a breathless, slightly annoyed-sounding, "Hello?"

"Hi, William. I'm sorry for calling so late but I just got finished with the work I had to do and I was wondering—"

"Who is this?" he interrupts, his breathing hard and heavy.

"Oh, sorry, it's Mattie. Mattie Winston? Your date from earlier this evening?"

"Mattie!" he says, his breathing slowly returning to normal. "What a coincidence. I was just thinking about you when the phone rang."

I wince and utter a silent prayer that his breathlessness and thoughts of me occurred while he was running on a treadmill, or doing sit-ups, or using a rowing machine.

I hear rustling noises and then what sounds like a zipper in the background as William-not-Bill says, "I'm surprised to hear from you. I figured you'd be . . ." He pauses, then says, "Busy all night."

"Nope, we're done for the evening, and Izzy, Dom, and I are going out for a drink to unwind a little. I wondered if you might like to join us."

There is a long silence on the other end of the phone and for a moment I think the call has been dropped. "William? Are you still there?"

"I am," he says quietly. "Is this a joke?"

"What do you mean?"

"Is this one of those things where I get dressed and run out to meet you but you never show up?"

"No, William, it's not a joke." Clearly the guy's been stood up a time or two, and I feel a touch of sympathy for him. Then a wave of guilt washes over me as I remember that my own motives aren't exactly pure. "I felt bad that our date got cut short and thought you might want to join us for a drink."

Another long silence follows before he finally says, "Okay. Where are you going?"

There are three hole-in-the-wall bars located in downtown Sorenson, and even though they are all independently owned, at some point in time they decided to join forces when it came to names. As a result, we have the Nowhere Bar, the Somewhere Bar, and the Anywhere Bar. At times it leads to conversations that sound like an Abbott and Costello routine.

Where should we go tonight?

How about Nowhere?

Aw, come on, we have to go to Somewhere.

Well, we could go there, or to Anywhere, but I'd rather go to Nowhere.

I tell William, "We're going to the Nowhere Bar. We're headed there now."

"You're sure?" he asks. His voice has that breathless quality again and I can't help but wince.

"Yes, William, I'm sure."

"Okay. I'll meet you there in ten minutes."

"See you then." I end the call and hand Izzy back his phone. "It's a go," I tell him. "But I'm having second thoughts about this. Do you think the Nowhere Bar serves any drinks with saltpeter in them?"

Chapter 8

Lest I have any doubts about William-not-Bill's level of excitement, it is eliminated when I see that he has beaten us to the bar and is already seated when we arrive. It's a little scary when you consider that the bar is across town from William's house but only a block from our office. I fear I may have bitten off more than I can chew and pray that Hurley really does show up so my efforts aren't for naught.

The Nowhere is doing a hopping business despite the late hour. Bars are one of the more stable staples of the Wisconsin economy. Wisconsinites love their beer, their Packers, and their cheese. Thanks to the proliferation of televised games and cable TV, bars have the ability to provide all three, making them a home away from home for many.

Because it's Halloween, the crowd tonight is a little scarier than usual, reminiscent of the bar scene in *Star Wars*. William, who has shed his Dracula persona for now, is seated at a small table in a back corner. He stands up and eagerly waves us over as we enter. After shaking hands with Izzy and muttering a hello to Dom, William shifts all of his attention to me. He pulls out my chair, a gentlemanly gesture I appreciate, but then scoots his own seat closer and settles in with his leg touching mine. I can feel the excitement radiating off him, which only enhances my guilt and anxiety. As I start to squirm beneath the weight of William's adoring gaze, I shoot Izzy a pleading look. And Izzy, bless him, sallies forth with the perfect solution.

"Boy, they don't do a very good job cleaning these tables, do they?" he says, rubbing at an imaginary stain. The reaction from William-not-Bill is instantaneous. His attention shifts from me to the tabletop and he starts flicking away at imaginary crumbs. The flicks are always done in sets of four and in a rectangular pattern. I grit my teeth and ball my hands into fists to suppress the urge I have to slap him out of it.

Izzy flags down a waitress and we order: a gin-and-tonic for Izzy, a screwdriver for me, and a rum-and-Coke for Dom. William-not-Bill orders a bottled beer and asks the waitress to bring a glass on the side.

"So," William says, making another set of flicks as the waitress departs, "what did you guys have to do tonight? Is it anything you can talk about?"

"Not really," says Izzy. "But I can tell you it's a murder investigation."

"Murder? Really? Was it someone local?"

Izzy nods. "I'm sure you'll hear something about it tomorrow."

"How awful," William says with a shudder. "And on Halloween even. That's kind of scary."

It is, and a moment of silence follows as we all contemplate that fact. Then I'm distracted by the feel of William-not-Bill's leg rubbing against mine.

"I'll bet it's messy work, isn't it?" William says, breaking the silence and looking even more horrified than he did a moment ago.

"Very," I say. Then I look over at Izzy and add, "Even after scrubbing in the shower I don't feel like I got all that blood off my legs."

William's leg pulls away from mine like he just got burned. Izzy shoots me a puzzled look but I'm saved from having to elaborate any further when the waitress brings our drinks. Izzy pays for the round and as the rest of us sample our wares, William picks up his glass, eyes it a moment, and then pulls a hankie from his pocket. He starts wiping down the glass both inside and out and I roll my eyes at Izzy and take a big gulp of my screwdriver.

Once he has his glass up to muster, William pours his beer and says, "I'm glad you asked me to join you, Mattie. I really enjoyed our time together earlier."

"So did I," I lie. An awkward silence follows and after waiting futilely for several beats for Izzy and Dom to fill the gap, I sigh and jump in. "So, William, since I can't talk much about my work, why don't you tell me a little something about yours."

"Well," he says, swiping at some imaginary dirt on his sleeve, "it's not anywhere near as exciting as what you do, I'm sure. Basically I handle investments, do taxes, and provide accounting services to a few businesses."

"Does it keep you pretty busy?" Dom asks.

William nods and I slug back more of my drink as he flicks away at imaginary dust motes. "I've got more work than I can handle most of the time," he says. Then he turns his doe eyes to me and adds, "But I'd be happy to take a look at your portfolio if you like and make some suggestions."

I try to stifle a laugh and end up snorting screwdriver out my nose. The closest thing I have to a portfolio is a file folder in my kitchen drawer that contains my bills and one bank statement. The current balance in my new checking account is just over a thousand bucks, barely enough to feed my ice cream habit for a month. My ex has everything else though I'm hoping to find a good enough divorce lawyer that I can at least get half the value of our house in the settlement. It's the only thing I have any hope of claiming since we have no kids and all of our other assets are either in David's name alone or were excluded in a prenup I happily signed in my then, starry-eyed state.

The house is worth close to a million, though, and since I have no desire to live in it anymore, I'm hoping to force David to either sell it or pay off my share of its value. Until then I am living more or less hand to mouth, the grateful recipient of Izzy's beneficence in that he not only gave me a job, he is letting me rent a small cottage behind his house that used to belong to his mother, Sylvie. Unfortunately the cottage is next door to the house David and I once shared, a proximity that makes it difficult to let go of my old life, though it does make for easy spying, a fact that has already gotten me into trouble.

"I don't think I have enough assets to need an accountant or financial advisor," I tell William. "Check back with me after my divorce is final."

William's eyes drop from my face to my chest and he says, "I think your assets are just fine."

As I roll my eyes I hear a noise that sounds like a snort, and it takes a moment to realize it came from behind me. Then the voice I most want to hear says, "May I join you?"

I look up and see Hurley standing there. Given that I was hoping to see fiery jealousy, his expression of bemusement is disappointing.

"Sure," Izzy says. "Grab a seat."

William frowns at the invitation and his expression darkens considerably when Hurley grabs a nearby empty chair and swings it around to our table, setting it right between me and William. His blatant rudeness annoys me and I decide to challenge him.

"What could possibly bring you out here tonight, Detective?"

"I come bearing gifts," he says, flashing me an enigmatic smile and handing over a large manila envelope stuffed with papers. I give him a puzzled look and he explains, "They're copies of those letters you found. I kept the originals for evidence. You said you wanted to read them."

I'm surprised, even though I suspect he made the copies so quickly only so he would have an excuse to venture out and find us. "Good detective work, Hurley," I say. "I'm sure it wasn't easy tracking us down here, and so quickly, too."

For a second Hurley looks guilty, making me suspect that Izzy was right—Hurley was watching me to see where I'd go, and who I went there with. Then Hurley shrugs. "It wasn't that hard," he says with great nonchalance. "This is the closest bar to your office so it made sense to look here first."

"Well, thank you for these," I say, folding the envelope full of letters and tucking it into my purse. And though I know I'm being petty, I can't resist tossing off one last jab. "But really, couldn't it have waited until morning?"

"It could have but I also found out a few things about our chief suspect that I thought you might be interested in," Hurley counters.

"Such as?"

He shrugs and tips back his chair, his hands laced behind his head. "I can't elaborate right now." He glances around but avoids looking at William. "This is too public a place, with too many ears."

William blushes a bright shade of red, and I can't tell if he's embarrassed, angry, or both. Guilt washes over me as I realize I set William up for this, and I feel a sudden surge of anger, part of it aimed at Hurley, part of it at myself.

"Seeing as how you're busy, I guess it will just have to wait," Hurley says, dangling the bait a little closer. "Unless you can free yourself up tonight."

William looks down at his shirt and starts plucking away at imaginary lint with a ferocity that's frightening. "I . . . I can leave, if you like," he stammers.

He looks so wounded, so pathetic, that I hate myself for what I've done. And Hurley's smug expression is just screaming at me for a slap-down.

"That's okay," I say, shooting a scathing glance at Hurley. "It can wait." I reach over and place my hand on William's arm. "What do you say you and I go back to my place for a nightcap?"

William's jaw drops and his plucking fingers freeze on his sleeve. Hurley leans forward, the front legs of his chair meeting the floor with a loud *thump*. I hear Dom mutter, "Whoa!" under his breath. Izzy doesn't say a word, but it's obvious from his expression that he's amused.

William finally snaps his mouth closed, swallows hard, and says, "I'd love to."

"Good." I push my chair back and stand. "Gentlemen, if

you'll excuse us. Izzy, I'll see you in the morning. Is eleven-thirty okay?"

"That will be fine," he says, his eyes twinkling.

Hurley opens and closes his mouth like a fish out of water, but says nothing. I smile at him and then crook my arm at William. "Shall we?"

William almost trips over his own feet in his rush to get to me. He takes my arm in his and I can feel him trembling as he leads me out of the bar. I start to have second thoughts about what I'm doing, and pray I haven't gotten myself into a situation I can't get out of gracefully.

Chapter 9

When we reach the parking lot I ask William, "Do you mind giving me a ride home? I don't have my car."

"Of course."

He is a perfect gentleman, opening the car door for me and making sure I put my seat belt on. I note that his car is a Toyota Prius and my estimation of him, and his financial status, jumps up a notch. I'm starting to think I didn't give the guy a fair shake when he climbs behind the wheel and says, "There's some mouthwash in the glove box. Can you get it out for me?"

I do so, then sit and watch, stunned, as he gargles and spits out his window. I half expect him to offer me a slug but realize that this sharing of germs is probably high on his list of phobias. Then I consider telling him I have a canker sore or some other infection, in hopes of warding off any attempts at a kiss.

My house is less than a mile away so it takes only a minute or two to get there. Along the way William glances at himself in the rearview mirror several times—taming his comb-over with a lick of spit, examining his teeth, and looking up his nose once, presumably for stray hairs.

He follows my directions and parks in front of my cottage. I climb out of the car quickly, not wanting to encourage the suitor scenario any more by waiting for him to open my door. Once we get inside he stops, looks around, and assumes an expression of obvious distaste.

"You're a bit of a clutterbug, aren't you?" he says.

"Sorry." I take the envelope Hurley gave me out of my purse and toss it onto a nearby chair. "Neatness is not one of my strong suits."

William looks like he is about to say something else but sneezes instead. Then he does it again. Three more follow in succession, like rapid-fire gunshots. "Do you have a cat?" he sniffles, taking out his hankie and dabbing at his nose. "I'm allergic to cats."

Suddenly I see light at the end of the tunnel . . . a way out of all this without rejecting William outright. "I do. He's a kitten, actually, about four months old, and his name is Rubbish because I found him in a garbage Dumpster."

William glances around the room with an utterly horrified expression and I half expect him to bolt for the door.

"Don't worry. He's probably in hiding somewhere. He does that when I come home, like a game of hide-and-seek." I gesture toward the couch. "Why don't you have a seat and I'll get us some wine."

He walks over to the couch and bends down to examine it carefully. When he starts brushing at the cushion, I head into the kitchen with my purse and grab the closest thing I have to wineglasses: a couple of juice tumblers. As I hear William sneeze several more times, I dig in my purse, find a tube of lipstick, and put some on. Then I take both of the glasses and wrap my lips around their rims, one at a time. When I'm done, I examine the glasses carefully in the light and deem the lip prints satisfactory. Then I open a bottle of Chardonnay and fill both glasses.

I return to the living room to find William sitting on the couch, red-eyed, sniffling, and tearing. He sneezes twice more as I approach and they are violent enough that his comb-over springs loose, standing up on one side of his head like a lopsided rooster comb.

"You poor thing," I tell him, handing him a glass of wine.

He takes the glass and true to form, holds it up for inspection. Despite the fact that his eyes are swollen halfway shut, he manages to widen them to startling proportions when he spies the lipstick mark. "Did you wash this glass?" he asks nasally.

I shrug. "I gave it a good rinse. Why? Is there a problem?"

He sets the glass down, blows his nose, and then sneezes again. I notice movement behind him and realize Rubbish has finally appeared, climbing up the back of the couch to perch just behind William's head.

William leans back into the couch and dabs at his eyes and nose. He looks truly miserable and I feel a pang of pity for him. Then I notice that Rubbish has hunkered down, his furry little ass wiggling in the air, his pupils dilated like a meth addict's. His eyes are focused on the flopping strands of William's comb-over, and I realize with horror that he is about to make a kill.

William retrieves his glass as I start forward in hopes of grabbing Rubbish before he can attack but I'm a step too late. The kitten launches himself forward, all claws out, and lands on top of William's head. William shrieks and pushes himself off the couch, managing to spill wine all over his shirt and knock over the coffee table in the process. Rubbish loses his grip, slides down the side of William's head, and then scampers into my bedroom.

At least now I don't have to worry about William trying to take me to bed.

"Jesus Christ!" William yells, holding a protective hand over his scratched face. He sets his now-empty wineglass down and takes out a second folded, cloth hankie from his pants pocket, which he uses to dab at the blood.

"I'm so sorry, William. Let me get something to clean up those scratches for you." I grab a towel from the linen closet, and fetch some gauze, hydrogen peroxide, and antibiotic ointment from the medicine cabinet. As I return to the living room, I half expect to find William gone but to his credit he is still here, though he is standing much closer to the door. His eyes dart back and forth crazily and I'm not sure if he's looking for Rubbish or planning a hasty escape.

His shirt front is soaked with wine so he unbuttons it and uses the towel to dry off his chest. In the meantime I dab at his wounds, clean them the best I can, and apply some ointment to each of the scratches. His comb-over is still standing at attention but there is something oddly endearing about it so I leave it alone. When I'm done, I stand back and tell him, "There you go. Good as new."

"What if I get an infection?" he asks. "Cats are notoriously dirty animals, aren't they?"

His questions remind me of someone else's recent comments and an idea begins to bloom in my brain. "Their *bites* are prone to infection," I admit, "but the scratches less so. I think you'll be fine."

He gives me a look that says he's doubtful. Then his head rears back and shoots forward as he lets loose a rapid triple sneeze. Between the movement and the comb-over, he looks like one of those bobbing glass bird toys with the colored liquid inside.

"It doesn't look like things are going to work out with us, William," I say, trying to sound disappointed.

"Clearly not." He blows his nose again.

"Would you be open to dating an older woman?"

He eyes me suspiciously. "Who did you have in mind?"

"My mother."

He looks offended.

"She's only a few years older than you and a very attractive woman," I add quickly. "Plus she's very, very clean." It's true. My mother is more of a neat freak and germophobe than William ever dreamed of being. She's also single, several years out from her fourth divorce, lonely, and a cat hater.

He considers my offer a moment and then shrugs. "I'm game for anything at this point, I guess."

"Great! I think you two will be perfect for one another. I'll give her a call and see if I can set something up, okay?"

He dabs at a trickle of blood on his ear and sneezes again. I take it as a yes.

"I think it would be best if I left," he says.

"I understand. And again, I'm sorry." I lean over and give him a quick buss on the cheek which, thanks to my freshly applied lipstick, leaves a perfect kiss imprint behind. I consider wiping it off but then decide to let it stay.

The kiss brightens his countenance considerably, and when he turns to leave he is wearing a silly-assed grin. I walk him to the door, flip on the outside spotlight, and watch as he gets into his car and drives away.

Only after he's gone do I realize I'm not alone. Standing at the back door to Izzy's house are Izzy and Hurley, both of them staring slack-jawed at me. Izzy looks amused and surprised, Hurley looks like a thundercloud. I give them both a little finger wave before going back inside.

Spying the envelope Hurley gave me earlier still sitting where I tossed it, I pick it up and settle in to read. It proves to be a depressing endeavor. Clearly Erik was both surprised and devastated by Shannon's desire to split, and their differing views about having children was at the heart of a good part of it. Erik wanted them and Shannon didn't, but in later letters Erik made it clear he was willing to forgo the children if it would help save the marriage.

Erik's love for Shannon is evident in every letter. I can find no hints of craziness or angry desperation in his words, only heartache. He mentions Luke Nelson in a letter dated nearly a month ago, so he apparently knew about him for a while. But he also wrote that he was willing to move past this bump in their marital road if Shannon would give him a second chance.

Basically, the letters support what my instincts are already telling me: that Erik loved his wife very much and was incapable of killing her. Granted, the separation paperwork Shannon hit him with might have been a finality he wasn't willing to accept. But I still can't make myself believe he would kill her over it.

Somehow I have to prove it.

Chapter 10

The next morning I drop my costume gown off at the dry cleaner. The lady behind the desk looks at it with a puzzled expression.

"Is this mud?" she asks.

"No, blood."

Her eyebrows shoot up and she drops the part of the dress she's holding like it's a hot potato. "Real blood?"

I nod. "Afraid so."

"It looks like a lot," she says, her voice shaky. Since she's eyeing me like she expects I'm about to go batshit crazy and hack her to death, I figure an explanation is in order.

"Sorry about that. I work for the medical examiner so I'm afraid blood is something of an occupational hazard. Last night I got called out to the scene of a homicide while I was at a Halloween party. This"—I finger the dress—"was my costume."

Her shoulders relax and she smiles. Then she leans across the counter and lowers her voice. "I heard about that," she says in her best conspirator's voice. "Someone said it was that waitress over at Dairy Airs, the one who models from time to time."

Ah, the ubiquitous but mysterious "someone" and "they," basic gossip fodder in any small town.

"They said she was shot," the woman goes on. "Is that true?"

"I can't say," I tell her, smiling back. She frowns, but looks at me with a new level of respect.

Though I enjoy a juicy bit of gossip as much as the next person and have partaken of fact swaps in the past, I've also been privy to knowledge on many occasions that I couldn't and wouldn't share. As a nurse, I always followed a strict code of confidentiality, even before the whole HIPAA thing started. With this job, I find myself once again bound to secrecy often as not. But that's okay because I've discovered two things over the years. One is that not sharing what I know can be as satisfying as doling out a juicy tidbit. And that's because of the other thing: status when it comes to gossip is less about what you actually know than it is about what people think you know. And my new job jumps me up to a whole new level because now people realize I'm a gatekeeper for some of the town's juiciest tidbits ever.

I leave the curious and frustrated dry cleaner behind and head for the office, arriving a little after eleven-thirty. Izzy is already there, sitting in the library with a cup of coffee and the Sunday paper.

"Morning," I tell him, pouring a cup of java and scrounging a cruller from a Dunkin' Donuts box left over from yesterday. I drop a ten-dollar bill on the table in front of Izzy and then settle into a nearby chair. "Congratulations," I tell him. "You won."

"Easy money," he says, pocketing the bill. "I knew Hurley would be there. You forget how predictable we men can be."

"I'll have to remember to tell that to my divorce lawyer."

"First you have to find one."

"I will. I just need some time."

"I thought last night's events might prompt you to speed that process up," he says, his voice laden with innuendo.

I give him a puzzled look. "I don't follow."

"Well, it looked like you and William hit it off pretty well. I told you he wasn't that bad."

"Are you kidding? It was an unmitigated disaster."

"Oh, sure," Izzy says with a smirk. "I saw him leave your place last night. Hurley and I both did. We saw the lip imprint on his cheek, the mussed-up hair, the unbuttoned shirt, and the big-assed grin on his face. Hell, you even scratched him, you wildcat you."

I stare at Izzy, blinking hard for a moment, before I realize what he's inferring. "No, no, no," I say, holding my hands out to ward off his evil thoughts. "You have it all wrong. William is allergic to cats, so his hair was all messed up because he sneezed a bazillion times. The scratches were from when Rubbish attacked his comb-over. The lip print—well, that was legit, but I only kissed him the one time on the cheek because he looked so miserable and I felt sorry for him."

I decide not to admit to the reason why my lipstick was so fresh.

"The evening wasn't a total loss, though," I continue. "I'm going to fix William up with my mother. I think they'll be perfect together."

"Well, if your intent was to make Hurley jealous, it worked. You should have seen the look on his face when he saw William leaving. He was fuming."

I smile, recalling Hurley's thunderous expression and imagining the thoughts that might have been going through his mind. "What was he doing there anyway?"

"He said he wanted to fill me in on some case facts but I'm pretty sure he was using that as an excuse to come by and check on you. He could have just called or waited until this morning."

As if on cue, I hear the door open behind me and see Izzy's gaze shift over my head. "Good morning, Detective," he says.

I turn around and smile at Hurley. "Good morning, Detective," I echo in the cheeriest voice I can muster.

He scowls at me, mutters, "Morning," and then shifts his attention to Izzy, effectively dismissing me. "Are we still on for noon?"

"Ready anytime," Izzy says, draining his coffee mug. "Let's get to it."

That's my cue so I scarf down my cruller, take one more swallow of my coffee, and head to the morgue.

Arnie, who functions as our primary lab tech, sometime autopsy assistant, general gofer, and resident conspiracy theorist, had tucked Shannon's body in the cold storage room last evening. It's the only body in the room so it isn't hard to find.

I grab the clipboard at the end of the stretcher and examine the checklist of items on the top page—all the things that have to be done before the actual cutting part of the autopsy begins.

A weight is obtained on each body, something that is relatively simple since the stretcher weights are known. Once a body arrives in our office and gets loaded onto a stretcher, the whole thing is wheeled onto a scale built into the floor. The scale automatically deducts the stretcher's weight and flashes the remainder, which is the body's weight, on a digital screen.

We also obtain vitreous samples—a needle aspiration of the fluid inside the eyeballs. Whereas blood and other bodily fluids deteriorate rapidly once death occurs, a process that can affect certain lab values or the presence of residual drugs, the vitreous fluid remains more stable. It can also help narrow down the time of death as there is a somewhat predictable rise in the potassium level in the vitreous fluid after death. Each body is also X-rayed soon after arrival, before it is removed from its body bag.

According to the checklist, Arnie did all of these things last night when the body arrived. I'm glad, not only because it makes my job that much easier this morning, but because I hate having to obtain the vitreous fluid. The process of pushing a needle into someone's eyeball, even knowing they are dead, gives me the willies.

I wheel the stretcher into the main autopsy room where Izzy and Hurley are already waiting. Izzy and I move Shannon's body from the stretcher onto the autopsy table, then Izzy, who is already suited and gloved, opens the body bag and starts taking photos while I don my own protective gear. Thirty minutes later we have photographed and examined her body and clothing for trace evidence, undressed her, scraped for evidence beneath her nails, and hosed her down. Izzy is posed over her upper chest with his scalpel, ready to make the first incision.

Hurley is standing off to one side and has been quiet up to now, watching us with an intensity that makes my pulse quicken every time I look at him. This is my fourth autopsy with him and so far he's followed a regular modus operandi: standing by quietly, observing, and occasionally asking a question or two about the significance of a particular finding. Today, however, he breaks with tradition just as Izzy is making the first cut. Taking out his notebook, he flips it open and begins a running commentary on his investigation thus far.

"Turns out Erik Tolliver was at work both yesterday and the day before. He met with Shannon at Dairy Airs on the day he said he did and, according to the workers there, things ended on a fiery note when Erik threw the papers at Shannon, called her a bitch, and stormed out. His dinner alibi holds up for the day of the murder but after about six P.M. his whereabouts are unaccounted for.

"Shannon was alive at three o'clock on the day she was murdered because that's when she left work, but I haven't found anyone who saw her after that. So that narrows down our time of death to sometime after three P.M. on the thirtieth. Yesterday's mail was still in the mailbox, presumably delivered sometime after Shannon was killed. The box is out by the street and the mailman said he drove up at about ten in the morning, put the mail inside the box, and continued on. He didn't pay particular attention to the yard display.

"The only other information I have is that her coworkers said she ate lunch around twelve-thirty on the day she was killed: a roast beef sandwich, some cream of tomato soup, and an order of fried cheese curds."

Izzy says, "That might help us narrow down the time of death even more once I get a look at her stomach contents."

Hurley says, "I'm betting she was killed after six that night. The husband definitely has some issues and I think that whole thing with the separation papers set him off."

I frown and Hurley catches it. "What? You still think he's innocent?"

I shrug. "I'm having a hard time believing he could do this, based on what I know of him."

"Want to make a friendly wager on it?"

"I don't know. It sounds like you already have your mind made up. How do I know you'll even try to find another suspect?"

Hurley sighs and gives me an *are-you-kidding-me?* look. "I always keep an open mind," he says.

"You seem pretty convinced that Erik did this."

"At the moment I am."

"See, I knew it." I look pointedly at Izzy, who wisely shrugs and says nothing. "Taking this wager would be a sucker bet."

"Then find me someone who looks better for it," Hurley says.

"Will you let me do some of my own investigating?"

"As long as you keep me in the loop, don't do anything that would interfere with the official investigation, and promise to share anything you find with me."

"And you'll share evidence with me?"

"Tit for tat," Hurley says with a suggestive grin.

I consider the idea. I'm competitive by nature and something about Hurley brings that trait out even stronger in me. "What are the stakes?" I ask.

Hurley shrugs, thinks a moment, and then says, "How about dinner? The winner picks the place and time, and the loser gets to pay."

"Deal," I say without hesitation, so excited over the prospect of dinner with Hurley that, for a moment, I don't care who wins the bet.

"Good." He closes his eyes, licks his lips, and says, "Mmmm. I can already taste my filet mignon from Harvey's, medium rare, wrapped in bacon, with a baked potato on the side."

I'm so transfixed by the sight of Hurley licking his lips and moaning that it takes me a second to remember that a dinner at Harvey's will cost me more than half a week's pay. My hands start to shake and I'm not sure if it's out of fear or lust. I realize Izzy has finished cracking Shannon's chest and is in the process of removing one of her lungs, so I tear my gaze from Hurley and try to focus on the work instead. Trembling hands, sharp scalpels, and slippery organs make for a bad combination.

Shannon's chest cavity is filled with clots of blood, and as Izzy scoops some of them out of the way, the idea of a medium rare filet mignon is suddenly nauseating. Izzy severs the connections for the right lung, removes it from the chest cavity, and hands it to me. I weigh it on the scale, noting that its color is a dull gray rather than the healthy pink it should be, an indication that Shannon was a smoker. Once I take it from the scale and lay it on the dissection table, I can see that it also has two bullet holes in it: one in the front of the lower lobe, which is most likely the entry point, and a second on the back of the middle lobe, the probable exit point.

Izzy confirms my suspicions when he finds a bullet lodged next to Shannon's thoracic spine. He pulls the bullet out, cleans it off, and shows it to Hurley. "Looks like a .38," he says.

"Yup," Hurley agrees. "And guess who owns a .38 caliber handgun?"

"Half the people in Wisconsin?" I offer, knowing it's not the answer he's looking for.

"I don't know about half," he says, "but I know Erik Tolliver owns one. He bought it two years ago."

I sigh, and start calculating how many pints of ice cream I'm going to have to forgo in the future so I can save up enough money to pay for our dinner date. I might have to ask Izzy for a raise, which would be rather brazen considering that I've only been on the job for a couple of weeks.

"Lots of people have guns," I counter. It's a feeble argument, but a true one. The NRA is alive and well in Wisconsin, where deer season means closed-down businesses, hunting widow parties, and men who become live oxymora by dressing in camouflage clothes topped with blaze orange vests. Every year, one or two yahoos are mistaken for a deer and get shot . . . Darwinism in action.

"A .38 is pretty common, isn't it?" I continue. "That alone isn't enough to convict the guy."

"Maybe not," Hurley says. "But it's one more piece of the puzzle."

"Did you find Erik's gun?" Izzy asks.

Hurley shakes his head. "Apparently he was smart enough to ditch the thing. I had a couple guys execute a search warrant on his place early this morning."

We have removed the second lung, and after noting that Shannon had a hiatal hernia—a typically benign condition where there is a hole in the diaphragm that allows a portion of the stomach to slide into the chest cavity—Izzy cuts loose Shannon's stomach. As soon as it's out, he slices it open.

"Her stomach is empty," he says.

"What does that mean?" Hurley asks.

"Well, it takes four to six hours after ingestion for food to empty out of the stomach and move into the intestines. So if Shannon ate around twelve-thirty as her coworkers said, it's unlikely she was killed before four-thirty. Once I get a look at her intestines I might be able to finesse that estimate some more."

For the next half an hour the room is relatively silent except for the sounds of slicing, dicing, and sloshing organs. We find a second bullet in the abdominal cavity and my initial suspicion that Shannon's liver was hit by one of the bullets is confirmed. The damage to the organ is extensive and would have caused significant bleeding. Some of the blood, most of it eventually, would have oozed out through the bullet wound. But a fair amount had also spread throughout the abdominal cavity, a condition that would have been excruciatingly painful. It might also have been a blessing of sorts since the bleeding into the chest cavity, along with the gradual collapse of the shot lung, would have caused a slow form of suffocation had she not bled out from the liver first.

For a moment I imagine Shannon, wounded, frightened, weak, and in pain, dragging herself down the hall of her house and out onto the porch in hopes of finding help. She had to have known she was seriously wounded and likely dying, and her will to live must have been strong. That she lost her life in such a cruel, horrifying, and painful way both saddens and angers me.

Nothing new is discovered during the examination of the remaining organs other than the fact that Shannon's uterus is riddled with large, fibroid tumors, something that would have made it very difficult, if not impossible, for her to get or stay pregnant. With Shannon's abdominal cavity now devoid of organs, Izzy shifts his attention to her intestines, which we'd removed earlier and placed in a large basin on the dissection table. He runs the twenty-some feet of small intestine like a garden hose, examining it inch by inch, opening sections along the way. Then he does the same with the large intestine.

"The only food I see here is in the ascending colon," he says when he's done. "That would take, on average, about eight to twelve hours. So if we assume she ate nothing else after her lunch at Dairy Airs, it's likely she was killed sometime between the hours of eight P.M. and midnight, give or take an hour or two."

"What a coincidence," Hurley says, shooting me a smug look. "Our primary suspect has no alibi for those hours."

"You mean *your* primary suspect," I grumble.

Hurley ignores my comeback and instead closes his eyes and licks his lips, an action that leaves me with my jaw hanging. "I can taste my steak already," he says.

His display of arrogant confidence brings out my competitive side. But though I want desperately to be right about Erik and his innocence, I know I have to be careful not to lose my objectivity.

"Don't get too cocky," I tell Hurley. "It's still only an estimate and I'm sure crow doesn't taste nearly as good as filet mignon."

Chapter
11

Hurley's challenge leaves me more determined than ever, so Monday morning I phone the office to tell them I'll be in late. Cass takes the message and informs me that Izzy is also tied up this morning so my delay shouldn't be a problem. I then make a phone call to the hospital to see if Erik Tolliver is on duty. He is, but I have another stop I want to make first.

Ten minutes later I pull into the parking lot of Dairy Airs, head inside, and settle in at one of the tables.

The waitress who serves me is Jackie Nash, an ex-classmate of mine and the owners' daughter. I know Jackie not only because of our school connection, but because she's had a number of surgeries at the hospital. Back in high school she had big plans, as did the rest of us, for escaping her small-town roots and moving to the big city. But a tragic car accident in her junior year left her burned over seventy percent of her body, and that changed everything. She still bears some horrific scars despite several plastic surgeries for grafts and scar revisions, and the gnarled tissue on her legs has given her a chronic limp. It might not have been so bad had the damage been contained to her torso and limbs but the flames also reached one side of her face. As a result, she resembles the Batman villain Two Face, looking relatively normal—and quite pretty—from one side, and horribly maimed from the other.

Jackie has been working the family business ever since her recovery from the accident. Those of us in town who know her are used to her scars, but occasionally, when strangers drop in, she is forced to face the awkward stares and rude comments of brutally honest children and tactless adults. Not surprisingly, those moments along with the trauma of the accident and the disruption it caused to her personal life have left her with more than a few emotional scars to go with the physical ones. During the years I worked in the hospital ER, I took care of Jackie during several of her mental breakdowns, though I've heard she's doing better these days.

Today she greets me with a smile, takes my order for a bowl of peach ice cream—I figure fruit is a good choice for breakfast—and brings it back a few minutes later. As I watch her walking back to the table something about her seems different, though I can't figure out what it is. I finally decide it's her face, which seems to have a new glow to it. Had she had another graft revision surgery, or was she simply using new make-up?

"What's new?" she asks, sliding into the chair across from me as I swallow my first spoonful. "What's this I hear about you and David?"

As if the whole town didn't know already. "It's true," I tell her. "We split up. I'm filing for divorce."

"I also heard you changed jobs. Someone said you're working for the coroner now."

I suspect Jackie is merely being nosy, trying to earn a little leverage in the gossip commodity. But it's okay because her veiled inquiry offers me the perfect opening.

"That's also true," I say after swallowing another bite. "In fact, that's one of the reasons I'm here. I'm looking into Shannon Tolliver's murder."

She shakes her head, looking stricken. "It's a terrible, terrible thing that happened to Shannon. Do they have any idea who did it?"

"Nothing solid yet. Do you have any ideas?"

Jackie rears back and looks at me, clearly startled by the question. "Me? Why would you ask me?"

I shrug. "You worked with Shannon so I figured you might have some insight into her life and the people in it."

Jackie glances around at the other tables and then looks down at her hands in her lap, her fingers fidgeting. "I suppose they'll suspect Erik," she says in a low voice. "Things *have* been kind of strained between him and Shannon ever since they split up."

"I heard they had an argument of some sort a couple of days before she died. Were you here when it happened?"

"Oh, yeah," Jackie says, rolling her eyes. "It was pretty intense. Shannon served Erik with separation papers and he didn't take it too well."

"Do you remember what they said?"

Jackie cocks her head to one side and looks up at the ceiling for a moment, giving me time to eat another spoonful of ice cream. "Well, I remember Erik telling Shannon he didn't want a divorce. He told her he wanted to try to work things out. But Shannon was pretty adamant about going ahead with it. Erik got mad, called her a bitch, and threw the papers at her. Then Shannon yelled at him to leave."

"Did he?"

Jackie nods. "He stormed out, got in his car, and peeled rubber out of the parking lot."

"What did Shannon do or say after that?"

"Well, she was pretty upset, crying and all. It was the end of her shift so she went into the back room for a bit to try to collect herself. Then she came out, ordered a bunch of food to go, and as soon as it was ready, she left."

"Did you see Erik again after that?"

Jackie shakes her head. "Nope, but he never did come around much. He's lactose intolerant so there isn't much here he can eat."

"Who else was working that day?"

"It was me and Shannon up front here. Mom was working in back."

"Did your mom witness the argument between Shannon and Erik?"

She nods. "Mom spent some time afterward trying to calm Shannon down."

"Is your mom here today?" I doubt it since I haven't seen her, and Jackie confirms my guess with a shake of her head.

"Dad's here today. Mom had a doctor's appointment." She takes out her order pad, scribbles something on a blank page, rips it out, and hands it to me. "Here's our home phone number," she says. "Give her a call if you want."

I take the paper and slip it into my purse. "Thanks. I will. If you can think of anything else about Shannon that might be significant, let me know. You can reach me at the ME's office." I give her the number, she writes it on another blank page of her order pad, and stuffs it in her pocket.

"Will do," she says. As a new customer enters, she gets up and adds, "Gotta run, but it was good talking with you, Mattie. Good luck with the whole marriage thing."

It only takes me another minute to finish my ice cream because I manage to resist the urge to lick the bowl. Then I get back in my car and head for Mercy Hospital, my old employer.

The hospital is an emotional place for me. Not only is it where both the birth and death of my marriage took place, it's where I worked for over twelve years. A good portion of my adulthood has been spent there, and I have tons of memories, both good and bad.

Many of the good ones are from my years in the ER. Things there can go from monotonous to chaotic in a matter of seconds, and it can be wonderfully, disgustingly messy—emotionally messy, blood-and-guts messy, and life-and-death messy. I left the ER to go work in the OR so I could be closer to my husband, David. But in the end, I lost two things that were very important to me: David and my job in the ER.

These days I'm a topic of lively gossip at the hospital—the nurse who caught her husband playing tonsil hockey with someone else in one of the operating rooms; the nurse who was suspected of murdering the lipstick on the dipstick; and the nurse who now slices and dices in a whole new environment. Oh, yeah, and the nurse involved in the infamous nipple incident.

It's been a few months since David and I split and since then there have been other topics to occupy the hard-core gossipers. While those events offered some distraction, they weren't enough to divert attention away from me altogether. I still get stared at and I swear I hear my name whispered in corners every time I go there.

Hoping to minimize the scrutiny today, I bypass the main hospital entrance and go in through the ER instead. The ER staff is a little less judgmental than your average hospital worker. The scale of what's weird, newsworthy, and important gets altered once you've cared for a man with a flashlight up his rectum, a condition that was later dubbed a "butt light."

As I walk through the ER doors, I can feel that familiar surge of excitement thrumming just below my skin. The air here always feels different. Today it sounds and smells different, too. Instead of the typical antiseptic smells, there is a distinct odor of feces in the air, and the low thrum of heart monitors, vital sign machines, and soft-soled shoes has been replaced by the sounds of a woman screaming like a banshee from behind one of the curtains. A nurse sitting behind the desk, a veteran ER warrior of some twenty-plus years named Debbie Hanson, greets me.

"Mattie! Welcome to the madhouse."

I smile and nod toward the noise. "That sounds ominous."

"It's a major Code Brown," Debbie says, lowering her voice. "She's been on Vicodin for a month without any stool softener and now her bowels are backed up to her eyeballs."

The screaming reaches a new crescendo and then suddenly stops, replaced by exhausted panting. A moment later, one of the ER techs emerges from behind the screaming woman's curtain carrying the bucket from a bedside commode. Debbie hops up and walks over to the tech.

"Let me see," Debbie says.

The tech proffers the bucket and a pungent fecal smell permeates the air.

"Wow," Debbie says with a look of respect. "I might have to give that one a name and an Apgar score." She looks over at me. "Want to see?"

"No, thanks."

Debbie hands the bucket back to the tech and says, "Don't even try to flush that down the hopper without breaking it up first or we'll be mopping for the rest of the day."

The tech nods, makes a face of disgust, and disappears into the dirty utility room carrying her prize. Debbie shakes her head with amazement. "I think that one might have set a record," she says, stepping back behind the desk and plopping down in front of a computer to make an entry in the patient's chart. "So what brings you here?" she asks as she types.

"I was hoping to talk to Erik Tolliver about what happened to his wife, Shannon."

Debbie frowns. "Oh, yeah, I heard about that. Scary stuff." She pauses and her eyes grow big. "Do you think Erik did it?"

I shrug, not willing to commit one way or the other. "It's very early in the investigation. I'm still trying to sort through the pre-liminaries."

She nods thoughtfully. "How's the new job going? Do you like it?"

"I do," I answer honestly. "Like anything new, it has a learning curve and an adjustment period, but so far I'm enjoying it."

"Good," Debbie says. "And today your job is a little easier because it just so happens Erik is down here doing a portable in room twelve."

This is a stroke of luck. "Do you guys have an empty room we can use for a few minutes?"

"Sure. Take the ENT room."

The ENT room, or ear, nose, and throat room, is one of the few beds in the ER that is contained inside its own room and has a real door as opposed to a giant shower curtain for privacy. Kind of ironic when you consider that it's typically the only room that doesn't require the exposure of delicate body parts during treatment.

I stake out room twelve, waiting for Erik, and moments later he emerges, pushing his portable X-ray machine. When he sees me his first impulse is to smile and say hi, but before the word leaves his lips he remembers I'm no longer a coworker, and possibly no longer a friend. His smile fades.

"Hi, Erik," I say, trying to sound nonthreatening and friendly. "I was wondering if I could talk to you for a few minutes about Shannon."

"I'm pretty busy," he says, pushing his way past me and parking his machine in the hallway.

"Please?"

Something in my voice strikes home because he stops.

"Look, Erik, I'm just trying to figure out the facts here. I'm not making any judgments, I'm just gathering information. I want to find out who did this to Shannon."

He turns to face me and I see the faint sheen of tears in his eyes. "I didn't kill her," he says in a low voice. "But I sure as hell would love to kill the bastard who did."

"Then talk to me," I plead. I gesture toward the ENT room and he walks that way, his head hung low. Once we're inside he sinks into a chair, leaning forward with his elbows on his knees and his face buried in his hands.

I lean against the wall and give him a minute to collect himself. Then, as gently as possible, I say, "Talk to me Erik. Give me your thoughts on all of this."

He looks up at me with a surprised expression.

"What?" I ask.

He shakes his head and smiles. "I was expecting more of a third degree, not a request for my thoughts."

I shrug. "I figure you knew Shannon better than anyone else and might have some insight into what was going on in her life recently."

"First tell me honestly. Do you think I did this?" He is watching me closely, no doubt to gauge the sincerity of whatever answer I give him.

"No, I don't," I answer without hesitation, looking him straight in the eye. "I've known you since grade school and I can't imagine the guy I know you to be doing something like this. But I'm well aware that people keep secrets, dirty little secrets that hide aspects of their personalities and lifestyles that most people will never know. I've been fooled by people who were much closer to me in life than you are, so let me caveat my answer by saying that I'm only about ninety percent sure you didn't do it."

He considers my answer and nods. "You're right. Everyone has secrets. Just when you think you know someone . . ." His voice trails off and we exchange knowing glances. Erik, like everyone else who works at the hospital, is well aware of my recent history with David and it seems that the destruction of our respective marriages has created an odd sort of bond between us.

"So tell me your thoughts," I say again. "Why would anyone kill Shannon?"

Erik shakes his head and stares miserably at his feet. "I wish I knew. The only person I can think of is this shrink she was dating. He strikes me as a shady character but I realize I'm biased."

I nod thoughtfully, acknowledging his prejudice. "What is it about him that you don't like, other than the obvious?"

Erik shrugs. "He's got veiled eyes. You know what I mean, the kind of eyes that always look like they're hiding something. And he never answers a question directly. Instead he always asks another question."

This doesn't surprise me and I'm not sure I agree with Erik's assessment. Psychologists, psychiatrists, and counselors in general are trained to answer questions with questions. It's a standard tool taught in Psych 101. What Erik is interpreting as veiled eyes may simply be Nelson's attempt to look objective and impassive when others are talking to him.

"How long had Shannon been dating him?"

"A couple months, I think, but I can't be sure."

"Did she share any thoughts about him with you?"

He looks sheepish. "We didn't discuss him much. I admit I had a tendency to get rather, um, emotional whenever the topic arose."

"Understandable," I say. Then I quickly shift gears on him. "Shannon was shot with a .38 and Detective Hurley says you own one."

Erik nods. "They came early yesterday morning and tore my place apart looking for it and any other evidence."

"Did they find any?"

"How could they? I didn't do this, Mattie."

"So where is the gun?"

"I left it with Shannon." He pauses and lets forth a pained, ironic laugh. "I figured she could use it for protection since she was living alone. She said she was afraid of the stupid thing and would never touch it, but I left it with her just the same and suggested that she get some lessons on how to use it."

"Do you know where she kept it?"

"Last time I saw it, it was in the spare bedroom closet."

"When did you last see it there?"

His brow furrows as he thinks. "I'm not sure. Several weeks ago, I think. I came by to pick up some of my clothes and I saw the box in its usual spot up on the shelf." He pauses a moment and then asks, "Do you know the time of death yet?"

"It looks like she was killed around eight P.M., give or take a couple of hours."

Erik's shoulders sag and I know he comprehends the significance of this finding. "It doesn't look good for me, does it?" he says, looking utterly miserable.

"There's no hard evidence pointing to you. Everything is circumstantial and it's still pretty early in the investigation."

His expression brightens for a second, but it's short-lived because the door to our room opens and I turn to see Hurley standing there with a couple of uniform cops.

"Erik Tolliver," Hurley says, "you are under arrest for the murder of Shannon Tolliver. You have the right to remain silent. Anything you say . . ."

As Hurley recites his Miranda warning, the two cops approach Erik, who willingly succumbs to being handcuffed. He mutters an acknowledgment of his rights when asked, then allows the officers to steer him from the room. I watch as he's paraded through the ER, looking ashamed, humiliated, and completely without hope. The ER staff and patients watch in silence, but I can tell they are all mentally rehearsing their respective recital of the events for later.

My heart goes out to Erik and, as the cops lead him out the doors toward a waiting patrol car, I give Hurley a dirty look. "That was tacky. Couldn't you have done this somewhere other than his place of work? And aren't you being a bit premature?"

"Not at all," he answers. I expect him to look smug but seeing the effect Erik's arrest has had on me, he looks sympathetic instead. "I'm sorry," he says, and I think he means it.

But it doesn't change the facts, and after seeing the pathetic look of dejection on Erik's face, I'm more motivated than ever to get to the truth.

Chapter
12

After saying my good-byes to the ER crew, I head for my car, knowing what I have to do next but dreading it. Erik is going to need a lawyer, a good one, and I know one of the best: my brother-in-law, Lucien. Unfortunately, being a good lawyer doesn't require charm, finesse, or good taste, and Lucien is a shining example of this fact. He behaves like a sexist pig and lacks any sense of tact or political correctness. He is famous, or perhaps infamous, for his free use of words like *poontang, diddlywhacker,* and *rib bumpers.* Once, at a party David and I had, Lucien vocalized his fondness for women who cater to fast-food restaurants because, "we are what we eat and that means they're all fast, cheap, and easy."

I've never understood what my sister, Desi, sees in Lucien, though as far as I can tell he is a faithful and loving husband despite his belief that developing a hard-on is a form of personal growth. He is also a wonderful father to his daughter, Erika, and his son, Ethan, who despite some odd idiosyncrasies are both bright, sweet kids. Twelve-year-old Erika seems to have inherited her father's flair for attention-getting behavior, a trait she exhibits through her appearance rather than her speech. Her clothes are typically dark, mismatched, and oversized, and her hair color changes on a regular basis, ranging from raven black to hot pink. Ethan, who just turned ten, is brilliant but far less out-going and flamboyant. Desi calls him her mini nerd. He prefers to hole up in his room alone much of the time, though that might be because no one else wants to go in there. The kid is en-thralled with bugs of all kinds and his room holds a creepy but fascinating collection.

As I dial Lucien's office number and listen to the phone ring on the other end, part of me hopes he won't be available. Talking to him is an exercise in extreme patience that I'm not sure I'm up for today. But as luck would have it, he's not only in, he answers his own phone.

"Lucien, it's Mattie."

"Well, hello, Sweet Cheeks! What goodly deed did I do to warrant a call from you?" In my mind I think it's more the other way around—what horrible thing did I do to deserve the punish-ment of having to talk to him? "If you're calling to thank me for that picture thing, there's no need. It's all in the family, so to speak." He lets forth with a salacious chuckle.

The picture thing he's referring to is a shot of me standing bare-chested next to Joey, a gigantic hulk of a man who despite being a little slow in some areas has a savant ability when it comes to computers and programming. Joey also fancies himself something of a superhero and even dresses the part by wearing a skintight, red hero suit—complete with cape—under his regular clothes. How I came to be standing bare-chested next to Joey is a story in itself, one that nearly rivals the infamous nipple incident. Unfortunately, it was Alison who took the picture, and in an ef-fort to keep her from publishing it in the local paper, I had Lu-cien serve her with an injunction. In the process, he got a copy of the picture. I shudder to think what he's been doing with it since then.

Still, as trying as Lucien can be, he's a successful criminal de-fense lawyer who, more often than not, wins his cases. I've long held the belief that he wins by embarrassing, harassing, or simply talking his opponents to death. However unbecoming his behav-ior might be, it's effective. Bracing myself, I tell him why I'm calling.

"No, it's not that. I'm calling to ask a favor."

"Let me guess. You're starting to feel a bit pent up with your new single life and you want me to fix you up with somebody, right? Can do, Babycakes. With those headlights of yours you should be able to snag a great bosom buddy, if you know what I mean." In my mind's eye I can see him wiggling his eyebrows. "And you're smart to get right to it while you still have them on high beams, if you get my drift."

Sadly, I did. But despite the fact that any moron would get one of Lucien's crass innuendos, he clarifies.

"You're no spring chicken, anymore, Mattie. With tatas the size of yours, it won't be long before you'll have to pierce your belly button so you've got something you can hook your bra onto." His comment makes me straighten up and pull my shoulders back. "Dally too long and you'll be well beyond your freshness date. I'm only telling you this, Sweet Cheeks, because you're family and I want you to be happy."

I mentally calculate the odds of anyone Lucien would fix me up with making me happy and figure I'd be better off strutting my stuff on the streets.

"So give me some guidelines," he goes on. "Are you looking for a serious commitment kind of thing, or just a fuck buddy?"

"I'm fine in that regard, Lucien, but thanks."

"You sure? 'Cause I got a friend who's also going through a divorce and he's been answering the bone-a-phone so much lately he's about worn his johnson out. "

"Yes, Lucien. I'm sure." I barely take a breath before my next sentence, not wanting to give him another chance to pursue his current line of thinking. "I'm calling because I want to know if you'll consider representing someone who I don't think can afford your usual fees."

"You want me to do a pro bono thing?"

"Well, discounted rather than totally free, but yes."

"Who, and what's the rap?"

I fill him in on the case against Erik, sharing what I know, which to be honest, isn't much.

"You think this guy is innocent?" Lucien asks me.

"I do, but I don't have anything concrete to base it on right now," I admit. "I need to look into some things."

"Are there any other suspects?"

"Nothing definite yet, but there's a boyfriend I need to talk to, some new shrink here in town."

Lucien groans. I know from past conversations with him that he doesn't like shrinks of any kind. I suspect it's because he's had dealings with them in the past and been told things he didn't want to hear, giving him a prejudice I'm hoping will work in my favor for now.

"Okay," Lucien says. "Because you're family I'll talk to the guy and look at the case against him, but I'm not making any promises yet."

"That's fine. Let me know what you think after you do."

"Will do, Sweet Cheeks."

"Thanks, Lucien."

"Don't thank me yet," he cautions. "I'm not promising to take the case, and even if I do, you don't know what I might ask for as a return favor."

The possibilities are frightening.

"I'm sure we can work something out," I say warily.

"Oh, yes," Lucien says, as I suppress a shudder. "I'm sure we can."

Chapter 13

I stop at home long enough to check on my kitten, Rubbish. He is glad to see me and mews cutely as he runs figure eights around my feet, darn near tripping me up. After a few minutes of kitty nuzzling, I get a call on my cell from the office. It's Cass, our receptionist/file clerk/secretary. As an amateur thespian, Cass likes to dress up and play her roles on a 24-7 basis. As a result, in the month or so I've worked there I've seen her come to work dressed as a sixties-era hippie, Little Orphan Annie, a pregnant yuppie mom, an old woman, and a Goth queen. Her makeup, hair, clothing, and body language are usually so well done that if it wasn't for her voice, I wouldn't know it was Cass most of the time. She's good enough with accents that even the voice isn't a guarantee. I wonder what she looks like today.

"I have some work for you, Mattie," she says when I answer. "Izzy is getting his annual physical and he's close to being done but needs a little more time. So he wants you and Arnie to go to the site and get things started."

"Where and what?" I ask.

"It's two bodies from some kind of car accident." *Two* bodies? Things were starting to hop here in Sorenson. "Apparently a couple kids looking for an isolated place to smoke some weed found a wreck in the trees off Crawford Road. The bodies are pinned inside the wreckage. Based on the plates and make of the car, the cops think it's a couple from Illinois who went missing weeks ago."

"Okay," I tell her, mentally rearranging my day. This kind of unpredictability might throw some people off but I thrive on it. That's one of the reasons I was attracted to the ER, where Murphy's Law always seems to rule. If there is a snowy field surrounded by barbed wire, some drunken yahoo is going to go flying across it on a snowmobile in the middle of the night. If there's a major trauma case coming in, that's when the X-ray machine always breaks. If someone mentions how quiet the shift is, you'll have a Smurf—someone in severe respiratory distress—appear within seconds. And heaven help you if you decide to order food delivered for your shift meal. As soon as the order is placed, everyone in town will flock to the ER. Most ER nurses excel at eating on the run and in some very strange places. I just excel at eating.

"Is Arnie in the office?" I ask Cass.

"He is."

"Tell him I'll be there in about five minutes."

"Will do. And . . . um . . . Mattie?" There's a short pause before she adds, "There's one other thing Izzy wanted me to tell you."

Based on her hesitation, I suspect it won't be good news. "Go ahead."

"The car was pretty well hidden in the trees so these bodies have been out there a while, most likely for the whole two weeks they've been missing."

"Oh." I swallow hard. "I see."

Bodies that are weeks old mean serious decay, and I haven't yet done a bad decomp. But Izzy, who has referred to such bodies as "bloaters" and "slippers," has talked about them enough that I know I'm in for a challenge. Rotting bodies don't look or smell very good, and while I feel pretty comfortable dealing with blood, guts, and ghastly wounds, I've never seen or smelled a rotting corpse. This is virgin territory for me.

"Hold on a sec," Cass says. "Izzy wanted me to call him on his cell and conference with you."

I wait nervously, wondering just how awful this is going to be. A minute or so goes by and then I hear Izzy's voice on my phone.

"Mattie, you there?"

"I'm here."

"Cass filled you in on the situation?"

"She did."

I am about to elaborate when I hear a male voice in the background speaking to Izzy. "Do you want to bend over now or should I wait until you're done on the phone?" Izzy tells me to hold on a second and I hear his muffled voice as he answers, though I can't make out any of the words.

"Mattie?" he says, returning to the phone. "I should only be here another half hour or so. You and Arnie snap some photos, get what info you can from the cops, and do your basic scene sketches. But wait until I get there to do anything with the bodies."

"Okay."

"This will be your first experience with serious decomp. Are you okay with that?"

"I'll be fine," I tell him with far more conviction than I feel.

"All right then. Go ahead, but take it slow." I'm about to ask him another question when I hear him suck in his breath and yelp, "Damn it, Adam! I was talking to her, not you," followed by the doctor's hasty apology.

I can't help but giggle and when Izzy hears me he says, "Knock it off or I'll start revealing your real name to everyone."

"My lips are sealed," I say, suddenly serious. Other than Izzy, no one outside of my family knows my real name. I've always assumed my mother was on some really good drugs when she gave it to me. Fortunately, the only place it can be found is on my birth certificate. Mother apparently took pity on me afterward and nicknamed me Mattie. It's the only name anyone has ever used since.

"See you out there, Izzy," I say, and then I disconnect before I can hear anything else.

Five minutes later I'm at the office, changed into a pair of scrubs, and on my way upstairs to Arnie's lab. I'm still trying to shake off the mental image of Izzy bent over an exam table getting his where-the-sun-don't-shine probe, and I'm almost looking forward to the distraction of badly decomposed bodies.

Arnie spends most of his time entrenched in his second-floor lab. Our facilities are well equipped and larger than one might expect to find in a town of this size because the ME's office covers not just Sorenson, but the entire county, even overlapping into adjacent counties at times. When Izzy took the ME's position seven years ago, he was pretty aggressive in securing some of the very best and latest equipment for the office. As a result, we now process some of our own evidence whereas in years past it was all sent to Madison, a practice that led to increased expenses and considerable delays. But our machinery capabilities are far greater than our manpower. As our only lab tech, Arnie does on-call time twenty-four-seven and typically puts in sixty-plus hours a week, a situation that is beginning to wear on him. Izzy has hinted that he would like me to take some classes and become certified to work as Arnie's assistant but he hasn't pushed it too hard yet, given that I'm still learning what I need to know to function as Izzy's assistant.

In the meantime, Arnie manages what he can and ships the rest off to the Madison lab. He hates sending anything out and would prefer to keep it all in-house, but as a one-man department, his abilities are limited.

Before coming to work with Izzy, Arnie was as an evidence technician for the L.A. Coroner's office. I'm not sure why he left there or how he ended up in Podunk, Wisconsin, and when I've tried to ask him or Izzy about it, they always skirt around the issue. I suspect it might have something to do with Arnie's fixation on conspiracy theories. He believes there are eyes in the sky watching our every move, spies circulating among us disguised as homeless people, and that the moon landing was faked but aliens really did crash in Roswell. Despite his paranoia and my suspicion that most of his friends wear aluminum foil hats, I like Arnie.

I find him in his lab, his head bent over a microscope, and he hails me by name without looking up, before I can say a word.

"It creeps me out the way you do that," I tell him.

He shrugs, switches the magnification on his microscope, and says, "I can tell from the scents and the way people walk. It's a talent you hone after a while." He finally looks up at me, squinting as his eyes adjust focus. "What can I do for you?"

"There are a couple of bodies in a car wreck in the woods off Crawford Road, and Izzy wants the two of us to go out and start the preliminaries."

"Without him?"

"For now. He'll meet us there as soon as he's done getting his alien anal probe."

Arnie's eyebrows shoot up with interest.

"He's getting his annual physical," I explain.

"Ah," Arnie says. He grimaces and squirms a bit in his seat before pushing back from the table, shrugging off his lab coat, and gathering up his scene kit. "Tell me what you know," he says.

"The cops think it's a couple from Illinois who went missing two weeks ago. Apparently the bodies are in an advanced state of decomp."

Arnie looks intrigued. "I wonder if it's the Heinrichs."

"Who?"

"Gerald and Bitsy Heinrich?" he says, looking at me like he can't believe I don't know them. "The oil magnate and his trophy wife?"

I shrug and he shakes his head, clearly disappointed. Then he enlightens me.

"Gerald Heinrich is the only child and sole heir of 1940s Chicago oil baron Dietmar Heinrich. Estimates list Gerald's wealth in the billions. His first wife, Maggie, died from some type of cancer and he remarried a few years ago to a woman named Elizabeth, or Bitsy, Conklin. Bitsy used to be a . . . hmm, how should I say it . . . a specialty dancer."

"You mean a stripper?"

"That, yes. But rumor had it she went a little farther than that in her heyday, providing private lap dances to certain clients, if you get my drift."

I did.

"Come ride in the evidence van with me and I'll fill you in on the rest," Arnie says, rubbing his hands together gleefully. "This promises to be an interesting day."

Chapter
14

I follow Arnie down to the garage where our one evidence van is stored. We stash our equipment inside and, as soon as we are underway, Arnie continues the Heinrich saga.

"Gerald Heinrich became quite smitten with Bitsy after a private lap dance or two and then paid her to quit dancing for anyone but him. It was assumed he'd keep her on the side as a mistress but he surprised everyone, especially his kids, when he married her."

"How many kids does he have?"

"Four: two daughters and two sons by his first wife—a bunch of spoiled brats, if you ask me. They're in their late twenties and early thirties and not a one of them has ever worked for a living. They sponge off their father's money and spend their time partying, jet-setting, and trying to avoid the tabloids. As you might imagine, they marked Bitsy as a greedy gold digger right from the get-go and immediately declared her the enemy. Bitsy has a son and daughter of her own: father or fathers unknown, and about the same age as the Heinrich kids. And trust me, there is no love lost between the two camps."

"Sounds like quite the tempest."

Arnie laughs. "You have no idea. Ever since Bitsy and Gerald went missing, the rumors have been flying. Bitsy's kids accused

Gerald's of killing the couple so they could inherit the money. Gerald's kids countered by saying they thought Bitsy killed Gerald and took off with his money. The two sides have been battling it out in the gab rags ever since."

I shake my head in disgust. "So if our bodies are Gerald and Bitsy, and they died as the result of a car accident, both sides may be eating crow."

"Oh, I doubt the battle will end that easily," Arnie says. "There's too much money at stake. If this does turn out to be Gerald and Bitsy, our little town is going to be in for a lot of attention."

He sounds excited at the prospect and I can't help but wonder if he'll end up contributing to the conspiracy mill at some point. So far, despite all his suspicions and paranoia, Arnie has shown himself to be objective and open when it comes to his work. He believes in the power and truth of evidence, and gracefully accepts it when he's proven wrong, though it never stops him from speculating about things and developing some pretty wild theories. Occasionally, his outside-the-box thinking is helpful, but most of the time, it's simply entertaining.

We pull up to the scene, identifiable by the ambulance, sawhorses, and police cars parked along the shoulder of the road. A storm has moved in, blanketing the sky with a morose shade of gray, and rain is coming down in big fat drops that hit the ground like overripe cherries. Apparently it's not much of a deterrent, however, since there is also a TV truck parked on the shoulder with its antenna raised high in the air.

Arnie says, "This isn't good. It looks like the media has already heard."

"How do they find out so fast?"

"They have people with police scanners who monitor all the emergency calls twenty-four-seven. Whenever something sounds potentially juicy, they'll send a crew out to investigate."

Arnie passes by the TV truck and parks at the front of the line of vehicles. Almost immediately there are several people running in our direction carrying microphones, cameras, and lighting equipment.

"Brace yourself," Arnie warns me. "They aren't going to be allowed near the crime scene so they'll be desperate for any clues they can get. Questions will be coming at you faster than a BMW on the Autobahn. Don't say a word."

Before Arnie has finished issuing his warning, several faces are peering at me through the van window. I reach behind me to grab my scene kit, then push back the news-hungry horde by opening the van door. As I climb out, I catch the faint odor of rotting flesh with my first breath and switch from breathing through my nose to through my mouth.

A perfectly coifed brunette wearing a tight-fitting business suit over a body not much bigger around than one of my pant legs runs up to me and says, "Is it true that the bodies you found here are those of Chicago oil baron Gerald Heinrich and his wife?" Then she shoves her microphone in my face.

I don't say a word and smile enigmatically instead, but when I do I accidentally breathe in through my nose and the smell nearly gags me. As I'm struggling to subdue my body's desire to recycle my breakfast, a bright light flashes in my eyes.

"Perfect!" says a voice I recognize.

Belatedly I see that Alison Miller is among the group of newspeople. I shoot her a dirty look but she has already turned around and is taking shots of all the emergency vehicles, pretending to ignore me.

I slam the van door closed, and when I try to take a step toward the grassy hillside leading down into the trees, I am once again accosted by the first woman, whom I recognize as a reporter for one of the major network TV affiliates in Madison. She begins a machine gun interrogation.

"Are there two bodies? Are there any signs of foul play? Has the Heinrich family been notified yet? How long have the victims been dead?"

I ignore the questions, glare at the cameraman, and shove my way past everyone. It's not hard to get past the newswoman since she's as short as Izzy even with her three-inch heels, and can't weigh more than one hundred pounds soaking wet, which she is, thanks to the rain. But the camera guy proves a bit more challenging. He dodges around me and aims the camera in my general direction. I try a similar dodge but as soon as I step on the wet grass it's like I'm on ice; one foot is heading downhill at a breakneck speed and the other is fixed on the shoulder of the road. Just as my legs start to feel like the wishbone in a turkey, I hear a loud ripping sound and my second foot finally gives way.

Chapter 15

I slide down the wet grass for twenty feet or more, most of it on my butt. When I finally come to a stop in a position that looks like a gymnastic maneuver gone horribly wrong, I look down and see that the crotch of my scrub pants is ripped out. Above me Alison is snapping away and the cameraman appears to be filming also.

I manage to drag my legs together as Arnie appears at my side. "That was impressive," he says. "I give it a nine and a half. I would have gone the full ten but the landing was a bit off."

"Very funny." I get up from the ground and try to adjust my pants.

"Uh-oh," Arnie says. "Did you have an accident?"

I give him an exasperated *duh!* look.

"I don't mean your fall," he says, pointing to my behind with barely contained laughter.

I crank my head around, trying to see, but my circus contortionist genes don't seem to be working. So I grab a handful of my scrub pants material and pull at the fabric. Just as I see the dark smear on the seat of my pants that looks like a Depends failure, I hear a distinct ripping sound and realize I've enhanced my crotch vent.

"Damn it!" I say, glaring at Arnie as he doubles over with

laughter. I hear several more clicks from above and quickly turn around so my backside is facing the trees. Then I mentally strangle both Alison and the TV camera guy while making a few ineffective swipes at my ass.

"Go ahead and laugh, you heathen." I scowl at Arnie.

"Sorry," he says, struggling to get himself under control. "But it is quite the sight."

"If you don't knock it off, it will be the last thing you ever see."

He makes a *yeah, right* face so I put my hands on my hips and give him The Look.

The Look is one of my more powerful tools, something I learned from my mother. When I was a kid, my sister, Desi, and I both trembled with fear whenever my mother gave us The Look. It came most often when we were lying about something, or screaming at one another, or had been caught doing something we knew we were forbidden to do, like the time we gave each other haircuts and indelible Magic Marker facial tattoos the day before our class pictures were taken. Mother would never say or do anything; she would just cock her left eyebrow and stare at us with this intense look that was mysterious, scary, and very powerful. It pierced our kiddie armor every time. I've seen her do it to grown men and make them weep. Though I've never mastered it to the degree my mother has, being six feet tall helps a lot with the intimidation factor.

It definitely has an impact on Arnie. Within three seconds of arching my brow he's straight-faced and all business. "Sorry," he mumbles.

"Can we please get going?" I say, picking up my scene kit, which has managed to slide down the hill with me.

Arnie nods, bows, and swings his arm toward the trees. "After you, milady."

"Walk behind me so those bloodsucking camera goons can't get any more shots."

"Happily," Arnie says, his voice excited as his gaze shifts to my butt.

I roll my eyes, turn toward the trees, and let Arnie fall into step behind me. A police officer is standing at the edge of the woods, and judging from the expression on his face, he hasn't missed any of what just happened. He looks like he's about to say something but Arnie shakes his head at him. "I wouldn't if I were you," he warns.

I arch my brow at the cop and he clamps his mouth shut and waves us along a barely discernible path of broken-limbed bushes amid the trees. Most of the deciduous trees have already dropped their leaves but there are enough pine trees to provide a fair amount of cover. The ground isn't nearly as wet here, but the shrubbery is so high and thick it keeps snagging at my feet like a snare. And the slope is a precipitous one, forcing me to turn sideways rather than face straight ahead. It makes for slow going but that's okay since with every baby step I take, the smell grows stronger and more pungent.

"Have you done any heavy decomps yet?" Arnie asks me.

I shake my head.

"It's not as bad as you think. The first few minutes are kind of tough but then it's like your body gets used to it and you don't even smell it anymore. I have some Vicks VapoRub in my scene kit if you want. Dab a little under your nose and it cuts the odor some. I don't use it anymore but I still carry it because a lot of the cops like to use it."

"No, thanks," I say, sounding as if I have a bad head cold because I'm so focused on not breathing through my nose. I am determined to tough it out and prove my mettle. After all, I've smelled some pretty nasty things in my time, like the time I found the weekend-old plastic bag with an amputated gangrenous foot in it that an OR tech forgot to put in the biohazard bin. But as we draw closer to the scene, the smell becomes so intense that even breathing through my mouth doesn't help.

I hear muffled voices and an odd buzzing sound ahead and grip my scene kit tightly, bracing myself for what's to come. As I push aside a dense growth of bush, the mangled front corner of a silver Cadillac Escalade comes into view.

Then I see Hurley standing with a couple of sheriff's deputies off to my right and lose sight of everything else, including the big root in the ground in front of me. I catch my foot on it and fall headlong toward the passenger side of the car. I try to break my fall against the wreck with my left hand but it hits something squishy, gelatinous, and slippery. I half fall, half slide to the ground, landing on my left side just below the passenger door.

"Aw, shit," I hear Hurley mutter. "There she goes again."

The smell of decay is suddenly so pungent, it's as if I'm bathing in it, and the source of the buzzing sound becomes apparent as I swat at the hordes of flies hovering around me. My stomach lurches as I look at the disgusting, smelly mess on my hand and arm, and just when I think it couldn't possibly get any worse, I see that it's all down the side of my scrubs as well. Then, just to make matters more interesting, I realize some of it is moving.

Maggots!

I brush frantically at the ones clinging to my arm and though some of them fall off, most of them prove surprisingly tenacious.

"What is that?" I say, gesturing toward the nasty pile of goo on the ground.

Hurley and the two sheriffs stare at me like I'm a life form from another planet and none of them offer up an answer. But Arnie does.

"My guess is it's what's left of the upper part of that person," he says, pointing toward the car.

Belatedly I look above me and see the remains of a well-clothed, bug-ridden, rotting corpse hanging halfway out of the broken passenger side window. One arm, or what's left of it, is hanging down the outside of the door and a steady flow of reddish brown goo is dripping off the fingertips into a puddle on the ground. Adding to the pool is what's left of the corpse's head, which is hanging onto its body by the thinnest of sinewy threads. Oozing from this is a grayish-colored jellylike substance. Both of the eye sockets are empty and I can see maggots crawling around there as well as in the nose, mouth, and ears.

I tear my eyes away from the horror of the hovering corpse and realize that everyone is watching me, waiting to see how I'll react. As the new kid on the block, this will be one more test to deem my worthiness and I'm determined to pass muster. I summon my resolve, set my scene kit to one side, and stand up. My scent receptors must be growing numb because already the smell doesn't seem quite as bad, despite the fact that my skin and clothing are covered with putrid goo.

As calmly as I can, I open my kit and remove a container of disinfectant wipes. Then I begin the arduous task of trying to bathe with a chemically ridden washcloth the size of a square of toilet paper. Realizing I'm not going to have a meltdown, the group shifts their attention back to the wreck. Relieved to be out from under their scrutiny, I do the same, wiping absentmindedly at the pungent miasma on my arm as I examine the scene.

I can see now that there are two bodies. The driver—most likely a man, based on the hair and clothing—is lying on the ground near the front bumper on the driver side. Both legs are badly fractured, and judging from the fact that the windshield is shattered but intact, I guess that he most likely dragged himself out of the car and along the ground as far as he could, where he then died.

Peering inside the passenger side I see that the legs of the corpse closest to me—this one appears to be a woman—are pinned beneath the dashboard. The front grille of the car is crumpled against the trunk of a large oak tree. In the back of the SUV are several suitcases, and beside the body in the front seat, covered with blood and Lord knows what else, is a lockable briefcase. Behind the car I see a mowed-down trail leading back through the brush and trees, presumably the path the car took before it came to rest.

Arnie echoes my thoughts by saying, "They must have been really moving when they left the road to have made it this far into the woods."

I nod in agreement and pluck another wipe from my container, feeling something tickle along my shoulder as I do. I idly scratch at the spot and watch as Arnie starts taking camera shots of the scene from a variety of angles. Three disinfectant wipes later, with my hands relatively clean, I don a pair of gloves and take in the condition of my scrubs, which are smeared down one side with the death goo. Remembering that Izzy will be coming to the scene, I take out my cell phone and try to call him, thinking I can ask him to bring me a change of scrubs. But my phone can't find a signal. I snap it shut, grab another wipe, and attempt to remove the worst of the muck from my scrubs using that.

I feel another itch—this time on my chest—and something about it makes me pull at the front of my scrub top and look down inside. To my horror I see a handful of maggots slowly crawling their way across my torso and around my cleavage. Panicked, I try to reach in there and pluck them out but then I feel that same itchy sensation in the middle of my back and realize the little varmints are now in places I can't reach. I do a jiggly jump-and-hop, hoping to knock them loose, but the itching only grows more intense. Suddenly I feel little itchies all over my body so I do the only sensible thing I can think of. Standing in the middle of the woods on a cold November morning in front of four men and two corpses, I strip off my scrubs and start swiping and swatting at myself like a full-blown detox in a lockdown room.

Chapter
16

"Get them off me! Get 'em off!" I yell, jumping around in the woods wearing nothing but my underwear. I'm brushing frantically at myself, my entire body suddenly alive with creepy crawling sensations. As soon as I've rid myself of the maggots I can see on the front of me, I crane my head around in an attempt to examine my back. I can't see a thing, and just as I feel my panic rise to an explosive crescendo, a steadying hand settles on my shoulder.

Hurley's breath is warm on my neck as he says, "What is it with you wanting to get naked all the time? Does it have something to do with that nipple incident you never told me about?" His fingers flick a couple of times on my back and then he turns me around and says, "There you go. They're all gone, at least from the places I can see."

He is grinning down at me suggestively, and after tearing my eyes from his face, I look around at the rest of the group to see if I've made as much of a spectacle of myself as I think. Apparently I have. Arnie is standing off to my right, mouth agape, his eyes riveted to my chest.

A cold breeze rustles the nearby trees, making my skin come alive with goose bumps, which only enhances the crawling sensation. I look down at my chest expecting to see more maggots crawling on me but the only bumps I see are in my bra. My nipples are protruding out from the cold, standing at attention like Madonna on steroids. What is it with me and nipples?

The two sheriff's deputies have their hands clamped over their mouths, their bodies shaking with mirth. I'm about to give them The Look when I hear a distinctive click-and-whirl sound over near Arnie. I'm thinking he has used his camera to sneak off a couple of shots, but when I look in his direction I see that he's still standing frozen and transfixed, a small string of drool hanging from one corner of his mouth. Some branches behind him flutter and I see a flash of movement.

I take a couple of steps closer and peer into the brush, quickly identifying the source of the noise. "Damn it, Alison, you might as well present yourself. I know you're out there."

The bushes rustle again and a sheepish-looking Alison steps out into the clearing.

Hurley shakes his head and sighs heavily. Then he shrugs off his jacket and hands it to me. "This is starting to feel like a habit," he says. As I put the jacket on, he walks over to Alison and holds his hand out. "Alison, hon, you know better. Give it over."

Hon? Since when did she move into *hon* position? Hun, perhaps, but *hon?*

Clearly the endearment isn't lost on Alison since her guilty expression is fleetingly replaced with a smug one. Then she shakes her head at Hurley and pouts cutely. "No one gets my camera, Stevie, not even you."

At the utterance of "Stevie" the two deputies both snigger but a death ray look from Hurley shuts them right up, making me a bit envious.

Hurley turns back to Alison and says, "You don't have to give me the camera, just the film."

"It's digital," Alison says with an unmistakable *duh* tone in her voice. "There is no film."

My natural endowments put a definite strain on the buttons of Hurley's jacket but I finally manage to get the majority of my chest under cover. As a result, Arnie snaps out of his coma and tunes in to the conversation.

"It's all stored on a little memory card," he tells Hurley. "Make her hand over the card." Then his eyes grow huge as a thought hits him. "In fact, give it to me. She might have taken some valuable evidentiary shots. I should review it all to make sure there isn't anything, um"—he pauses and his eyes briefly dart toward my chest before he looks back at Hurley—"anything critical on there."

I whirl around and glare at Hurley. "If that memory card goes to anyone but me I swear I'll sic my crazy-assed brother-in-law on all of you."

The crowd grows silent. Everyone here knows that being the focus of Lucien's attention is to risk public embarrassment and shame the likes of which most people have never imagined, much less experienced. The man is a master rumor monger and in a small town like this one, rumors spread faster than cold sores at an orgy.

"Give her the card," Hurley says to Alison. "And then get your ass out of here. I could have you arrested for this, you know."

I turn back and smile smugly at Alison, but she is clearly undaunted by Hurley's threats. She bats her eyelashes at him and says in a breathless voice, "Ooh, does that mean handcuffs, Stevie?"

Hurley shoots her a thunderous look and she pouts again, removes the memory card from her camera, and tosses it to me. Her aim is a bit short and I have to bend and reach in order to catch it. As I do so, Hurley's jacket rides up my backside and I hear him suck in his breath behind me. He leans forward and whispers, "I'll give you twenty bucks to do that again."

As I slip the memory card into one of the jacket's pockets, I feel a blush spreading over my body, but it's quickly forgotten when the bushes rustle again and Izzy steps into the clearing.

He pauses a moment to take in the scene. "Dare I ask?" he says, his gaze settling on me.

"I wouldn't," Arnie says.

"Not if you know what's good for you," Hurley warns at the same time.

The two sheriff's deputies just shake their heads.

Izzy nods. "Okay, then. Let's get to it."

Chapter
17

After cleaning my scrub pants off the best I can, I reluctantly put them back on. My top is a total loss however, so I keep Hurley's jacket, which fortunately helps to cover my crotch vent. By the time I don a plastic gown over it all—better late than never—I feel like the Michelin Man. Finding a place to hook my voice recorder proves challenging, but after testing its ability to pick up what I'm saying from beneath the plastic gown, I end up sliding it down into my cleavage, much to the amusement of all the men.

The contents of a wallet and pocketbook we find in the car support Arnie's suspicions about the victims' identities, though it won't be enough to establish a definite ID. For the male victim, it will likely require a forensic dentist, but Izzy informs me that identifying the female might be easier since we find a pair of breast implants sitting in her lap. Implants all have serial numbers on them, allowing us to trace them back to the surgeon who used them, and from there, to the patient who received them.

A couple of hours later we have finally bagged what can be bagged, and tagged what can be tagged, including samples of all the maggots, flies, and other insects found on and around both bodies. The remains of the two bodies have been removed—a task made no easier by the degree of decomposition—and sealed up inside special body bags. One of the sheriff's deputies who had been on site originally left to make arrangements for towing the car from its resting place back to a special garage. As a result, a four-wheel-drive, flatbed truck arrived ten minutes ago. Once we were sure the trail the Caddy had taken through the trees was thoroughly examined and photographed for evidence, the truck backed its way along the same path. The men who came with the truck are now winching the car into place and trying not to vomit.

It's almost entertaining at this point to see the reactions of the newcomers since everyone else has become more or less immune to the odor. My own nose hasn't so much as wrinkled for the past hour and a half.

Despite the temperature, which is a seasonable forty-nine degrees, I'm sweating like a pig beneath my many layers and can't wait to get back to the office and into a shower, though at this point, regular body odor is the least of my worries. I strip off my outer suit and bag it to get some relief, but the outfit beneath still leaves something to be desired.

The task of getting all the evidence from the scene back to the office is our next challenge. Not only do we have to haul the two body bags and all the evidence we have obtained through the woods to our vehicles, there is the matter of the news gauntlet waiting back at the road. Given my current state of attire and the fact that I've made myself plenty newsworthy already today, I'm desperate to avoid anyone with a camera. And as I watch the tow truck guys do their thing, I have a brainstorm.

"Izzy, why don't we load the evidence onto the flatbed of the tow truck along with the car and take it back to the office on that?"

Izzy shakes his head. "We need to ensure our chain of evidence."

"Easy enough," I counter. "I'll ride with the truck and the evidence. In the meantime, you and Arnie can carry a few items back to the cars the way we came in and give the news crew that sound bite they're so desperately seeking."

Izzy considers the idea for a moment. "Maybe," he says

thoughtfully. "But how would we secure everything down on that flatbed?"

Damn, I hadn't considered that. And I'm guessing the image of the ME's office won't be enhanced much by body bags flying off the back of the truck and onto the highway. I'm about to kiss my brilliant idea good-bye when Arnie saves the day.

"I'm pretty sure they have tarps they use to strap stuff down to the bed. Put everything under the tarp and it should be fine."

Izzy nods approvingly and I feel hope spring once again in my chest—at least I pray it's hope I'm feeling, and not another maggot.

Izzy says, "Let me run it by the truck driver," and then he walks over to the tow truck's head guy and starts talking and gesturing up a storm. The driver is frowning pretty hard, and just when I'm thinking it doesn't look good, Izzy points to me. Suddenly the guy's face splits into a broad, slightly lecherous grin and he nods vigorously.

A second later Izzy trots back over to us. "They're willing to do it," he says.

"What the hell did you promise them for payment?" I ask, watching as the head guy says something to the other two men and they all turn to stare at me.

"Just the usual," Izzy says enigmatically.

I'm hardly reassured since we've never done this before and there is no "usual" established for this situation. I chew on my lip, debating my alternatives, and decide I'd rather spend half an hour squeezed into the cab of a tow truck with three sweaty, drooling men than have to face the news cameras again.

But then Hurley walks up to me and whispers low in my ear, sending a little tingle down my spine. "Those guys look a little rough. If you want me to ride with you, I will. I can leave my car out here and pick it up later."

I look up at him, an action that carries a thrill all its own since there aren't a lot of men who are taller than me, and flash him a grateful smile. "Thanks. That would be great."

An hour later, we have everything loaded onto the truck except for a few evidence envelopes that Izzy and Arnie are carrying. The Caddy is secured and tarped at the front end of the flatbed and all the other evidence is tied down under a second tarp at the back.

A member of the truck crew approaches me, chewing on the large wad of "tobacky weed" I heard him borrow from his buddy. That's how he worded it—"borrow," like he was going to chew it and then give it back. He looks directly at my chest, smiles at me with a handful of brown stained teeth, and says, "You kin ride in the back seat with me."

I look to Hurley for help but he's wearing a cocky grin that tells me he's enjoying my predicament far too much to intervene. Resigned, I climb into the back seat of the king cab, sandwiched in between Mr. Tobacky Weed and his supplier, while Hurley climbs into the front seat with the driver, a huge behemoth of a guy named Manny. We are about to take off when Mr. Tobacky Weed sniffs the air a few times and makes a face.

"Holy shit," he says. "What on earth is that smell?" He sniffs the air a few more times and his nose eventually settles somewhere in the neighborhood of my cleavage. His eyes drift up toward my face with a look of disgust. "It's her," he says, rearing back. "Lord, lady, you smell worse than the rat what died under Bubba's outhouse."

Mr. Tobacky Weed's supplier wrinkles his nose and rears back like he's been slapped. "Man, you ain't kidding," he says, pinching his nose shut. He pushes open the little vent window beside him and sticks his face in the crack. "Aw, that's bad. I don't think I can take it, Manny."

"Me neither," Mr. Tobacky Weed says, opening his window vent and mimicking his partner. "Aw, geez," he says, gagging. "I think I'm gonna ralph."

Hurley turns around and looks at me with a sympathetic smile. "You are kind of ripe," he says, making a face like he just tasted something rancid.

"Well, what do you want me to do about it?" I snap back. "It's not like there's a shower out here anywhere. I don't see what I can do short of stripping naked and wiping myself down with the chemical cloths."

All four men stare slack-jawed at me for a moment before Mr. Tobacky Weed breaks the trance. "I can't ride with that smell," he declares, taking a last, woeful look at my chest.

"Me either," says his partner.

"Well, I have to ride somewhere," I tell them. "I can't leave my evidence."

They all look at each other, temporarily dumbfounded. Then Mr. Tobacky Weed's one mental light bulb turns on, sealing my fate.

Banned from the truck's cab, I am forced to ride on the flatbed along with the car and the evidence. My ride isn't exactly legal, but Hurley pretends not to notice, an act I vow to make him pay for.

I've never understood the appeal of convertibles. It sounds romantic—the wind in your hair, the sun on your shoulders, Mother Nature all around you—but the truth is, nature has nasty things like stinging, cold raindrops, and the wind can tie knots in your hair.

The flatbed of the tow truck is the convertible ride from hell and by the time we arrive back at the morgue I look like something the dog barfed up. Since Izzy and Arnie aren't back yet I'm able to get into the office garage without any further camera incidents, but it also means I have to sit and wait for them to arrive to ensure the security of our evidence.

Hurley heads outside to make some phone calls—the morgue garage is a dead zone for signals as well as people—and the tow truck crew head down the street to the Nowhere Bar for a bite of lunch and a pint or ten of ale. I perch myself on the back end of the flatbed and start scraping chunks of God-knows-what out of my hair while dreaming of a long, hot, soapy shower.

The door opens and I get excited thinking my shower is imminent, but it's only Hurley coming back from his phone calls. His presence causes an excitement all its own, but when I see him look at me and purse his lips to bite back a laugh, I figure now isn't the best time for me to make a move.

"Christ, Winston, you certainly are a sight." He holds his camera phone up and sights me through the viewer. "Can I snap a picture of you?"

"I don't know," I answer, smiling sweetly. "Can I snap your family jewels?"

His phone clicks closed and disappears into his pocket. The garage door opens again and I breathe a sigh of relief at the sight of the van pulling in with Arnie behind the wheel. As he parks alongside the truck, I see Izzy in the front passenger seat, staring out his window at me with an expression of shocked disbelief. Once Arnie shuts the engine down, Izzy hesitates for a few seconds before slowly opening his door. But instead of getting out, he stares at me from the safety of the van's confines like he expects me to spring on him and eat him alive.

"What the hell happened to you?" he asks. "Your hair looks like you stuck your finger in a light socket."

I scowl at him and make a self-conscious swipe at my head. Before I can say anything, Hurley jumps in with an explanation. "The guys in the truck deemed her too rank to sit inside so they made her ride back on the flatbed."

Izzy's eyes grow wide and he gives me a cautiously sympathetic look. "I'm sorry, Mattie. I know this has been a rotten day for you," he says gently.

Hurley snorts and says, "Yeah, it stinks that you had to ride in the back."

Arnie, who is out of the van and standing beside Hurley, chuckles and says, "No kidding. That really reeks."

"A truly rank day," says Hurley.

"Utterly foul," adds Arnie.

The two of them are wearing shit-eating grins and I give Izzy a pleading look. For a split second he manages to look disgusted by the humor, but then he turns on me faster than a starving dog on a steak.

"Totally putrid," he tosses out, and then all three of them start guffawing like they're at a hillbilly hootenanny.

I fold my arms over my chest and glare at them with my best Look but it doesn't even begin to penetrate. I fear I'm losing my touch. So I move on to threats instead. "I think I need to give each and every one of you a great big bear hug," I say, jumping down from the flatbed and spreading my arms wide as I move toward them. Hurley and Izzy both back up without hesitation but Arnie stands transfixed for a moment, clearly weighing the nastiness of being stunk up against the sweetness of a possible cleavage nestle. Ignoring Arnie, I close in on Izzy and Hurley. Izzy, realizing he might get backed against the wall and no doubt aware of his inability to outrun me, holds his hands up, nods in the direction of the other two men, and says, "Do it and I'll tell them your real name."

Hurley's eyebrows shoot up with curiosity and I stop dead in my tracks, silently cursing Izzy. "I'll make you pay, all of you," I seethe. Then I stomp off toward the shower, leaving the boys behind me giggling like a gaggle of little girls.

Chapter
18

Tuesday morning, freshly scrubbed and showered for the fourth time since yesterday afternoon's fiasco, I take the jacket Hurley loaned me the day before, which I have tied up inside two plastic bags to try to mask the odor, and drop it off at the dry cleaner. The same woman is on duty and the first thing she says when I walk in is, "Your dress isn't done yet but it should be ready later today."

"That's fine," I tell her. I didn't expect the dress to be done yet but I didn't want to hang on to the jacket any longer than necessary, fearful it would stink up my car. "I'm here to drop something else off." I toss the bag onto the counter, and when she starts to open it I stop her.

"I wouldn't do that if I were you," I caution. "It's a bit pungent. You'll want to wear gloves and such to handle it."

Her expression is a mix of intrigue and fright. "What is it?" she asks, trying to peer through the white plastic.

"It's a jacket. A man's jacket. Unfortunately it was exposed to some pretty nasty stuff at a scene with some decomposed bodies."

Her eyes grow wide. "Was it that car accident thing that was on the news last night?" She leans closer. "Was it really the Heinriches in there?"

"We don't know for sure," I tell her. "And I can't say anything more until we can confirm the IDs."

She frowns, clearly disappointed. "This is going to cost extra," she says, nodding toward the bag. "A lot extra."

I suspect she's being punitive because of my unwillingness to share and is enjoying what little power she can wield over me. So I flash a smile of indifference and say, "That's fine. And there's no rush. Whenever you can get to it."

I leave the disappointed dry cleaner behind and drive to the office, where Arnie informs me that Izzy is out doing some follow-up tests for his physical and isn't planning to do the autopsies on the Heinrichs until the afternoon. Preferring to spend time at home with Rubbish rather than holed up in the library—which is the closest thing I have to an office—I grab some textbooks and drive back to my house, where I spend a couple of hours studying up on how weather affects decomposition rates.

At a little past eleven my cell phone rings and a look at the caller ID tells me it's Lucien. I wince, knowing I have to talk to him in order to get an update on Erik's situation, but reluctant to spend any time in conversation with the man who once declared himself a "vagitarian."

"How's it going, Sweet Cheeks?" he says when I answer.

"Fine. Have you had a chance to look at Erik's case yet?"

"I have. The case against him is mostly circumstantial at this point."

"Can you help him?"

"I'm willing to give it the old college try," he says. "I told him I'd cut him a break on the fees as a favor to my favorite sister-in-law."

Not much of a compliment considering I'm his only sister-in-law.

"His arraignment is tomorrow morning. I'll update you when I know something more."

"Thanks, Lucien." I'm about to disconnect, feeling relieved that my conversation with him was a relatively normal one this time, when he tosses out another tidbit.

"Gotta run, Sweet Cheeks. I'm due in court. I'm representing an Australian woman who got slapped with a DWI." That sounds normal enough until he adds, "She told me she's a lesbian. That lends a whole new meaning to the term *down under*, doesn't it?"

After I hang up the phone, I turn my mental efforts toward Shannon's murder by digging out a telephone book and looking up Luke Nelson's address and phone number. I expect to reach a receptionist or an answering machine, but Nelson himself answers.

"Hi, Dr. Nelson. This is Mattie Winston. I'm a deputy coroner with the medical examiner's office."

There's a bit of a pause before he responds. "I'm guessing this is about Shannon Tolliver?" he says rhetorically. "I heard about it yesterday. What a terrible thing."

"Yes," I agree. "It is terrible. I'm wondering if you might have some time for me to come by and talk to you about it."

"I've already arranged to meet with a Detective Hurley on the matter. Won't that suffice?"

I mutter a curse under my breath at hearing that Hurley has beat me to the guy. "Well, while my office does work with the police, we also conduct our own, separate investigation into these matters." This isn't totally true but Nelson doesn't need to know that.

"I see," he says, emitting a heavy sigh. "Can't you do it together so I don't have to set up two separate appointments? I'm a very busy man."

His tone, and the implication that his time is more important than the investigation into Shannon's death, irks me, but I swallow down my ire, not wanting to alienate him this early in the process.

"Perhaps we can accommodate you in that regard," I tell him. "When are you meeting with Detective Hurley?"

"He's coming by this evening at six, after I'm done with my patient appointments."

"Darn," I say. "I have plans this evening and won't be able to make it then." It's a lie. I have no plans, and much as I would love to spend more time with Hurley, I can't resist the chance to scoop him. "I don't suppose you'd have any free time before then? Like now?"

He rewards my request with another world-weary sigh, letting me know he thinks I'm a huge pain in the ass. "Fine," he says, clearly perturbed. "I'm eating at my desk right now since I typically use my lunch hour to review the charts of my afternoon patients. I have forty-five minutes before my next appointment, and if you can get here before then, I'll give you whatever time is left."

"I'll be there in a few minutes."

I hang up and make a quick scan of my fridge for something of my own to take along and eat while I'm there, but despite my love of food, I'm not much of a cook. My idea of a home prepared meal is when I set the table before the delivery guy shows up. The best I can come up with for now is a half-eaten tub of cottage cheese and some strawberry jam. I hastily toss the two together in the cottage cheese container, and shove it and a spoon in my purse.

Five minutes later I pull into the parking lot of a small strip mall that contains a karate school, a mail store, one of those dollar stores, and Dr. Luke Nelson's counseling services. Not the most auspicious location but perhaps it's only meant to be temporary.

The front room of the office is set up as a small waiting area with a smattering of chairs, a couple of end tables, and one coffee table bearing a dozen or so out-of-date magazines. A sign on the wall by the door at the back of the room instructs visitors to take a seat and wait for the doctor. The chairs look worn and used and it makes me wonder just how well Dr. Nelson is doing. Given his self-proclaimed busy schedule, I expected something a little classier.

At the moment, the back room door is open and I get my first look at Luke Nelson as he gets up from behind a desk and walks out to greet me. He's a tall and relatively handsome man, with a head of thick blond hair, blue eyes, and the slender build of a runner. He's wearing glasses but, rather than making him look bookish or nerdy, they combine with his rather patrician features to lend him an air of sophistication and casual intelligence.

"Ms. Winston, I presume?" he says, and I note that his voice has the practiced smoothness I've come to associate with most people in his profession. It's supposed to sound objective, encouraging, and soothing, but to me it always sounds as if there's a hint of oily slickness in there.

I walk over and extend my hand. He takes it, and though his handshake is just the right amount of firm and friendly, his skin is cool and clammy.

"Thank you for taking the time to meet with me," I tell him, pulling my hand back and resisting an urge to wipe it on my pants. "I'll try to be as brief as I can."

He glances at his watch and says, "Well, you have a little over half an hour. Come on into my office."

I follow him into the adjacent room, which is furnished with the same worn, well-used-looking furniture I saw in the waiting area. A desk—bearing the half-eaten remains of a Subway sandwich—and a high-backed office chair are set against the back wall. There is a computer on one side of the desk and the other end holds a stack of charts, leaving Nelson and his lunch in the opening in the middle. A smaller, upholstered chair sits on the opposite side of the desk, angled so that it looks toward the side wall of the room. A bookcase filled with a variety of hefty medical tomes covers the wall to my left, topped off by what appears to be an artificial plant. To my right there is an open door leading into another room. The glimpse I get of this adjacent area is a bit of a surprise. I see a cushy-looking stuffed leather chair, a comfy couch, what appears to be a Tiffany floor lamp, and a tasteful but expensive-looking Persian rug. Clearly the bulk of Nelson's expenses have gone into his consultation room, which I have to admit looks cozy and welcoming.

He gestures toward the chair in front of his desk and then settles into the larger one behind it. "I hope you don't mind if I finish eating," he says, picking up his sandwich and taking a bite, making it clear that it doesn't matter to him whether I mind or not.

"Not at all," I say, setting my purse on the floor. "In fact, I brought along something myself and if you don't mind, I'll join you." I fish my container of cottage cheese and my spoon out of my purse. Playing at his own game, I rip the top off the container and have a spoonful at the ready in seconds. I think I see the hint of a smile on his face as I shove the concoction into my mouth, but it's there and gone so fast I can't be sure.

He swallows but my mouth freezes midbite as I realize my cottage cheese is one step away from being rancid. Belatedly I glance at the freshness date and see that it came and went well over two weeks ago. I force myself to swallow what I have and set the rest of it aside.

"So," I say, wishing I had thought to bring something to drink, "tell me about your relationship with Shannon Tolliver."

He arches one brow at me. "Well, no one can accuse you of beating around the bush. What happened to her is truly tragic." He tries to look the part but it feels forced. "There isn't much to say, really. I liked her. She was a very attractive lady. We went out a few times but it wasn't a real steady thing. In fact, I hadn't seen her for a week or so before her death."

"How long were you dating her?"

He looks up at the ceiling a moment, then says, "Off and on for a couple of months."

"Were you intimate?" I expect to startle him with this question, but I'm disappointed.

"Yes, though not at first," he answers without hesitation.

"And were you exclusive? Or were you seeing someone else?"

He stares at me for a few seconds, then further delays his answer by picking up his sandwich and taking another bite. Given that he didn't blush or hesitate in the least when answering the intimacy question, I'm curious as to why this one would throw him. It's apparent he wasn't expecting it.

He chews slowly, swallows, and then says with a smile, "I don't really see how my dating life outside of Shannon is material to your investigation."

"Where were you on the night Shannon was killed?"

"Let's see. That was Friday, wasn't it?"

I nod.

"I came into work around ten in the morning and did my usual chart reviews. Then I had patient appointments every hour from noon to six. I took an hour for dinner here in my office and made some phone calls. I ordered a pizza, so I'm certain that can be verified, as can the phone calls. Then from seven to eight-thirty I headed up a group therapy session here. After that I went to Somewhere until one o'clock or so."

I start to ask for clarification on the somewhere but then realize he means the bar.

"Then I went home to bed."

I nod thoughtfully. "It should be easy enough to check on the bar and the pizza delivery," I tell him, realizing his alibis cover our new window of time for Shannon's murder, "but I'd like verification of the appointments from your patients."

He makes a frowny face and says, "Well, I'll have to ask my patients for permission first. Confidentiality and all that, you know."

"Of course. I don't need to know why they were here, just that they were, and that they saw you."

"I'll see what I can do but it may take me some time. I don't have an office assistant so I'll have to contact each patient myself in between appointments."

Clearly he is running the office on a pretty tight budget. It makes me curious about his past. "You've been here what . . . six months or so?"

He nods. "Yes, give or take a week."

"Where were you before you came here?"

"Florida."

"Wow, that's quite a change. What made you move up here?"

"I didn't like the heat and humidity. Plus I grew up in the Midwest."

"Here?"

"Indiana."

He is being careful to answer my questions with the bare min-

imum of information, offering nothing extra. Though it could be
nothing more than good old-fashioned Midwestern reserve, I
suspect he is being intentionally cautious and wonder why.

"Did you have a practice in Florida?"

He nods, eats the last of his sandwich, and then says, "I got my
degree down there and opened a solo practice right out of school.
It was mostly elderly patients with the typical aging and depres-
sion issues. It got boring after a while and to be honest, it was a
bit of a challenge trying to make a go of it with the pathetic
Medicare reimbursements. I'm sure there were wealthy retirees
down there but as the new kid on the block, I couldn't seem to
attract them."

"How is your practice doing here?"

"Better than expected. I had forgotten what a hotbed of dys-
function a small town can be," he says with a practiced smile.
"I'm hoping to move into a better office soon and then I'll be
looking for an assistant. But I haven't one yet, so . . ." He makes
a pointed glance toward his watch and I decide to let him off the
hook, knowing I'm not likely to get much more out of him anyway.

"I appreciate you taking the time to talk to me," I tell him,
scooping up my disgusting cottage cheese dish and slapping the
lid on it.

"No problem," he says, though we both know he doesn't
mean it. "I suppose I'll have to go over it all again when that cop
comes by later."

"Well, I'll try to share what you've given me with him and
maybe that will help to expedite things."

"Thank you."

"In the meantime, if you could get me a list of the patients you
saw that day and permission to talk with them, I'd appreciate it."

"I'll do what I can but I'm not making any promises."

"I'm sure you'll find a way," I say with forced sweetness. "You
can assure all of them that I'll keep the information in the
strictest confidence."

"I'll let you know when I have something."

"Please do." I wouldn't be at all surprised if he stalled on the matter, so I add, "And if I don't hear from you in the next day or so, I'll be back in touch."

Back outside in my car, I take a moment to reflect on our conversation. My gut tells me Nelson wasn't as forthcoming as he could have been and I suspect he might be holding back critical information. But until I can follow up on his alibis, there isn't much else I can do here.

I can't wait to talk to Hurley and let him know I beat him to the punch interviewing Nelson. Of course, I'll do so under the guise of sharing information with him but that won't stop me from gloating. I wonder if he's planning on attending the Heinriches' autopsies and decide to call and ask him.

The light at the approaching intersection turns green and I speed up to go through it. Since I haven't yet figured out how to put anyone on speed dial, I am momentarily distracted by trying to find the right numbers to punch on my cell. As a result, I never see the car hurtling toward me from the side, its driver oblivious to the red light.

The impact knocks the wind out of me and my car is tipped up on the driver side wheels. It seems to teeter there for a second before it finally goes over the rest of the way, coming down hard on the roof, rolling and rolling like a barrel. I feel a blinding pain on the top of my head and then I don't feel anything at all.

Chapter
19

I hear voices—one very loud one in particular—and the sounds of someone retching. The loud voice is yelling, "Get back! Move away, people. We need some space here."

My eyes are glued shut and I can feel something sticky and gooey all over my face. At first I can't remember where I am or how I got here, but then the male voice is speaking again, closer to me and softer in tone.

"Miss? Can you hear me? My name is Hal and I'm an EMT. You were in a car accident and we're here to help you."

I try to nod but a horrible pain knifes through my head and neck, freezing me in place. I manage a moan.

"Damn it, Chuck," Hal says. "Get a grip and get in here. She's got a pretty extensive head injury and I need some help."

Then I hear another male voice, this one much shakier. "Sorry," the second voice mutters. "It's just that I've never seen brain matter all over the place like that." With that he gags and I hear the retching sounds again.

Then his words sink in. *Brain matter? Is he talking about me? That can't be very good. How is it I'm able to think if my brains are leaking?*

In order to survive as a nurse, particularly an ER nurse, there is a certain skill you must have: the ability to override your natural instinct to panic in highly stressful situations. For some it comes naturally; for others it must be learned. I am one of the lucky ones; my fight or flight reaction is so dulled that theoretically I should have been weaned from the gene pool centuries ago, my kind stomped to death by charging wooly mammoths. But a number of people like me survived the odds and you'll find the majority of us in fields like emergency medicine, police work, and search and rescue.

That instinct kicks in now as I try to make sense of how I can hear, see, and feel things if my brains are playing Humpty Dumpty. Logic tells me it can't happen but there's no one else in my car.

Wait. Maybe I'm dead. Maybe this is what it's like in the after-life, or in those few moments before your soul says *I'm outa here* and flees the premises. Except I feel pain. Do dead people feel pain? Having never been dead before, this question momentarily stumps me.

Then I take a strange mental segue and remember how my hairdresser, Barbara, helped me plan out my funeral. I recall how good I looked when we were done and find some solace now in the knowledge that if I have to be dead, at least I'll look stunning during those last good-byes. I have absolute faith in Barbara's ability to put Humpty Dumpty back together again.

Then I hear another voice, one I recognize, one that makes my pulse quicken—though I suppose that could be because I'm hemorrhaging.

"Christ, that's Winston," Hurley says. His voice sounds a bit shaky.

"You know her?" Hal asks.

"I do. Is she okay?"

"Too soon to tell," Hal says, sounding worried. "It appears she has a serious head injury and as soon as my partner here can get his stomach under control enough to help me, we'll get her im-mobilized and out of the car. Then I might be able to give you a better idea of her condition. In the meantime, if you want to talk to her, offer some encouragement, there's a good chance she'll be able to hear you even if she's in a coma. You never know what might make a difference."

A second later I hear Hurley's voice again. "Damn it, Winston. This is no time for games. You get it together now. And if you think this is going to get you out of our steak dinner bet, you have another think coming."

I assume, based on the tremor in his voice, that this is what passes for concern in Hurley's world. I'm touched, and I want to open my eyes and see him, but they are glued shut.

I hear the second EMT, Chuck, clear his throat and say, "I think I'm okay now, Hal. Let me help."

Hands gently cradle and move my head as I feel the cold plastic of a cervical collar being slid into place behind my neck. As the collar is being secured, a gloved hand rubs up against my cheek, pushing something wet and sticky onto my upper lip. And then it hits me: the smell of strawberries. At first I think I might be having an olfactory hallucination, smelling things that aren't there because of whatever damage has been done to my brain cells. Then another smell registers, one that bears a faint resemblance to sour milk.

Suddenly it all makes sense. I raise one of my hands and take a swipe at my eyes. It makes the smells intensify and I manage to get one eye open a slit's worth, though the other one is staying stubbornly closed. Through the open one I can see a red haze mixed with a few whitish-gray chunks on my fingers. I stick them in my mouth and give the goo a tentative taste test.

Just as I thought: it's the remains of my lunch.

I hear a symphony of gasps, a sickly moan, and then a loud *thud*.

"Shit," Hal mutters. "There he goes again. Damn it, Chuck!" Then I hear sniffing sounds. "I'll be damned," Hal says. "I think this is cottage cheese and jelly."

"Huh?" Hurley asks.

Hal leaves my side, presumably to attend to his fallen partner. "I thought that crap all over her head and face was blood and brain matter but it's not. It's food. It must have gotten spilled on her during the accident."

"So is she okay?" Hurley asks.

"I think I am," I manage to mumble.

"Hey! There you go," Hal says. "I think she's in better shape than my partner here. I'm going to have to call for a backup ambulance for him. I'm afraid seeing a patient eat her own brains was simply more than he could take."

Forty-five minutes later I'm safely ensconced on a cot inside the ER with Dr. Allan Connor examining my injuries. I can hear Hurley beyond my curtain asking one of the nurses on duty if he can come in and see me. He says it's so he can get information about the accident though I'm pretty certain traffic accidents don't fall within the scope of duties for a homicide detective. But since I was planning on finding him anyway before I was broadsided, I'm anxious to have him come in and chat. I want to share what I uncovered about Luke Nelson.

I'm glad Allan is the doc on duty. I worked with him years ago when I staffed the ER and I know he's a thorough, no-nonsense guy with superb diagnostic skills. He's already cleared my cervical spine and removed the collar, and one of the nurses was kind enough to clean the jam off my face, allowing me to open both of my eyes.

Allan finds a small laceration on the back of my scalp that will need a few stitches, but other than that I'm home free. He warns me that I'll likely be plagued with aching muscles tomorrow, but doubts I'll have any other symptoms. "You're damned lucky," he says. "The EMT showed me a picture of your car and the damage was quite extensive."

"Is it totaled?" I ask.

Hurley pushes aside the curtain, steps in, and provides the answer. "Yup. It's crusher fodder."

"What about the other car? Who was in it? Are they okay?"

Allan, abiding by the strict confidentiality requirements imposed on all healthcare providers, says, "All I can tell you is that there was just the driver, who sustained a few injuries, though nothing that appears life-threatening at this point."

I blow out a sigh of relief.

Allan says, "I need to go check on a couple of other things and then I'll be back to stitch up your head." He disappears from my tiny cubicle, leaving me with Hurley.

"You're not bound by the privacy requirements," I say to him. "Can you fill in any of the blanks for me?"

"I can tell you that the driver was a teenager and that it looks like he was texting someone on his phone when he hit you. Several witnesses saw him blow through the red light."

I wince, knowing I'm almost as guilty as the kid since I was trying to make a call on my cell phone when I was hit.

"He busted one of his legs but his car had air bags and he was wearing his seat belt so at least he wasn't totally stupid," Hurley goes on. "The car is his dad's Lexus so I'm guessing the kid will be suffering more pain at home than he will be here."

"I'm just glad he's okay."

"Where were you headed?"

"Back to the office to help Izzy with the autopsies. Actually, I was hoping to hook up with you there, to share some information. I managed to wrangle a lunch meeting with Luke Nelson."

"Really?"

"Yup." I try not to look or sound too smug but I can't resist skewering him just a little bit more. "He mentioned that he was supposed to meet with you later today so I figured I could make that easier for you by sharing what I managed to find out. You know, to keep us from duplicating our efforts."

"I see."

I expect him to look put out, or at least chagrined, but instead he looks amused.

"So, do you want to know what I found out?"

"Sure, one second." Up to this point he has been standing beside my stretcher. Now he disappears from the cubicle only to return a few seconds later with a chair. He sets it down beside my cot, settles into it, and then takes a notebook and pencil out of his shirt pocket. "Go ahead," he says.

I tell him about Luke Nelson's alibis and that he is going to ask the patients he saw that day if it's okay for us to know they were there and, if necessary, talk with them. Then I tell him about Nelson's history, his practice in Florida, and his claim that he hadn't seen Shannon for a week before her death.

"It seems odd that they didn't get together more recently," I say. "He claims it's because he was busy but I got the feeling there was more to it than that."

Hurley shrugs. "It's a guy thing. We don't feel the same need to be together with a romantic partner twenty-four-seven the way women do."

I arch a brow at him and scoff. "That's a bit stereotyped, don't you think?"

He shrugs again. "There's a reason stereotypes are stereotypes. It's because they hold true much of the time."

"You're right," I say, setting my jaw and folding my arms over my chest. "You men do tend toward a love-'em-and-leave-'em mentality. It seems rather lonely and sad to me."

"It's a defense mechanism," Hurley counters. "Like the way you women are always being so secretive."

"I'm not secretive," I say.

"Really? Then what was Izzy referring to the other day when he threatened to tell us your real name?"

Crap. A little kid's voice echoes in my head: *You sunk my battleship!*

"That was just a stupid inside joke," I say dismissively, but I can tell from the way Hurley is studying me that he isn't buying it. "Anyway," I say, hoping to shift the subject, "I figure Allan will spring me from here as soon as I get my stitches and then I'll check in at the office so I can help Izzy post the Heinrich couple. Then later tonight I'll hit up the Somewhere Bar and see if Nelson's alibi there holds up."

Hurley sighs. "I still say the husband did it."

"Maybe. Maybe not. Either way, we need to check out all the possibilities, right?"

"Right."

"I'd also like to go back to Shannon's house and have another look around."

"Looking for anything in particular?"

I shake my head. "Not really. It's just a feeling I had when we were there the other night. Something I was missing."

"Okay, but I want to go with you. How about I give you a call?"

"That's fine."

There is a moment of silence and then Hurley pushes out of his chair and shoves it off to one side. "I have things to do so I'll catch up with you later."

I nod, cursing the whole love-'em-and-leave-'em thing.

He turns to leave, but then hesitates and looks back at me. "I'm glad you're okay, Winston. You gave us a bit of a scare there."

He shoves the curtain aside and is gone in a flash. But his words make me smile so wide that the cut on my head starts to throb. And the memory of the way those blue eyes looked at me makes other parts of my body throb, too, but in a much nicer way.

Chapter
20

By the time my head is stitched and cleaned and I'm ready to go, I realize I have no way to get anywhere. With my car totaled, I'm stranded without wheels. I also don't have my cell phone and assume it is still inside the wreckage somewhere. I curse myself for not realizing my dilemma sooner and asking Hurley for a lift. The idea of using him as my personal chauffeur, even for a little while, is pretty appealing.

I run through a mental list of possible rides and use one of the ER phones to start making calls. There's no answer at Izzy and Dom's house and I can't remember Izzy's cell number, which was the only number programmed into my own phone, done by Izzy himself when he gave me the thing. I call the office and Cass informs me that everyone is very busy, and that Izzy heard about my accident and called in a couple of coroners from another jurisdiction to help him with the Heinrichs' autopsies. They are in the midst of doing them now so the good news is I won't have to assist with the rotting bodies, but the bad news is there is no one in the office that has the time to ferry me around.

Next I try my sister, Desi, but there is no answer there, either. Fortunately the paramedics did bring my purse with me and, after cleaning off the cottage cheese and jelly remnants, I dig out my wallet and check my cash status to see if I have enough for a cab.

One of the advantages of living in a small town is that the cab service is relatively cheap. They'll take you anywhere in town for three bucks. But the flip side is that the cab service only runs until sundown. That's because it's owned and staffed by a group of senior citizens whose ability to see and drive in the dark is limited. Based on the number of dents I've seen on their vans, their ability to see and drive in the daytime is not much better. But the risk of a fender-bender is offset by their maximum speed. Those images you see on TV of New York City cabdrivers busting speed limits and weaving in and out of traffic couldn't be further from the Sorenson truth.

Though I'm not too keen on risking my involvement in another car accident, my choices are limited so I place the call. The cab's office is only a few blocks from the hospital and the dispatcher assures me she has someone there waiting to go, but it takes a full half hour for my van to arrive.

Behind the wheel is Bjorn Adamson, an eighty-something gentleman I know from working at the hospital. I took care of him a few times in the ER: once when he was having problems regulating his blood pressure, once for a nosebleed, and once for a minor heart attack. I'd also cared for him in the OR twice not long ago when he had hernia and cataract surgeries. I recall how his daughter said he was having problems passing his urine because of an enlarged prostate and that she thought he might be showing the beginning signs of senile dementia.

Trying not to worry over the fact that my cabdriver's current state of health could probably generate enough medical bills to send an internist's kid through college, I climb into the front seat of the van. I do a quick physical assessment honed from my years of nursing and note that his white hair is much sparser since I last saw him—except for the tufts growing out of his ears and nose— and his skin has so many age spots he appears to have a tan. His clothes are wrinkled and I detect the distinct odor of stale urine.

I greet Bjorn by name and ask him how he's doing.

He doesn't answer my question; he just sits there staring at me. I assume he's trying to figure out who I am and how he knows me, so I offer up a little help.

"I'm Mattie Winston. I'm a nurse here, or used to be, and I've taken care of you a few times. Remember when you came in for your hernia surgery a few months ago?"

I think I see a faint spark of recognition in his rheumy eyes and he smiles. "You're a nurse?" he says.

I nod.

"Thank goodness. I could sure use some help with this daggummed thing." With that he reaches down and pulls up the leg of his pants. There, strapped beside his knee, is a urinary catheter leg bag. I can see the catheter snaking its way up his pants and the bag itself is so full it's about to burst. "Doc says I need to have this goddamned tube stuck up my wiener so I can pee because my prostrate is so big."

"Prostate," I correct him.

"Yeah, that's right, my prostrate. Anyway, my arthritis has gotten so bad these days that my fingers don't always work like they should and managing this little cap thingy here about drives me nuts. Every time I try to empty this bag I end up with piss all over my hands and my shoes, everywhere but the toilet. See, it's supposed to just pop off here when you grab this little tab but I never can seem to. . . ."

With that, he manages to pop the cap off just fine and nearly half a liter of urine starts draining out onto the van floor.

"Aw, dammit!" he whines. "See what I mean?"

I do indeed. It's pretty hard to miss a river of urine flowing toward your feet. I manage to open the van door and hop out before the flow reaches me. It spreads across the floor in a giant pool.

"I'll be right back," I tell him. "Let me run inside and get some stuff so we can clean that up."

He nods, pulls a tissue—one individual, two-ply tissue—from his shirt pocket, and starts dabbing at the urine pool. It's like trying to wipe up the Mississippi River with a single roll of paper towels.

Inside the hospital I round up a bunch of towels, some sanitizing cloths, some isolyzer powder—a nifty substance that will turn any liquid into a dry, sweepable solid—and some linen, and trash bags. Ten minutes later the cab is as clean as it's going to get—though the stale urine aroma is still present—and Bjorn's bag is empty and recapped.

Since I never did get to eat lunch, I ask Bjorn if he'd mind taking me to Dairy Airs before he takes me home. I'm hoping Jackie Nash's mother might be there. He is so grateful for my assistance with his catheter and the parting of the yellow sea that he offers to take me to Dairy Airs for free. When he finds out that my car was totaled in an accident and I have no idea when I'll be able to get a replacement, he tries to work out a deal with me.

"Tell you what," he says. "If you'll empty this dag-gummed bag for me a couple of times a day, I'll take you anywhere you want to go for free in return. Whaddaya say?"

I give his proposition some thought. It does offer me an alternative means of transportation temporarily, but I'm also afraid of Bjorn getting a little too used to the idea of me caring for him and getting stuck doing it for a lot longer than I'd like. So I counter his offer with one of my own.

"Tell you what, Bjorn. We can try that for a few days but then I want to reevaluate things. I'm pretty sure I can get you a different kind of leg bag, one that has an easier gizmo for opening it. It might cost a little more and it's something I'll have to order so it will take a few days to get here, but I think it will solve your problem. In the meantime, we can help each other out."

He thinks about my offer for a few seconds and then says, "Okay. But if this newfangled bag doesn't work any better, will you help me out a little longer?"

"We'll deal with that when the time comes," I answer evasively, hoping it never will. He seems satisfied with that answer and we finally pull out into the street at a blistering ten miles an hour.

Dairy Airs is just over a mile from the hospital but it takes us nearly fifteen minutes to get there. Along the way at least ten drivers honk, yell obscenities, and make rude gestures as they pass us by in a cloud of disgust.

Unsure how long I will be here, I suggest to Bjorn that I call for him when I'm done but he insists on coming in with me, saying the length of the wait won't matter. "They have the best cheesecakes in this place," he says, pulling into a parking place and nudging the van's front tires into the curb. "I try to get a slice at least once a week."

Cheesecake sounds pretty darn good to me, too, and Bjorn and I spend a few minutes at the cake case, staring through the glass at the day's choices and trying to decide what to get. Finally we settle into a booth and moments later our treats arrive: caramel pumpkin for Bjorn, and for me a delicious, melt-in-your-mouth lemon chiffon with a grilled cheese sandwich yet to come for dessert.

Jackie is the waitress again. I'm relieved when she greets Bjorn by name, letting me know that the two have met and I don't have to worry about any awkward comments from Bjorn. When Jackie asks him how his health is doing, he dodges the question with a polite "Fine, thanks."

I ask Jackie if her mother is on duty and she shakes her head. "She's a little under the weather today," she says. She hesitates a moment, looking nervous, then slides into the booth beside me and asks in a low voice, "Anything new on Shannon's case?"

"Nothing concrete. They've arrested Erik but most of the evidence is circumstantial. He's retained Lucien as his lawyer."

"Well, that's good," she says, looking unconvinced. Mention of Lucien triggers a mixed reaction in most people. She leans closer to me and whispers, "Do you think he did it?"

I shake my head, swallowing a bite of my cheesecake. I look over and realize Bjorn has already scarfed down his slice, and decide I need to try to get him to drive as fast as he eats.

"No," I tell Jackie. "I don't think Erik did it. But there are some things that don't add up."

Jackie chews on her lip looking worried for a moment. Then she sees that my sandwich is up and goes over to get it. As I watch her walk, I'm once again struck by the feeling that something about her is different.

Before I can ponder it much, Bjorn says, "Do we have to talk about dead people? When you get to be my age, it's kind of an uncomfortable subject, you know."

"Sorry," I say.

"Besides, I thought you just came here for some cheesecake. Speaking of which, when am I going to get mine?"

"You already ate it."

He turns and glares at me. "I think I'd know if I just ate a piece of cheesecake, missy."

"You did, Bjorn. Look, there's your empty plate in front of you. See the crumbs?"

Jackie returns and hands me my sandwich. Bjorn, who is staring at his plate with a puzzled expression, shrugs and says to Jackie, "Best bring me another piece then."

Jackie leaves to fetch Bjorn's second piece of cheesecake while I bite into my sandwich, relishing the mixed flavors of fresh cheese and butter.

As soon as Jackie brings Bjorn his second piece of cheesecake, he stabs a chunk of it onto his fork and waves it at us. "If you ask me," he says, "the husband did it. I watch that crime channel on cable all the time. You know the one, with all the court cases and forensic shows? It's fascinating stuff, but the outcomes are pretty predictable. Nine times out of ten it's the spouse."

"Erik *was* pretty jealous," Jackie adds, sounding as if she's trying to convince us. "So I guess it would be foolish to rule him out too quickly."

She turns to leave but I say, "Wait a second," and grab her arm to stop her. I can feel the ridges of her scars beneath her sleeve, and when she looks back at me with an expression of panic, I release my grip. "Sorry," I say looking apologetic. "But there's one more thing I wanted to ask you. Do you know that new psychiatrist in town, Luke Nelson, the man Shannon was dating?"

Jackie glances nervously over her shoulder and I'm not sure if it's to see what's going on in the rest of the place, or if it's to see if anyone else is listening. Finally she nods and says, "He's been in here a few times. He likes our Very Berry ice cream."

Maybe there's hope for the guy after all, I think, finishing off the first half of my sandwich and grabbing the rest. The Very Berry is excellent.

"How did he and Shannon get along?"

Jackie frowns. "Okay, I guess," she says with a shrug. "I never saw them argue or anything. But they never showed much affection, either," she adds quickly. She looks around again, her eyes blinking fast, her hands stuffed inside the pockets of her apron, jingling her tip change. "If you'll excuse me," she says biting her lip again, "I need to make a dash to the ladies' room. You guys have a good one, eh?"

She is gone in a flash and her reaction to the last line of questioning leaves me wondering if there is more to her knowledge of Luke Nelson than she let on. Determined to find out, I fish some cash out of my purse, slide it across the table to Bjorn, and ask him to pay for our meal. Then I head into the ladies' room, eating the remains of my sandwich along the way.

I find Jackie standing in front of one of the sinks, staring at herself in the mirror. I move beside her and check out my own reflection, horrified when I see what a mess my hair is and the faint reddish discoloration on my right cheek—most likely from the strawberry jam—that looks like a faint port-wine stain birthmark.

"I thought you might come in here," Jackie says, as I dampen a paper towel and try to wash the red off my face.

"I'm sorry, Jackie. I don't mean to impose, but I want to find out what happened to Shannon and make sure it doesn't happen to anyone else."

She nods wearily, squeezes her eyes closed, and sighs heavily. Her hands have a white-knuckled grip on the edge of the sink.

"Are you a patient of Luke Nelson's?" I ask as gently as I can.

She turns and looks at me with a startled expression, like a deer caught in headlights. Then a montage of emotions flit across her face: surprise, curiosity, and then relief. "Yes, I am," she says finally, sighing. "I'm not crazy or anything. It's just that . . . well . . . this . . ." She waves her hand around the scarred side of her face and I nod sympathetically. "And then to top it off, my mother was just diagnosed with breast cancer, which means I'm at risk, too."

"Oh, crap, Jackie. I'm sorry. I didn't know."

"No reason you should since you don't work at the hospital anymore, but between trying to hold down the fort here and at home, worrying about Mom's health, and dealing with my dad . . . well . . . it does stress me out at times."

"That's perfectly understandable. It's nothing to be ashamed about."

She casts a wary look at me. "You won't tell anyone, will you? I don't want anyone to know I'm seeing a shrink. People jump to conclusions. I don't want everyone in town knowing about my personal life. You know how it is." *Boy, do I.* "No one knows I've been going to Dr. Nelson, not even my family."

"And I won't tell them," I assure her. "But I would like to ask you a couple of questions, just between us."

Her shoulders sag in resignation. "Go ahead."

"Did you see Dr. Nelson on Friday at all?"

She thinks for a minute, then nods. "I had an appointment with him at two o'clock."

I breathe a sigh of relief when I realize that her appointment is outside the time frame needed to verify Nelson's alibi, which means I have no need to share the information with anyone else. So I move on to my next inquiry.

"What do you think of him? Is he helping you?"

For a moment her face takes on an almost beatific expression. Then she shrugs. "I guess so."

"What does he do for you?"

"We just talk mostly," she says, her cheeks flushing pink. "He's a very good listener and that seems to help me." She looks down at her hands and starts picking at a cuticle. "Why so many questions about him?' she asks.

I can see how uncomfortable she is with the topic and figure it's either because she's still worried that I will share her information with others, or that too much rumor and speculation will chase Luke Nelson away. Patients do tend to develop strong attachments to their shrinks. Sensing that I've pushed her as far as I can, I say, "I'm trying to get a feel for all the people in Shannon's life, that's all. And I promise that what you've told me will stay between us. I'm sorry I had to pry."

"It's okay. I understand."

I turn to leave but she calls me back. "There is one other thing I forgot to mention earlier. It might not be important but . . ."

I look back at her, waiting expectantly.

"I had a really bad day a couple of weeks ago and I called Dr. Nelson in a panic. It was late in the evening but he was kind enough to agree to meet me in his office for an emergency session." She flashes me a wan smile. "Since it was so late, he walked me out to my car when we were done and, just as I was getting ready to leave, this woman showed up. I got the impression he wasn't very happy to see her."

"How so?"

"Well, she approached us and said, 'I see you're up to your old tricks, Luke.' At that point he practically shoved me into my car and made a hasty retreat for his own. But the woman followed him and the two of them began yelling at one another. I started my car up but rolled down my window and dawdled a bit before driving away because I was curious. I heard the woman tell Dr. Nelson he'd be sorry he screwed with her and that she would make him pay. She was totally in his face and tried to block him from getting into his car. But he shoved her aside, got in, and drove away."

"I don't suppose you know who the woman was?"

Jackie shakes her head. "No, I've never seen her before. But I did see her get into a little cherry-red convertible sports car of some type and it had a vanity plate on it."

I raise my eyebrows in question.

"It was an easy one to remember," Jackie adds with a smile, "because the lady was rather well-endowed and her license plate read HOT 44D."

Chapter 21

After borrowing Dairy Air's phone to make a quick call, I drag Bjorn away from the ice cream display and ask him to drive me across town. He stares at me, blinks hard several times, and asks, "Who are you again?"

It seems his daughter's suspicions about possible senility might be on target.

"I'm Mattie, remember? The nurse? I emptied your bag for you?" I say, gesturing toward his leg.

He nods, but still looks confused. It doesn't exactly warm the cockles of my heart knowing that I have a half-blind, slightly confused, incontinent old man for a chauffeur. So I offer Bjorn a deal.

"Tell you what. How about if I drive the cab for a while and you ride along? It's going to be dark in a couple of hours and I have a few other places I need to go."

Bjorn considers my proposition for a second or two, then counters with, "Okay, but will you empty my bag again?"

"You betcha." It's a no-brainer. Either I empty the bag or risk the explosion of urine all over the cab.

We climb into the van with me behind the wheel and I drive us to the Keller Funeral Home. As I pull up out front, Bjorn looks at the building and then gives me a questioning stare.

"Is there something you're not telling me?" he says. "I know I'm old but I think I'm in pretty good shape."

"Relax," I reassure him. "I'm just here to get my hair done."

He looks back at the building, then at me and mutters, "And they think *I'm* senile."

I laugh. "I know it looks odd but there's a woman named Barbara who works here as a beautician and she is quite talented, with both the living and the dead."

We get out and head inside. I steer Bjorn toward the main office because in order to get to Barbara, who works her magic down in the basement, we will have to get past a locked door. An elderly woman who looks a little too close to casket-ready is sitting behind a desk in the office. She starts to get up from her chair to greet us but then recognizes me and plops back down. This is a good thing because the first time I came here I had to watch her negotiate the distance from her chair to mine and feared I'd be doing CPR before she reached me. Her name is displayed on a metal bar on her desk: Irene Keller.

"I'm guessing you're here to see Barbara again," she says to me.

I nod. "Yes, I just spoke with her on the phone."

She gives me a quick once-over, clucks her tongue several times, and shakes her head, though I'm not sure if the shaking is a tremor or a judgment. "You know, a little basic maintenance goes a long way," she chastises. "Barbara is very talented but if you don't do your part, you're just wasting her time."

"It's been a rough couple of days," I explain. "I haven't had the time to tend to myself the way I should."

She rolls her eyes at me. "I don't understand you young folks these days. You need to find the time. If you don't care how you look, why should anyone else? I mean, seriously, even at my age I manage to find the time to work at my appearance." She waves a hand around in front of her face. "Do you think this look is easy to maintain?"

Yikes! I'm not sure a monster special-effects expert could duplicate her look. Her skin has more wrinkles than a shar-pei, and her white hair has a faint green tint to it and is so sparse I can count the individual follicles in her scalp. Her eyebrows are drawn on and the rest of her make-up is boldly colored, a garish contrast to her translucent skin and pale coloring. And her lipstick is drawn on so far outside the normal lines of her lips that it looks like a three-year-old did it.

Bjorn apparently thinks it all looks fine because he says, "You are a beautiful woman. How is it I've never met you before?" Obviously his cataract surgery wasn't as successful as I'd thought.

Irene shifts her attention from me to Bjorn and does another quick once-over. I notice that her eyes stall briefly and widen when her gaze nears his crotch. There is a noticeable bulge there, thanks to Bjorn's catheter, but Irene has no way of knowing that's what it is. She shifts her gaze to his face and smiles. "I'm Irene Keller," she says. "I own this place and I'm a widow."

"Bjorn Adamson," Bjorn says with a sideways nod of his head. There is a definite twinkle in his eye. "I drive a cab and I'm a widower."

Nothing like getting the preliminaries out of the way, though I guess when you get into Bjorn and Irene's age group, time is a valuable commodity.

"Barbara is expecting you. She's just finishing up with another customer," Irene says to me, never taking her eyes off Bjorn. "The door is unlocked."

"Is the other customer dead or alive?" I ask.

"Alive," Irene says, still maintaining eye contact with Bjorn.

I look over at Bjorn. "Do you want to wait up here or come with me?"

"I think I'll wait up here. That is if Irene doesn't mind."

"Of course not," Irene says, smiling broadly and revealing a mouthful of yellowed, lipstick-stained teeth.

"Do you have anything to eat?" Bjorn asks.

"I have some cookies."

"I love cookies."

As I leave the office and head for the basement door, I hear Irene ask Bjorn if he's done any preplanning for his funeral. He says he has not, but would love to hear what she has to suggest. Foreplay for eighty-year-olds.

I head downstairs and enter the main prep room. There is an elderly female corpse stretched out on one of the tables and for a minute I think Irene must have been confused. But then I hear voices in a room off to the side and head that way.

Barbara sees me and waves me into the room. A tall blond woman is standing beside her looking picture-perfect and utterly radiant in a tight-fitting pencil skirt, tailored blouse, and peep-toe pumps. As I take in the sleek hair, the deftly applied make-up and the long-legged, stylish grace, something about her strikes a familiar chord. A second later it hits me.

"Chris!"

"Hey, girlfriend," Chris greets back. "Good to see you again." Chris, despite the feminine good looks, is actually a transvestite. I met him a few weeks ago at a trendy bar outside of town while investigating the Karen Owenby case. I found myself then feeling much as I do now—envious as hell and amazed that a man can look that good as a woman, not to mention that much better than me.

"I took your advice and met with your stylist here," Chris says. "You were right. Her talents are magical."

Barbara smiles at me and says, "Thanks for the referral."

"My pleasure."

"Oh, the pleasure is all mine," Chris says, admiring himself in a mirror hanging on the wall. "And the ambience here is so . . . so . . . delicious."

That's not how I would describe it, but hey . . . different strokes and all that.

"And it's like a two-for-one deal," Chris goes on. "Barbara helped me pick out all my funeral accessories, everything from the coffin and satin pillow down to the music and flowers." He pauses and sighs delicately. "I'm going to be a knockout as a corpse." He walks over to a counter, picks up a large ring-binder notebook, and starts flipping through it. I see several color head-shots of women on the pages. Chris settles on one—an adorable Audrey Hepburn–style cut—and hands me the book.

"I'm considering trying this one next time," he says. "What do you think?"

"I think it will look stunning on you," I tell him honestly, noticing as I do that the eyes on the model in the picture are closed. I flip through a couple more pages and realize that all of the models are corpses—fine-looking corpses, mind you, but dead nonetheless. I make a mental note not to use the word *permanent* around Barbara because I'm not sure it means the same thing here that it does in other salons.

With one last wistful glance in the mirror, Chris picks up his purse, bids us both good-bye, and sashays out of the room.

Barbara turns her attention to me and takes a moment to survey my hair and make-up. "Looks like you ran into some trouble," she says.

"You have no idea," I say, rolling my eyes. "First I fell into a pile of decomp goo and then I had to ride back from the scene on the flatbed of a truck. Today I wrecked my car and managed to get cottage cheese, strawberry jelly, and blood in my hair. Oh, and I have a couple of stitches up here." I touch the area and wince, surprised at how tender it is. The lidocaine used to numb the area has worn off. "I'm a mess, Barbara. Can you help?"

"Lie down," she says, gesturing toward an empty stretcher. "Let me see what I can do."

Though it took some coaxing to get me to lie on a stretcher for dead people the first time I came here, I eventually got past my heebie-jeebies. I'm glad I did, because Barbara is truly a miracle worker. Just shy of an hour after my arrival I arise from my stretcher like a two-bit actor in a Bela Lugosi movie. My hair has been shampooed, conditioned, trimmed and blown dry. My face has been washed, treated with some kind of herbal stuff, and adorned with make-up. I feel renewed, refreshed, and attractive again.

After thanking Barbara, I write her a check and say good-bye, then venture upstairs to look for Bjorn. I find him and Irene in one of the sitting rooms, holding hands. Judging from the red smear on Bjorn's cheek and the further spread of Irene's lipstick,

I'm guessing they were doing more than hand-holding. Pretty fast moves, if you ask me, but then there is that age thing.

I manage to tear Bjorn away from Irene, but not before hearing that they have a date planned for two nights hence to play bingo at the senior center.

I slip behind the wheel of Bjorn's van and as soon as he's seated inside I say, "Looks like you two hit it off, eh?"

He smiles and gazes off into the distance. "A gentleman never kisses and tells," he says. Then he looks over at me and his smile fades. "Who are you again?"

Chapter
22

Within a few minutes of leaving the funeral home we pull up in front of the police station. I tell Bjorn I won't be long and hint that he might want to wait in the van, but he's having none of it.

"I'm coming in," he says. "I need something to eat and maybe they'll have some snacks or something."

I can't believe he's still hungry after scarfing down two huge slices of Dairy Airs cheesecake and who knows how many cookies with Irene.

"And I'm sure they have a bathroom in there, don't they?" he goes on. "'Cause my bag is feeling kinda full."

Resigned to having Bjorn as my sidekick, I head into the station with him in tow. Sitting behind the glassed-in reception area is the day dispatcher, a woman named Stephanie whom I know well. She greets me warmly and says hi to Bjorn as well, who nods and asks, "Do you have any vending machines here?"

"In the squad room," Stephanie says, hitting a buzzer that opens the door to the inner sanctum. As soon as we step through she hands me a cell phone and says, "Here you go. It's a bit sticky with something and I meant to clean it off for you but didn't get to it yet. It seems to be working okay, though. How did you know I had it?"

"I didn't," I say, taking it. "How did you get it?"

"One of the guys found it in your car when they towed it to the impound lot."

"Thanks." It is indeed sticky and I grab a tissue from a box on Stephanie's desk and try to wipe it down. Instead, all I manage to do is cover it with fuzz.

"So if you didn't know about the phone," Stephanie asks, "what brings you here?"

"I need you to run a license plate for me."

"I need to eat something," Bjorn adds. "And empty my piss bag."

Stephanie's eyes grow big at that and she wheels her chair a few inches back.

"I'll help him," I assure her. "While I do that, can you look up this plate for me?" I take a pen and paper from her desk and write down "HOT 44D" and "cherry-red convertible" on it. "I don't know the make of the car but it shouldn't be too hard to figure out."

Stephanie nods, takes the paper, and turns to her desk while I steer Bjorn into the back. We stop in the restroom, a unisex room with one toilet, one urinal, and a sink. The urinal height is perfect for Bjorn's catheter bag and it doesn't take me long to empty and recap it. I stop at the sink, wet a paper towel, and use it to clean off my phone. A minute later we are on our way to the squad room and as soon as we enter, Bjorn makes a beeline for the refrigerator. On the door is a set of those magnetic poetry words and several lines of them have been put together. One reads HAVE CAR AND GUN DON'T LIKE TO RUN. Below it, with TASER handwritten on a blank magnet is LET'S PLAY TASER TAG. Just above the door handle is another one: EAT IF YOU DARE.

"I wouldn't eat anything out of there if I were you," I warn Bjorn. "God knows how long some of that stuff has been in there."

He ignores me and opens it anyway. I'm surprised to see that it's relatively empty; someone must have gotten ambitious and cleaned it out recently. Its only contents are a half pint of cream, a couple of sodas, a package of hemorrhoid suppositories, and a box of bullets.

Bjorn and I scratch our heads over the contents for a moment before he grabs a can of Mountain Dew and closes the door. It's not the best choice; the caffeine in the Mountain Dew is a diuretic, meaning his leg bag will be refilling in no time, but I let it go. He then turns to the snack machine and fishes some change out of his pocket.

"Damned inflation," he grumbles. "I remember when you could buy stuff out of these machines for a dime." He proffers his hand and shows me that he has one quarter, one nickel, three pennies, and a lint-covered cherry Lifesaver. "I don't think I have enough," he says mournfully.

I fish out my wallet. "Here," I tell him, handing him a dollar bill. He puts his change back in his pocket, pops the linty Lifesaver in his mouth, and takes the money. The dollar is enough for two purchases and Bjorn opts for a bag of nacho cheese-flavored tortilla chips and a package of Oreos.

Back at the front desk, Stephanie starts to fill me in but is waylaid when her radio to the 911 center goes off.

"Officer needs assistance at the medical examiner's office, 400 E. Sixth Street. Code 10-103f and 103m."

"What the hell?" I say. I stand and listen as Stephanie responds and then dispatches all available officers on duty to the site. "What's 103f and 103m?"

"The 103 is code for a disturbance, the f means there's a fight, and the m means there might be a mental patient involved."

A mental patient at my office? I briefly wonder if it might be Arnie but quickly dismiss the idea. He's a bit off the radar but I'm pretty sure he's not insane.

Steph's phone rings and I wait impatiently while she answers it. As soon as she hangs up she says, "That was one of the officers over at your office calling to fill me in. Apparently there is some kind of family squabble going on with the Heinrichs' offspring and it's getting kind of dicey."

Great. The spoiled rich kids. Just what I need.

"Oh, and here's the report on that tag you wanted," she adds, handing me a piece of paper. "The car belongs to a lady over in Smithville."

I mutter a curse under my breath. Smithville is a half hour away and not within Bjorn's jurisdiction. Apparently reading my mind, Bjorn says through a mouthful of Oreo crumbs, "Hey, I don't mind if you do the driving."

"What about your dispatcher?" I ask him.

He shrugs, swallows, and wipes some excess crumbs off his lips with the back of his hand. "I'll take a few days off and we can use my car. But you'll have to pay for the gas."

I nod and say, "That seems fair. Shall we plan it for tomorrow then?"

Bjorn nods; at the moment his mouth is too full to talk. But as soon as he swallows he looks at me with a puzzled expression and says, "Who are you again?"

Chapter
23

As we pull up to the main entrance of the ME's office, I see that the street is crowded with TV vans and reporters. Clearly the Heinrich tragedy has piqued the public's interest, not surprising given their wealth and social status. I have no doubt their story will be a feature in newscasts for the next several days, and fodder for magazine articles for weeks to come. When I spy Alison amidst the crowd I have to smile, knowing she must love all this attention. This is the second time in a month she's had insider status on a huge national story. With any luck some big-city news station will offer her a plum position, getting her out of my hair and away from Hurley.

Not wanting to run the media gauntlet, I pull the cab around back and park in the secured garage. When Bjorn and I finally make our way to the front lobby, we find it packed with people: two regular-duty cops, Hurley, Cass, Izzy, and six other people, five of whom are yelling and gesturing at someone else. There aren't any media people that I can see, but a few of them are peering through the glass in the front doors, trying to see what's going on. Fortunately for us, the glass is tinted, making it easy to see out but impossible to see in.

I take a moment to admire the extremely well-fitting jeans Hurley is wearing, and wish for a moment that I was Barbara

Eden and could nod all these other people out of here. Then, reluctantly, I shift my focus to the rest of the room.

Standing in front of Cass's desk are three women. Two of them are Barbie doll twins: personal-trainer thin, artificial D-cups, dyed-to-blond perfection, dressed in designer clothes, artificially tanned, skillfully made up, and adorned in jewelry that costs more than I make in a year. They are screaming at a third woman: a mousy, wallflower type dressed in shabby chic and clutching a pocketbook the size of a small suitcase. The odds may be two to one, but there is a fierce light in the mousy woman's eyes that makes me think she could easily prevail.

On the adjacent wall is a uniformed police officer who is doing his best to keep two men apart. One of the men, a lanky blond guy with a dark tan and a sun-etched face, is dressed as if he's ready to hop on a sailboat. The other is heavy-set, balding, and wearing a suit and tie, though the jacket has a worn-to-death sheen to it. I suspect his shirt was at one time white, but several faint stains have blurred the original color beyond recognition. As the officer does his best to keep the two men from coming to blows, they glare at one another with obvious venom—their faces suffused red with anger and their fists clenched tight. If the cop between them fails, I'm putting my money on Mr. Frayed Suit since Sailor Boy has a spoiled, soft look about him and is only half the other man's size. I am about to award Sailor Boy a couple of grudging points for moxie when I realize it's more likely he's being driven by drunken stupidity. He has the bloodshot eyes and slightly bulbous nose of a long-term drinker.

Holding center stage in the middle of the room is Hurley and another man. In stark contrast to the other groupings, these two appear to be carrying on a reasoned and calm conversation. The third man, who is as tall as Hurley and built with a sinewy strength, has dark blond hair, brown eyes, and an air of calm self-assurance. He is dressed in casual slacks and a white dress shirt with the sleeves rolled up, revealing a pair of sexy looking tanned and muscular forearms. After a few seconds of study, I gauge his age to be somewhere around my own—in his mid-to-late thirties—and guess that he and Ms. Mousy are the oldest ones in this group.

Bjorn, who is standing beside me taking it all in, says, "Is there a vending machine in this place?"

I'm beginning to think Bjorn might be infected with a tapeworm but decide not to say anything. If I do, I know he'll have me handling his poo as well as his pee and I don't want to go there. So I fish in my purse, hand him some change, and direct him down a hallway off the lobby. "Halfway down that hall," I tell him. "By the bathrooms."

"Oh, good," he says, taking the money. "That will work out well because I need to go lay some cable."

I shoot him a puzzled look. "Lay some cable?"

"Yeah, you know, punch a dook?"

I stare at him, confused.

"Pinch a loaf?" he says.

With that one I finally catch on, but before I can indicate so, he throws his hands up in the air and yells, "I need to take a shit. Okay?"

The entire room falls into a sudden, awkward silence and everyone turns to look at me and Bjorn. We stare back for a few beats and then Bjorn turns and shuffles off down the hallway. Though it seems his outburst provided a distraction, rather than calming the crowd, it gives one of them an opening for an attack.

Ms. Mousy takes her suitcase-sized purse and smacks the crap out of the closest Barbie doll twin, who shrieks and lunges at the woman with her hands extended like claws—albeit well-manicured claws flawlessly painted in Mojave Desert Red. I half expect the other Barbie doll to join in but instead she grabs her twin and pulls her off Ms. Mousy.

"Let's take a breather, shall we?" the second, saner twin says to the other two women. "We're all adults here. Why don't we try to behave so?" Her voice is smooth, silky, and very sexy. I see Hurley staring at her with keen interest and feel a sudden pang of jealousy.

"I agree," says the man standing by Hurley. "Clearly we've

been drawn together under some less-than-ideal circumstances. Let's try to do the best we can with it and honor the dignity of our respective parents, shall we?"

Like the woman I assume is his sister, this guy's voice is luscious: mellifluous, rich, and a bit sultry. There is also the faintest hint of an underlying British accent, suggesting he spent some time there. Between the voice and his demeanor, he manages to gain control of the room, at least for the moment. All eyes are on him. Mine are on him, up and down him, and all around him. Two can play at this infatuation game and this guy is worth a goggle or three.

As if sensing my ogling he turns and looks at me, making me blush.

"I don't believe we've been introduced," he says, walking toward me with one hand extended. "I'm Aaron Heinrich."

"Mattie Winston, Deputy Coroner," I return, taking his hand. We exchange a brief shake, but as I'm about to let go he tightens his grip ever so slightly and smiles at me. "You're far too pretty to be doing this kind of work," he says. Coming from anyone else it would have sounded stupid and sleazy but he manages to make it sound sexy and flattering. I blush deeper and say a silent prayer of thanks to Barbara.

"I'm ... um ... not sure one's looks ... um ... matter with this job," I stammer. "But thank you." From the corner of my eye I can see Hurley scowling at us.

"Well, Mattie Winston," Aaron goes on. "Perhaps you can lend a voice of sanity to our proceedings here today. As you may have guessed, we are the Heinrich and Conklin families." He gestures toward the Barbie twins and says, "These are my sisters, Katrina and Grace, and this gentleman over here"—he shifts his attention to my left and nods at Sailor Boy—"is my brother, Easton."

Sailor Boy winks at me. I nod politely toward the twin Barbies but make no effort to approach them since Aaron still has a warm but firm grasp on my hand.

"These other two people," Aaron continues, "are our stepsiblings, Sarah and Tom."

Both stepsiblings look mad enough to spit fire and I fear that neither of them will be easy to deal with. I've already seen Sarah attack one of the Barbies with her purse, and if it wasn't for the cop standing between Easton and Tom, I'm pretty sure Easton would be out cold by now.

The Heinrich sibs are a little harder to gauge. Easton has a clueless look about him that makes me think he's the youngest and easiest going. The twins, however, are a toss-up. The sister named Grace, who ironically is the one showing the least of it at the moment, looks like she wants to kill someone. Based on the way she is glaring at Sarah, I'm guessing she's visualizing a big bull's-eye on the other woman's forehead.

Katrina, on the other hand, has the same calm, refined expression her brother Aaron has. Her face reveals nothing and I'm at a loss to gauge how difficult or easy it will be to work with her.

With introductions out of the way, Aaron turns his attention back to me and says, "It's a sad thing that brings all of us here today. I understand you have found the bodies of our father and his wife, Bitsy."

"Based on evidence we found with the bodies, it does appear that way," I tell him. "But I'm not sure if their identities have been confirmed yet." I look over at Izzy, who is standing behind Cass's desk. He looks like he wants to run and hide somewhere, but to his credit he takes a step closer. After swallowing so hard that his Adam's apple looks like the weight on one of those strong man things at the carnival, he introduces himself and volleys this first question.

"I'm Dr. Rybarceski, the medical examiner. I performed autopsies on the victims we found and can tell you that the bodies have been identified as those of Gerald and Bitsy Heinrich."

"Can you tell us how they died?" Aaron asks.

"It appears they both died of injuries sustained in the motor vehicle crash. That's only a preliminary finding, however, as we still have some test results we are waiting on."

"Were they killed instantly?" Katrina asks. Sarah shoots her an evil look that impresses me. That stare could melt icebergs.

"It doesn't appear so," Izzy says carefully. "There was evidence to suggest they both survived the initial crash, but I can't be sure how long at this point."

The evil stepsiblings all exchange pointed looks and then Grace fires away with another question. "Can you tell which of them died first?"

Izzy takes a deep breath before answering. "Perhaps we can once we analyze all the evidence a bit more. But at this point I can't answer that question."

"Well, when can you?" Grace asks, sounding impatient. "We need to know."

"It will probably take a few days at least," Izzy says. "Maybe longer. We need to analyze certain fluids and examine, um, the insect activity."

If anyone has any concerns that the idea of bugs munching on the dead bodies of their parents would bother anyone in this group, we are quickly enlightened.

"Well, get on it then," Grace says irritably, and the others all nod. "Do whatever you need to do with what you've got and get us an answer."

Izzy looks like he wants to snap back at the woman but to his credit he manages to maintain his composure. "May I ask why this information is so important to you?" he asks.

"Oh, for Christ's sake," Grace says, rolling her eyes and placing her perfectly manicured hands on her hips. Aaron holds one hand up to shush her and smiles at Izzy.

"It seems there are some issues with the wills," he explains. "As you may or may not know, Bitsy wasn't my father's first wife. I think he knew some of us didn't approve of her or their arrangement so when he married her he changed his will. Now it says that if he dies before Bitsy, she inherits the bulk of his money. But if Bitsy precedes him in death, the money goes to us, Gerald's children.

"Bitsy had a will as well, and it states that her entire estate will go to her children, Sarah and Tom." He gestures toward the twosome as he says their names, then sighs heavily. "There are millions of dollars at stake here," he says, turning his gaze on me. "And where that money goes will be determined by who died first. If Bitsy survived the crash longer than my father did, then she inherits his money and it all goes to Sarah and Tom. But if my father survived longer, it goes to us. You see our dilemma here?" He bestows that charming smile of his on me again and I find myself smiling back before I know what hit me. To add to my delight, Hurley sees it and his scowl deepens.

Izzy says, "I can't promise you that we'll be able to distinguish the times of death with the degree of accuracy you need. Often the best we can do is narrow it down to a chunk of hours."

Sarah is the one to roll her eyes this time and she stomps her foot in anger. "Goddamned spoiled rich brats!" she mutters. "You don't need the money. The trust fund your father set up already gives each of you an annual income that's greater than most people will see in a lifetime. You're just being greedy."

Katrina glares at Sarah and grits her teeth. Grace says, "It's not your money to begin with, you stupid bitch. Your mother was nothing but a cheap gold-digging whore who bewitched my father so she could get her hands on his money."

"My mother is not a whore!" Sarah screams.

"You're right," Grace says, smiling smugly and catching Sarah off guard. "At least not anymore. All she is now is worm food."

"Fuck you!" Sarah screams. She launches herself at Grace, grabbing a chunk of that dyed-perfect hair. Katrina jumps to her sister's defense, which forces Tom to abandon Easton and join the fray to assist his outnumbered sister. Easton watches for a second, shrugs, and then joins the melee.

The air fills with shrieks of anger and a cacophony of cuss words. Within seconds the group becomes a blur of swinging hands, kicking feet, ripped clothing, and flying chunks of hair. The two uniform cops do their best to break it up and regain control but it's clear they have their work cut out for them. Then one of them heightens the interest by taking out his Taser.

Aaron, Hurley, and I step back toward the desk out of the way seconds before the Taser fires. The prongs fly out and bite home accompanied by the electrical static noise of 50,000 volts of electricity. Someone screams—it's a low, male sound—and falls to the floor. The ploy is successful; the group immediately grows quiet and breaks up, distancing themselves from the victim.

I hear Hurley mumble "dumbass" under his breath just before the group parts enough for me to see who got fried. There on the floor, his body rigid with agony, is Taser cop's uniformed partner.

Chapter
24

An hour later we have managed to clear out the various members of the Heinrich-Conklin debacle and I'm sitting in the office library with Izzy, Hurley, and Bjorn, who has just made it onto my hit list by finding and eating the pint of Ben & Jerry's I had hidden in the break room freezer.

"I've got all the insect evidence from the bodies collected," Izzy tells us, "but the only forensic entomologist in the state is on vacation and won't be back for another four days. I can try to find someone else but I'm not sure how long it will take so it may be a while before we can get any data."

"Great," I say. "Somehow I don't think patience is a strong suit for anyone on either side of that family. I don't understand why they can't just work it out between themselves. Hell, there's plenty of money to go around. Why not just split it up evenly between all six of them?"

"Because that would make too much sense," Izzy says. "The more money these rich people have, the more they want."

"Frigging spoiled rich people," Hurley mutters. "I hate them."

His comment cheers me at first because I suspect it might be driven by his jealousy toward Aaron. Then I remember the rumors I've heard about Hurley's past. Prior to coming here he worked as a homicide detective in Chicago. But a brusque run-in with a well-connected, rich man whom Hurley suspected of killing his wife cost Hurley his job, even though the man was later arrested and convicted of the crime.

"Well, I'm ready to switch gears and get back to focusing on Shannon's case," I tell the group.

"Speaking of which," Hurley says, pulling a slip of paper from his jeans pocket. "That shrink gave me a list of names for the patients who had appointments on the day of Shannon's murder. They all agreed to talk to me as long as they wouldn't have to testify." He unfolds the sheet and shows it to us. I recognize five of the names, including Jackie's, and note that Hurley has made checkmarks beside all but one of them.

"What do the checkmarks mean?" I ask.

"It means I've spoken with them and verified their appointments. The only one I couldn't reach was the noon appointment, this woman named Catherine Miller," he explains, tapping a finger next to the name. "But since we know Shannon was killed sometime after noon, I don't think it matters. The shrink's alibi is looking pretty solid. So we're back to the husband."

"We'll see," I say, frowning.

"I hear your brother-in-law is representing him," Hurley says.

"Yes, I asked him to."

"You're that convinced he's innocent?"

"Not one hundred percent, but I can't see him doing it. And so far the evidence is still circumstantial, isn't it?"

Hurley gives me a conceding nod. "It is, but there's a lot of it. We dumped the calls from Shannon's cell phone."

"And?" Izzy and I say at the same time.

"It's mostly calls to her mother in Tennessee, a sister in California, and some local calls to friends, work, and such. There was one call to Erik on the day he showed up at Dairy Airs and argued with her. But there was also an incoming call from him at five forty-five on the day of her murder. He conveniently forgot to tell us about that."

"See," Bjorn tosses in. "I told you the husband did it. It's always the spouse."

Hurley gives me a self-satisfied smile.

I try to recall what Erik told us about his whereabouts and activities the day of the murder. "Wasn't that when he said he was having dinner with Jacob Darner?" I ask Hurley.

"It was, and while he did have dinner like he said, Mr. Darner says he left the restaurant around five-forty, meaning Erik was on his own when he made the call and, as far as we know, for the rest of the night."

"You say he called Shannon, but did he talk to her?" I ask.

"The call only lasted thirty seconds so I'm guessing he got her voice mail." I open my mouth to ask the next obvious question but Hurley beats me to it. "And no, he didn't leave a message."

"Have you asked him about the call?"

Hurley shakes his head. "I planned to interview him at the station this afternoon but I got tied up checking into some other stuff and then the fracas here started."

"So all you really have is more circumstantial evidence."

"For now, but give me time."

Izzy gets up and tucks his chair in under the table. "Well, while you two battle things out here I've got a ton of paperwork to finish. Let me know if anything of interest comes up."

Taking my cue from Izzy, I also get up and push my chair in. "I have some things I want to follow up on. I still want to go back to Shannon's house and look around. I have a feeling there's something there I'm missing."

Hurley says, "We can do that tonight if you like."

"That would be great." I'm delighted at the prospect of spending more time with Hurley, even if it is at a murder scene. Sometimes you take what you can get. "Unfortunately my only set of wheels at the moment is Bjorn here and I need to get him back to the cab garage. Would you be willing to be my chauffeur?"

He glances at his watch. "I'm meeting with Luke Nelson in ten minutes and expect it to take a half hour or so but I can pick you up somewhere after that."

Bjorn, having finished off my Ben & Jerry's, says to me, "I got a bulge here in my pants that needs tending to."

Hurley's eyebrows shoot up halfway to his hairline. He opens his mouth to say something, but I cut him off. "Don't. It's better not to know some things." I turn to Bjorn. "Don't worry, Bjorn. I'll take care of it."

Hurley grins wickedly and says, "Anything I can help with?" Though I'm pretty sure he means it as a joke, Bjorn is under no such illusion. "Hell, no, you can't help," he says irritably. "I don't want another man having anything to do with my wanker." Just in case Hurley might be dense enough to miss the meaning, Bjorn grabs his crotch and gives it a jiggle.

Hurley, barely containing his laughter, says to me, "How about if I meet you at the cab garage at six-thirty? That way you and Bjorn here can have some private time together."

Bjorn and I pull up to the cab garage a little after six. The place is dark and looks deserted. Bjorn has trouble finding his personal car in the lot in part because it's a moonless night. Fortunately there is only one car in the lot that can be his and as I'm steering him toward it, he looks at me with a frown and asks, "Who are you again?" He scans the parking lot with a bewildered expression. "Are we going somewhere? And where's Beatrice?"

Uh-oh. Beatrice is his wife, who's been dead for some ten years now. I'm beginning to suspect Bjorn is a sundowner, an affectionate term those of us in healthcare use for people whose confusion worsens after dark.

I take Bjorn's keys and open his car, letting him sit on the passenger side to keep him from trying to drive off somewhere in his confusion. We settle in and wait for Hurley, who pulls up a short time later. Leaving Bjorn for a minute, I walk over to Hurley's car and tap on the driver's side window. He lowers it, smiling at me.

"Do you and Bjorn need a little more time together?" he asks.

"As a matter of fact, we do. Would you mind following me to his place? He can't see well enough in the dark to drive and he's gotten a little disoriented now that the sun has gone down."

He grins wickedly at me but says nothing. I head back to Bjorn and drive him home with Hurley following. I help Bjorn into his house and then spend ten minutes in the bathroom with him removing his leg bag and connecting him to his nighttime bag, one that hangs at the bedside. As I steer him to his bedroom with him carrying the urine bag in one hand like a pocketbook, he stops for a moment and stares at his feet.

"I really should try to get some shoes to match this bag, don't you think?" he says.

After making sure Bjorn is tucked in and his door is locked, I walk over to Hurley's car and climb in the passenger seat. He pulls out, not saying a word but smiling from ear to ear. Five silent minutes later we are standing at Shannon's front door and Hurley cuts the crime scene tape. When he opens the door, goose bumps race down my arms and the carnal odor of stale blood makes my stomach lurch.

As if sensing my hesitancy, Hurley places a hand at the small of my back and says, "It's always hard to come back to these places. The initial horror wears off but it gets replaced by an overwhelming sense of loss and sadness." He sighs and his breath is warm and oddly reassuring on my neck. "It's truly disheartening to see the horrors that human beings are capable of inflicting on one another."

I'm surprised at the level of emotion in his voice. I've developed an impression of him as a hardened, tough guy and this unexpected peek at his soft underbelly is both surprising and erotic. The air around us feels charged, and when I look up at his face he gazes down at me with a warmth I've never seen there before. The pressure of his hand at my back increases slightly and when he lowers his head I realize he is about to kiss me. A sensation like warm molten wax courses through my body, centering in my groin area. Then I remember where we are and know in an instant that this is the wrong place and time.

Reluctantly I pull back from him and sigh. "Not here."

He holds me tight a second longer before the pressure of his hand lightens. "You're right," he says, matching my sigh. "Let's get back to business."

We enter the house and I wrinkle my nose at the smell of stale death. We pause a moment in the living room to look around and don some gloves. My gut is telling me to head back to the bedroom, that there's something in there I missed. But I hold off and walk through the rest of the house first.

Nothing strikes me as odd until I reach the kitchen and start examining Shannon's food stocks. Her monthly grocery bill must have been huge. There is enough here to feed a family of six and at least a quarter of it is designed to satisfy someone with a hellacious sweet tooth. There are four different flavors of Dairy Airs ice cream in the freezer, dozens of packages of cookies and cakes stashed in the pantry, and a wide assortment of candies in the cupboards.

Hurley, who followed me to the kitchen but stopped in the doorway, is leaning with one shoulder against the doorjamb, his hands in his pockets, his eyes watching my every move. I'm not sure if his close scrutiny is because he's worried I might somehow contaminate the crime scene or if he's reflecting on the moment we had on the porch.

I finish examining the kitchen and head for the bedroom, but Hurley won't step aside to let me by. I stop inches in front of him and we look at each other for several seconds before his face breaks into a smile.

"What?" I ask.

"You've taken to your new job pretty quickly. And you seem to have good investigative instincts."

"It comes from being nosy, which is a survival tool in a small town like this. And it's come in handy during my nursing career, too. The ability to read the small clues can really help when you're trying to size someone up and get a grasp of their lifestyle."

Hurley nods. "Whatever the reasons, I just wanted to let you know that I think you're doing a good job so far despite your tendency to get naked under the oddest of circumstances."

My face flushes hot at his words and I feel my heartbeat speed up. Desperate to escape that penetrating gaze of his I tell him, "I'd like to move into the bedroom now." His eyebrows arch and his smile broadens as I realize what I've said. "To look at Shannon's stuff," I add quickly. He doesn't move at first and I tag on a beseeching, "Please?"

He finally steps aside and I hurry past him, hoping he won't follow me. The idea of being in a bedroom with him after the sexually charged moments we just shared makes me nervous. Perhaps sensing my level of discomfort, he wanders off into the living room and starts rummaging through a corner desk instead.

Once again I am struck by the level of femininity in Shannon's bedroom. It's a very girly room—too girly for me—and I imagine it would prove uncomfortably girly to any man who may have entered. That gets me to wondering about the intimate moments she shared with Luke Nelson. Did they take place here, his place, or somewhere else that offered a more neutral setting? Somehow I sense that this room was something of a sanctuary for Shannon, a place where no man was welcome.

As I look at the bedside tables I remember the letters I found in there and holler out to Hurley, "Hey, I forgot to tell you that I read those letters from Erik to Shannon." He doesn't answer me and I assume he didn't hear so I move closer to the door to try again. I look out into the living room and see him seated at a corner desk, his face frowning as he examines some papers.

Curious, I walk over to him. "Find something?"

He shrugs. "Don't know if it's all that significant but Shannon had quite a bit of credit card debt. On this one card alone she owed over ten thousand dollars and there are two other bills here I haven't gotten to yet."

"Hey, it's the American way," I tell him, feeling a twinge of guilt. I ran up some pretty significant credit card bills myself when I was living with David. Once I left him, I was afraid to use the cards since they were all in his name and I didn't know if he had flagged the accounts to prevent me from using them. So to avoid that embarrassment, I never tried.

"What kind of stuff did she buy?" I ask. Hurley hands me the bill he's holding and I scan the contents. There are several orders from a health food company, which seems in total opposition to the contents of the kitchen. In addition I see charges for several visits to her personal physician and a whopping charge of several thousand to a cosmetic dentist located in Madison.

I make a mental note to chat with Shannon's doctor, a woman physician I know from working at the hospital. And though I'm momentarily surprised that someone of Shannon's obviously modest means would spend so much money on cosmetic dentistry, I then remember her side career as a model.

I hand the bill back to Hurley and venture into Shannon's bathroom, which is just off her bedroom. It's a typical woman's bathroom, full of make-up, lotions, fancy soaps, and a variety of hair products. When I open the medicine cabinet I find the usual collection of over-the-counter medications: aspirin, Tylenol, cough syrup, laxatives, and an allergy drug. I also find the reason behind all of the health store charges. The rest of the cabinet is jam-packed with vitamins, minerals, and herbal supplements, most of them bearing labels that promise some type of assistance with weight loss.

Once again I feel a kinship to Shannon and every other woman who has ever had to struggle with her weight. It's a constant battle and there are days when I swear I can gain weight simply by thinking of eating something, or sitting in the same room with it. When I do cave in and gain a few pounds, at least I can hide the results beneath my larger sized, loose-fitting, fat clothes. But Shannon didn't have that luxury if she wanted to maintain her modeling career.

Also in the medicine cabinet is a supply of birth control pills, which reminds me of what Erik had said in his letters to Shannon about wanting children. Was Shannon's obsession with her figure the reason she held out? Was she afraid of ruining her modeling career if she got pregnant? Or was it something else altogether?

Something is nagging at me, a little itch in the back of my mind, but I can't seem to reach and scratch it. I move back to the bedroom and stand there a moment, trying to figure out what it is that's bothering me. But it remains elusive so I head back to Hurley.

"Any chance you're up for a drink?" I ask him.

"Are you asking me out on a date?"

"No, I just want to check out Luke Nelson's alibi at the Somewhere Bar."

"I already did. Several people verified that he was there."

"Oh."

There's an awkward moment of silence before Hurley adds, "We can go anyway if you want, and have a nightcap. I don't know if you found what you want here, but I'm not seeing anything too exciting."

I put my hand on my hip and give him an injured look.

"Evidence-wise, I mean," he adds, his eyes twinkling.

"Good, because I'm not that kind of girl." One of his eyebrows arches and he gives me a smoldering look that makes my stomach go all squishy. "Although I suppose I could be," I add as I head out the door.

Chapter
25

All of the bars in town have their frequent fliers: the pasty-faced, doughy-looking, smoky-smelling, weekday regulars, folks who look like they live in the place. They're the ones who have a "usual" seat, are greeted by the bar staff by name, and are served their drink of choice without having to ask for it. But on any given night there will also be some outsiders in the bars, the occasional drop-ins, the celebrators, the lonely, the bored, the out-of-towners, and others like us, who are simply looking for a brief break in the day.

Even if you're not a regular at one of the bars, Sorenson is a small enough town that a lot of the patrons know each other simply because they are neighbors. Both Hurley and I know the bartender on duty tonight, a redheaded, fifty-something woman named Cara. She greets us both by name and as we settle in at the bar, I order a Miller Lite on tap while Hurley opts for a bottle of Sam Adams. We also know several of the patrons, as well, though different ones for different reasons. In my case it's because they are people I've grown up with or cared for when I worked at the hospital. Hurley, being relatively new in town, knows most of his acquaintances "professionally."

When Cara brings our drinks, we exchange some polite chit-chat with her. But when there's a brief lag in the conversation, I ask her if she knows Luke Nelson. I see Hurley shoot me a side-long glance but pointedly ignore him.

"I do," Cara says. "He comes in from time to time. He isn't a regular or anything but he probably drops in a couple of times every month. I think he fancies himself some kind of Frasier Crane or something. Boring shit, if you ask me," she concludes with a roll of her eyes.

Hurley snorts a laugh and Cara looks pleased that her commentary has amused him. She leans on the bar, shifts her attention to him, and asks, "So, are you seeing anyone these days, Detective?"

Hurley practically spews the beer he just sipped and turns cherry red.

"'Cause I'm free tomorrow night and have tickets to the opera in Madison," Cara continues with an exaggerated wink.

Realizing she is merely yanking his chain, Hurley laughs, swallows his beer, and says, "Good one."

"Hey, a girl can dream, right?" Cara says.

Indeed.

Since neither of us has eaten dinner, we order a couple of sandwiches and then I challenge Hurley to a game of darts baseball. Despite my competitive nature, I spend the entire time not caring if I ever hit the board, as long as I can watch Hurley walk up to retrieve the darts. In fact, I quickly realize the view is greatly enhanced when I miss altogether and he has to bend over to pick up my darts from the floor. He beats me handily and, by the time we decide to call it quits, I'm embracing my loser status and struggling to rein in my hormones.

We order two more beers and settle back in at the bar. I can feel the sexual tension growing tauter by the moment and we spend a few moments sitting side by side sharing another awkward silence. There is a foot of space between us but I can feel the heat radiating off his body and my mind is imagining how it would feel to nestle my head against the broad expanse of his chest and the soft flannel of his shirt. It's Hurley who finally breaks the silence with a husky clearing of his throat before he speaks.

"So, Winston," he says. "Can I ask where things are with you and David?"

"Nowhere," I tell him. "He's made some overtures about trying again but I've made it pretty clear I'm done with him. I can't forgive him for cheating on me with Karen."

"People screw up sometimes," he says with a shrug. "You must have some residual feelings for the guy. Are you sure you want to throw away your marriage because David made this one mistake?"

I give him a disbelieving look. "It's a pretty big mistake, don't you think?" I say, angry that he's defending the slime bag. "I mean, it's not like he didn't pick up his clothes, or came home late for dinner, or tracked mud in on the carpet. He risked everything we had, everything we'd built, everything I believed in. He showed a total disregard not only for my feelings, but for my life. So yeah," I conclude, my ire hitting a crescendo. "I'm sure."

Hurley has hit a nerve and the feelings I've been working so hard to suppress over the past few months come boiling to the surface. I feel the sting of tears in my eyes and swipe irritably at them, turning away from him and staring at the dwindling head on my beer.

"Sorry," he says, his voice soft. "I just . . . I wanted . . . I wondered . . . shit."

He lowers his head and starts scraping the label off his bottle with his thumbnail. The awkward silence returns, hovering between us like a noxious gas. After several, agonizingly long minutes of it, he pushes his bottle away and says, "Come on. I'll drive you home."

Not trusting my emotional state enough to speak, I simply nod and climb down from my bar stool. I follow him to the car and when he gallantly opens my door for me, I nearly burst into tears. The drive is blessedly short but uncomfortably quiet, and as he turns into my driveway I feel the need to say something to try to salvage the moment, and my future with him.

"It's not easy for me," I manage, twiddling my thumbs and staring at my lap.

"I'm sure it's not," he says, sounding weary.

"But I'm very certain where I stand on the matter. David and I are through. I know I haven't taken the steps to make it official yet, but that doesn't mean I'm having second thoughts. I promise you, that part of my life is over. Done with. Finis."

"I believe you," Hurley says, pulling up in front of my cottage and shifting his car into park. "But based on what I see here, I'm not sure David does."

Confused, I look over at him but his eyes are focused on my front porch, his expression grim. I follow his line of sight and understanding glimmers. There, sitting on the porch, is David.

"Damn it," I mutter.

"Do you need me to stay or will you be okay?"

Every fiber of my being wants him to stay but I know that now is not the time. Reluctantly I shake my head. "I'll be okay," I tell him. Keenly aware of David watching us, I make an impulsive decision. I lean over and kiss Hurley on the cheek. His skin is soft and warm on my lips, and his smell is heavenly. "Thanks for driving me tonight," I whisper in his ear.

He turns to look at me and the normal blue of his eyes has darkened into something edgy, smoldering, and electrifying. It takes every ounce of willpower I possess to open the car door and get out.

As I approach the porch, Hurley turns his car around and heads down the drive. I hear his wheels squeal as he pulls out onto the road, and a terrible sense of loss washes over me. Part of me wants to go running after his car and beg him to take me away. Part of me wishes I'd asked him to stay. But I do none of those things. Instead I climb my front steps and brace myself for whatever David has in store.

Chapter 26

"Hello, David."

He stares at me with an annoyed expression. "Just what the hell was that?" he grumbles.

I ignore him, open my front door, and head inside. David follows, firing questions in machine-gun fashion.

"What the hell was that, Mattie? Did you just kiss that guy? Is there something going on between you two? Are you dating him? Are you *sleeping* with him?"

This last question piques my ire enough to make me whirl on him and fire back. "Who are *you* sleeping with these days, David, now that Karen's gone?"

He pulls back, blinks hard several times, and then his whole body sags. "Okay," he says miserably. "I had that coming. I'm sorry."

He plops down in a nearby chair and stares at his hands, picking at a cuticle on one of his fingers. I study him, taking in the waves of his blond hair, the taut patrician angles in his face, and the tall, lean lines of his body. I still find him handsome, but its effect on me at this point is nil.

"Why are you here, David?"

"I heard you were in a car accident. I wanted to make sure you're okay."

"I am, as I'm sure the ER staff told you. So if that's all you want, you—"

"I wanted to talk to you about something else, too."

"What?"

"Us."

"There isn't any *us* anymore, David." The words come out harsh and angry, and he shoots me a wounded look that momentarily softens me. Then I remember what he did and my spine stiffens again. "For a relationship to work there has to be trust. And I don't trust you anymore. That's it in a nutshell."

He nods wearily. "I understand that, and I deserve it," he says. He leans forward with his arms on his knees and looks up at me with that wounded, puppy-dog look again. "What I did was wrong, but I've learned from my mistakes, Mattie. I'm asking you to consider forgiving me and to maybe, just maybe, give me . . . give us a second chance. I know it will take time and I'm not here to push you, but I don't want you to rush into anything else either." He pauses and I know the "anything else" he is referring to is Hurley. "Don't close all the doors yet, Mattie," he says, making his final appeal. "Don't throw away everything we had."

I stare at him a moment, and even though I feel bone-weary tired, I remain standing, not wanting to give him the impression that this discussion is going to continue. "What we had was a façade, David. It wasn't real. I can't forgive what you did, at least not to the degree necessary to make things work between us."

"Not now, maybe," he appeals. "But if we give it some time I'm sure we can—"

"I don't love you anymore, David." The words stop him dead, and as I utter them, the truth of the statement rings through to my core. It's oddly releasing, but it also leaves me feeling terribly sad. "I'm sorry," I say honestly.

There must be something in my expression that drives home the truth of my claim because his shoulders sag with resignation.

"So that's it then," he says.

"Yes."

He digests things for a few seconds, then pushes himself out of the chair and takes a last look around the small confines of my cottage. Rubbish appears from the bedroom, strolling languidly into the room, pausing for one of those luxurious cat stretches. He eyes David then dismisses him as handily as I have, walking over to me instead and winding himself around my feet. He purrs contentedly and when David takes a step in my direction, I quickly reach down and pick Rubbish up, holding his warm, soft, vibrating little body close to my chest. As barriers go, he isn't much of one, but the action has the effect I want; David stops moving toward me.

"Are you seeing that detective who drove you home?" he asks.

"That's none of your business." The words come out harsher than I mean them to but if it bothers David, he doesn't show it. In fact, he smiles.

"You're still hurting and angry with me," he says, turning toward the door. "But despite what you're feeling now, I think your feelings will change over time. And I'm willing to wait."

For a brilliant surgeon, he's pretty clueless. Not wanting him to feel encouraged in any way, I blurt out a last parting shot. "I'm filing for a legal separation and, as soon as our waiting period is up, I plan to file for a divorce. I hope you'll be fair in the settlement rather than spiteful."

I see a tiny shudder course through his body, but he doesn't look back at me. After a moment he says, "We'll see."

I'm not sure if his equivocation is referring to my threat of a divorce or my plea for him to be fair, but I let him go without asking for clarification. As the door closes behind him, I nuzzle my nose in Rubbish's fur and whisper, "It's just you and me now, kiddo. Just you and me."

I make my way to the kitchen and treat Rubbish to a plate of tuna. Then I search the fridge for a treat of my own and, finding nothing of interest, I move to the freezer where I find a brand-new pint of Ben & Jerry's Cherry Garcia. I take it and a spoon back out to the living room and settle in on the couch with the remote control. After flipping through the channels I settle on an old episode of *Frasier*. It reminds me of Cara's statement about

Luke Nelson and that gets me to thinking about the name and address I have for the woman who owns the HOT 44D license plate. I make a mental note to try to find her tomorrow and figure out what her connection to Nelson is. Something about the man just feels wrong to me and maybe this woman is the key.

By the time *Frasier* ends I realize I've eaten the entire carton of ice cream. Feeling disgusted with myself, I set the empty container aside and silently wish I could go back in time and undo all the calories I just consumed. The thought niggles something in my brain and a seemingly unrelated montage of images flashes through my mind: the food in Shannon's kitchen, a pathetically skinny teenager I took care of once in the ER, the clothes in Shannon's closet, the contents of Shannon's medicine cabinet, Jackie's description of Erik's visit to Dairy Airs, the discovery that Shannon had a hiatal hernia, and the abrasions I found on her right hand when I first examined her body.

It all comes together in a startling explosion of insight. I explore this new path some more, taking all the detours, considering the various implications, and examining the potential outcomes. And in the end it leads me to a stunning conclusion . . . one that will very likely change everything regarding the investigation into Shannon's death.

Chapter
27

Despite not going to bed until well after midnight, I'm wide awake at six A.M. Last night's revelation is still at the forefront of my thoughts and I plan my day accordingly. At seven A.M. I make several quick phone calls: one to Bjorn to make sure he's up, ready, and remembers who I am, one to Dairy Airs, one to my brother-in-law, Lucien, and one to Sally Hvam, the owner of the red convertible. I get lucky on the call to Lucien and reach his assistant, Caroline, instead.

"He headed for the courthouse a little bit ago," Caroline tells me. "Erik Tolliver's arraignment is later this morning."

My call to Sally Hvam doesn't go quite as smoothly.

"Who the hell is this?" she asks in a husky voice, clearly annoyed. There is an underlying grogginess that tells me I have most likely wakened her.

"My apologies if I woke you up," I start. "But I'm—"

"Of course you woke me up," she snaps. "What hours do you think bartenders keep anyway?"

"I'm sorry. I didn't know you were a bartender."

"Who the hell are you?"

I introduce myself, explaining that I'm a deputy coroner and that I'd like to ask her some questions about an acquaintance of hers.

"Coroner? Doesn't that mean you investigate deaths?" she asks, sounding more alert now.

"It does. I'm looking into a murder."

"Whose?"

"A woman here in Sorenson by the name of Shannon Tolliver. Do you know her?"

"Name doesn't ring a bell but my bell's like the Liberty these days. A bit cracked." She chuckles at her own joke. "Was she the one I heard about who got shot around Halloween?"

"Yes."

"Well, I'm afraid I can't help you. I suppose I might have served her at some point in my career. The bar I work is a busy place. But I don't know the woman."

"She's not the one I want to ask you about. I'm checking background information on someone the victim was dating, a psychiatrist here in town by the name of Luke Nelson." When I hear a quick inhalation of air on the other end of the phone, I know I've hit pay dirt.

"Oh, yeah, I know him all right. What's the asshole gone and done now?"

"What do you mean? What has he done before?"

She lets out a deep throaty chuckle that makes me suspect she's a smoker. "How much time do you have, honey?"

"As much as you need," I tell her. "How about if I meet with you later this morning so we can talk?"

She hesitates, then says, "I can meet you in a couple of hours, if you want. But you'll have to come here to Smithville."

"That's fine. Do you want to meet somewhere public or should I come to your house?"

She names a small café and gives me directions. After agreeing to meet there at twelve-thirty, I hang up and watch Izzy's back door through my window, while sipping my coffee. As soon as I see Izzy emerge, I head out to greet him.

"Looking for a ride to the office?" he asks.

I shake my head. "Actually I was wondering if I could take the day to follow up on some things in the Tolliver case."

"I suppose," Izzy says, looking pointedly at the empty parking pad beside my cottage. "But how are you going to get around?"

"Bjorn is willing to drive me for now. We worked out a deal. I'm going to need to buy a new car at some point since the other one is totaled, but I have no idea how long it's going to take to get a check from the insurance company. Plus, there's a complication."

"I'm afraid to ask."

"The insurance was in David's name, so the check will go to him."

"I saw him sitting on your porch last night, waiting for you. Is that why he was here? To discuss the car?"

"Hardly. He was looking for another chance, hinting at reconciliation."

"And?"

"And I told him I'd give up food first."

"Ouch," Izzy says, flinching. "I guess you slammed that door shut for good."

"I'm glad you see that, but I'm not so sure David does."

"Time will tell, I guess. Do you think you'll get into the office at all today?"

"It will be this afternoon if I do. Is that a problem?"

"Shouldn't be, but take your cell and your pager with you just in case. If I need you I'll give you a call. Want to share what it is you're looking into?"

I shake my head. "Not yet. It's just a theory for the moment. I need to check on some things first."

The sound of an approaching engine makes us both turn and seconds later Bjorn pulls up. He parks the car, turns off the motor, and climbs out carrying his urine leg bag in one hand and the full bedside bag in the other, the connecting tubing snaking its way out of his trousers.

"I need my sack emptied really bad," he says, proffering the full bag at me.

Izzy raises a brow, but before he can utter a word I hold my hand up and say, "Don't ask. It's part of my cab fare."

I escort Bjorn inside and into my bathroom, empty the bed-side bag, switch him over to his leg bag, and make a mental note to remember to order him the new ones with the easy-open valve.

"Where to today?" he asks me as soon as I have him clamped and ready to go.

"I want to start with Dairy Airs, then the police station, then the hospital, and after that I need to go to Smithville."

"Pretty full day," Bjorn says, licking his lips. "I think I need a piece of cheesecake to get me started."

Cheesecake sounds good to me, too, but if I ate it as often as Bjorn does, I'd end up resembling the body suit Robin Williams wears in *Mrs. Doubtfire*.

Bjorn seems alert and aware this morning so I let him drive and, thanks to his eagerness for cheesecake, he manages to briefly hit the speed limit on a thirty-five-mile-an-hour street. The two-mile trip only takes a little over seven minutes, darned near light speed for Bjorn. We settle into a booth at Dairy Airs and order our respective items: a decadent-looking slice of turtle cheesecake for Bjorn and a bagel with cream cheese for me. Once again Jackie is our waitress—I knew she'd be working be-cause I'd called earlier—and as soon as she brings our food, I tell her the reason I'm here.

"There's something about Shannon that's bothering me and I'm wondering if you can help shed any light on the matter."

She shrugs, looks a little nervous, and says, "I can try."

"You mentioned that on the day Erik was here and got hit with the separation papers, Shannon ordered a bunch of food before going home. Is that something she did on a regular basis?"

"Oh, yeah," Jackie says with a roll of her eyes. "That woman had a truly blessed metabolism. She ate like there was no tomor-row and never seemed to gain an ounce. Maybe it was her stom-ach problem."

"Stomach problem?"

"She mentioned once that she had some kind of stomach problem and that was why she spent so much time in the bathroom." She pauses a moment, thinking. "It did seem like she had to go pretty often, and sometimes she would stay in there for quite a while."

"Did she usually eat here when she worked, or did she take stuff home with her?"

"A little of both, I guess."

I thank Jackie for her time and she looks puzzled but relieved when she realizes I'm done questioning her. Apparently Bjorn is puzzled, too.

"How do eating and toileting habits help solve murders?" he asks.

"You'd be surprised," I tell him, and though he still looks perplexed, he lets it go. We finish our meals in silence and as soon as we are done, we hop back in his car and head for the police station.

At the back of the Sorenson City Police Department are four jail cells. Most of the time they're occupied by town drunks who need a place to sleep off their latest alcoholic stupor and the doors to the cells are often left ajar. But every once in a while the jail houses someone charged with an actual crime, like Erik Tolliver.

After getting clearance from the front desk and depositing Bjorn in the squad room with some change for the vending machines, I head for the cell area, where I find Erik sitting on the bunk in cell number two, reading the morning newspaper. There is a desk area in front of the cells where an officer would typically sit, but at the moment it's empty. Erik is hardly alone, however. Cameras mounted near the ceiling are aimed at each of the cells and connected to monitors out at the dispatcher's desk. There is also a button on the wall of each cell that connects a prisoner to an intercom system in case they need to call for help. I know from past conversations with the cops that the intercom system also allows for eavesdropping, should the need arise. Push a button on the other end and you can hear everything that goes on inside a cell.

Hearing my approach, Erik peeks over the top of his news-

paper and then greets me with a weary "Good morning." I return
the greeting, grab the chair behind the desk, and wheel it over in
front of his cell.

"I'm almost afraid to ask why you're here," he says, setting his
paper aside.

"I have a few questions about Shannon."

He gives me a wary look. "Is this part of your investigation?
Shouldn't I have Lucien here?"

"It *is* a part of my investigation but not anything official, at
least not yet. I'm following up on a hunch and just want to ask
you a couple of questions about Shannon's eating habits."

Erik looks surprised. "Her eating habits? What's that got to do
with anything?"

"I'm not sure yet. It might be nothing, it might be everything.
If my suspicions are right it could work in your favor but I'm still
only theorizing at this point. I don't see any reason to call Lucien,
but if it will make you feel more comfortable to do so, go ahead.
I'll wait."

He weighs his options and decides to trust me. "Okay," he
says. "But if I start to feel uncomfortable about anything you ask,
I'm going to call a halt."

"Fair enough. To start with, can you tell me how Shannon's
modeling career was doing?"

He shrugs. "Okay, I guess. I mean it wasn't anything huge and
the work was pretty irregular. It was mostly local jobs. You know,
modeling clothes for flyers and ads in the paper, that sort of stuff.
She called the money she made from it her funny money."

"Did she typically diet when she had a job coming up?"

"Hell, it seemed like she was dieting all the time. She was always saying she needed to lose a few pounds. I remember a couple of times when she consumed nothing but those diet drinks
for a few days." He grimaces and shudders. "I tried one of them
out of curiosity once. I don't know how anyone can subsist on
those things. They're nasty."

"Were there ever times when she ate a lot? You know, way
more than usual?"

Erik smiles. "Don't we all?"

I wisely decide to take the Fifth on that one.

"She called them her binges," he goes on. "Some days she'd eat as if it might be the last food she'd ever see. And boy, did she have a sweet tooth. Her job at Dairy Airs was quite the challenge for her at times, what with all the ice cream and cheesecake and such."

"Did she ever show any remorse over her binges?"

He shrugs. "Sometimes she'd blame it on her hormones. You know, say it was that time of the month and all."

I nod. I'm familiar with that excuse since I've used it myself rather often, ignoring the fact that if it was true, my time of the month would be nearly every day.

"Sometimes she'd moan about what a pig she was and complain about her lack of willpower, but no more than any other woman I know."

I smile, pausing a moment as I try to find a delicate way to ask my next question. "Do you think that she spent an unusual amount of time in the bathroom?"

"Well, yeah," he says, giving me one of those *duh* looks. "But that was because of her IBS."

IBS is an acronym for irritable bowel syndrome, a condition that can cause frequent bouts of diarrhea, constipation, and abdominal pain. It's not rare but it's not all that common either. And I'm pretty sure Shannon didn't have it, unless she developed it within the last six months.

"How long had she had IBS?"

"The whole time we were married." I frown and Erik picks up on my confusion. "What?" he asks. "I can tell something is bothering you."

"It's just that I remember when Shannon had that emergency appendectomy a few months back. I was the scrub nurse on her case and she never mentioned having IBS. It wasn't in her history."

"Maybe she forgot," Erik says with a shrug. "Or maybe she

was just too embarrassed to mention it. I know she didn't like to talk about it."

"Maybe," I say, but I don't believe it. I had an up-close and very personal view of Shannon's bowels during that surgery. In fact, I held them in my hand. And there was no indication of a disease of any kind, much less IBS. Nor was there any sign of it during her autopsy.

"Why does it matter?" Erik asks. "Where are you going with all of this?"

I shake my head. "I don't want to say just yet," He gives me a look of exasperation so I try to explain myself more. "It's for your own good, Erik. If I tell you what I'm thinking and I'm wrong, it will get your hopes up for nothing. And if I'm right, telling you too soon could compromise the investigation. But it might also exonerate you. So I'm asking you to sit tight, be patient, and trust me on this one."

He makes a sweeping gesture around the inside of his cell. "It's not like I have much choice."

"I promise you that as soon as I have anything solid, I'll let both you and Lucien know, okay?"

He studies me through the bars of his cell, seeming to weigh my trustworthiness. Apparently I pass muster because he sighs, nods, and says, "Okay, Mattie. My fate is in your hands."

I should feel relieved to hear him say this, but I'm frightened instead. The weight of this investigation is beginning to press hard on me, and Erik's fate is a responsibility I'm not sure I want.

Before I have time to consider it further, I hear a familiar voice coming down the hall, one that prompts me to prepare for a hasty exit. Seconds later Lucien enters the room accompanied by a uniformed officer and Bjorn.

At first glance Lucien appears to be a normal, decent-looking guy. He has an average build, strawberry-blond hair, blue eyes, and wears suits, button-down shirts, and ties when he's working. But his clothes always have that slightly rumpled, slept-in look, and often as not the colors he wears clash violently. His hair, which is just wavy enough to be a bit unruly, is usually slicked back with a ton of greasy gel that makes it look perpetually wet. It all works together to lend him an air of slick sleaziness, an image he manages to reinforce every time he opens his mouth.

The officer gestures toward Bjorn, whose hands and face are smeared with chocolate. "Does he belong to you?"

"He does," I say, taking Bjorn by the arm and steering him toward a chair. I grab some tissues from a box on the desk and start trying to clean off the chocolate. From the corner of my eye I see Lucien watching me with *that* grin, the one that means something crass is coming, so I brace myself.

"Aw, Sweet Cheeks," he says to me in a pathetic tone. "I know you're probably yearning for a churning now that David's out of the picture, but this guy's a little old for you, isn't he?"

"I'm not dating him," I say, adding a mental *you moron* tag to the statement. "Bjorn is a cabdriver, and since my car was totaled the other day, he's driving me around until I can find a replacement."

Bjorn doesn't help the situation when he adds his own two cents, which turns out to be more like a halfpenny. "We worked out a deal," he explains. "I take her where she needs to go and she takes care of the tube in my peter."

Silence fills the room and Bjorn senses that he might have said something dicey. He tries to remedy the situation but only makes it worse. "She handles my sac when it gets too full and I need to drain my tube."

"Hey, Sweet Cheeks, you can handle my sac anytime you want."

"Nice, Lucien. Are you forgetting about your wife, who also happens to be my sister?"

"Of course not. We can include her, too. I'm always up for a threesome."

The uniform snorts a laugh at that one and even Erik manages a smile. I'm about to snap off another comeback but I bite it back, realizing it's a waste of time. I know from past experience that Lucien has no shame. And while he talks a good talk, as far as I know that's all he does. Someday I'm going to take him up on one of his challenges just to see what happens. But for now, I think the wisest course is to ignore him.

"Come on, Bjorn," I say, walking over and hooking my arm through his. "Let's get going."

"Where to now?" he asks as we head out of the police station.

"I want to make a quick stop at the hospital, to order you those other bags I was talking about." That's only part of the reason I want to go there but Bjorn has no need to know the other. "After that I need to go to Smithville, but if you don't mind lending me your car I can drop you off at the cab office and you can spend the afternoon driving around some real customers for a change."

He shrugs and says, "A trip to Smithville sounds like fun. I don't get out of town much anymore." I start to protest but before I can get a word out he adds, "Besides, what about my bag? You said you'd keep me empty all day."

I sigh, wondering why his forgetfulness never includes this promise. "Okay, Smithville it is then, right after the hospital."

There's a brief moment of awkwardness when Bjorn and I both head for the driver's side door of his car, but I acquiesce and move to the passenger side. As he climbs in behind the wheel and shuts the door he says, "When we get to the hospital I think I'll head for the cafeteria while you order your stuff. I'm kind of hungry."

"Fine, but you have to promise me you'll eat some real food this time. No more sweets for now, okay?"

He shoots me a sidelong glance that is a mix of disappointment and calculation. "How about just one tiny dessert after I eat something healthy?" he tries.

I shake my head. "No, Bjorn. You've already eaten more sugar today than most people eat in a week. It's not healthy." He opens his mouth in preparation for his next protest and I cut him off, delivering my coup de grâce. "Besides, all that sugar makes you pee more so your bag is going to fill up faster."

He clamps his mouth shut and stares out the windshield for a moment, contemplating. I can tell he's suspicious about my claim but I also know he isn't likely to know if it's true or not.

When I see a look of resigned acceptance on his face, I know I've won, at least this round.

"Okay," he says, turning the key. He carefully backs out of his parking space and into a light post. The one advantage of his snail's pace is that these little fender benders don't cause too much damage or injury. A definite disadvantage is the road rage he triggers among those forced to share the streets with him. His driving skills, or lack thereof, create pockets of chaos everywhere we go. At least five cars honk angrily at us and I lose count of how many drivers make obscene hand and finger gestures. Bjorn is blessedly oblivious to it all as we crawl our way along.

I, however, am not. I take every glare, every gesture, and every unheard uttering personally. So when we finally pull onto the street where the hospital is located, I breathe a sigh of relief. But when I see the crowd of people and vehicles gathered in front of the building, I realize the chaos has followed us here.

Chapter
28

Cop cars, ambulances, TV vans, and half a dozen miscella-
neous vehicles are parked willy-nilly in front of the hospital
by the ER entrance. I see uniforms of all types amidst the crowd:
cops, hospital security guards, EMTs, and a few generic hospital
white coats. There must be close to fifty people milling about
and Bjorn is so captivated by the scene that he almost runs over
three of them in his efforts to negotiate the bedlam.

As soon as he's safely parked I take out my cell phone and dial
the ER. Fortunately one of my old nursing cronies, Phyllis—aka
"Syph"—answers, a coup for me since I know she'll tell me anything I want to know.

"What's going on out front of the hospital?" I ask her.

"It's one of those precious Hallmark family moments," she
says, her voice thick with sarcasm. "Apparently some family got
into a tiff about a will and things got physical. Ambulances were
called and one of the people involved was transported to the ER.
He's in here and his cereal bowl is a few flakes shy, if you get my
drift. A couple of cops are trying to deal with him but the guy's
gone totally off his rocker.

"The rest of the family members are out front, arguing. Rumor
has it two of the women got into a hair-pulling contest and an
EMT got punched when he tried to break it up. His partner

called for backup and that's when security and the police got involved. We've been told none of the injuries are serious but we have no way of knowing since the only patient we've seen so far is the Froot Loop in here."

This scenario sounds disturbingly familiar, and as I scan the crowd of faces my suspicions are confirmed. There, right in the middle of everything, is Aaron Heinrich. Having no desire to get caught in another of the Heinrich family melees, I grab Bjorn's hand, duck down so I can't easily be seen, and guide us both along the edges of the crowd. We make our way to a back entrance to the hospital, one that's mainly used by delivery personnel. It's locked on the outside but I remember the key punch code needed to open it and, within seconds, Bjorn and I are inside. I send him off toward the cafeteria and then take some back hallways that lead into the patient care area of the ER.

The curtains around bed four are wide open, and standing on top of the stretcher is Easton "Sailor Boy" Heinrich. He's yelling something at the two cops nearby, one of whom is Larry Johnson. Syph and another nurse are standing off to one side watching the show and I join them.

"Hey, Mets," Syph says when she sees me. Syph isn't her real name. Her real name is Phyllis but years ago when I worked in the ER, we got bored one night and gave one another nicknames that were disease related and sounded somewhat similar to our real names. This was our way of poking fun at how we tend to refer to patients by their bed numbers and disorders rather than their names, which is why Easton Heinrich is now known as the Whackadoodle in Bed Four.

Syph nods toward the Whackadoodle. "This is a good one. I haven't had anything this interesting since your nipple incident. I'm not sure if the guy is crazy or just drunk, but he sure as hell is entertaining."

The drunk part is obvious from Easton's bloodshot eyes and the alcohol fumes wafting from his body so strongly I can smell it from where I'm standing. "Is he under arrest?" I ask.

"Not yet, but I suspect he will be before he's done."

Easton screams at the cops, "You want me? Then come and get me, fuckers. I dare you." He makes a come-on gesture with his hands, waggling his fingers at the cops. Larry shrugs and glances at his partner. They look like they are about to take Easton up on his offer when Easton ups the ante by stripping off his shirt. This gives the cops pause and Larry opts for a little verbal coaxing instead.

"Come on, buddy. Don't make this more difficult than it has to be."

"I'm not your fucking buddy," Easton screams, tossing his shirt at the cops and then proceeding to loosen his belt. Seconds later his pants drop down to his ankles and he steps out of them, nearly falling off the stretcher in the process. He kicks them toward the cops and then wiggles his ass like some flaky pole dancer.

Larry and his partner take an involuntary step back as the pants fly at them, and this meager bit of success seems to fuel Easton's fire. Before I can blink he strips off his boxers and assumes a "ta-da" pose with his arms outstretched overhead.

"Wow," Syph says. "This guy really is crazy."

"And very well hung," observes the other nurse.

Easton hears the comment and thrusts his hips toward Larry. "You want me?" he taunts, shaking his impressive tallywacker at Larry. "Then come and get me, you one-bullet Barney."

"Hey," Larry objects, looking wounded. He looks at his partner and they apparently share a silent exchange because the partner nods and starts slowly moving toward the foot of the bed. Easton is flinging his hips from side to side and is so taken with the sight of his own penis whacking against his thighs that he misses this move. Nor does he see Larry remove his Taser from its holster.

"Go!" Larry yells.

This momentarily befuddles Easton who looks up at Larry with an expression of confusion. Meanwhile Larry's partner makes a quick dash to the other side of the stretcher, arriving mere seconds before Larry fires.

There's a brief buzzing sound as Easton screams like a girl and crumples. Larry's partner manages to catch him before he flops onto the floor and moments later, a subdued Easton is curled into a fetal position on the stretcher, crying like a baby.

"God, I miss this place," I tell Syph.

"Yeah," she says with a sigh. "It does have its moments."

The other nurse moves in and tries to soothe Easton. The cops are more than happy to step back and let the nurse do her thing, but they stay close by just in case. It seems the Taser has taken all the fight out of Easton because he willingly submits to being dressed in a gown and lets the nurse draw some blood and start an IV on him.

"Might as well start an alcohol pool," Syph says, looking over at me. "You want in?"

"Hell, yeah," I say, digging in my pocket and coming up with a dollar. "Are you doing *Price Is Right* rules or closest takes it?"

She thinks a minute, then says, "Closest."

"Okay. I'll take 389."

Larry fishes some change out of his pocket and walks it over to Syph. "Put me in. I'll go for 325."

Within minutes we have a pool of money totaling eight bucks, hardly enough to get rich off of but that's not the point. The ability to accurately estimate blood alcohol levels is a prized talent among ER workers and cops, and the esteem of winning goes a lot farther than the money.

While waiting for the blood test results to come back, I relay Bjorn's predicament to Syph and she manages to find me not only the necessary order form for the new urine leg bags, but a sample of one left behind by a sales rep. Next I explain to her that I'm curious about Shannon's health history and want to review her medical record. Normally this would be a violation of HIPAA, the law that makes it easier to get your hands on a nuclear weapon than a patient's chart. But because I'm a deputy coroner and Shannon's case is one we are investigating, I have a legal right to pull and examine her record.

Pulling a chart is a term left over from the days of Medical

Records departments that stored thousands of paper files documenting a patient's care. Nowadays everything is on computer and in less than a minute Syph has accessed the information I need and given me control of the computer.

Shannon's record isn't a huge one. There are a couple of ER visits: one from a few years ago for vaginal bleeding that turned out to be a miscarriage, and another for a small laceration on her leg that needed a few stitches. There is also the appendectomy from a few months ago that I already know about. Her doctor's office visits are a bit more interesting. Apparently Shannon was dead set against getting pregnant, fearful it would affect her figure so much that it would shatter her modeling dreams. Yet diet alone was obviously a problem too, since there were multiple requests for diet pills. One thing I don't find in the record is any mention of IBS.

When I'm done, I close the file and log off the computer. Easton's blood test is back and his alcohol level is a whopping 426, making me, who had the highest guess of anyone, the prized possessor of eight bucks. After thanking Syph for her help with the chart and gloating for a few minutes over my win, I head down to the cafeteria, where I find Bjorn finishing off the last of a food tray. Despite my cautions, I see that he's currently working on a piece of strawberry shortcake and still has a slice of peach pie to go.

I settle in with him at the table. "Are you about done here, Bjorn?" I ask, glancing at my watch and then eyeing all the empty plates on his tray. "I have another appointment to get to."

"Almost," he says around a mouthful of shortcake.

I'm about to lecture him on his poor diet when I hear voices approaching. A moment later a small crowd of people enters the cafeteria and, much to my dismay, I see that it's the Heinrich clan, minus Easton of course. Tagging along with them is a uniformed cop named Junior Feller, and Hurley.

Junior steers the Heinrich trio to a nearby empty table and motions for them to sit. Hurley, who saw me the moment he entered the room, approaches our table.

"What are you doing here?" he asks.

"Official business," I say vaguely. "Are you socializing with the upper crust these days?" I add, gesturing toward the Heinriches.

"Part of our divide and conquer strategy," he says. "Two of the uniforms inherited Bitsy's kids and took them down to the police station to get a statement. Junior and I inherited this bunch. Their brother is in the ER."

"Yes, I saw him," I say, smiling at the memory.

Over at the Heinrich table, Junior and the two sisters get up and head for the food line. Aaron looks like he intends to follow but then abandons the group and moves over to our table instead.

"Well, hello there, Mattie," he says to me. "It's nice to see you again."

Hoping to avoid getting caught up in the family's drama I say, "I'm just about to leave."

Aaron pouts handsomely and says, "Darn. I was hoping to have a little time to chat with you." He settles into a chair beside me and nods at Bjorn, who has finished his shortcake and is working on his pie.

"I don't have any more information on the death of your father, if that's what you're hoping for," I tell Aaron.

"Well, I suppose that would have been nice, but that really isn't my objective. May I ask you a personal question?"

This catches me off guard, and while I want to say no, my sense of politeness won't let me. But since I can't quite bring myself to openly invite him into my private life, I simply shrug instead.

"I see you aren't wearing a wedding ring," he says. "Does that mean you're single?"

"Um, yes, sort of," I say stupidly, squirming uncomfortably in my chair.

Hurley moves around the table and takes a chair next to Bjorn, his expression dark. He glares at Aaron, who appears oblivious.

"Sort of?" Aaron echoes.

"I'm separated and in the process of filing for a divorce."

"Ah, well, that's unfortunate for your ex but good news for me. Are you seeing anyone?"

I realize Aaron is flirting with me and apparently Hurley has figured it out as well because he shifts his attention to me and his glare intensifies. Despite the coldness in his stare, I feel myself warming beneath the heat of his gaze.

I hesitate for the briefest of seconds before answering Aaron's question, my evil side warring with my good side. The evil side wins. "No, I'm not seeing anyone in particular," I tell him, smiling. I start playing with my hair, wrapping a strand of it around my finger.

"Good," Aaron says, "That means you can have dinner with me tonight." His voice is warm and behind his eyes I sense something deliciously dangerous.

I smile and swallow hard, feeling my heart beat faster. A strange warmth courses through my body and centers somewhere between my thighs with a sensation like molten lead. I feel confused, unsure if these strange sensations are the result of Hurley's stare, Aaron's flirtation, or a combination of the two.

Before I can summon up a halfway intelligent response to Aaron's invitation, Hurley jumps in and says, "I don't think that would be a good idea." Aaron and I tear our eyes from one another to give Hurley a questioning look. Hurley stutters a moment, turns a bright shade of red, and then adds, "It would be a conflict of interest, given Mattie's attachment to the case involving your father."

It's a valid point. Score one for Hurley. "Hmm, yes," I say, unsure if I'm relieved or disappointed. "There is that."

Aaron looks momentarily distraught, but then he brightens and says, "Well, I guess you'll just have to hurry up and solve the case then. I'm a patient man. I can wait."

I'm not sure what to say to that. Aaron is a handsome and presumably wealthy man, who seems to have his head on straight, unlike his siblings. I can't deny some small attraction to him but I'm not sure I'm interested in dating him. Still, I'm amused enough by Hurley's growing discomfort to leave things open for now.

"I guess I better get to it then," I say, hoping my words sound both noncommittal and vaguely promising.

Aaron and I exchange a long, innuendo-laden look while Hurley watches us and steams. The moment stretches out between the three of us until Bjorn, who has finished his pie, drops his fork onto his plate with a clatter, making everyone jump.

"That was good," he says, leaning back in his chair with a self-satisfied expression. He looks at me and adds, "I'm ready to go now but I'm afraid my peter needs some attention first."

Chapter
29

Though Aaron looks amused and raises his eyebrows at Bjorn's comment, I offer no explanation. Instead, I say my good-byes and escort Bjorn to the nearest bathroom.

Within minutes I have switched the old urine bag over to the new one that Syph gave me, and after a brief demonstration on how to empty it, Bjorn does it himself without difficulty. He is delighted and I seize the moment by trying again to convince him to let me drop him at the cab office so I can go meet Sally Hvam on my own. But Bjorn is having none of it, particularly after I make the mistake of mentioning that it's a luncheon meeting.

"Lunch?" he says, rubbing a hand over his stomach. "Sounds good. I *am* kind of hungry."

I simply stare at him, speechless. I'm not sure if I'm worried or envious of his ability to eat everything in sight without gaining an ounce. Most likely it's a little of both. The worry stems from the thought that he might have something physically wrong, like cancer, diabetes, or a tapeworm. The envy is because I would kill to be able to eat like he does without getting fat.

Resigned to feeding Bjorn yet again, I drive the two of us to the Home on the Range café where Sally Hvam is supposed to meet me. Though I've never met the woman, I easily pick her out of the crowd as soon as we enter the place. For one thing, she is the only woman sitting alone. But the primary clue is the license plate thing, though I'm thinking these tatas look more like 50DDs.

I steer Bjorn over and introduce myself. Sally stares at Bjorn with a suspicious expression. "Who's this?" she asks.

"My chauffeur, sort of. It's a long story. Mainly, he just wants to eat."

Right on cue, Bjorn settles into a chair and says, "Where the hell is the menu?"

Sally hands him hers, which is nothing more than a computer-generated flyer folded in half. As Bjorn takes hold of it, his eyes settle on Sally's primary attribute and a whole new hunger starts to show on his face. "Good Lord, woman," he says. "If those ain't made for nuzzling, I don't know what is."

"Bjorn!"

"It's okay," Sally says with a chuckle. "I'm used to it."

A waitress comes by and delivers two more menus. As soon as she's gone I open mine, zero in on a grilled ham and cheese sandwich, close it, and go to work on Sally. "So how do you know Luke Nelson?"

"I was your victim's predecessor," she says, "along with several other women."

"Really?" For a second I think she means other women were murdered. Then it hits me that she's talking about dating, not about Luke Nelson being a serial killer.

"Yeah, the bastard suckered me big time. I thought I was his one and only but I found out later he was stringing me along with a couple of other women. He was smart, I'll give him that. He never dated two women in the same town. Made it less likely his sneaking around would get discovered."

Ah, a serial heartbreaker then. "So how did you find out?"

She lets forth with a throaty chuckle. "Actually, it was a fluke that brought him down. We'd been dating for several months and he was talking about making things permanent and planning for the future, that kind of stuff, you know?"

"You thought he was talking about marriage."

"Exactly! And I was pretty darned excited by the proposition, no pun intended." Again she laughs at her own joke. "I'm in my late thirties and the fruit ain't as ripe as it used to be, if you get my drift. I want to have kids someday and that window is closing pretty damned fast."

Her comment makes me wince since I'm in the same boat. When my marriage to David was getting stale it didn't seem right to think about having a child until we got things sorted out. Then he got someone else pregnant instead and the marriage ended. Now, like Sally, the big hand on my biological clock is hanging just before midnight.

"So I'm all worked up and giddy like a damned fool school-girl," Sally goes on, making me smile. "I'd heard about this place at the Dells that does weddings and it sounded nice, so I decided to take a little road trip and go check it out. But my car broke down on the highway and I ended up having it towed into some little Podunk town. That's when I got hit with the good news and the bad news."

With perfect timing, the waitress chooses this moment to come and take our orders, leaving me in suspense. Sally and I both order sandwiches, but Bjorn goes for the pot roast plate with mashed potatoes, veggies, and carrot cake for dessert.

As soon as the waitress leaves, Sally picks up her tale where she left off. "So the good news was that there was a mechanic in Podunk who could fix my car. The bad news was it was going to take him a couple of days because he had to order a special part. Then there was more good news because the guy had a loaner he was willing to rent me for only twenty bucks a day. So I did the necessary paperwork and was getting ready to leave when I got hit with the next dose of bad news."

Sally falls silent as the waitress returns with our drinks but resumes as soon as she's gone. "It turns out that mechanic's shop is right across the street from a little coffee shop. Want to guess who I saw walk in and sit down at a table just inside the front window, acting all lovey-dovey, kissy-kissy with some other woman?"

"Luke Nelson?" I answer unnecessarily.

"Damn straight. So I'm sitting there, shocked, wondering what the hell is going on and then I think maybe she's a relative and I'm jumping to conclusions. But then he plants a kiss on her that no one outside of West Virginia would use on a relation. The kind that makes you want to tell them to get a room, you know?"

I nod.

"So I just sat there watching for a while, trying to sort it all out, feeling stunned and wounded. My first impulse was to hurry home, lock myself in, and lick my wounds, you know?"

I did. I'd done just that for two months after catching David with Karen Owenby.

"Then I considered walking across the street and giving Luke a piece of my mind. But I didn't want to make a spectacle of myself and by now I was more curious than anything. So I waited. About half an hour later they got up to leave. I watched him plant another sloppy wet one on her lips and then they got into their respective cars and drove off. I memorized her license plate and then decided to follow Luke, thinking I would confront him back at his place. But he surprised me by heading north when he should have gone south. So I stayed behind him, realizing that the loaner car was yet another bit of good luck since he would have recognized my car.

"Half an hour later we arrived in Podunk's twin. This time he parked in front of an apartment building so I pulled in several spaces away and waited. He went inside and came out ten minutes later with another floozy on his arm.

"They got in his car and drove to a nearby movie theater. I followed them inside, being careful not to be seen, and sat at the back of the theater. It was some stupid Sundance movie, one of those celluloid nightmares that's supposed to have deep meaning but is really just some idiot's ego masturbation, you know? It didn't matter because I didn't pay much attention to the movie. My eyes were glued on dickhead, and his lips were glued to the floozy. Even in the dark I could tell he had his tongue halfway down her throat most of the time."

Sally is making no effort to lower her voice and several other diners cue in on her when they hear the words *dickhead* and *masturbation*. It makes me want to slink down lower in my seat but I resist the urge. Part of me wishes the waitress would come with our food, thinking that might derail Sally for a few minutes, long enough for people to quit eavesdropping and staring at us. But another part of me is fascinated with her tale and anxious to hear the rest. So I let her run on.

"I sat there the whole time watching them," she says, shaking her head sadly. "Just before the movie ended I got up and went back out to the parking lot. They came out a few minutes later and I followed them back to her apartment. This time I got out and followed to see which apartment she lived in. I wrote down the name I found on the corresponding mailbox, then went back out and sat in my car until Luke left. And that wasn't for another two hours. Based on the condition of his clothes when he came out, I'm guessing they weren't watching TV together."

"Ouch," I say, feeling her pain.

"Yeah," she says with a sigh.

The waitress returns finally, this time with our food. Bjorn digs into his like he hasn't eaten in weeks. Sally and I both take a couple of bites from our sandwiches before she puts hers down and continues talking.

"Needless to say, I didn't want to believe what I saw but the evidence was pretty overwhelming. I decided to try to get a few more facts before confronting Luke so I had a cop friend run the plates of the woman I saw in the coffee shop and got her name and address. Then I went to visit her."

Oh, how I would have loved to be a fly on the wall for that conversation.

"Her name is Julie Mathers and she lives in Cambria. As you might guess, our initial meeting was a bit intense. But eventually I convinced her that we were both being hoodwinked and that there was at least one other woman I knew about, and who knew how many I didn't. She finally got as angry as I was and I convinced her to follow me in my car over to the town of Randolph and the apartment of the second woman. There wasn't anyone home when we got there so we sat together in the parking lot in my car, comparing notes, and planning all kinds of evil paybacks that we'd never have the guts to carry out, but which made us feel better nonetheless."

This I could relate to, having indulged in several revenge fantasies myself over the past few months, a fact that didn't help my situation much when I became a suspect in Karen Owenby's murder.

Sally pauses and takes another bite of her sandwich. I realize I've become so enthralled with her story that I've momentarily forgotten about my own food. A truly historic moment! Bjorn, on the other hand, hasn't been the least deterred and has almost cleared his plate.

Once she has swallowed and taken a drink of her soda, Sally continues. "After an hour or so the second woman came home. Her name is Hannah Kvalheim, in case you're interested."

I can see a bit of lettuce stuck in Sally's teeth and a handful of crumbs resting on that shelf of a bosom. Though I'm tempted to tell her, I stay mum, not wanting to interrupt her flow of thought.

"It was much easier to convince Hannah, given that there were two of us there. We stayed nearly two hours discussing that slime bag and the various promises he made to all of us. The other two were content to simply stop seeing him and write it all off to bad judgment on their parts, but I was determined to confront the bastard, you know?"

"And you did," I say, remembering Jackie's description of the incident. "What was his reaction after that night?"

Sally shrugs. "Nothing. The bastard couldn't have cared less that he'd been caught. He never apologized, never attempted to call again, and never showed up at my door. I've talked to Julie and Hannah since then and they both say the same thing. They called him, delivered their Dear John speeches, and he simply accepted them and went on with his life." She pauses, finishes off the last of her sandwich, and then adds, "Clearly we were all gullible as hell, but I have to say the guy was really good. Very convincing."

"Did you ever talk to him again?"

She shakes her head. "After I confronted him in the parking lot that night, I wrote him off. I got my rant in and that seemed to do it for me."

"How about the other girls?" I ask, digging a pen out of my purse and writing their names and towns down on a napkin before I forget them. "Do you know if either of them tried to contact him?"

"I don't think so, but I can't be sure. If they did, they didn't tell me about it. Then again, I haven't talked to either of them in a while so who knows?"

This gets me to wondering if either of the other scorned women might have tried to patch things up with Nelson, only to discover there was yet another woman in the picture: Shannon. Could one of them have felt angry enough about it to try to eliminate the competition? I voice this question to Sally.

"I don't think either of those other two women would harm a fly," she says, shaking her head. "I was mad enough to hurt someone, but it would have been that bastard Nelson, not a fellow victim."

"Do you think he's capable of killing someone?"

She leans back in her chair, folds her arms over her chest, and gives the question some thought. "I don't know," she says finally. "But he did have some rather odd impulses in the bedroom."

"Can you be more specific?"

She leans forward and drops her voice several decibels. "Let's just say he liked to play rough."

Chapter
30

Bjorn drops me off at the ME's office after we return from Smithville and when I tell him he can go home for the night he frowns.

"What's the matter?" I ask him. "You can handle your new bag okay, right?"

"I guess," he says. "But hanging with you is kind of exciting. You get into all kinds of things. I don't usually get this much excitement in a day."

Or this much food, I think, suspecting that may be the bigger lure for him.

"Well, I don't have anything exciting planned for the rest of the day," I assure him.

"What about tomorrow?"

I hesitate. Much as I've grown fond of Bjorn, it's time to get my own set of wheels. "Tomorrow I plan to just hang in the office," I tell him, though truth is, I don't know yet what I'll be doing tomorrow. But I don't want to commit to anything with Bjorn yet because once he latches on to me, I'm not sure I'll be able to shake him. "And you need to make some real money, so why don't you plan on running your cab as usual and if something comes up and I need you I'll give you a call. Okay?"

He nods but looks crestfallen. For a moment I feel guilty but then figure that once the sun goes down, he's unlikely to remember any of this anyway. Looking lonely and pathetic, he drives away.

I find Izzy sitting in his office working on a stack of files taller than he is. I pull up a chair and start filling him in on my day, starting with the conversation I had with Sally Hvam. He listens but keeps working on his charts, making notes, looking at lab results, and filling out paperwork.

"I don't know what it is about Nelson," I say once I'm done. "There's something about him that bothers me. He's a little too slick for my tastes."

"Just because he's a philanderer doesn't mean he's a killer," Izzy cautions. "And from what I understand, he has a pretty solid alibi."

"Speaking of alibis, I have a theory about Shannon that might change her time of death."

Izzy stops what he's writing and looks up at me. "Really?"

"I think so. Hear me out and tell me if I'm totally off base."

He sets his pen aside and gives me his full attention.

"I noticed when we processed the crime scene that Shannon had an abrasion on the knuckles of one hand. But we didn't find any foreign material there."

Izzy nods but says nothing, so I continue.

"I also discovered she had a habit of eating a lot whenever she was working at Dairy Airs, and that she spent a lot of time in the bathroom. According to Erik and one of her coworkers, she claimed she had IBS, but when I looked through her medical records there was no mention of IBS, though there were several notes about her asking for diet pills. Then there are the contents of her medicine cabinet. There were several different kinds of laxatives in it. And Erik told me that Shannon was hoping to expand her modeling career but was always struggling with her weight."

I pause, letting Izzy put the facts together on his own. "You think she was bulimic," he says.

"I do," I say, trying to contain my excitement.

He thinks for a few more seconds and I see a light spark in his eyes. "It fits," he says, nodding slowly. "The knuckle abrasions could have been caused by her teeth scraping over them when she stuck her finger down her throat. It also explains the hiatal hernia she had—bulimics often develop one. And if she threw up her last meal, then you're right. It would change all of our assumptions about the time of death."

"And that might exonerate Erik."

Izzy gives me a cautious look. "It might, but to be honest I think it may simply widen the window on the time of death, rather than shift or narrow it."

"But if we don't base the time of death on Shannon's stomach contents, then couldn't she have been killed much earlier than we originally thought?"

"Yes, but it's just as possible that our original time frame is correct. The things we use to estimate the postmortem interval—the degree of rigor, body temperature, vitreous potassium levels—all have variances of several hours. So all this does is give us a broader window of time."

It's not the exoneration I was hoping for but at least it's a bit of hope.

"If nothing else, at least it increases the pool of potential suspects," Izzy says. "Have you shared any of this with Hurley?"

"Not yet. I wanted to run it by you first, to make sure my thinking was on target."

"I'd say you're spot on and we should let Hurley know ASAP." With that, he picks up his cell phone and dials Hurley's number. After listening for a few seconds, he says to me, "It's flipping over to voice mail." He then leaves a somewhat cryptic message, saying only that I have uncovered some critical new evidence in Shannon's case.

"Kudos," he says with a smile as he snaps his phone closed. "This should impress Hurley. It's a brilliant bit of detective work."

"Thanks," I say, blushing and hoping he's right. "In the meantime, I could use a favor. I need to get some new wheels. I have a little bit of cash saved, thanks to the generously low rent you charge me and what little I have left of my hospital severance pay. But it isn't much so I'm going to have to get something used." I pause and reflect on the paltry balance in my bank account. "*Really* used," I clarify.

"I can front you a small loan, if that would help."

I shake my head. "You've done enough for me already."

"What about an advance against your wages? We can set up a payment plan so it's deducted from your paycheck each week."

I consider this idea, which would give me a little more money to play with while still saving some face, and agree. "Thanks," I tell him.

"No problem. Will two thousand be enough?"

I have no idea but I nod anyway. I want to get up and kiss him but I know how much he'd hate it. Izzy isn't a very demonstrative person.

"Consider it done," he says.

"There's one more thing," I say. "I could use some help picking something out. I have no idea how to tell a good engine from a bad one."

Izzy gives me an apologetic look. "Sorry, I don't know my way around these modern engines any more than you do."

"What about Dom?"

Izzy snorts. "He might be able to help you pick out a color and upholstery, but that's about it. Tell you what I can do, though. I can give you the name of a reliable mechanic. That way, if you find something you like, you can have him go over it for you before you buy."

"I guess I can do that if I have no other options but I'd rather not. Any money I spend on a mechanic is money I can't spend on a car. Plus, if I pick a lemon on my first try, that means paying for at least two visits to a mechanic . . . and on from there. It could get expensive very fast."

"I see your point. You need someone who won't mind working on your engine for free before you commit."

Behind me the door opens, and I hear Hurley's voice. "Somebody call me?"

I turn and watch Hurley's long legs stride into the room, admiring the way his jeans hug his thighs. Izzy's last words hang in the air and suddenly they take on a whole new meaning as I imagine the many ways Hurley could work on my engine.

"Hi, Steve," Izzy says. "Did you get my message?"

Hurley shakes his head. "I was already on my way here and was pulling into the garage when you called. So I figured I'd come in and talk to you in person. What's up?"

"We have a few new things in the Tolliver case to tell you about," I say.

Hurley settles into a chair, takes a notebook and pen from his shirt pocket, and starts writing as I tell him about my luncheon date and the scorned women who were romantically involved with Nelson. Izzy takes over when I'm done and fills Hurley in on my discovery of Shannon's eating disorder and the potential impact it could have on the case. As Izzy is talking, Hurley turns sideways in his chair, stretching those long, blue-jeaned legs toward me. My eyes follow the line of his inseam until I reach a spot that makes my face feel like it's about to burst into flames, and I force myself to turn away and focus on Izzy's face instead, resisting the urge to fan myself.

When Izzy is done, Hurley closes his notebook, tucks it away, and says, "Nice work, Winston. Not only can't we be certain of the time of death, we have a whole new list of suspects."

I can't tell if he's being sincere with his praise or sarcastic, and though I'd like to ask, I'm reluctant to speak. As hot as my face and certain other regions of my body feel right now, I'm afraid I'll turn into a fire-breathing dragon if I open my mouth.

Izzy, who always seems to be able to sense when I'm stymied by Hurley's presence, saves the day. "Say, Steve," he starts. "Do you know anything about car engines?"

Hurley shrugs. "I'm fairly handy," he says. "I rebuilt an engine a few years back. Why do you ask?"

Izzy explains my car dilemma and five minutes later, Hurley and I are headed for Kohler's Used Cars, which is located on the north edge of town. The first minute of our ride is in silence. Then Hurley breaks it with a loaded question.

"So what do you think of Aaron Heinrich?"

Trying not to smile, I simply say, "I like him. He seems to be the only one in that family—in either of those two families, for that matter—who has his head on straight."

Hurley contemplates my answer for a second and then says, "He seems to like you."

"Well, it's mutual then."

In the periphery of my vision I see Hurley shoot a worried glance in my direction. I maintain my beatific Mona Lisa smile and say nothing. The remainder of the ride, which is a blessedly short couple of minutes, is utterly quiet until we pull onto the car lot.

"Let's take a look at what they have," Hurley says. He drives around, checking out the inventory. Most of the cars are only a year or two old—no doubt a sign of the economic times—and they come with scary price tags that are way out of my league. After a run up and down each aisle, Hurley parks outside the office.

Bobby Keegan, a classmate from high school, is on sales duty and he rushes out the door of the building to greet us. Back in the day, Bobby was a star player on our high school football team and he still looks like a jock. He's dressed very casually in jeans, a Polo knock-off shirt, and a letter jacket—probably the same one he wore in high school. If I look close I can see a couple of white hairs mixed in with his natural blond, but overall Bobby has aged well and looks much the same as he did nearly twenty years ago.

"Mattie Winston!" he says, greeting me with a big smile as I get out of the car. "To what do I owe this pleasure?"

I'm not sure if Bobby actually remembers me from high school. I didn't hang with him and the rest of the jocks-and-cheerleaders group, and wasn't the memorable type in general. I probably would have been marked as a wallflower if not for my popularity at the slow dances.

I haven't kept up with most of my high school acquaintances; heading off for college severed many a relationship and a lot of the kids moved on to bigger and better towns. But I do occasionally run into old classmates who stayed in Sorenson or who, like me, returned here after their college years. Bobby is a classic example. We crossed paths at the hospital a few months ago after his wife convinced him to get a vasectomy following the delivery of their fifth child. Knowing I'd be among the crew wielding a scalpel in the area of his love spuds allowed Bobby and me to reconnect in no time.

"I need a car," I tell Bobby. "My other one was totaled and until I can get the insurance situation sorted out, I need some wheels to get me around, something cheap but reliable."

"How cheap are you thinking?" Bobby asks.

"I have about three grand."

"That's a decent down payment," he says, turning to scan the parking lot inventory. He starts to head for a nearby row of cars.

"It's not a down payment," I tell him, stopping him in his tracks. "That's the total amount."

I see Hurley turn to stare at me, but I avoid looking at him. Bobby looks back at me and laughs. "That's a good one," he says with a chuckle. "Seriously, how much are you looking to spend?"

"It isn't a joke, Bobby. That's all I have."

Hurley says, "Christ, Winston, you can hardly buy a bicycle for that kind of money these days. Can't Izzy front you some cash?"

"He already did," I say irritably, shooting him a dirty look. I turn back to Bobby with my best pleading expression. "Look, Bobby, I'm in a tight spot. You know about my situation with David, don't you?"

He nods even though it's a rhetorical question. In a town this size, hot gossip is the one thing that disproves the theory of relativity by traveling faster than the speed of light. Plus, Alison plastered my private life all over the paper when she wrote up the article on Karen Owenby's death and the other murders that followed.

"David and I don't have any kind of official agreement between us yet so the whole money thing is a bit complicated for me right now. Plus, the insurance and title on my wrecked car are both in David's name. So all I have is three grand. Do you have anything for me?"

Bobby stares at me with an expression of disbelief and starts to shake his head but then he snaps his fingers and his face lights up. "You know what, I just might," he says. "Follow me." He leads us inside the showroom and directs us to a couple of chairs by a desk. "Have a seat. I need to talk to my manager but I'll be right back."

Hurley and I settle in as Bobby disappears through a door.

"Are you crazy, Winston?" Hurley says to me. "Do you have any idea what kind of heap you're going to end up with for that amount of money?"

"What do you want me to do, steal a car?" I snap back. "I thought my marriage to David was for a lifetime so I didn't worry much about the financial end of things. I have virtually no credit in my own name; everything we own is in his name. Not very savvy of me, I'll grant you, but I was in love and trusting. I got blindsided and now I'm paying for it." I pause, realizing the irony of my last statement. "No pun intended," I add.

He gives me a sympathetic look and shakes his head. "Can't you borrow money from your sister or something?"

"No. She's got two kids to raise and a husband who makes good money but who also spends it with abandon. Probably on porn," I add, rolling my eyes.

We fall silent for a few moments and then Hurley says, "I don't have a lot saved up but I can probably loan you another thousand or two if that will help."

I shoot him a look of gratitude. "That's very sweet of you," I tell him. "But I don't like borrowing money from friends. At least with Izzy it's being treated like an advance against my wages. He'll take a little out of each paycheck until I've paid it all back. If what I have isn't enough, then I'll go plead my case to the bank. There's a local banker I know who might loan me a few grand in exchange for some sexual favors."

Hurley doesn't respond but he studies me hard enough to make me blush, no doubt trying to determine if I'm joking or not.

Bobby returns, saving me from having to clarify. "Mattie Winston, this is your lucky day," he says with a big-assed grin. "It just so happens we have an older-model car in stock that just came in, and my boss is willing to let you have it for three grand. It's not real pretty, mind you," he cautions, "but it's been well maintained and the engine is solid. And it's never been driven hard. It should be good for another fifty thousand miles or so."

This is good news. Fifty thousand miles is a long time when you live in a town whose perimeters are only a few miles apart.

"What make, model, and year is it?" Hurley asks.

Bobby hesitates before answering. "It's a ninety-two Cadillac."

"You're going to sell her a car that's nearly twenty years old?" Hurley scoffs.

"It's old, yes," Bobby says quickly, holding up a hand to Hurley's objection, "but it's a Caddy. And it's got low mileage for its age, just over a hundred thousand."

Hurley frowns. "I suppose you're going to tell us next that it belonged to some little old lady who only drove it around town."

"Well," Bobby says with a sideways nod, "it *has* had only one owner and primary driver all these years. Lots of passengers, though," he adds with a wry chuckle. "Let's go take a look at it, shall we?"

After Bobby takes us into the back mechanic's area and shows us the car, Hurley pops the hood and starts looking over the engine. An hour later he wipes the grease from his hands and delivers his verdict. "He's right," he says. "It's in pretty good shape. I think you should buy it."

"You're kidding, right?"

"No, I'm not. I know it's not the most beautiful vehicle in the world but the engine is sound and the interior is in decent shape. Plus, the price is right."

I fold my arms over my chest and pout, knowing he's right but none too happy about it.

"Hey," Hurley says, "you can always stay with Bjorn."

My brain summons up the smell of stale urine and my objections begin to ease. Then Bobby makes me an offer I can't refuse.

Chapter
31

Bobby says, "I'll tell you what. Go ahead and take it for a day or two. Drive it around and see how it feels before you decide."

The offer makes perfect sense and thirty minutes later I drive out of the parking lot in a slightly used, midnight blue hearse, compliments of Sven Keller from the Keller Funeral Home. According to Bobby, Sven decided to upgrade his fleet with cars that look more like mini vans than traditional hearses, thinking it would be less offensive to the bereaved whose loved ones were being transported inside. I'm not sure where that leaves me, though I'm pretty certain it's going to be hard to get around town incognito if I buy this thing.

On the flip side, the car handles smoothly and the interior is nicely done up with leather and a faux wood grain. And the price is very reasonable, making it the only car I can currently afford. Still, it's a hearse. It looks like a hearse and it's had who-knows-how-many dead bodies in it. The pine-tree-shaped scented thingy dangling from the rearview mirror only partially masks the lingering scent of formaldehyde.

I'm not ready yet to show Izzy what his money can buy, and I'm eager to share my newfound theory about Shannon with Lucien. Given the hour, I suspect he will be home rather than at the office and it's always safer to be around Lucien when Desi's there, too. He tends to tone things down when his family is present.

I turn off the road to head for my sister's house. I wave at Hurley, who has been following me and laughing his ass off since we left the car lot. As soon as his car is out of sight, I convert my wave into a one-fingered salute.

When I pull up in front of my sister's house a few minutes later, I see my twelve-year-old niece, Erika, standing on the front stoop with a couple of her friends. Though the other girls are wearing items that are rather conventional, Erika is adorned in black tights, a long black shirt that hangs halfway down her thighs, black high-top shoes, and heavy black eye make-up. Her hair, which is naturally brown but has ranged in colors from pink to blue over the past year, is a matching shade of ebony. All three girls spare me a glance as I pull up and park at the curb, but when I step out of the vehicle, Erika stares at me with a slack-jawed expression, her eyes wide with amazement.

"Holy crap," she says as I approach. "That car is so rad." Erika has always been attracted to things dark and deathlike, so to her a hearse is the ultimate in cool. "Is it yours?" she asks.

"Possibly," I tell her. "I'm test driving it to help me decide."

"You *have* to get it," she says, walking over to the car and running her hand down the side of it. "Will you let me drive it when I get my license?"

"Sure." It seems a safe promise given that she's still several years away from a learner's permit, much less a license. "Is your dad here?"

Erika nods, her eyes focused on the car. "He's inside with Mom and Ethan," she says. "Can we look at the inside of the car while you're here?"

"Sure, just be careful. Technically it's not mine yet, so don't do any damage."

"We won't." She heads for the car, waving at her friends to follow, but they all hang back looking wary.

Inside the house I find my sister, Desi, in the kitchen cooking something that smells garlicky and delicious. Lucien is there with her, sitting at the breakfast bar with a glass of wine in his hand.

"Mattie!" Desi greets me, smiling. "What brings you here?"

"Mainly I'm here to talk to Lucien, but it's always good to see the rest of you, of course."

Lucien wiggles his eyebrows at me and gives me a quick head-to-toe ogle, but says nothing.

"Would you like to stay for dinner?" Desi asks. "I'm making baked ziti with Italian sausages." I'm about to accept when she adds, "Though I should probably warn you that I also invited Mom. She'll be here any moment."

Knowing my mother is coming almost changes my mind. Mother is a die-hard hypochondriac and spending time with her typically consists of listening to a recitation of her latest symptoms, followed by speculation on what her dreaded disease of the week might be. And Mom does her homework. She knows all the signs and symptoms for some of the world's most obscure diseases. I spent the better part of my childhood expecting the woman to drop dead at any moment. Then I got old enough to realize her only illness was a mental one.

David, being a physician, caught the brunt of Mom's hysteria whenever we were with her, plus she would call him several times a week to give updates. Marrying a physician was the one thing I did that made the woman proud of me. Now that he's out of the picture, my mother often looks at me with shame, disbelief, and disgust. She regards having a physician for a husband as the height of a woman's ambition. The mere fact that he screwed around on me is not enough to outweigh that fact.

Knowing I'll have to face both Mom's disappointment and her health paranoia makes me want to turn tail and run. But I do love Italian food, and the smells in Desi's kitchen have already seduced me. Besides, I have an idea of how to derail my mother tonight, or at the very least, shift her focus.

"I'd love to stay," I tell Desi. "And at the risk of sounding rude, do you think you have enough for me to invite someone else over? I'd be happy to go buy some extras, if need be."

"No need," Desi says, dismissing my concern with a wave of her hand. "I have enough here to feed an army. Is it that hunky cop of yours?"

I wish.

"What hunky cop?" Lucien asks, perking up. "Is there something you're not telling me, Mattiekins? Have you been bumping uglies with someone?"

"Lucien!" Desi chastises. "That's a bit personal."

"Relax, I'm not dating anyone," I tell them both. "The person I want to invite is a friend that I think might be a perfect match for Mom."

"Ooh," Desi says, raising her eyebrows. "That could be interesting. Give him a call."

I don't have William's number so I ring Izzy instead. "Having second thoughts about letting that one get away?" he asks.

"Hardly," I snort. "I'm going to invite him to dinner at Desi's so he can meet my mom."

I hang up and call William. The phone rings several times and I'm about to hang up when he finally answers, sounding impatient and out of breath.

"Hey, William, it's Mattie Winston."

There's a long silence before he says, "Okay," rather cautiously.

"I'm wondering if you're free for dinner."

There's another pause followed by a sigh. "I don't think I can survive another trip to your house," he says.

"You don't need to. It's at my sister's house, over on East Street. And while her daughter sometimes looks like she should have fangs, there are no animals here. My mother is coming and I'd like you to meet her. I think the two of you will hit it off."

He considers the proposal for a few seconds and then says, "Okay. What time?"

"Now. Dinner will be ready in about half an hour."

"Should I bring anything?"

"Just your handsome self," I say. I hear him suck his breath in so fast he whistles.

As I'm hanging up the phone I hear the front door open and my mother's voice holler out, "Lucien? Desi? Is everything okay?" Her voice sounds frantic and she enters the kitchen at a fast clip, looking paler than her usual color, which is about as pale as a living human being can be. When she sees me she stops cold and stares for a moment, blinks hard several times, and then looks around the room. "Is everything okay?" she asks again, clapping a hand to her chest. "There's a hearse parked out front."

"A hearse?" Desi says.

"That's mine," I explain. "I wrecked my other car and needed to find something else to get around in for a while."

"You're driving a hearse?" my mother says, her eyes wide.

"Well, I haven't actually bought it yet, but it seems to be in pretty good shape and it's about the only thing I can afford right now."

My mother shakes her head, clucks her tongue a few times, and looks at me as if I've just died and someone is getting ready to load me into the back of the hearse. It's bad enough that I've let a doctor get away and have taken a job cutting up dead bodies; in my mother's eyes, that's tantamount to sleeping in an alley with a screw-top bottle of wine wrapped in a brown paper bag. With the hearse I've hit an all-time low.

Desi pours a glass of wine and slips it into Mom's hand, no doubt hoping it will take the edge off her. Mom takes a sip and then settles onto a stool at the breakfast bar next to Lucien. She turns and looks at me with an expression of keen disappointment.

"Mattie, if you need money I can help you out a little," she says.

"Thanks, but I can manage. It's about time I established some credit in my own name anyway. I was a fool to give David the financial reins in our marriage."

"Well, he is the primary breadwinner, isn't he?" Mom says, taking another sip of her wine.

"He *was*," I say. "But I make enough to do okay on my own."

Mom dismisses my comment with a look of disgust and an impatient wave of her hand, as if she's wafting away some nasty odor. "What have I always told you about letting your husband feel as if he's the king of the castle?"

This is Rule #1 in Mother's Rules for Wives, a set of ten conventions she swears will keep any marriage strong and intact. She's been beating the rules into my and Desi's brains since we were old enough to walk. The fact that Mom's been married and divorced four times makes the validity of her advice a bit dicey, but she chooses to ignore that.

"You undermined David's masculinity by insisting on working all the time," Mom goes on. "It's no wonder he strayed."

Desi, who is stirring her sauce on the stove, sucks in a breath and gives me a wide-eyed look. Lucien wisely takes this opportunity to slip off his stool and escape from the kitchen.

"I've worked all my adult life, Mom. That was how I met David in the first place, if you'll recall. Had I not been working, I most likely never would have married him."

"Yes, but once you *did* marry him you should have quit your job. You should have focused on being a wife instead of a nurse, and on making a nice home."

"We had a nice home, until David wrecked it. And why shouldn't I be allowed to do something I love the same way David does?"

Mom shakes her head sadly. "You just don't get it, Mattie," she says.

"No, Mom," I say irritably. "You're the one who doesn't get it. David risked my life by sleeping with another woman. In *my* book of rules, that's an unforgivable sin."

Mom is about to come at me with another comment when we are all literally saved by the bell—the chiming of the front doorbell. I make use of the interruption to escape Mom and her insane list of rules. By the time I reach the front door, Lucien has already opened it and I see William standing on the stoop. I hurry over to greet him and make introductions.

Lucien is courteous but it's obvious he doesn't want to get caught up making small talk to an odd-looking man with a bad comb-over, so I steer William out to the kitchen, praying that my instincts on this one are correct. After doing a quick round of introductions, Desi pours a glass of wine for William and hands it to him. Making no effort to conceal what he's doing, he holds the glass up to the light and examines it carefully. Can't say I blame him after what happened at my place.

"William is a very talented financial analyst and accountant," I say.

"That's nice," Mom counters, watching him with a curious expression.

As soon as William is done inspecting his glass, he takes a sip and then focuses on the other two women in the room. He nods at Desi and then zeroes in on Mom. His expression softens noticeably and one of his eyebrows arches in surprise. With her porcelain skin, blue eyes, trim figure, and well-maintained blond dye job, Mom is an attractive woman, at least physically.

"It's a definite pleasure to meet you," he says, taking Mom's hand and brushing his lips over it. As I watch, I make a mental bet with myself as to which of these germaphobes will try to wipe the cooties away first but surprisingly, neither one does. "Mattie said you were attractive, but she didn't do your beauty justice. You are a very striking woman."

Mom makes a stuttering motion with her mouth but no sound comes out. For once, she is speechless. She smiles at William and does a coquettish tilt of her head as a faint tinge of pink colors her cheeks.

William stares for a few seconds more, then looks over at Desi, who has just finished scraping Italian sausage from her cutting board into a frying pan. As she takes the board to the sink and starts to wash it with one of those soap wand thingies, William's eyes grow huge.

"You need to use bleach," he says. "Meats can harbor all kinds of bacteria that soap alone won't get rid of. You'd be amazed at the horrible diseases you can get from something like that."

My mental uh-oh is quickly countered by the heightened interest Mom is now showing William. "You are so right," she says, apparently in control of her voice again. "I'm constantly on these girls about stuff like that. One can't be too safe when it comes to germs."

She locks eyes with William and I imagine love being born over the mental image of a Petri dish. I'm thinking this dinner is going to be a huge success on all counts when Ethan enters the room.

"Aunt Mattie," he says. "Check out my new pet." He thrusts his arm out as he approaches and there sitting on his sleeve is a three-inch-long bug. "It's a Madagascar hissing cockroach," he says proudly. And as if on cue, the bug sits back on its haunches, waves its hairy antennae in the air, and hisses.

The hissing sound is closely followed by a high-pitched screech and a loud crash as William faints dead away, taking one of the bar stools down with him.

Chapter
32

Despite all the drama, the evening isn't a total bust. When I couldn't arouse William right away and the gash on his head refused to stop bleeding unless I put direct pressure on it, Desi called for an ambulance. There was some brief confusion when the ambulance arrived and saw a hearse already parked out front, but that was cleared up with a few explanations.

William is now awake but foggy, his comb-over safely contained inside a gauze turban, his body loaded on a cot rather than in a coffin. We follow the entourage outside to the driveway and watch as the EMS crew loads William into the ambulance. Mom insists on riding along with him and makes a big enough stink with the ambulance crew that they finally cave and allow her in the rig. As the ambulance pulls away, I can see my mother sitting next to William, stroking his arm and murmuring in his ear.

Lucien, who briefly appeared in the kitchen right after the incident, has been ensconced in his office ever since, searching his law books in case William decides to sue. Ethan is in his room, hopefully locking his pet roach back inside its cage.

As Desi and I watch the ambulance disappear down the street she says, "I do believe you made a love connection there."

"Not exactly the way I hoped the night would go but hey, I'll take it."

"I'm sorry about Ethan," she says. "I keep telling him he needs to be careful about showing his bug collection to other people, but he gets so excited he forgets. The kid loves bugs. He reads everything he can get his hands on: books, Internet sites, magazines . . . you name it."

"It's okay. In fact, I think it bonded Mom and William faster than any quiet dinner would have."

"It could have been much worse, you know," Desi says as we turn to head back into the house. "Ethan could have brought out one of his fly farms."

I'm afraid to ask but do it anyway. "Fly farm?"

"It's an enclosed terrarium type of thing filled with maggots and flies. Ethan has six different ones in his bedroom because he's studying the reproductive cycles of various types of flies for a school science project." Desi pauses and shudders. "He's pretty much done with it at this point. All he has left is to organize his data and write a report. It can't be soon enough for me. I don't mind the flies so much but all those maggots give me the creeps."

I can sympathize and the mere mention of maggots has me feeling them crawling on me all over again.

Desi lets me eat a plate of her wonderful dinner and after scarfing it down, I say my good-byes, shoo Erika and her friends out of the hearse, and head for the hospital to check on William.

Most of the people on duty in the ER at this time of day are night-shifters, and I don't know them as well as I do the day folks. So rather than venturing into the ER proper, I head for the waiting room, where I find my mother sitting in one of the chairs, reading a magazine.

"Hey, Mom, how's William doing?"

She sets her magazine aside and motions for me to sit next to her. "They stitched up his scalp wound, but only after William made the doctor clean everything five times. He's down having a CT scan of his head now. The doctor said he's pretty sure it will be negative."

"That's a relief," I say.

"He's an interesting guy, very clean. Are you dating him?"

I shake my head. "We went out on a blind date once, but it didn't work out."

"I see."

"So he's all yours."

She gives me a sly look and says, "Is it that obvious?"

"Well, it is to me. After all, I've seen you court before. I know the signs."

She flashes me a grim smile. "I haven't had the best track record when it comes to husbands and beaux, have I? I've always been proud of you girls for marrying so well."

Here we go.

"Well, it turns out I didn't do as well as we originally thought," I counter.

She gives me her classic pish-paw wave of dismissal. "You did fine. David made a little mistake. That's all. I think you're writing him off too easily. It's every girl's dream to marry a doctor. You shouldn't be so eager to just throw all that away. It gives you social standing and credibility." She pauses, then adds, "The cream always rises to the top, you know."

So does pond scum, I think.

"Sorry to disillusion you, Mom, but that never was my dream. My dream is to be married to a man who loves me, a man who is faithful, a man who doesn't risk my health and my life for the sake of a little sexual gratification."

"Well, he wouldn't have looked elsewhere if he was getting what he needed at home," she says with a sniff. "You know what I've always told you girls about keeping things interesting."

I did. It was Rule #6 in Mother's Rules for Wives: don't be afraid to experiment in the bedroom. David and I did experiment some, but it was pretty chaste. Mostly it consisted of trying different positions and him asking me to wear sexy lingerie. I always went along until the day he came home with a Xena, Warrior Princess costume. I put it on but rather than looking sexy, I looked like the starring role in a Wagner opera. The only thing lacking was one of those Norsky Viking helmets, which would have been somewhat appropriate given my real name, though it also would have lent a whole new meaning to the term *horny*.

I'm groping for a way to get Mom off topic when a nurse comes out of the ER care area and approaches. It's Lucy "Lupus" Julseth, someone I used to work with and one of the people whose names was on Luke Nelson's patient list.

"Mattie!" she says, greeting me with a smile. "How the heck are you?"

"Good as can be expected," I tell her.

Lucy looks to my mom and says, "He's back from his CT so you can come and sit with him if you'd like."

"I would," she says. She looks over at me with a questioning expression and I wave her on.

"Go ahead. I have to get home but I'll call you in a day or two." As my mother heads for the care area of the ER, I say to Lucy, "So you're working the night shift these days?"

"Not by choice. Mark and I split up so I needed to make other arrangements for childcare." She sighs and looks longingly out the window toward the parking lot. That's when I remember that Lucy is a smoker.

"Want to step out for a puff?" I ask her. She nods and looks re-lieved. We head outside to an area just off the hospital property and Lucy lights up. She takes a long drag and blows it out slowly, taking care to see that the smoke blows away from me.

"It's hard to arrange childcare when you work these twelve-hour shifts," she says, taking another drag. "But I need the money and the night shift differential helps. So for now, the kids are spending the nights at my parents' house and I sleep during the day while they're in school."

"I'm sorry to hear about you and Mark. When did it happen?"

"A month ago. He said he needed to find himself." She finger quotes the last two words and rolls her eyes. "What a bunch of bullshit."

"Can I ask you a personal question?"

She puffs on her cigarette, shrugs, and nods.

"Is that why you're seeing Luke Nelson?"

Her brow furrows and she gives me a startled look. "How do you know about that?"

I explain about my investigation into Shannon's death and how I came across the list of names. "I assure you I'll keep the fact that you're seeing Nelson confidential," I tell her. "I don't really need to know why you were seeing him, but I'd like to ask you some questions about him, if you don't mind."

"If you want to know if I had an appointment with him on the day Shannon died, some detective already asked me. I did."

"What time was your appointment?"

"Three o'clock." She stubs her cigarette out on the sidewalk and stuffs the butt back in her pack. "I was there for an hour."

"Have you been seeing Nelson for a long time?"

"I started a couple of months ago when I sensed that Mark and I were drifting apart. I thought some counseling might help me figure out how to get things back on track."

"Did it?"

"Obviously not," she says with a wry chuckle. She turns to head back inside and I follow along beside her. "Maybe if Mark had gone with me it might have helped but I couldn't get him to do it and Nelson said he'd prefer to keep it one-on-one for the time being anyway."

This strikes me as odd since I've always heard that marital counseling is more effective when both parties are involved. "Has seeing Nelson helped you deal with the breakup?"

We are at the entrance to the ER waiting room and Lucy pauses with her hand on the door. "I started having panic attacks about a week after Mark left and despite trying several medications, they've been getting worse. So for my last few visits, Dr. Nelson tried something new, some sort of hypnotherapy. I guess it's working because I haven't had an attack since, though to be honest, I don't remember a whole lot about the sessions."

"Interesting."

"Look, I have to get back to work, but it was good to see you again. You doing okay since you and David split?"

"I have good days and bad days."

"Any chance of reconciliation?"

I shake my head. "No, we're done. I can't get past the whole cheating thing. I'm a pretty forgiving person, but that's a bit more than I'm willing to take."

Lucy nods and looks away. I sense she's uncomfortable with my comment and wonder if Mark has strayed, too.

"You take care," she says, and before I can ask her anything else, she opens the door and disappears inside.

Chapter
33

Lucy's comments about her experiences with Nelson get me to wondering, so I dig out my cell phone and give Hurley a call.

"Hey, Winston," he answers. That whole caller ID thing still freaks me out. "What's up?"

"I'm wondering if you could give me some information. You provided us with a list of names for Nelson's patients but not the times of their appointments. Do you recall who it was that had the four o'clock slot on the day Shannon was killed?"

"You're still focusing on him?" he says tiredly. "I know you don't want to believe your friend could have done this but Nelson's alibi is solid for the time in question. He didn't do it. Even with your discovery about Shannon's eating disorder and the change in the time of death, Erik Tolliver is still our most likely suspect."

"Humor me, would you? There's something about Nelson that bothers me. I can't put my finger on it, but I can't let it go yet, either."

Hurley sighs and says, "Hold on a minute."

I hear him set his phone down and shuffle some papers, and wait until he comes back on the line.

"Okay, here you go. The four o'clock appointment was a woman named Carla Andrusson. I've already talked to her and she verified that she kept her appointment that day."

"Thanks," I tell him, glad Carla is someone I know. She's the wife of my dentist, Brian Andrusson, and also a former patient of mine. I was on duty eight years ago when she came into the ER after having a seizure and was diagnosed with a brain tumor. The tumor was surgically removed and fortunately proved to be benign. But during the surgery Carla suffered a small stroke that left her with some left-sided facial paralysis and right arm and leg weakness.

After getting Carla's home phone number from Hurley, I hang up. It's well past nine o'clock, so I decide to head for home. I stop at the Kwik-E-Mart on the way to pick up some treats and discover they are out of Ben & Jerry's Cherry Garcia. I settle on Cookie Dough instead, and by the time I lug it and my other treasures to the counter, my hands are nearly frostbitten.

When I get home, Rubbish greets me at the door, winding his way around my feet and purring contentedly. I scoop him up before he can trip me, and carry him to the kitchen, where I fix him up a nice plate of the tuna I just bought for him. While he eats I kick off my shoes and plop down on the couch with my ice cream, turn on the TV, and flip channels until I settle on an old episode of *Cheers*.

Twenty minutes later, I've dug out all the cookie dough chunks and have nothing but melting ice cream left. I pour a little of the molten remains into a dish for Rubbish, who cautiously sniffs and then laps it up. Nice to know we share similar tastes. I wash the rest of the ice cream down the sink, feeling slightly virtuous for not having eaten the whole thing.

Sated, I head for the bathroom to take a shower but my cell phone rings. I curse, thinking it must be Izzy with a death call, but to my surprise it's Hurley.

"Hey, Winston, what are you doing?"

"I was just getting ready to hop in the shower before bed. Why?"

"Can I interest you in joining me for a drink?"

My heart skips a beat and I start to feel all flushed again. "Sure," I say. "Where?" Before he answers I start a mental chant: *your place, your place, your place.*

"How about the Nowhere Bar in fifteen minutes?"

I hope this isn't a sign our relationship is going nowhere. "Okay, see you there."

I'm disappointed we're meeting in such a public place, though I'm delighted to be meeting him at all for something that isn't work related. But the suddenness of the call throws me into a frenzy because I'm far from date ready. I don't have enough time to wash my hair because it takes me fifteen minutes just to blow dry and style it. So I pin it up and hop in the shower, washing everything from the neck down. I hesitate when I look at my legs. I haven't shaved in nearly a week; when the weather gets colder and long pants become a daily fixture, I tend to get lazy. Now I'm regretting it. What if I get lucky tonight? What if Hurley and I end up somewhere in bed together? Can I risk grossing him out with hairy legs?

I decide I can't and shave them in record time, leaving myself with two good-sized nicks that refuse to quit oozing blood. I get out of the shower and dab some toilet paper on them, praying that scabs are less of a turn-off than winter fur.

I do a quick fix to my hair and make-up, and then change my outfit five times in an effort to find a pair of pants that don't make my ass look bigger than the fender on a Buick. Rubbish thinks I'm playing with him and each time I remove a pair of pants and toss them aside, he pounces on them, biting and clawing like it's a life-and-death struggle.

I settle on a pair of pants I find the least offensive—black and made out of a very forgiving stretchy knit fabric—and smooth my blouse down over them. I grab my coat, purse and car keys, and head out with one minute to spare.

I find Hurley sitting at a table in a back corner. He waves to me when I enter and I meander my way through the crowd of people standing around the bar. When I get to the table, he stands and pulls out a chair for me. I catch a faint whiff of some exotic scent emanating from him and my hormones kick up a notch.

"Thanks for the invite," I say.

He settles back into his own chair and motions at a barmaid.

"Wait until you hear what I have to tell you before you thank me," he warns, his expression taut.

He takes a swig of his Samuel Adams as the barmaid arrives to take my order. I settle on a Miller Lite on tap and the second the barmaid turns away I lean toward Hurley.

"What is it?" I ask.

"We found Erik Tolliver's gun."

He just drops it out there, like a bomb, with no further explanation. Judging from his earlier warning, I'm guessing that the circumstances surrounding this find won't bode well for Erik.

"Where?"

"It was tucked in between some sheets in a linen cabinet in the radiology department at the hospital. One of the techs found it this evening when she was rotating the linens."

"Fingerprints?" I ask.

Hurley shakes his head. "It was wiped clean. But that reminds me. We got the fingerprint evidence back from Madison and several of the prints we collected in the house belonged to Erik."

"Of course they did. He lived there for a long time so I'd expect to find some of his prints. Were any of them found in blood, or in the mess in the kitchen?"

"No," Hurley admits.

The barmaid brings my beer and I take a swig to avoid looking at Hurley, knowing my disappointment is probably showing on my face. "Have you done any ballistics yet?" I ask, grasping at straws.

"No, but given where we found it . . ." He lets the thought hang there, knowing I'm smart enough to come to the obvious conclusion. Then he further depresses me by adding, "I did some follow-up this evening on those women whose names you gave me and their alibis check out. So if you're right about Erik, we have no suspects at all. I think it's time to admit defeat."

"I'll wait for the ballistics report."

Hurley smiles. "You are a stubborn woman, Winston."

"It's not stubbornness, Hurley, it's my gut. I consider myself a pretty good judge of character and I truly don't think Erik Tolliver could have done this."

"Despite all the evidence?"

"It's circumstantial, just like it was with David."

An awkward silence stretches between us. When Karen Owenby was murdered, the primary suspect, at least in Hurley's eyes, was my husband, David. But despite my anger and disappointment with David over his affair, I couldn't make myself believe he was a killer, despite some pretty damning evidence. Hurley and I butted heads then much as we are now. That time, I prevailed, but I have to confess that this time I'm a little less sure. I know Erik fairly well, but not nearly as well as I know David. And despite what I just said to Hurley about my gut, I'm clearly not as astute as I might think, given that David managed to carry on an affair for a long while without my knowledge.

Hoping to lighten the mood and keep my hasty leg shaving from being a total waste of time, I challenge Hurley to a game of darts. But my heart isn't in it tonight and he beats me handily. With my beer now gone, I tell Hurley I'm going to call it a night.

"Okay," he says, draining the last of his second beer. "I'll walk you out."

He gathers both of our coats from our table and holds mine for me while I put it on. As he settles the coat around me, his hands gently grip my shoulders and linger there for a second longer than necessary. I stand frozen to the spot, afraid to move and afraid *not* to move, until his hands finally drop away. My face feels like it's about one foot away from a blast furnace so I keep my eyes focused ahead, worried that if I look at Hurley the raw emotions I feel will be apparent from the color in my cheeks.

The cool night air seems to help some but I still avoid looking at Hurley until I get to my car. As he looks at the vehicle, a smile crosses his face. "How's it driving?" he asks.

"So far, so good. The engine seems to run well and the seating is pretty comfy. The lingering aroma of formaldehyde is a bit of a bummer but my niece now thinks I'm a truly rocking aunt and wants to know if I'll give her and her friends a ride in it with them lying down in the back."

Hurley chuckles. "So are you going to buy it?"

"I don't have much choice. It's the only thing I can afford right now." I pause and look up into Hurley's baby blues. There's a twinkle there, but I also see a hint of something else, something hot and smoldering that makes me squirm in a deliciously uncomfortable way. Something impulsive comes over me and before I can think about it, I lean up and kiss him on the cheek. His skin is warm and spicy smelling, and the bristles from his five-o'clock shadow make my lips thrum.

"Thanks for helping me find it," I stammer as I step back.

When I look at his face I see that his smile is gone. Embarrassed by my boldness, I start to apologize but all I can do is stammer.

"Sorry, I didn't mean . . . I didn't want to . . . I just . . ."

Any further attempts to explain myself are cut off when Hurley takes my shoulders and pulls me close. Our faces are only inches apart and since I haven't bothered to zip up my coat, I can feel his chest against my breasts. I'm close enough to be in touch with several of his other anatomical parts, too, and I'm pretty sure that's not a nightstick I'm feeling. My nipples harden into exquisite little bumps and I have to fight an urge to grind my pelvis against him.

"No apology necessary," he says, his voice thick and husky. "I rather liked it." His face lowers and our lips touch in a gentle spark that quickly explodes into a raging fire. He pulls me into him and my entire body comes exquisitely alive with wondrous sensations everywhere it's touching his. When his tongue probes its way between my lips, I part them willingly, ready to share every inch of myself. My hormones start flaring like sunspots, and just as I'm about to bodily toss my stud into the back of the hearse and do my best imitation of a kinky cowgirl, I hear a familiar male voice behind me.

"Well, well, isn't this interesting?"

Hurley pulls away from me and it's all I can do not to grab him back, wrap my legs around his waist, and rein his lips back into submission. But my ardor dies a quick death when I see the source of the voice: Luke Nelson.

Hurley looks embarrassed; his face is beet red and the front of his jeans make it obvious he was enjoying what we were doing. As was I, and I'm pretty pissed off at Nelson for interrupting.

"So are you two always a team?" Nelson asks, smiling at the two of us. "It makes sense, of course, given your jobs and all. I'm sure you share a lot of interests in common." He pauses and adopts an exaggerated expression of worry. "Though I'm thinking it might make for some conflict-of-interest issues, eh?"

Hurley's eyes narrow, as does the tent in his pants. "What do you mean?" he asks. "What conflict of interest?"

Nelson shrugs, his smile back in place. "Well, it seems that your respective investigations would require a certain level of objectivity," he says. "You two didn't look very objective just now."

Hurley's eyes narrow down to a dangerous glint. He says nothing but the look he's giving Nelson communicates volumes. I imagine the average person would feel rather intimidated—I do, and he's not even looking at me. But Nelson is no average person.

He stares Hurley down for several seconds and then shrugs again. "You two have a nice night," he says, and then he turns and heads into the bar.

Hurley's eyes shoot darts into Nelson's back. "I think I understand now why you don't like him," he mutters. "He's a smug bastard."

"That he is," I concur, wishing Hurley would shift his attention from Nelson back to me. Some of those delicious tingly feelings he triggered in me are still circulating. But Nelson has successfully killed the mood.

As soon as Nelson disappears into the building, Hurley finally turns to look at me. "It makes me want to try to get a search warrant for his office, just to teach him a lesson. But there's no cause."

I frown, realizing that what he says is right but not liking it.

"You okay to get home on your own?" he says.

My hopes sink faster than William did after seeing Ethan's cockroach. I nod reluctantly, angrier than ever with Nelson. I desperately want to make him pay.

"Drive carefully," Hurley says. He stands there looking at me and I realize he's waiting for me to get into my car. I turn and open the door, wishing I could come up with some way to make the evening last a little longer. But the moment is gone, utterly and sadly irretrievable.

As soon as I settle in on the front seat, Hurley says, "See you soon," and then he's gone.

I stick my key in the ignition and turn it. The engine starts up without a hitch, purring contentedly. And as I back the hearse out of the parking lot, I find myself wishing Luke Nelson was riding in the back the way most of the prior passengers did.

Chapter
34

My night is filled with dreams about Hurley, some of them erotic, most of them just warm and cuddly. It's one of the latter that's interrupted when my alarm goes off. I groan as I roll over and hit the snooze button, praying that I can fall back to sleep and pick the dream up where it left off, but it's not to be. Nine minutes later the alarm goes off again, and after slapping it irritably, I drag my butt out of bed.

After taking care of my morning ablutions, I head over to Izzy's house and knock on the back door. Dom answers moments later.

"Good morning!" he says cheerfully. "You're just in time for breakfast. I made blueberry pancakes."

Dom's blueberry pancakes are orgasmic and I figure they might be just the medicine I need to quit mourning my lack of Hurley. I follow Dom into the kitchen—a bright, cheery room with east-facing windows that take full advantage of the morning sun—and find Izzy seated at the table with a cup of coffee and the morning paper.

"Good morning," I say, slipping into my usual chair. The smell of the pancakes has me practically drooling.

Izzy sets his paper aside and stares at me.

"What?" I say, knowing he's seeing something but not sure what it is.

"You have something to tell me?"

I shrug. "I don't think so."

He stares a little longer, his eyes narrowing into slits. Curious, Dom turns from the stove and starts staring at me too. "I think you're right, Izzy. Something is different."

I look back and forth between the two of them, my expression rife with skepticism. "You guys are nuts," I say dismissively.

"No, no, I can see it," Dom says. He turns back to the stove, scoops a stack of pancakes onto a plate, and then walks over to me. "Spill it or I won't let you have any," he says, waving the plate under my nose.

Thumbscrews and Chinese water tortures have nothing over the aroma of warm, juicy blueberries stuffed into fat, fluffy pancakes. I cave in a half second flat.

"Okay, Hurley and I met at the Nowhere for drinks last night and afterward we made out in the parking lot."

Dom scoops three pancakes off the top of the stack and plops them on my plate. The next two go to Izzy. Dom takes the last one for himself and settles in beside me. "Do tell," he says. "Was this a date?"

I cut a pat of butter from the stick on the table and start painting my pancakes with it. "Not really," I say. "Turns out he wanted to tell me they'd found Erik's gun."

Izzy asks, "Where?"

"It was under some sheets in a linen closet in the radiology department at the hospital."

Izzy grimaces and gives me a sympathetic look.

"I know, I know," I say with a sigh. "It doesn't look good for Erik. But until the ballistics report comes in, I'm not convinced."

"All right, enough," Dom interjects. "Quit talking shop and let's get back to the making out part."

Now that my pancakes are thoroughly coated in melted butter, I grab the warm syrup Dom has on the table and bathe my stack with it. "We had a couple of beers and played some darts," I tell them. "Then, when we left, he walked me to my car."

"Wait, you have a car?" Izzy says. "Did you actually buy something?"

"Not officially, but I'm thinking I will. Bobby Keegan is letting me test drive it for a day or two to help me decide."

"Is it something reliable?" Izzy asks. Dom gives him an exasperated look. I know Dom could care less about the car; he wants the smooch scoop.

"It seems to be," I tell Izzy. "But it has . . . other issues."

Izzy frowns and I take advantage of the moment to have my first bite of pancake. As I chew, the flavors of maple, pancake, and blueberries start a small orgy in my mouth.

"Get to the kissing stuff," Dom says, trying to get the conversation back on track. "Was it good? Did he use tongue? Did you share any, um, friction?" The expression on his face is devilishly delighted.

I smile enigmatically and wiggle my eyebrows at him. "You could say there was some friction, but we were interrupted before things could get too heated."

"Interrupted how?" Dom asks.

"That shrink, Luke Nelson, was there. He looked pretty smug at finding the two of us in a clutch and made some innuendos about how our pairing up might be a conflict of interest."

Izzy frowns at that. "That's ludicrous. Besides, what difference would it make to him? Didn't Hurley say Nelson had been cleared with regard to Shannon's death? As I recall, his alibi was pretty solid."

"It is," I admit. "But there's something about that guy that bothers me. I can't put my finger on it but I get the distinct feeling he's hiding something."

"Well, he is. Or was," Izzy says. "He had all those women he was stringing along."

I nod thoughtfully, enjoying a few more bites of breakfast heaven before I speak again. "I'd like to talk to one of the patients Nelson saw the day of Shannon's death, Carla Andrusson. She's my dentist's wife and I've socialized with her a few times in years past when David and I attended some parties. I plan on going into the office first thing this morning, but do you think it would be okay if I took a little time away later today to do that?"

Izzy shrugs. "If there aren't any autopsies pending, I don't see why not. But what do you hope to accomplish? Hasn't Hurley already verified all the appointments?"

"He did. But I just can't let go of this nagging feeling I have that something is off. Maybe it's just my dislike of the guy, but I want to look into it."

Izzy stares at me with a worried expression and shakes his head. I know he wants to say something but I refuse to take his bait. We both go back to eating and the room is utterly silent for a few minutes other than the noise of forks scraping against plates. As I stab the last bite of my pancakes and let them melt in my mouth, I have to resist the urge to run my fingers around my plate so I can snag the remaining few crumbs. "Dom," I say, once I have swallowed and dropped my fork onto the empty plate with a clatter, "that was heavenly."

Dom beams and his lily-white skin blushes an adoring shade of pink. "Thanks." He hops up and starts clearing the table, carrying the dishes to the sink. As soon as he starts loading the dishwasher, Izzy leans toward me and says, "Be careful, Mattie."

"Of what?"

"Losing your objectivity. I know you haven't taken a liking to this Nelson guy but don't let a first impression override your common sense. It could get you into trouble. And the same thing goes for Erik."

"What do you mean?"

"The evidence against him is pretty strong. I think you need to start entertaining the idea that you might be wrong about him."

I shake my head vehemently. "I don't believe Erik did this."

"No, you don't *want* to believe Erik did this. But if you're honest with yourself I think you'll realize that it's not only possible, but probable that he did. He had motive, opportunity, and the weapon."

"We don't know if that gun was the murder weapon yet," I say irritably, hearing how feeble it sounds even to me. "Can we at least wait for the ballistics report before we convict him?"

Izzy doesn't answer. He just sighs and gives me a sympathetic look that sucks all the wind from my sails.

"Okay," I say, feeling defeated. "I realize it's not looking very good for Erik, and I admit that if the ballistics report comes back showing that the gun they found was the murder weapon, it will be pretty damning. But let me have my presumption of innocence until all the evidence is in, okay?"

Izzy smiles and pushes back from the table. "Okay. Now let's go take a look at this car of yours. Dom, are you coming?"

Dom turns off the water in the sink and grabs a dish towel. "Right behind you," he says. I lead the way to the back door and as soon as I open it, there is my car, displayed in all its morbid glory. Dom and Izzy stand quietly for several seconds taking it in. Izzy's face slowly breaks into a wide grin. Dom clucks his tongue and tosses his towel over his shoulder. "Well, hell," he says. "There goes the neighborhood."

Chapter
35

After thanking Dom again for breakfast and hearing Izzy say he'll be right behind me, I drive into the office, one of three places in town where the sight of a hearse pulling in doesn't raise an eyebrow. As soon as I verify that there aren't any autopsies pending, I head for the library and take out the phone number Hurley gave me for Carla Andrusson. I get an answering machine and leave a vague message stating who I am and that I want to talk with her about something important.

As I'm doing so, the door to the library opens and Arnie walks in.

I finish my message and then give Arnie a cheery "Good morning" as I hang up.

"You're sounding chipper today."

"I had breakfast at Izzy's this morning. Dom made blueberry pancakes."

"Ah," Arnie says, nodding knowingly. "Being the recipient of anything Dom cooks is enough to cheer anyone up. That man should have been a chef."

"Tell me about it," I say, starting to drool again from the memory.

"Where is Izzy?" Arnie asks. "In his office?"

"I guess so. He said he had a bunch of paperwork to catch up on."

"Well, then, you get to hear the news first," he says, smiling enigmatically. I see that he's holding some papers behind his back and he looks like a cat inside a room filled with clipped-wing canaries.

I brace myself, thinking he is about to pound another nail in Erik's coffin by sharing the results of the ballistics report with me, but instead he says, "You'll never guess what I found in that briefcase we retrieved from the Heinriches' car."

I think for a moment, trying to guess what kind of find would have Arnie looking so excited. "Proof of alien life?"

"Nope."

"A top-secret government document?"

He shakes his head.

"A million bucks?"

"No, but you're definitely getting warmer."

I shrug. "I give up."

He pulls the papers from behind his back and tosses them onto the table in front of me. "These are copies of the real ones," he says.

I turn the papers around and see that they are the wills for Gerald and Bitsy Heinrich. I scan what follows but it seems to be pretty routine legalese. I shrug again, failing to see why Arnie is so excited.

"Look at the last page," he says.

I do so and see a page full of signatures and what looks like a notary stamp at the bottom.

"Check out the date," he says.

I do so, noting that the signatures were made on October twentieth of this year. The meaning starts to dawn on me and I quickly flip through the rest of the pages, scanning the text.

Arnie is shifting from one foot to the other, his face alight with delight, his excitement barely contained.

"Oh, my," I say when I've read enough. I look up at Arnie. "Is this for real?"

"The original papers seem to be in order. And I contacted the notary. She verified everything."

"Wow," I say, smiling and sliding the pages back to Arnie. "This certainly changes things."

"I know. I can't wait to see the reactions."

My cell phone rings and as I grab it, Arnie takes the papers and says, "I'm going to show this to Izzy. Catch ya later."

"Don't do anything with them until I'm there to watch," I tell him. "I wouldn't want to miss this for anything."

He nods and heads out as I answer my phone. "Hello?"

"Mattie? This is Carla Andrusson, returning your call."

"Hi, Carla. Thanks for getting back to me so quickly."

"Well, you said it was urgent. Are you having some kind of dental emergency? Because if you are, you're better off just calling the office. I don't have—"

"No, this is about you," I tell her, interrupting her spiel. "I need to talk to you about something personal and I wondered if we could meet somewhere?"

She hesitates, then says, "Well I'm trying to get ready for a dinner party I'm having tonight. Can this wait for a few days?"

"Not really."

She lets out a sigh to let me know she's perturbed and I decide I'll need to be more forthright if I'm going to get her to cooperate. "I don't know if you heard or not but I'm working for the medical examiner's office now."

"No," she says, sounding genuinely surprised. "I didn't know that."

"I need to ask you about something related to a murder investigation and time is of the essence here."

There's another pause before she caves. "Okay, but you'll need to come over here. I have too much to do to afford any time away from home."

"Not a problem. Can I come over now?"

"Fine," she says, sounding as if it's anything but. And then she hangs up without so much as a good-bye.

I head for Izzy's office to let him know I'm leaving and find him talking on the phone. Arnie is pacing outside the door, waiting for Izzy to hang up so he can share his latest news. Though

I'm dying to see Izzy's face when he hears about the wills, I don't want to keep Carla waiting. So I tell Arnie where I'm headed and make him promise to give me a blow-by-blow description of Izzy's reaction later.

Belatedly I realize that pulling up in front of Carla's house in a hearse isn't likely to help my cause any. Apparently she was watching for me because she is at the front door wearing a panicked expression before I can turn the engine off. She is a cute, petite, redhead with exquisite porcelain skin that is quite pale under normal circumstances. Right now, standing in her doorway, she looks like a ghost. But as soon as I climb out of the car, her face relaxes and a bit of color returns to her cheeks.

"You scared the life out of me," she says as I approach. Then she seems to realize the irony of her statement because she slaps a hand over her chest, giggles, and says, "Oh, my."

"I know," I say, nodding and smiling. "It's not the most inconspicuous ride, is it?"

"Hardly. Do you have to drive that thing as part of your new job?"

"No, that *thing*, as you call it, is my new set of wheels. I totaled my regular car, and for now, this is all I can afford."

She looks confused for a second, then dawning hits her face. "I see. Things with David aren't going well then, I take it?"

"You could say that."

"Well, come on in. I have some great coffee and some fresh-baked muffins that might cheer you up."

I follow Carla inside, realizing that the hearse might not be the curse I originally thought it was. It has helped to break the ice and lighten her mood, rather than darken it. She leads me into her kitchen, points to a chair, and then goes about setting up her coffeemaker. While her back is to me, I take a moment to examine my surroundings. The kitchen looks brand-spanking new and judging from the travertine floor tiles, granite countertops, cherry wood cabinets, and high-end, stainless appliances, her husband's practice must be doing well.

"I was sorry to hear about you and David," she says over her shoulder, measuring coffee into a basket. "You two always seemed like the perfect couple."

"Yes, well appearances can be deceiving," I say. "I imagine most marriages look good on the outside, but what goes on behind closed operating room doors is another matter."

The statement is a test to see if Carla has heard the sordid details behind my breakup with David. Her next statement tells me she has because she knows exactly what I'm talking about.

"Yes, an unfortunate choice for David," she says, shaking her head. "You have to wonder what the hell he was thinking doing something like that at the hospital."

"Thinking with the wrong head, I imagine," I say. She lets forth with a warm, throaty chuckle and I decide to take advantage of her relaxed mood. "How are things going with you and Brian?"

She hesitates for a beat longer than necessary, and even though she still has her back to me, I know whatever she says next will only be a part of the truth.

"We're doing okay." She shrugs. "I wish his practice didn't take up so much of his time, but I've learned to adjust."

She has finished setting up the coffee, and after turning on the machine, she grabs a plate of muffins from the counter and sets them on the table in front of me. I note that even though her mobility appears fine, she does very little lifting with her right hand, making me suspect she still has some residual weakness on that side.

"How are the kids?" I ask.

"They're doing great." I can tell from the change in her tone that this is a huge source of pride and joy for her. "They're both attending the U of Dub down in Madison. Carrie is a freshman majoring in business and Tom is one year away from finishing medical school."

"You must be very proud," I say, taking one of the muffins from the plate—raspberry with a crumb topping—and picking a chunk off the top. I pop it in my mouth and relish the flavors.

"I am," She beams for several seconds, and due to her linger-

ing facial paralysis, the smile is slightly lopsided. She takes a
muffin for herself but she doesn't eat any of it. She peels the
paper cup from around it and then sets it on the table. Her smile
fades and her expression turns sad. "I miss them." Her gaze wanders about the room. "The house feels kind of big and empty
these days."

"Is that why you're seeing Luke Nelson?"

It's an abrupt segue and Carla's slight flinch reflects that. She
shoots me a wary glance and then quickly looks away. "Something like that," she says vaguely. "I've been a bit depressed
lately. You know . . . the kids being gone, Brian working so much,
being alone all the time, getting older, losing my looks . . ." She
lets out a mirthless laugh and makes a dismissive wave with her
hand. "All the usual midlife crap I suppose."

I sense her shutting down and scramble to find a way to reconnect. "Tell me about it," I say over a mouthful of muffin. "My
marriage has fallen apart, my finances are a wreck, and I'm living
in a friend's cottage that he had built for his ailing, aging mother.
I'm at an age where I thought I'd either have, or be starting a
family, but instead I'm facing reentry into the dating game." She
smiles sympathetically. "And to be honest, the whole idea of dating terrifies me. I can feel all my insecurities and the pressure of
time bearing down on me. I jiggle in places that I never used to
have, gravity is getting the better of several of my body parts, and
in just a few more years I can expect my hormones to start taking
extended vacations, which means my chances of ever having
children grow smaller every day." I pause and flash a wan smile.
"So I think I understand what you're going through, Carla.
Growing old alone seems like a very real, very scary possibility to
me these days."

"So what's the answer?" she asks. "How do we deal with all
this stuff?"

"Hell if I know. I'm long on questions and short on answers
these days." I hesitate for the merest beat of a second before taking the plunge. "I've given some thought to getting therapy," I
lie. "But I'm a little wary. I've never done anything like that before and it seems kind of, I don't know, scary."

She nods thoughtfully. "I know what you mean. The whole idea of it scared me, too. But I figured it was worth a try and these days there isn't as much of a stigma associated with that sort of thing the way there used to be. Hell, half of Hollywood boasts about their problems and their shrinks. It's given psychotherapy a whole new cachet."

The coffee has finished brewing and she gets up and makes herself busy pouring two mugs full. I finish decapitating my muffin and peel the paper away from the body of it as she sets the coffee cups on the table—one at a time since she apparently doesn't trust her right arm to hold one of them—along with a little pitcher full of cream and a sugar bowl.

"Yeah, I guess you're right," I say, topping my coffee off with a dollop of cream. She leaves hers black and takes a sip of it. Her muffin is still sitting in front of her, naked but otherwise untouched. I pinch off a section of the body on mine, but hesitate before popping it into my mouth, not wanting to lose my momentum. "But even though therapy is more acceptable these days, it's hard for me to shake off this belief I have that it's all a bunch of hocus-pocus. Has it helped you any? Has Dr. Nelson given you any tips or tricks or wonder drugs to try?"

Carla frowns. "Maybe," she says hesitantly. "I've only seen him a few times so far, so it's a little early yet to tell if it's really helping."

"What does he do? What kind of therapy does he offer?"

She looks away from me, her expression thoughtful. "It's a bit . . . unusual," she says, staring at the wall.

I sense there is more to come so I scarf down the bite of muffin I'm holding and wait. It doesn't take long.

"He uses some kind of hypnosis or something. Most of the time when I leave his office it's as if I was there, but I wasn't. It's hard to explain. I can remember talking with him and feeling very relaxed, but something about it always seems surreal, like I was dreaming it, or watching it in a movie."

"I've heard that hypnosis can be very therapeutic. How does he do it? Does he dangle a watch or something, like you see on TV?"

"No. Though he does have a wall clock that ticks rather loudly" she adds, managing a quick smile. She prods her muffin but still doesn't eat any of it. "He has me sit back on this big comfy couch he has and gives me a cup of warm herbal tea to help me relax. Then he just lets me talk."

"About what?"

"My life, I guess. He asks me what I like about it, what I don't, what I feel about people, things, myself. And then at some point he takes over the talking."

"What does he say?"

"He calls it ego building. You know, telling me I'm a bright, intelligent, attractive woman and that I have the power to be whatever I want. That kind of crap."

"Crap?"

She shrugs. "In some ways it does make me feel better about myself when I leave there. But when I play it all back in my head it just seems so . . . I don't know . . . fake. Like a cheap come-on or something, you know?"

I do, and I can't help but think that Carla's discomfort with Nelson somewhat mirrors my own, though apparently it hasn't been enough to make her stop seeing him.

My cell phone rings, and after glancing at the caller ID and seeing that it's Izzy, I apologize to Carla and explain that I need to take the call. She nods, and politely excuses herself from the room.

"Hey, Izzy, what's up?"

"Can you get back here to the office?" he asks. "I just called Hurley and told him about Arnie's find. He's on his way here and plans to call the various family members in to give them the news. I thought you might want to be in on it."

"Heck, yeah," I say, relishing the thought. "I wouldn't miss that for all the money in the world."

I hang up and Carla's timely reappearance makes me suspect she was eavesdropping despite her apparent attempt to give me some privacy.

"Do you have to go?" she asks.

"I do. But maybe we can get together again sometime and chat some more."

"I'd like that," she says, giving me a feeble smile.

I grab the last of my muffin and proffer it toward her. "These are phenomenal," I tell her.

"Thanks. Why don't you take a couple with you? I have more than enough," She lets out a self-deprecating laugh. "I still bake as if I have a whole family living here."

There is something painfully sad in the way she says this, and I almost walk over and hug her. But my gut tells me it would be the wrong thing to do, so I hold back and take the muffins instead. Carla shows me to the door and I thank her for letting me stop by. As I turn to step off the porch she calls me back.

"Mattie?"

"Yes?"

"What's the real reason you're so interested in Dr. Nelson?"
Busted.

"It's part of a routine investigation," I say vaguely, but Carla isn't about to let me off that easily.

"What kind of investigation?"

"He used to date Shannon Tolliver. That makes him a person of interest in her case." It's the truth, though not the whole truth. Still, I'm hoping it will suffice.

Carla weighs what I've told her for a few seconds, scrutinizing my face. I try to keep my expression placid but Carla is savvier than I gave her credit for.

"There's more to it than that," she says. It's not a question.

"Maybe."

She leans against the door frame and looks up at the sky. "There's something about him that bothers me."

"What?"

"I don't know exactly. I can't put my finger on one specific thing. On the surface he seems professional, affable, and kind. But . . ." I want to grab her and shake her to make her spit it out. But I manage to restrain myself. "Something just feels wrong," she says finally. "Every time I leave there I feel . . ." She hesitates and then shrugs. "I feel wrong. I can't explain it any better than that."

She doesn't need to. "I think I understand what you're trying to tell me, Carla. To be honest, there's something about him that rings wrong with me, too."

"I have another appointment with him tomorrow. Will you let me know if you turn up anything?"

"Sure."

"Thanks, Mattie."

"Thank you," I say in return. "You've been a big help to me."

With that, Carla turns and goes back inside. As I climb into the hearse and start it up, I have a strong feeling that she's watching me leave. And oddly, I also have the feeling that neither of our lives will ever be the same again.

Chapter
36

I head back to the office, anticipating the upcoming meeting with the Heinrich and Conklin families. Even more exciting is the knowledge that Hurley will be there. As I pull into the parking lot, I see Aaron Heinrich pulling in at the same time. He hails me as I get out of my car.

"Hello, Aaron."

He is positively beaming as he approaches. "I take it we've been called here because your office finally has some answers for us," he says, falling into step beside me.

"Yes, we do."

"That's great news."

"How can you be so sure? You don't know the outcome yet."

He smiles at me and dismisses my question with a wave of his hand. "I don't really care about the money all that much."

"Really?" I say, my skepticism obvious.

"Yes, really. Unlike my siblings, I've managed to put away most of my money rather than squander it. I'll be okay no matter what happens."

"Then why are you glad to hear we have an answer?"

"Well, for one thing, it will put an end to all this bickering." He opens the door to the office and holds it for me, his smile broadening. "But even better," he adds as I walk inside, "is the fact that once your investigation is done, you no longer have a reason to avoid having dinner with me."

"I see," I say, feeling myself start to blush. Cass is on duty; at least I assume the long-haired, hippy-looking girl behind the desk is her. Standing beside her is Hurley, who starts to smile but then quickly scowls when he sees Aaron and I walk in together.

"What about this coming Saturday?" Aaron says as we approach the desk. "Are you free? Because I'd love to take you to this fabulous restaurant I know in Green Bay."

Hurley's scowl deepens and my wicked side takes over. "Let me think on that, Aaron," I say, smiling sweetly at him. "I'll let you know before you leave today, okay?"

"Great!" He claps his hands like a little kid, a gesture I find somehow charming.

Cass walks over to us and says, "Mr. Heinrich, if you'll follow me I'll take you to the conference room. The rest of your family as well as your stepsiblings are already there."

I hand my muffins over to Cass, and as she leads Aaron out of the reception area, Hurley walks over to me wearing an expression that looks like thunderclouds. "You aren't seriously going to go out on a date with that yahoo, are you?" he grumbles.

I shrug and smile. "I don't know yet. He's handsome, charming, and seems to be the only member of his family with any brains or common sense. So why not?"

"Handsome?" Hurley scoffs. "You find that coiffed playboy look appealing?"

"I find many looks appealing," I tell him. I turn to head for the conference room but before I can take a second step, Hurley grabs my arm and pulls me back.

"Don't do it," he says.

"Are you kidding? I wouldn't miss this denouement for anything. I can't wait to see those spoiled brats get their comeuppance."

"I don't mean that," Hurley says, looking nervous. He still has a hold on one of my arms and he grabs the other one and turns me to face him. "I mean the other thing. You can't . . . I mean, you shouldn't . . . damn it!" He blows out a breath of exasperation. "I don't want you going on a date with Aaron Heinrich," he finally spits out.

His hold on me is firm but not tight and I briefly consider shaking his grip loose. But I like him touching me too much to do so. So I issue a verbal challenge instead. "Give me one good reason why I shouldn't."

Hurley pulls me closer and wraps a hand around the back of my head. Then he launches a full-frontal lip assault. Our mouths collide in a deliciously sensual lock and then his second hand is at the small of my back, pulling me into him. As his tongue starts a gentle probe, I feel the hot, throbbing parts of him against my own. My nipples jump to attention and I cop a cheap feel by rubbing my chest ever so slightly over his.

And then I hear an "Ahem" behind us.

Suddenly all that wonderful heat is gone as Hurley breaks his lip-lock and steps back, away from me. The action leaves me breathless, longing, slightly befuddled, and a tad pissed off. I look to Hurley for an answer and see that his eyes are no longer focused on me, but rather behind me. I turn and find Izzy standing there wearing a smirk nearly as wide as he is tall.

"I'd offer the two of you a private room," Izzy says. "But I'm afraid the best I can come up with on such short notice is the morgue fridge. And not only are those tables kind of uncomfortable, I'm afraid the two of you would thaw out all the bodies."

"Sorry," Hurley mumbles, adjusting his pants in a vain attempt to hide the conspicuous bulge that has sprung up.

"No need to apologize," Izzy says, still grinning from ear to ear. "But we are about to get started in the other room so if you want to attend, you might want to get yourselves together and head that way."

"Be right there," Hurley says.

Izzy turns and leaves the room. I look back at Hurley, expecting him to appear embarrassed or chagrined, but instead he's wearing a smirk.

"So, was my reason good enough for you?" he says.

"Huh?"

"Did I persuade you?"

"Persuade me?" My mind can't seem to wrap itself around what he's asking because it's still muddled up in a haze of glorious sensations and raging hormones.

Hurley shakes his head at me. "How quickly they forget," he says. "You asked me to give you one good reason why you shouldn't date Aaron Heinrich. So I'm asking you, was my reason good enough?"

"Oh. That."

"Yes, that."

I lick my lips, relishing the lingering taste of him there. "Yeah," I say, giving him a silly-assed grin. "I'd say you made your, um, point"—I shoot a salacious glance toward his crotch—"exceedingly well. Now you better find a way to make it go away or Easton Heinrich might think you're coming on to him."

"Want to help me?"

Oh, boy. Suddenly the Heinrich/Conklin fiasco doesn't seem so interesting. But before I can answer, the main door to the office opens and two cops stroll in: Junior Feller and Larry Johnson.

At first I think the presence of the cops means the families in the other room must have gotten out of hand already, but the relaxed manner of Junior and Larry as they stroll into the room suggests otherwise.

"Hey, Steve," Larry says, acknowledging him with a nod. He looks at me and his voice warms up several degrees as he says, "Good to see you again, Mattie."

Hurley doesn't miss the subtle change in Larry's tone, but even if he did, the puppy-dog eyes Larry has every time he looks at me is a dead giveaway.

"What are you guys doing here?" Hurley asks, his tone gruff.

Junior says, "Izzy called us and wanted us to stand by. He said he's got some news to deliver to that nutcase family that went bonkers at the hospital the other day and he wanted some backup on hand just in case."

"Probably a smart idea," I say.

Hurley puffs out his chest a bit and says, "I think I can handle things on my own."

Apparently I'm not the only one whose hormones got a workout during that kiss. Clearly Hurley has more testosterone than brains at the moment. Not only do the Heinriches and Conklins have him clearly outnumbered, they're also nuttier than squirrel shit. After working in the ER for a number of years, I can vouch for the added strength insanity imbues in people.

As soon as Hurley throws down his awkward gauntlet, a deafening silence fills the room. Larry, who is known for his painful bluntness and lack of verbal filters, remains thankfully quiet and continues to just stand there making moon eyes at me.

Junior, who is a bit more tactful, finally breaks the silence and says, "Oh, I'm sure you can, Steve. But to be honest, we want to be in on whatever's going down. One of those crazy-assed Heinrich women nailed me in the cojones the other day during that melee at the hospital. And from what Izzy told us, the Heinriches aren't going to be very happy with what he has to tell them. So personally, I'd like to be here. I can't wait to see their hopes get crushed into tiny little pieces."

Yikes! I make a mental note to never do anything that will piss Junior off.

Hurley ponders Junior's request for a moment, and then says, "Okay, after you." He gestures toward the door to the back part of the office and Junior and Larry head that way. I fall in behind them with Hurley bringing up the rear. As soon as the two cops are through the door, I pause, turn over my shoulder, and whisper to Hurley.

"Is it safe to let you walk behind me?"

He grins and arches his left eyebrow at me. "Absolutely not."

Ride 'em, cowboy!

Chapter
37

The "conference room" is actually the library since it's the only space other than the morgue fridge big enough to hold this many people, and Hurley and I already have dibs on that other room. As we enter the library, a cacophony of noise greets us. Everyone is talking to everyone else and most of the voices are a mere gnat's ass away from shouting. Hurley's little pup tent is safe, assuming it's still up, because our entry into the room goes unnoticed by everyone other than Izzy.

Larry and Junior hang out by the door, leaning against the wall. Hurley and I make our way to the head of the table and take the two empty chairs, me next to Izzy and Hurley between me and Grace Heinrich. I take a moment to observe the rest of the group. Grace and Katrina are seated to our left and Easton is seated at the opposite end of the table. On the other side are Sarah and Tom Conklin, with Aaron at the end near his brother.

Grace is leaning across the table lecturing Sarah about the importance of family heritage. Sarah is lecturing right back at her about the ills of greediness and how righteous it is to share. Katrina is mostly listening to this exchange, though she punctuates her sister's comments periodically with "Damn right!" and "You know it's true!"

Farther down, Easton is leaning in front of his brother and

shaking a finger in Tom's face, ordering him to "just give it up, put your tail between your legs, and go the hell home."

Aaron, once again the cool, detached observer in the group, is smiling past his brother's arm at me. I hear Hurley mutter, "Asshole," under his breath and know he hasn't missed the focus of Aaron's attention.

Izzy makes a couple of attempts to get the attention of everyone, but his efforts are wasted. It's not until Hurley cuts loose with a shrill whistle that the conversations cease and everyone's attention shifts to the head of the table.

"Thank you all for coming," Izzy says.

"Cut the crap and just get on with it," Easton snaps. Judging from the red roadmap I can see running over his eyeballs, I guess his blood is somewhere around ninety proof about now. "Which one of them died first?"

Izzy nervously shuffles the folder of papers in front of him. I know the others in the room probably think he has autopsy results in there, but I know otherwise.

"We aren't one hundred percent sure," Izzy begins, "but—"

"What the hell!" Grace yells. "If you don't have any answers for us, why are we here?" The rest of the group chimes in with their own grumbles but another whistle from Hurley silences them.

"I do have an answer for you," Izzy says. "Just not the one you think."

I expect more grumbling, but to my surprise, they all remain quiet, waiting.

Izzy opens the folder in front of him and takes out a stack of stapled papers. He doles out one of the stapled packets to each family member in the room, sliding them across the sleek surface of the table.

"As you can see," Izzy begins, "the papers in front of you are copies of two wills and testaments. The originals are currently tagged as evidence and in the hands of an attorney. We found these wills inside a briefcase that was in your parents' car."

Aaron and the women start reading, flipping the pages as they go, their faces taking on disbelieving expressions. Easton, however, tries in vain to focus on the first page and then tosses his packet aside.

"We don't need to read any goddamned wills," Easton slurs. "We all have copies already."

"Not of this one," Izzy says. "If you'll look at the last page, you'll see that they were drafted, signed, and witnessed the day before your parents disappeared."

Aaron flips a page and starts to chuckle.

Grace flips a page and mutters, "What the fuck?"

Katrina stares at her packet and says, "How could they do this?"

Tom remains silent and keeps reading; Sarah looks up at Izzy and says, "Are you sure this is for real?"

Izzy nods. "We found the lawyer who drafted the wills as well as the witnesses who signed them. They verified both documents."

Easton, clearly curious now that he's seen his siblings' reactions, snatches his packet back and tries once again to bring the words into focus. He doesn't appear to be having much luck so Izzy summarizes for him.

"So, as I'm sure you can all see, it doesn't matter which of your parents died first because the outcome is the same either way. All of their money is going to a select group of charities."

"Are you fucking kidding me?" Easton screams. "No fucking way."

Aaron tries to placate his brother by placing a hand on his arm. "I'm afraid it's true, bro," he says calmly. "They've cut us all out."

"Fucking sonofabitch!" Easton yells, pounding a fist on the table.

Grace sets her packet of papers down, glares across the table at Sarah, and in a scarily calm and quiet voice, says, "This is all your fault, you fucking bitch."

"My fault?" Sarah comes back. "If you and your siblings hadn't been so goddamned lazy and greedy, maybe our folks wouldn't have felt the need to do this."

"Greedy?" Grace shrieks. "I'll give you greedy, bitch!" With that, Grace flings herself across the table and smashes into Sarah head first. Sarah yelps, grabs a chunk of Grace's hair, and screams, "Get off me, you crazy bitch!" Grace manages to grab Sarah by the throat and at that point Tom joins in and starts trying to pry Grace's hands loose. That sets Katrina off, who mimics her sister's maneuver by flying across the table and trying to gouge Tom's eyes out. Easton, who I'm now convinced is not only a lush but several Froot Loops shy of a full bowl, stands up, rips his shirt open, and dives across the table into Tom.

Seconds later, the room is utter chaos, with Hurley, Junior, and Larry joining the fray. Izzy and I hop out of our chairs and pin our backs to the wall behind us, huddling in the corner farthest from the melee. Across the room I see Aaron slide along his wall and then slip out of the room altogether.

I hear fabric ripping, people screeching, and the sickening sounds of flesh and bone crunching together. At one point blood flies and hits the side wall but I can't tell whose it is. One of the chairs gets broken and the table is slowly pushed all the way to the other side of the room.

"Well, that went well, wouldn't you say?" Izzy says to me as we stand watching. He grabs a nearby chair and positions it in front of us like a barricade.

"Thank goodness you had Junior and Larry here."

Izzy nods. "Think we can get past them to the door?" he says as somebody's purse flies across the room and hits the wall beside us.

I shake my head and watch as Tom Conklin takes a swing at Easton, who either ducks or falls, allowing Tom's fist to connect with Junior's face instead. "Too risky," I say, grimacing as Junior staggers sideways.

Oddly enough, the Heinrich and Conklin clans seem to be pulling together for a change, ganging up on Hurley and the other two cops. It's not looking too good for our side when the door to the library crashes open and an unbelievable sight appears.

There, filling the entire doorway, is a behemoth of a man wearing a Lone Ranger–type mask. His feet are encased in red boots and his body is outfitted in tight, red spandex: body suit, tights, and cape. He stands there with his legs spread apart, his fists on his hips, and his arms cocked wide. On his puffed-out chest is printed a giant, yellow, capital letter *H* for Hacker Man. As odd as this apparition is, it's one I've seen before. Beneath that superhero costume is Joey Dewhurst, the computer savant who saved my life once before.

The sight of him now worries me more than it reassures me. Despite his intimidating presence, Joey is a big softy and I'm afraid he's going to get hurt. He steps into the room and grabs for the person closest to him, which happens to be Easton. Joey, who probably outweighs Easton by a good two hundred pounds, easily pulls his quarry aside. Easton whirls around angrily, ready to throw a punch, but he freezes, staring at Joey with a look of horror on his face. And then he screams like a little girl.

"Get it off of me!" he screeches. "Oh my God, oh my God! Make it go away!" With that, Easton collapses and starts to sob. This spectacle is enough to distract the others in the room, who glance over to see what's going on and then freeze where they are, stunned into submission. I can't say I blame them; Joey the superhero is a rather incredulous sight.

"What the hell is that?" Tom Conklin asks, his eyes wide with fright.

Since Hurley and the other cops know Joey and his predilection for costumes, they aren't as riveted as the rest of the group. As a result, they are finally able to gain the upper hand and cuff Tom, Sarah, and the two Heinrich sisters.

That leaves Easton, who is lying on the floor at Joey's feet, still sobbing. He appears to have wet himself, and once Larry and Junior realize that, they look at each other, sigh, and do a quick game of rock-paper-scissors. Junior wins and a reluctant Larry carefully approaches Easton and zip-ties his hands behind his back.

By now, I can see there are other people lurking in the hallway just beyond the doorway to the room: Arnie and Aaron Heinrich. I hear Arnie tell Larry, "Yeah, Joey and I were just coming back from lunch and we ran into this guy out front." He gestures toward Aaron. "He told us about the meeting in here, and when we heard the commotion going on beyond the door, Joey went into hero mode, stripped off his regular clothes, and made his entrance."

With everyone in the room secure, Hurley makes his way over to me and Izzy. His hair is attractively mussed, one sleeve is torn nearly off, revealing a sexy shoulder beneath, and his lower lip has a small cut on it.

"You guys okay?" he asks.

"We're fine," I say. "But you look a little the worse for wear." I reach up and gingerly dab at a drip of blood on his lip. And as soon as my finger touches that soft flesh, I remember how those lips felt against mine. I feel myself growing hot and quickly pull away.

"I'm fine," Hurley says.

"Thank goodness for Joey," I say. "Who knows what would have happened if he hadn't shown up when he did?"

Hurley looks offended. "We were managing just fine on our own."

"You're kidding me, right?" I say, looking askance. "Those nut jobs were beating the crap out of you guys."

"The hell they were," Hurley sulks.

I look at him and break into a grin. "Well, well. Aren't we the macho man? You can't stand the fact that a bumbling superhero-wannabe saved your ass, can you?"

"He didn't. We almost had them by the time Joey showed up," Hurley argues. He looks over at Izzy. "Didn't we?" It's a rhetorical question. Hurley fully expects Izzy to agree with him, but instead Izzy just shakes his head.

"Crap," Hurley says, looking crestfallen.

"It's okay," I say, patting him on the shoulder. "Cheer up. Nobody's perfect. Now quit sulking, put on your big boy pants, and let's get out of here."

As I turn to leave the room I hear Hurley utter a parting shot behind me. "Women," he huffs. "Can't live with 'em, can't get 'em to wear a leather bustier."

Chapter
38

Oddly enough, Hurley's parting quip gives me an idea. As soon as the Heinrich and Conklin clans are hauled off to jail, I make a phone call to Carla Andrusson and ask her if I can stop by again. She isn't happy with yet another interruption in her dinner party preparations, but after promising to be quick, she relents.

I let Izzy know I'm heading out and make a beeline for Carla's house before she has a chance to change her mind. When I tell her what I want her to do she is resistant at first, but after some reasoning and cajoling, she finally buys into my plan and we agree to implement it the following day.

From Carla's house I head to the dry cleaner to pick up my gown and Hurley's jacket. As I'm headed into the store my cell phone rings and, as I fumble for it, I run into someone who is coming out. I look up to apologize but the words freeze on my lips. Standing in front of me is Luke Nelson.

"Ah, so we meet again," he says. He is smiling but it looks forced and the tone of his words is flat, tired, and exasperated sounding.

"Hello," I say. I start to push by him but he stops me with a question.

"Anything new with Shannon's case?"

I turn to look back at him, my hand on the door. "We've made a little progress," I say vaguely, studying his facial expression. If my words worry him at all, he isn't showing it.

"I hear they found the gun her husband owned."

"Yes," I say. "But we don't have the ballistics report yet so we don't know if it's the murder weapon." Then it hits me. "How did you hear about it already?"

"I have a few connections," he says cryptically. His evasiveness annoys me but I can hardly complain since I've been that way myself. "I take it my alibi patients from the day in question have been cooperative?"

"Yes."

"Good. So I can safely assume we won't be having lunch again anytime soon?"

There is a hint of smugness in the way he says this that makes my hackles rise. I suspect he is deliberately taunting me. "You are safe from me," I tell him, flashing him my best plastic smile. "At least for now."

His eyes narrow ever so slightly when I utter this caveat and a muscle in his left cheek starts to twitch. For several intolerably long seconds we stand there staring at one another. I'm pretty certain he's playing a game of intimidation with me so I stand my ground, refusing to break eye contact even though every nerve in my body is screaming at me to escape. It's all I can do not to smile with relief when he finally says, "Good day," and leaves.

Belatedly I remember the phone call I never answered. I take my cell out, look at the call history, and see it was Izzy. There is no message in my voice mail so I call him back.

"Hey, Izzy, what's up?"

"Arnie says he's found something of interest in the blood samples we collected from Shannon's house. I thought you might want to be here when he tells us what it is."

"Give me ten minutes and I'll be there."

I disconnect the call and head inside the cleaner's, where the same lady is on duty behind the counter. She looks nervous when she sees me and I brace myself for some bad news. Which will it be? The gown or Hurley's jacket?

"I have your stuff ready," she says. She disappears into the back and returns a moment later with both items placed on hangers and covered in plastic. "That was one nasty jacket," she says, wrinkling her nose. "We had to process it three times to get the smell out." I nod, waiting for the kicker. "So your total comes to sixty bucks. I had to charge extra for the jacket treatment."

I wince at the price and dig out my wallet. All I have is forty-two dollars. "I guess I'll have to wait until payday to get both items," I tell her. "How much was the dress?"

She chews her lip in thought for a moment, then says, "Tell you what. How about I give you a half-price deal?"

I raise my eyebrows in surprise. "You mean thirty bucks for both of them?"

She nods.

"That's a deal," I tell her. I pay her and walk out to the car feeling pretty chipper. Today must be my lucky day. But as I drive to the office, something about the whole transaction bothers me. It was easy, maybe too easy.

I take the dress into the office with me and give it back to Cass, thanking her for letting me borrow it. Then I head for Arnie's lab.

Izzy is already there and he waves me in as soon as he sees me. "Come on in. You're going to love this, I think."

Arnie is sitting at his desk holding a small plastic plate about the size of a playing card. On top of the card are a series of circles, each one with a red dot in it. "Check it out," he says, handing me the card. I look at it and see that it's a blood typing test. "I've spent all week wading through those two-hundred-plus blood samples we collected from Shannon's house," he says. "And every one of them has tested out as Shannon's blood type."

"Okay," I say slowly, confused as to why this news would interest me.

"Shannon's blood type is A positive but that sample you have in your hand is B negative, which is a very rare type."

"It's not Shannon's blood?"

Arnie grins and shakes his head.

"Where was it found?"

"I pulled it off of one of the glass shards we found in the kitchen."

"So it's most likely the killer's blood?"

"Yep. And here's the part you're really going to like," Arnie adds, his grin getting bigger. "Erik Tolliver's blood type is O positive."

My eyes grow wide.

"And since we can assume the owner of this blood was injured by the glass, it might rule Erik out even more if there were no cuts of any kind found on him when he was arrested."

My heart is leaping with joy; this really is turning out to be my lucky day.

"Have you told anyone else about this yet?" I ask.

"Not yet," Izzy says. "I was going to call Hurley but I thought you'd want to be here when I deliver the news."

"Damn right I do," I say, smiling and rubbing my hands together with glee. "One free dinner coming up, compliments of Hurley. I can hardly wait."

"Don't get too excited," Izzy cautions. "It isn't a full exoneration yet, just a lot of very reasonable doubt. Arnie is going to send the blood sample to Madison for a DNA test and that might give us even more ammunition."

"Might?"

Arnie says, "Well, it was a small sample to begin with and there isn't very much of it left so I'm not sure if they'll be able to get a full profile."

"Still, the blood type alone is something, isn't it?" I ask.

"It is," Izzy agrees.

"Can I tell Lucien about this?"

Izzy shrugs and looks at Arnie, who shrugs back. "I don't see why not," Izzy says. "Why don't you call him and I'll get a hold of Hurley."

I nod eagerly, realizing that for once in my life I'm actually looking forward to talking to Lucien. I take out my cell phone and dial his number, but it flips over to his voice mail. Rather than trying to explain everything on the phone, I leave a brief message to let him know we have discovered some key evidence in the case and ask him to call me back.

Izzy has already finished his call by the time I hang up. "Hurley will be here momentarily," he announces.

I'm excited to hear this, not only because I'm eager to let Hurley know my faith in Erik's innocence was valid, but because it means getting to see him again. I can't wait to pick up where we left off and I figure any time spent near him enhances the chances of that happening.

I dash to the restroom to do some primping in preparation, and pop a breath mint just in case I might get lucky. By the time I come out, I hear Hurley's voice outside Izzy's office and hurry toward it.

As I round the corner high with anticipation, I stop dead in my tracks. Just as I'd hoped, there stands Hurley in the doorway of Izzy's office. But standing beside him, looking doe-eyed, dewy-fresh, and lovely, is Alison Miller.

Chapter
39

Alison looks at me standing in the hallway and smiles. "Hello, Mattie."

Hurley looks too, and I struggle to keep my expression impassive and not let on how badly I want to scratch Alison's eyes out.

"Alison, what are you doing here?" I ask.

"I was with Stevie when Izzy called. I was interviewing him about the Heinrich case." She hooks her arm around Hurley's and leans into him. "When I heard there was something new in Shannon's case, Stevie here was kind enough to let me tag along."

Hurley turns back toward Izzy, forcing Alison to let go of his arm. If she feels at all slighted by his action, she doesn't show it. "So what have you got for me?" Hurley asks.

Izzy fills him in on the blood evidence and then asks if Erik Tolliver had any injuries on his body when he was arrested.

Hurley, who is frowning, shakes his head. "Not a scratch," he admits. He turns to look at me again and the smile he bestows on me makes my irritation with Alison evaporate. "Damn, Winston. It looks like you might have been right about Erik Tolliver after all."

Seeing my chance to put Alison in her place, I smile back and say, "So I guess that means dinner is on you, correct?"

"Looks like it," Hurley says.

Alison's smile disappears faster than a Whack-A-Mole. "Dinner?" she squawks. "What dinner?"

"Oh, it's nothing," I tell her with a dismissive wave of my hand. "Just a little bet Hurley and I had going." I look back at Hurley and smile sweetly. "I'm thinking lobster rather than steak."

"Ouch," he says, smiling in a way that lets me know he doesn't find the idea at all painful. He starts to say something more when his phone rings. He answers it, frowning as he listens. "Okay," he says into the phone. "I'll be right there."

He hangs up looking chagrined. "I have to go. I'll catch you guys later."

Alison falls into step beside him. "Where are we going?" she asks.

Hurley pauses and holds a hand up to stop her. "I'm done for today, Alison. We can finish this up some other time, okay?"

Alison pouts and starts to say something back at him but Hurley doesn't give her a chance. In seconds, he's gone. Alison looks so stricken that for a brief second I feel sorry for her. But then she turns, gives me a flippant little smile, and says, "I guess I'll just have to hook up with him again later." Then she flounces out of the room in Hurley's wake.

I spend the rest of the afternoon in an exceptionally good mood. Between the new evidence exonerating Erik and my pending dinner with Hurley, even sitting in the library and reading up on all the horrible ways people have found to kill one another doesn't dampen my spirits. Nor does the prospect of talking to Lucien when he returns my call.

"What's up, Sweet Cheeks?"

"I have some news for you. We found blood evidence at the scene of Shannon's murder that isn't hers. And it isn't Erik's either."

"Seriously?" Lucien says. "You're not just yanking my chain, are you? I mean, don't get me wrong, there are things on me I'd love to have you yank, but my chain isn't one of them. Unless it was hooked up to my—"

"I'm serious, Lucien," I say, cutting him off. Then, before he has a chance to start up again, I explain what Arnie found with all its implications. When I'm done, I tell him I have to run and hang up, not giving him a chance to thank me in his uniquely sordid way.

I leave the office a little before five and on my way home I stop at the grocery store. Not wanting to attract any unneeded attention with the hearse, I pull into the far side lot where the employees park. Inside the store I grab some cans of tuna for Rubbish, and some fruit, rolls, and chicken salad for myself, managing to pass up the ice cream aisle.

Back outside I unlock the hearse and toss my bag onto the passenger seat. I'm about to get in when I hear a whimper behind me and pause, wondering if I imagined it. But then I hear it again, this time accompanied by an odd scratching sound. I turn to investigate and focus on the back area of the lot where two large Dumpsters sit. Sandwiched between the bins is a dirty, skinny dog that looks to be barely more than a pup. It's standing on its hind legs, clawing at the side of one of the Dumpsters with paws much too big for the rest of him. Its color is a dingy, brownish yellow—though I can't tell how much of that is natural and how much of it is dirt—and I can see ribs protruding through its fur. Its eyes are huge, round, chocolate brown, and the ears are flopped over like a lab's.

As I get closer it sees me and drops down to all fours. I expect it to run away but instead it plops down into an awkward sitting position, hind legs akimbo, revealing that it's a he.

"What's the matter, boy?" I say, slowly moving closer. "You hungry?" He cocks his head at me and whines, his tail thumping a few times. I stop and squat down about ten feet away from him. "Come here, boy."

He thumps his tail a few more times and stands, but doesn't approach. I try coaxing him again and though he looks like he wants to come, he stays put. Deciding I need more of an enticement, I get up, go back to my car, grab the chicken salad I bought, and begin another slow approach. When I pass the point I was at before, he stands and backs up a few steps, so I stop and squat. He stops, too, and wags his tail in a steady rhythm. I can tell he's both hungry and curious so I pop the top on my container of chicken salad and set it on the ground in front of me.

"Come on. Come get a bite. You look like you could use it."

He wags his tail so hard his butt wiggles from side to side. He takes a tentative step forward, ducks his head, pauses, then another step. A minute or two of this and he is only an arm's length away. His nostrils are flaring wildly as he sniffs the chicken salad. I reach for him and he cowers but holds his ground and lets me give him a little scratch behind the ears. I slide the chicken salad an inch or two closer and it's enough to overpower his fear. He closes the last little distance and starts sucking up the food with amazing speed. His efforts inch the container closer to me. By the time it's empty it's nearly touching my feet and the pup's head is between my knees. I stroke the top of his head, and though he flinches, he doesn't back away.

"Good boy," I say softly, petting him gently. He lifts his head from the empty dish, looks at me briefly, and then glances away. He plops his butt down and lets me continue to pet him, but he avoids making eye contact, clearly letting me take on the role of alpha dog.

After a few minutes I stop petting him and he looks at me again, his tail stepping up its rhythm. I pick up the empty container and stand, expecting him to run off, but he stays at my feet. I walk over to the Dumpster and toss the empty container inside. I'm surprised to see the pup has followed and when I turn to head back to my car, he stays on my tail.

When I reach the door to the hearse, the pup sits down at my feet and looks up at me with those huge, chocolate-brown eyes, his rump wiggling with excitement.

"What?" I say, and the rump wiggles faster. "Don't you have a home?" Judging from his condition and the lack of a collar, I doubt he does, and those beseeching eyes are starting to tug at my heartstrings. I consider trying to take him to a nearby shelter but in the back of my mind I worry that if I do, it will be a death sentence for him.

"Okay, here's the deal," I tell him. His butt wiggles with tail-wagging delight. "If you want to come home with me for tonight, you can." His butt moves even faster, as if he understands me. "But it's only temporary, just until I can find you a home, okay?" He bobs his head and pants happily and if I didn't know better, I'd swear he just nodded his agreement.

I turn to open the door to the hearse and faster than I can say "okay," the pup is sitting in the front passenger seat, tongue lolling, his face showing the first light of real happiness.

I slide in behind the wheel and the pup's excitement reaches a tail-wagging crescendo. "Settle down," I tell him, and amazingly he does. "Remember, this is only temporary."

He leans over, nuzzles my ear with his warm, wet nose, and then licks my cheek. It's the most affectionate, nonsexual gesture anyone has shown me in a very long time and it totally melts my heart.

"Crap," I mutter as I start up the engine. "I really need to stay away from garbage Dumpsters."

Chapter
40

I'm a little worried about how Rubbish is going to deal with the addition of this new boarder so I make the pup stay in the car while I carry my groceries inside. Rubbish greets me at the door as usual, winding his way around my feet and purring up a storm. As soon as I set my purchases on the kitchen counter, I scoop Rubbish up, nuzzle him for a few seconds, and then promptly shut him inside my bedroom. Then I go back to the car.

I wonder if the pup will try to run once I let him out but he stays dutifully at my heels and follows me inside without hesitation. I lead him out to the kitchen and give him a bowl of water, which he makes disappear in about five seconds flat. After giving him a refill, I put my groceries away and rummage through the cupboards and fridge for something else to feed him. I figure as hungry as the little guy obviously is, it will be better if I fill him up before he meets Rubbish, lest he try to eat him.

There's not much to offer but I manage to find a couple of hot dogs and some peanut butter. I cut each of the hot dogs into four pieces and then mix them in a bowl with some peanut butter, figuring the gooey consistency will force the pup to eat a little slower. But it has no such effect. The bowl is emptied in ten seconds flat.

"Wow," I say to him as he looks up at me gratefully, licking his chops. "That's impressive. Even I can't suck food up that fast. You're like a vacuum cleaner."

A faint mewing sound emanates from the other room—Rubbish letting me know he wants out. The pup hears it too, and cocks his head from side to side a few times before heading into the living room to investigate. I follow him, watching him track his way to the bedroom door with his nose to the floor. When he reaches it, he sniffs at the crack beneath it, then suddenly jumps back, scared by something.

From beneath the door I see one long furry paw extending into the living room. It feels around a bit, then disappears. It returns seconds later—with the claws pointed upward this time—and wraps itself around the door.

The pup makes a leaping lunge toward the paw and then quickly backs away from it, letting out a yippy bark. His tail is wagging, his ears are pricked, and his eyes are totally focused. Rubbish, clearly not intimidated by the action and noise on the other side of the door, extends his paw even more. I watch the two of them play at this game for a minute or so and then decide it's time for introductions.

I tell the pup, "Sit." I move toward him, expecting I will need to push him into a sitting position so he learns what the word means, but to my amazement, he takes a step back, sits, and looks at me.

Rubbish is still feeling around with his paw, but as soon as I crack the door, he withdraws it and appears at the opening. He looks out at the pup, who looks back at him and then at me. The pup whimpers a little, wags his tail, and starts to get up, but when I tell him to stay, he does. Clearly, judging from his knowledge of basic commands, the dog isn't just a stray. I realize I'll need to do a lost-and-found ad and surprisingly, the idea depresses me. The little furball has already wormed his way into my heart.

Shoving the ad thought aside, I open the bedroom door wider and let Rubbish out. He stands his ground for a minute, studying the new intruder, and even tries a tentative hiss, turning sideways and arching his back. The pup looks from Rubbish to me several times, whimpering in an excited but friendly manner. I repeat the stay command and he does, but it's obvious it's killing him to do so.

Rubbish is curious, too, but seems determined not to show it. He ventures a little closer and then turns away and heads for the kitchen as if he couldn't care less that another furry, four-legged critter is in the house. As soon as Rubbish disappears into the kitchen, I follow, calling the pup to come along with me. This time I let him approach Rubbish, who tolerates a brief butt sniff before turning and smacking the pup across the nose with his paw. Can't say I blame him. I'd probably smack anyone who tried to sniff my butt, too.

Rubbish takes off running and the pup follows. The two of them race into the bathroom, where I hear a familiar *thump-ump* sound. It's Rubbish entering his favorite hiding place: the floor cabinet beneath my sink. I find the pup sitting in front of the cabinet door, his head cocked sideways, staring at it and whining.

I figure that as long as I have the pup in the bathroom, I might as well take advantage of the fact to bathe him. I shut the door to the room, closing all of us inside. Then I start filling the tub.

Fifteen minutes later, both the pup and I are soaked and Rubbish is sitting on top of the sink cabinet rather than in it, looking at us both with disdain. The pup's true color, which is a nice shade of blond that nearly matches my own, is revealed. I towel the dog off and as I'm starting to clean up the water mess, he walks over to the bathroom door and whines. I open it, thinking he just wants out, but he heads for the front door and repeats his behavior. Finally catching on, I walk over and let him out to do his business.

I make a mental note to pick up a collar and leash for him in the morning, though he makes no attempt to wander and returns to the house as soon as he's done. I spend the next fifteen minutes blowing him dry and then shower myself.

Less than an hour later I am in bed, with a furry body cuddled on either side of me. And I have to confess, it feels nice to be sharing my bed again, even if it is with creatures who have four legs instead of three.

Chapter
41

The next morning I let the pup out again to do his business just before I head for work. We run into Izzy, who is backing out of his garage, and he stops and rolls down the window of his car.

"What is that?" he asks, pointing to the dog.

"It's Hoover. I found him last night hanging out by a Dumpster behind the grocery store."

"Hoover?" Izzy repeats.

"Well, yeah. It's only temporary. I don't know what his real name is. But given the way he sucks down food, I thought it appropriate. He was obviously hungry so I fed him and then he sort of insisted that I bring him home."

Izzy shakes his head woefully. "Judging from his output, I'm guessing you fed him a lot."

I look over at Hoover and see him in a grunting squat, his haunches quivering with the effort as he deposits a huge, steaming pile of dog doo-doo in the grass beside the cottage.

"I plan on taking out a lost-and-found ad in the paper. It's only temporary," I say again, worried that Izzy is upset about me having another pet in his cottage.

Having finished his morning ablutions, Hoover runs back to me and sits at my heels, his tail wagging.

Izzy studies the dog a moment and says, "He's cute. And he seems well behaved."

"He is," I say hopefully.

"What are you going to do if no one claims him?"

"I haven't given it much thought." Actually, that's not true. I've given it a lot of thought and sort of hope no one *will* claim him but I'm not about to fess up to that fact. "I don't know," I say with a shrug. "I guess I'll deal with that if and when it happens."

"I see," Izzy says, and I suspect he does. "Are you coming in this morning?"

I nod. "I'm right behind you. But if you don't need me right away I thought I'd stop by Kohler's and take care of the final paperwork for the car."

Izzy's gaze shifts to the hearse and a hint of a smile crosses his face. "No problem," he says, shifting into drive and pulling away slowly. "Just keep your cell handy in case I need to get a hold of you."

"Will do."

I breathe a sigh of relief that Izzy didn't have a major melt-down over the dog and head back inside. I instruct both Hoover and Rubbish to behave and guard the house, give them both an ample supply of food and water, and then head out.

Bobby Keegan comes outside to greet me as I pull into the lot of Kohler's Used Cars. "So what do you think?" he says. "It's in great shape, no?"

"It is," I admit grudgingly. "It seems to run fine and it's quite comfy inside."

"So do we have a deal?"

"I think we do."

He claps his hands together with glee. "Great! Come on inside and we'll finish up the paperwork."

It takes me the better part of forty-five minutes to finalize all the details. When I'm done, I start to head for the office but then decide to take a quick detour instead. After a stop at the bank to replenish my empty wallet, I pull into a strip mall that contains, among other things, a pet store. I head inside and quickly fill up a basket with an assortment of doggie items: a collar, a leash, a spray can of flea and tick repellant, tennis balls, a brush, a chew bone, and a box of treats. I carry the basket up to the counter and set it down, then head back into the aisles for a bag of dog food. I toss a twenty-pound sack over my shoulder and when I pass a stack of stuffed doggie pillows on my way back to the register, I grab the top one by the corner and drag that with me, too. My mind keeps telling me I'm insane since there's a good chance Hoover belongs to someone and I may lose him in a matter of days. But I'm in total denial.

Close to a hundred dollars later, I load the dog food and the pillow into the back of the hearse and toss the bag containing my other treasures into the passenger seat up front. Just as I start the engine, my cell rings. I see from the caller ID that it's Izzy and my first thought is that he somehow knows where I am and is about to lecture me on the foolishness of spending money I can't afford on a dog that I likely won't be able to keep.

"Hey, Izzy," I say, answering the phone. "I finally got everything tied up with the car and I'm heading your way." It's the truth in essence, even if I am leaving out a few significant details. In case he knows where I am at the moment, I don't want to lie and say I'm just leaving the used car lot, but if he doesn't know, I see no reason to clue him in, either.

"We have a death over on King Street," he says, and I breathe a sigh of relief. "It's an elderly person and probably a natural, but we have to investigate. Want to meet me there?"

"Sure." He gives me the exact address and I plot a course through town that takes me along Hanover Avenue toward King Street. I'm halfway there when I come up on the Johnson Funeral Home, which is located on the corner of Hanover and Chestnut, another well traveled street. Apparently there is a funeral in progress because just ahead of me I see a hearse pull out of the funeral home parking lot onto Hanover and then make a quick turn down Chestnut. Two more cars follow before I catch up, putting me momentarily in the midst of the procession. Apparently my presence causes some confusion because rather than turning onto Chestnut, the remaining cars all fall into line behind me. It takes a couple of blocks before I look in my rearview mirror and realize what's happening.

I try to shoo the cars away by waving my hand in the air but the driver of the car immediately behind me merely waves back. So I roll my side window down and try more hand gestures, but to no avail. Half a mile later I turn onto King Street with a fourteen-car entourage at my heels.

There is an ambulance parked in front of the house along with two cop cars. I see the EMTs and two uniformed officers standing on the front porch of the house. As I pull up and park behind one of the squad cars, the cars behind me start pulling to the curb as well. In less than a minute, both sides of the street are filled with parked cars going back an entire block.

I climb out of the hearse and head back to the first car in the funeral procession to inform them of their mistake. But before I can get to them, an unmarked sedan pulls up with Hurley at the helm. And right behind him is our office van with Izzy in the passenger seat and Arnie driving. They stop in the middle of the street since there's nowhere else to park, and Hurley gets out of his car in a huff, looking annoyed.

"What the hell are all these lookie-loos doing here?" he asks me, shooting an angry look at the cops on the porch. "Don't those uniforms know their job?" He starts toward the clueless cops looking like he wants to rip them both a new one, so I stop him by grabbing his arm.

"Hurley, hold up a sec. These people aren't lookie-loos. They followed me here and those cops had no idea they were coming."

"They followed you?" he repeats. "What, you have a fan club now?"

"No, it's this stupid car," I say, gesturing to the menace behind me. "I drove into the middle of a funeral procession and it confused some of the drivers. They followed me instead of sticking with the rest of the motorcade."

Hurley looks from me to the cars and back to me again. Izzy, who has rolled down the window in his van and overheard our conversation, is trying vainly to suppress a smirk. Several of the drivers in the funeral procession have rolled down their windows as well, including the car directly behind me.

Hurley says, "They think this is a funeral?"

"My thoughts exactly," the guy in the car behind me snaps. "What kind of Mickey Mouse operation is this, anyway? Are we burying Charlie in somebody's backyard?"

"Who the hell is Charlie?" Hurley asks, sotto voce.

"I'm guessing he would be the deceased," I surmise. I make a sweeping gesture toward all the parked cars. "And they all think he's in the back of my hearse."

Funeral Guy hears this and says, "You mean he's not in there? What the hell did you do with him?" He gets out of his car, walks up to the back of mine and peers through the window, then turns and storms toward us, making me back up a few steps. Judging from his physique, I'm pretty sure Funeral Guy is a weightlifter on steroids. His thigh muscles are so big he walks like he just came in from a month of riding herd on his cattle. His arms are slightly extended because he can't put them down at his sides and his biceps look like they are about to burst out of the sleeves of his suit. He's almost as tall as Hurley, and judging from the way his fists keep opening and closing, I'm guessing his patience will burn out quicker than a magician's flash paper.

"Sir, you need to calm down," Hurley says, planting a hand on the man's chest to stop his approach. "There's been some confusion here."

Funeral Guy's face is the color of a ripe plum and I'm guessing his blood pressure is rising faster than a retiree on Viagra. "Damned right," he grumbles. "Where's the casket? Where the hell is Charlie's body?"

"You followed the wrong car," Hurley tries to explain calmly. "There isn't any body here."

"Well, technically there is," I toss out, earning an exasperated glance from Hurley. "Just not the one you think."

Funeral Guy looks momentarily confused, then the one brain cell that wasn't killed off by the steroids finally fires. "What the fuck!" he yells, his voice resonating like thunder. "You assholes put the wrong body in Charlie's casket?"

"No, sir," I say quickly, trying to ameliorate the misunderstanding. "That's not what I meant at all. There is no casket. The body I'm talking about is in that house over there. The body you want is—"

"You dumped Charlie in a house? You sonofabitchingcocksuckingbastards!"

Before I can so much as blink, Funeral Guy rears back and plants his fist in Hurley's cheek with a sickening, bone-crunching *thunk*. Out of the corner of my eye I see one of the policemen and both EMTs leap off the porch and start running toward us. Hurley staggers sideways and then crumples to the ground. I let out a little yelp and start to head for him to see if he's okay, but Funeral Guy stands like an incensed bull between us and his attention is now focused on me.

I backpedal quickly, stealing a glance at the cop and EMTs heading my way. I can tell they aren't going to make it in time, and judging from the crazed look on Funeral Guy's face, the time for calm persuasion came and went some time ago. I turn, grab the handle to my car door, and p it open. I dive across the seat and quickly turn to try to grab t.. door to close it, but Funeral Guy is too quick for me. He catches the top of the door in one of his meaty hands and yanks it wide open. Realizing that the idiot could kill me, I look around frantically for something I can use to forestall him until the cop gets to me. As Funeral Guy grabs hold of my leg and starts to pull me from the car, I let out a blood-curdling scream, kick him with my free foot, and then fire off the only weapon I can find.

"Arrgghhh!" Funeral Guy screams, releases my leg, and clamps his hands over his eyes. "What the fuck!" He backpedals away from my car and straight into the arms of a uniformed police officer. "My eyes! My eyes!"

Hurley gets up from the ground, massaging his jaw, and makes his way over to me. "You okay?" he asks.

I nod.

"I didn't know you carried pepper spray."

"I don't. It's flea and tick repellant."

Hurley starts to smile but it fades to a grimace as he massages his jaw again. "I'd say he's been successfully repelled," he says. "Serves the bastard right."

Chapter
42

A second patrol car arrives and Funeral Guy is cuffed and hauled off to jail. It takes me a good ten minutes to explain to the other funeral attendees what has happened and to direct them back through the streets to the cemetery. Some of them are angered by the snafu, one guy is amused, and the others simply look embarrassed.

As soon as Funeral Guy is safely away, Izzy and Arnie get out of the office van and follow Hurley into the house with the corpse.

By the time I join them, Izzy is on the phone and Hurley and Arnie are standing in the living room staring at the dead man, who is sitting in a recliner. The man's face is pasty white and his hands, which are hanging at his sides, are swollen and purple with lividity, as are his feet. He looks peaceful, though very dead, and I'm guessing he's been this way for several hours.

"Who is Izzy talking to?" I ask Hurley.

"His physician," he answers, nodding toward the corpse. "A neighbor told one of the cops that the old guy was a ticking time bomb and it was simply a matter of time before he cashed in his chips."

"Who found him?"

"The same neighbor. Apparently he and Dead Guy have

breakfast together every day. When Dead Guy didn't show, the neighbor came in to check on him and found him like this."

Izzy hangs up his phone and turns to address the rest of us. "In addition to diabetes, he had an extensive cardiac history that included three myocardial infarctions, CHF, and an ejection fraction of fifteen percent."

"In layman's terms?" Hurley says, wincing and massaging his jaw.

"Basically he's been a dead man walking for several months. Judging from what we know and what we can see here, I think it's safe to say this was a natural death."

"Okay, then," Hurley says, wincing again. "We're out of here."

"You need to get that looked at," I tell Hurley, watching him rub the now faintly discolored area on his jaw.

"I'm fine," he grumbles. "The guy just caught me off guard."

Realizing Hurley's male pride has been damaged, I say, "Yeah, who knew he was going to go nuts like that?"

Hurley eyes me warily, and I suspect he's trying to determine if I'm busting on him or serious.

"I think he had 'roid rage," I continue. "That kind of physique isn't found in nature. It had to have come from steroid abuse. And the strength it can give people is frightening." I reach up and gently palpate along Hurley's jawline. He has a day's worth of beard stubble that is surprisingly soft, and as I move my fingers over his cheek I can feel the muscles beneath my hand twitching. He is watching me intently, and though I can feel his gaze on me, I don't return it. I'm afraid of what I'll say or do if I become entranced by those soft pools of blue.

Arnie clears his throat and says, "Should we get you two a room?"

Izzy snorts a laugh and I drop my hand from Hurley's face. After shooting a death-ray look at Arnie, I tell Hurley, "I don't feel any obvious fractures but you have quite a bit of swelling and bruising there. You should probably have it X-rayed."

I leave the room and head out to the dead man's kitchen, where I open a few drawers and, after finding what I want, head for the freezer. A moment later I return to the living room with a plastic baggie full of ice cubes wrapped in paper towels and hand it to Hurley. "Put this on your cheek," I tell him. "It will help reduce the pain and swelling."

He takes the baggie, does as I instructed, and says, "Thank you." His voice is soft and tender and I don't think it's all because of his jaw. The way he is looking at me makes my skin hot and my toes curl.

I realize Izzy and Arnie are already outside, meaning Hurley and I are alone together . . . well, that is if you don't count the dead guy. It seems most of my moments with Hurley occur near a dead body, hardly the best setting for a romantic interlude. I head outside and join Arnie and Izzy at the van.

"Are you coming back to the office?" Izzy asks. I nod. "Try not to bring a crowd with you, okay?" he adds with a twinkle in his eye.

"Ha, ha." I head back for the hearse and as soon as Arnie pulls out, I fall in behind him. Hurley is still inside the house and I mourn the fact that I'm leaving him there, vulnerable and alone. Then I curse the fact that the dead keep interfering with my love life.

Back at the office, I settle into the library with a forensic textbook and spend some time reading about the analysis of stab wounds. It's fascinating stuff but I'm still glad when my cell phone rings and offers me a break from the grim reality of how much damage sharp penetrating objects can do to the human body. A quick look at my caller ID tells me it's Carla Andrusson calling.

"Hi, Carla."

"Hi, Mattie."

"How did it go?"

"I don't know. Like all the other times, I guess. I did what you said." Her voice sounds oddly flat and devoid of emotion.

"Good. Thank you. Can I come by now to pick up the equipment?"

"Sure."

I hang up, stop by Izzy's office to let him know I'm going to run a quick errand, and then head for Carla's house. She greets me at the door and smiles, but it comes across as a plastic, social nicety, an expression worn solely for appearance' sake.

"Thanks again for doing this, Carla," I say as she waves me in and leads me to the kitchen.

"Sure." She sounds and looks like a Stepford Wife.

"Are you okay?" I ask, seriously concerned.

"Of course." She flashes the plastic smile again. "Why do you ask?"

"I don't know. You seem different somehow. Subdued. Not your usual self."

She waves away my concern. "I'm just a little tired. My nerves kept me awake last night worrying about this appointment today."

"Sorry."

"Don't be. It's done now." She hands over the digital recording device I gave her yesterday—the one Izzy gave me for recording my observations at death scenes. "I kept it in my purse during the appointment so I'm pretty sure Dr. Nelson didn't suspect anything," she says.

"Did you listen to it?" I ask. I know I would have found it close to impossible not to do so had our roles been reversed. My curiosity is insatiable. It's not that I can't keep a secret; I can and do all the time, and will probably take several of them to my grave. But I hate being out of the loop.

She doesn't hesitate at all with her answer. "No. I figured I'd leave that up to you. You will let me know what you find, won't you?"

"When I can," I say evasively. Truth is, anything I hear on the recorder will probably be inadmissible as evidence. I didn't have her do it to gather evidence but rather to bolster—or dismiss—my own suspicions about the man. But if I do find something that might be usable, sharing that information too soon might compromise the investigation.

I'm eager to get back to the office and listen to whatever Carla recorded on the device, but I don't want to seem too rude or ungrateful, so I force myself to be social and take a sip of the coffee she pours for me. Shockingly, it is ice cold.

As I spit it back into the cup, Carla looks at me with that flat smile and says, "Is it too strong?"

"No, it's cold."

She blinks her eyes several times very rapidly. "Silly me," she says in a goofy manner that seems very unlike the Carla I know. "I must have forgotten to turn the burner on." For just a second her smile fades. She rubs both her temples and looks momentarily frightened and confused. But the change is fleeting and the smile is pasted back in place so quickly I start to wonder if I imagined it.

"I'm going to head back to my office now, Carla," I say, getting up from the table. "Call me if you need anything, okay?"

She laughs and there is a hint of the old Carla in the sound. "Let's hope I don't need what you have to offer," she says.

I thank her again for helping me and leave, but as I drive away I keep replaying the scene at her house over and over again in my mind. Her behavior was disturbing, and while something about it nudges at my brain, I can't quite pull out the message my subconscious is trying to send.

I arrive back at the office and plan to head straight for the library to listen to the recording. But in the main lobby I run into a crowd. Cass is seated at her desk and today she is dressed as a punk rocker complete with spiked, purple hair, striped tights, Doc Martens, an oversized shirt, and lots of piercings I assume are fake since I'm pretty sure she didn't have any holes in those places before. Standing in front of the desk are Izzy, Aaron Heinrich, and Hurley, whose cheek looks more colorful but a little less swollen.

"There she is," Aaron says, turning to greet me. He flashes his thousand-watt smile and leans back against Cass's desk.

Izzy says, "Aaron stopped by to thank us for the work we did investigating his father's death. And he also wanted to know if it would be allowable for him to ask you out for dinner, now that the case is closed."

"Dinner?" I say stupidly, caught off guard by the invite.

Izzy says, "There're no conflict-of-interest considerations any-more."

If looks could kill, Izzy would be reclined on one of the back tables right now judging from the way Hurley is glaring at him. Izzy appears not only oblivious, but amused.

Aaron says, "Change of plans. I thought we could head down to Chicago instead of Green Bay. I know some great restaurants and there's a show in town I'd like to see. So what do you say, Mattie? Will you do me the honor of joining me tonight?"

I consider the invitation for a moment and my hesitation wins Izzy a momentary reprieve from his death sentence because Hurley focuses his glare on me instead. His attempts at intimidation annoy me, making me want to dish a little back. But I'm not sure I'm ready to go on a date with Aaron.

"I'd love to," I say, smiling at Aaron. I swear the thunder-clouds on Hurley's face make the barometric pressure in the room drop precipitously. "But I can't do it tonight."

Aaron looks disappointed but he brightens quickly when I add, "Perhaps another time?"

"Sure," he says. "Give me your phone number and I'll call you later and set something up." He pulls a pen from his jacket pocket, turns around to take a slip of paper from Cass, and then looks back at me expectantly with pen poised.

I figure the phone number thing is a safe bet since, in my experience, most men who say they'll call never do. Plus, I'm abiding by Rule Number Seven in Mother's Rules for Wives: men are like mascara—they run at the first hint of emotion, so try to keep them guessing. Giving my number to Aaron should keep Hurley guessing, or at least squirming, for a while. There is one teensy problem, however: I don't know my own number. As I open my phone and start scrolling through menus to find it, Aaron laughs.

"Is your phone number top secret?" he asks.

"Not exactly," I say with a grimace of a smile, hoping I don't look too stupid. "Izzy wrote it down for me once but since I never call myself and the key people who need it already have it, I haven't managed to memorize the number yet."

I see Hurley shift uncomfortably and presume it's because my implication—that Aaron is now about to become a "key" person—isn't sitting well with him. Izzy is grinning from ear to ear.

"Oh, hell," Hurley grumbles. "I'll give it to you." He rattles off a string of ten numbers, which Aaron scribbles down and then tucks away into his pocket.

Whoa. I didn't see that coming and, frankly, the fact that Hurley would so glibly pass out my number to a potential rival annoys me. I thought our history of a spontaneous kiss or two and what might be construed as a second base hit in the parking lot of the Nowhere Bar meant he felt something for me. Now I'm not so sure.

"Thanks, man," Aaron says.

Hurley just nods. His scowl is gone and in fact, he looks downright chipper. I focus on keeping my expression neutral, hoping not to show how devastated I am by his actions.

"Yes, thanks, Hurley," I echo, snapping my phone shut. "That was very sweet of you."

"Anytime. Now if you folks will excuse me, I have some business to tend to." With that, Hurley strides across the lobby and out the front door.

"I'm sure you folks have things to do as well," Aaron says, "so I guess I'll be going too. I'll give you a call in a day or two, Mattie."

"Sure. Okay." I try to force a smile onto my face but it isn't easy. On the inside, I'm one hormone release away from crying. Aaron walks over, gives me a quick buss on the cheek, and then follows Hurley's path to the parking lot.

"Very interesting," Izzy says as soon as the front door closes.

He is still grinning and I give him a hurtful look. "I'm so happy my agony amuses you," I whine.

"Agony? Why are you in agony? You have two incredibly handsome, eligible bachelors interested in you. I should think you'd be dancing."

"Apparently Hurley doesn't give a crap who I date," I pout. "He was more than happy to help the matchmaking along. And I doubt Aaron is seriously interested. I know his type. They like to play with a new toy every week or so. I doubt I'll ever hear from him."

"I doubt it, too," Izzy agrees. "Especially since Hurley gave him the wrong number."

I settle into the library, which is empty, and shut myself inside. I'm not sure if Hurley wanted me to know what he was doing when he gave out my number but the fact that I do has boosted my spirits considerably. Now all I have to do is decide whether or not to let him know that I know.

Putting those thoughts aside, I take out the recorder I retrieved from Carla and start playing it back. At first it seems pretty routine. I hear Nelson talking to Carla, offering her a cup of her favorite hot tea, and reviewing what they discussed at their last session. I feel a twinge of guilt, knowing how private this discussion is meant to be. Even though Carla has given me permission to listen to it, I still feel a little slimy doing so. Carla discusses the fact that she and her husband have been sleeping in separate bedrooms for several months, and when Nelson asks her how she feels about that, she offers up a one-word answer: "frustrated."

Less than a minute later, just as I'm beginning to doubt my motives and hate myself for what I'm doing, the tone of the session takes a dramatic shift. Carla's voice becomes slurred and muted. I hear Nelson call softly to her but her only response is a grunt. And then all I can hear are background noises; rustling, a sliding sound, a wet sound, heavy breathing, and more grunting. After a few minutes there is an odd, rhythmic noise followed by a distinctly male sound that is unmistakable.

I'm sitting on the edge of my seat now, my ear glued to the recorder. I start to feel ill and swallow hard, glad I haven't eaten anything. The only sounds I can hear on the tape are more rustling and an occasional exertional type grunt. Then there are several minutes of relative silence where all I can hear are two people breathing.

Finally, some forty-five minutes into the session, I hear Nelson call to Carla again and this time she answers. Then they pick up their conversation where it left off.

I turn the recorder off and sit stunned for a moment, considering what I just heard. Suddenly Carla's odd demeanor starts to make horrifying sense. I toss the recorder into my jacket pocket and quickly head for the parking lot.

Less than five minutes later I'm at Carla's house but she doesn't answer when I ring the bell. I peek through her garage windows and see that her car is gone. Frantic, I pull out my cell phone, ready to call Hurley. But before I can dial, the phone rings. It's Izzy.

"Hello?" I answer impatiently.

"Where are you?" Izzy asks. He sounds a bit testy himself and I can't say I blame him since I didn't tell him I was leaving the office.

"I had an errand to run," I say vaguely. "Sorry, I forgot to tell you."

"Well, drop whatever you're doing. We have a death to investigate and I figure you'll want in on this one since it's at the office of that shrink you dislike so much."

Chapter 43

I drive the hearse as fast as I can toward Luke Nelson's office. I'm in a state of panic and kicking myself for believing Carla when she told me she hadn't listened to the tape and not recognizing the meaning behind her mood change. Of course she listened to the tape. How could she not? I'd been a fool to believe her.

Now I fear she has killed Luke Nelson, and while I am no fan of the man, particularly after what I heard on the tape, I feel somewhat responsible.

The usual crowd of onlookers and emergency vehicles are already on the scene and the entrance to Nelson's office is being guarded by a uniformed police officer. There are two ambulances parked out front. One of them is empty and I assume the EMTs are inside, but the crew for the other rig is lounging around outside their rig.

I pull in behind the loungers and as I get out of my car, one of the EMTs says, "You're a bit premature, aren't you?"

I know most of the EMTs in town from working at the hospital, but this guy is a new face. I give him a puzzled look and say, "Why do you say that? Isn't there a death here?"

"Well, yeah," he says in a manner that makes it clear *dumbass* should follow. I adore our local EMTs but this newbie clearly has a bit of an attitude. "But the ME's office hasn't even arrived yet so I don't think they're going to let you take the body."

"I *am* the ME's office," I tell him, using my own *you nitwit* inflection.

He looks confused for a moment and glances from me to my car and then back to me again. And suddenly I understand. I keep forgetting that my car is now a hearse.

"That's a little tasteless, isn't it?" he says, nodding toward the car.

Newbie has picked the wrong time to screw with me. "You want to know what's tasteless, buddy?" I snap at him. "Tasteless is hanging around a crime scene when you're obviously not needed just so you can gawk at the dead bodies. Now why don't you get your ass out of here? Your village is missing its idiot."

Newbie looks stunned by my outburst, causing me a nanosecond of regret before my larger misgivings take priority. As Newbie backs away from me and climbs into his rig, Izzy pulls up and parks behind my hearse. My guilt over Carla must be apparent because as soon as Izzy gets out of his car, he says, "What's wrong?"

"I think it may be my fault that Luke Nelson is dead," I tell him sotto voce.

"He's not," he says, closing his car door and heading for Nelson's office. This response is so far from what I expected, I'm rendered speechless. I fall in behind him and, because the length of my one stride equals nearly three of his and I'm so wildly distracted by all the questions racing through my mind, I nearly run him over twice along the way.

Even though I now have reason to believe the world would be a much better place if Nelson wasn't in it, I'm relieved he isn't dead. Not only because of my own guilt but because I want to see him suffer. Death would be much too easy an escape for him.

I start to relax a little when I realize I've jumped to some pretty incongruous conclusions about Carla. I assumed that if she wasn't home, she would be here. But she could be anywhere. Maybe she didn't listen to the tape after all. Maybe her strange attitude earlier really was due to a lack of sleep, like she said.

As we enter the office's anteroom, I see Hurley standing just inside the far door that leads to Nelson's office area, staring grimly into the room where Nelson sees his patients. Off in the corner to my left, three EMTs are huddled around someone in a chair. I push past Izzy, taking care to avoid the trail of bloody footprints I can see leading from the office into the anteroom, and take a stand beside Hurley, who acknowledges me with a quick glance. Then I look into the counseling room.

Reclined on the sofa is Carla Andrusson—at least I think it's Carla since the build and distinctive hair color look like hers and the clothing matches what I saw her wearing earlier. But the face is unrecognizable, misshapen and covered with gore. There is blood everywhere—on the walls, the ceiling, the carpet, the sofa, the chair—and one of Carla's arms is hanging off the sofa, her hand cupped on the floor, pooled with blood. Inches away from her hand lies a mean-looking gun, and a nasty, acrid smell that I now know is a combination of blood and gunpowder, permeates the air.

My initial instinct is to dash into the room and check her for vital signs. But I quickly realize it would be a waste of time. I feel sick as my hope that Carla had nothing to do with this shatters into pieces.

Izzy steps up beside us and takes in the scene.

Hurley turns to us as if to say something, but then hesitates, staring at me intently. "Are you okay?" he asks, looking concerned. Then he backs away from me. "You're not going to puke on my shoes again, are you?"

I shake my head.

"What's the story?" Izzy asks.

"According to the shrink, that's Carla Andrusson, one of his patients. Apparently she busted in here carrying a gun and went off on the doc about the awful state of her marriage, and how hopeless her life was. Then she shot at the doc before turning the gun on herself."

"She shot Nelson?" I ask.

Hurley nods.

"Where is he?"

Hurley gestures toward the anteroom and I step back to look out the way I came. I see now that the patient the EMTs are tending to is Luke Nelson. He looks pale and shaky, and there is a blood-soaked bandage around his left arm, but he appears otherwise fine.

Izzy says, "Well, I guess we best get to it." He sets down his scene case and then dons a biohazard suit, goggles, and gloves. When he realizes I'm not dressing for duty he says, "You coming?"

"In a sec. I need to talk to Hurley first."

As Izzy makes his way into the room, I turn and speak to Hurley in a low voice. "This is all my fault."

"*Your* fault? How do you figure?"

"Carla was helping me with something and we . . . um . . . sort of discovered something about Nelson."

"Such as?"

"You have to hear it."

"Hear it?" Hurley says, looking confused. "From whom?"

I start to tell him but I'm interrupted by the sound of Nelson's voice behind me.

"This is an awful thing," he says. "Clearly I missed something. I didn't think she was suicidal. I feel so responsible."

I whirl around and find myself face-to-face with the creep. "Of course you're responsible, you snake. What did you expect? You—"

I'm cut off when Hurley grabs my arm and pulls me back. "Mattie, what the hell?" he hisses.

At the same time, one of the EMTs says to Nelson, "Sir, you really need to go to the hospital to get checked out. Even though the bullet only grazed your arm, you might need a couple of stitches. And your blood pressure is extremely high. You need something to lower it."

"A couple of deep slices across your throat ought to do it," I toss out angrily.

"Damn it, Mattie," Hurley says. He yanks me by the arm to

the far corner of the room, positioning himself between me and Nelson. He grabs me by the shoulders using his body to block my view of the others, but I can hear the EMTs walking Nelson back out to the anteroom. Hurley turns and shuts the door behind them before shifting his focus back to me. "What the hell has gotten into you?" he asks. His tone is more concerned than angry but I can tell he is a little peeved.

When I look up at him, I manage to calm myself some, momentarily afloat in the serene blue depths of his eyes. His body is so close I can feel the heat radiating from him, and a part of me wants to collapse into him, have him wrap his arms around me, and just stay there. Forever. But I'm too sick with disgust, guilt, and sadness to do anything but sag against the wall beneath the weight of his hands.

"Nelson is a sick, perverted bastard," I tell him. "He was drugging Carla Andrusson and having sex with her during her appointments without her knowing it. And if he was doing it to her, I'm betting he was doing it to others, too."

Hurley's eyebrows shoot up nearly to his hairline. "And you know this how, exactly?"

"I have it on tape."

"You have videotape of Nelson having sex with drugged patients." It isn't a question, but rather a statement, made with more than an innuendo of skepticism. I'm not sure if his doubt is due to disbelief or shock, but either way, it's partially justified.

"No, not videotape. It's audio."

Hurley closes his eyes and shakes his head as if he's trying to rattle something in there loose. "Let me see if I've got this right," he says, dropping his hands from my shoulders. I miss the warmth of them immediately. "You have a tape of the *sound* of Nelson having sex with a drugged patient?"

"Yes, with Carla."

"How can you tell she's drugged? And how can you be sure what you're hearing is the sound of sex?" I start to answer but he doesn't let me get a syllable out. "And even if you're sure that's what it is, how do you know it wasn't consensual? How do we know who exactly is making the noises? Do they announce themselves on the tape? And just how the hell did you get your hands on something like that in the first place?"

I realize he's going to be pissed when I tell him what I did. Worse yet, I'm afraid I might have compromised any case we have against Nelson since the tape likely can't be used as legal evidence.

I see movement from the corner of my eye and see Izzy standing in the doorway to the counseling room eavesdropping on our discussion. And that's when I wonder if my foolishness might also cost me my job.

Belatedly I see the ramifications of what I've done, and the very steep price I might have to pay for my dogged suspicions of Nelson and my half-baked plot to catch him out. Though it's chump change compared to Carla's cost. With this one single act I may have let a killer go free, ruined a handful of lives, and lost my job, Hurley's respect, and Izzy's friendship. I can tell tonight is going to be a two-carton session with Ben and Jerry.

I take the recorder out of my purse and hand it to Hurley. "I met with Carla Andrusson yesterday to talk with her about Nelson and his alibi. And in the course of doing that, I discovered that something about her sessions seemed wrong. Carla thought so too, though she didn't know why. So I convinced her to take my recorder along in her purse. It taped her entire session."

Hurley squeezes his eyes closed and pinches the bridge of his nose. "Why would you do that?" he asks. His question has the same ring to it my mother has when she asks me why I'm divorcing David: abject disappointment.

"I've had the sense all along that something is wrong with that guy," I tell him. "And I was right. The tape proves it."

"Not in any way we can use in court," he counters. He looks at me with a pitiful expression that makes me want to cry. The last thing I want Hurley to feel for me is pity. "Did Carla listen to the tape before she handed it over to you?" he asks.

"She said she didn't," I tell him. "But in hindsight . . . well . . ."

There's no need to complete the thought because the bloody

scene in the next room says it all. I hang my head in shame and tears start to burn behind my eyeballs.

"What's your verdict, Izzy?" Hurley asks.

At first I think he's asking Izzy to pass judgment on me and my stupidity, and maybe he is. But judging from the answer, it's obvious Izzy thinks Hurley is asking about Carla.

"Too soon to tell," he says with a shrug. "The location and angle of the head wound and the stippling around it don't rule out suicide. I'll have to take a look at Nelson's wounds to determine if that part of the story holds up, and of course I'll know more once I complete my autopsy, but for now Nelson's version of the events fits the evidence."

"But there is one part of his story that doesn't fit," I say. "If Carla did listen to the tape and came here with a gun, I don't think it was her marriage she was upset about."

I take things a few steps further, desperate to redeem myself in any small way. "What if Shannon found out what he was doing? That would give him a motive to kill her. And if he was drugging his patients with something that allowed him to have sex with them without them knowing about it, he could also have left his office during any one of those appointments without the patients knowing. That negates his alibis."

"What kind of drug would do that?" Hurley asks. "I would assume he'd need something that can be given orally."

"On the tape I heard him offer Carla a cup of tea and it's about fifteen minutes after that when her speech starts to slur."

Izzy jumps in. "There are several hypnotics that are fast-acting and quickly processed that would produce short-term sedation and anterograde amnesia: midazolam, Zaleplon, ketamine, or GHB."

Hurley considers this. "Can we test for those?"

Izzy grimaces. "You can, but it would have to be shortly after ingestion. Most of these drugs metabolize pretty quickly." He looks at me. "When was Carla's appointment?"

"Early this morning."

"Then we might get lucky."

"We still have the issue of the gun that killed Shannon," Hurley says. "We know it belonged to Erik and it was found at the hospital in the department where Erik works."

"That's easy," I tell him. "Nelson was dating Shannon so he would have had access to the gun, which was in Shannon's house. And as a doctor, he has free rein to go anywhere he wants in the hospital. Nelson could have easily planted that gun where you found it, knowing it would implicate Erik."

Hurley nods thoughtfully and then says, "I guess I need to have more of a chat with the doctor." He turns and opens the door to the anteroom, and Izzy and I follow him out. The EMTs are gathering up their supplies and preparing to leave. Nelson is nowhere in sight.

"Where's your patient?" Hurley asks the EMTs.

"He declined any further treatment," one of them answers. "So we had him sign a waiver and he lit out of here."

"You let him leave?" Hurley says, clearly pissed.

The EMT shrugs. "No one said we needed to detain him. Not that that's our job anyway," he adds pointedly.

"Damn it!" Hurley mutters. He takes out his cell phone, dials a number, and then starts barking out instructions.

Izzy and I head back into the office area and before I get bloodied up by the body, I decide to have a look around Nelson's office. I don a pair of gloves and start going through the drawers of his desk. Though I'm still feeling morose and stupid for what I did, I can see a bit of hope on the horizon. Hurley has the tape and even if it isn't admissible as evidence, it at least validates my suspicions and accusations. If Carla tests positive for some type of sedating drug, that might be evidence we can use legally. And I realize that whatever drug Nelson used on his patients had to come from somewhere, so maybe we can track that and use it as evidence, as well. So all isn't lost. We might nail the bastard yet.

Assuming, of course, that Hurley can find him.

Chapter
44

While Izzy processes the scene in the consulting room, I opt to remain in the office area. I don't think I can bring myself to look at Carla's corpse yet so I continue going through Nelson's desk, pulling files from his drawers and flipping through them. I'm alone with my thoughts trying unsuccessfully to focus on the files, when Hurley, who disappeared half an hour or so ago, returns with Alison in tow. My mood is dark enough as it is, and Alison's presence doesn't help the matter any, especially when she starts rubbing up against Hurley.

"It's a bit inappropriate for her to be here, isn't it?" I say to Hurley.

Before he can answer, Alison pipes up with "Oh, I'm not here as a reporter. The police station is a bit short-staffed right now so they hired me on as a freelance photographer to help out for a while."

I look questioningly at Hurley, who nods and shrugs. I'm not happy with this turn of events and I suspect Alison knows why. Not only don't I trust her not to use the pictures for the paper, it gives her more excuses to spend time around Hurley.

After flashing me a smug smile, she takes her camera in hand and starts shooting pictures of Nelson's office. Apparently Hurley has his doubts about her trustworthiness, too, because he warns her, "Remember, Alison, none of the pictures you take here can be used in the paper unless they're cleared by me first. Understood?"

After Alison nods, Hurley heads for the front of the office, leaving me alone with her while Izzy works on Carla's body in the next room. I'm sorting through some files in Nelson's desk drawer when Alison starts snapping pictures of me.

"I can't believe all the death we've had here in town lately," she says. She pauses and cocks her head at me. "Ever since you took your job at the ME's office, Mattie, it seems people are dropping like flies."

I'd like to drop her at the moment, out a twentieth-story window.

"Or maybe," I counter, "it's just that you're more aware of the deaths now that you're following Hurley around like a bitch in heat."

She smiles but there's no warmth to it. "Aw, are you jealous?" she taunts.

"Not at all," I say, smiling back with matching iciness. I suspect half of Alison's interest in Hurley is simply her desire to take a jab at me. As a reporter, it's her job to be provocative and trigger emotional outbursts. It makes for good pictures and good copy. I figure if I feign disinterest, maybe she'll move on to something, or someone else.

"Are you saying you have no interest in Hurley?" she asks.

I focus on the files I have stacked on the desk, not wanting to meet her gaze when I lie to her. "None at all," I say with great nonchalance.

"Then you won't mind if I make a move."

"Have at it," I say with a shrug. "Hurley is just a toy to pass the time with. I have no romantic designs on him whatsoever. In fact, I'm dating someone else right now. I'm having dinner with Aaron Heinrich."

This isn't altogether true since I haven't actually accepted Aaron's invitation, but I'm banking on Alison not knowing that.

I hear someone clear their throat and know from the masculine sound of it that it isn't Alison. When I look up expecting to see

Izzy, I see Hurley instead, standing in the doorway, staring at me with a wounded expression. Panic sets in as I wonder how long he was there and how much he heard.

"Hurley, I—"

His cell phone rings, cutting me off. He answers with a brusque "Hurley here," and then listens for a minute. When he hangs up he turns away from me and addresses his remarks to Alison.

"It seems our Dr. Nelson has flown the coop," he says tersely. "I've had the office issue a statewide APB on him so we'll get him eventually." He looks back at me then, his expression cold. "I listened to the tape and you were right. It's obvious what was going on. But I'm afraid it's not going to be usable for evidence given how it was obtained."

"I'm sorry, I didn't think things through very well," I say, trying to convey my apologies for more than just the tape.

He stares at me for several seconds and as I struggle to read his face I try to communicate volumes with my own. Then he says, "I'm outa here. I'll leave a couple of uniforms behind to help you with the evidence." And just like that, he's gone.

Alison raises her camera and snaps a picture of me, one I pray won't show the disappointment and hurt I'm feeling. Then she smiles. "Wait for me, Stevie," she yells over her shoulder. "I need some quotes for the paper." She flounces out of the room, leaving me angry and alone.

I spend some time shuffling the files around but I'm too upset to focus: upset with Alison but even more upset with myself. I'm relieved when the Keller Funeral Home shows up to load Carla's body and take it to our morgue because at least it's a distraction. As I follow them out into the anteroom I look for Hurley, but he's nowhere to be found.

As soon as the funeral home vehicle takes off, Izzy turns to me and says, "Arnie is still at the office so he can do the intake. I don't plan to post Carla until tomorrow morning and I know this has been a rough day for you, so why don't you take the rest of the day off?"

Knowing I'm dangerously distracted, I take him up on his offer, stripping off my gloves and tossing them in the trash. I drive home in a somber mood, where I find Hoover curled up in the middle of my bed sound asleep. Nestled between his front paws sleeping just as soundly is Rubbish. I strip down to my undies and crawl in beside them. They waken, but when they see I'm joining them, they both settle down and go back to sleep.

Surrounded by my warm, snuggly little furballs, I curl up into a ball and start to cry.

After a fitful night of pacing, crying, and occasionally sleeping, I awaken the next morning to the ring of my cell phone. Daylight is peeking in through my windows and a quick glance at the clock tells me it's a little after seven. Memories of the previous day's events come flooding back as I grab my phone and I mutter a silent prayer that it's Hurley on the other end, calling to give me another chance and forgive me for my stupidity.

"Hello?"

"Did I wake you?" My spirits sag as I realize it's Izzy, not Hurley.

"No," I lie. I sit up and rub the sleep and dried tears from my eyes, then look over at Rubbish and Hoover, who are curled up together on the other side of the bed. "What's up?" I ask, throwing the covers off and climbing out of bed.

"Have you seen this morning's paper?"

I shake my head, then remember that I'm on the phone. "No. How bad is it?"

"Well, your picture fills the front page above the fold, right beneath a headline that reads, LOCAL WOMAN DEAD, INVESTIGATION ONGOING. You look appropriately stricken. Beneath that is another, smaller headline that says, PSYCHIATRIST ON THE LAM, with a picture of Luke Nelson. The article doesn't say anything about the sexual abuse or that Carla killed herself, just that Nelson is wanted as a person of interest and can't be found. Hurley said he wants to keep the details quiet for now."

"You talked to Hurley this morning?"

"Yep, I called him right before I called you. My mother fell yesterday and she's in the hospital so I need to run up there and see her this morning."

"Sylvie fell? Is she all right?" I'm concerned not only because of my friendship with Izzy, but because the cottage I'm living in was originally built by Izzy for Sylvie when her health was failing. She gradually improved and moved out after a year because she's fiercely independent and has little tolerance for Izzy's lifestyle. She's been going strong ever since at the ripe old age of eighty-something, but if she's had a setback and needs to move back in, I might lose my digs.

"Not to worry," Izzy says, reading my mind. "The hospital said she didn't break anything. They diagnosed a mild case of pneumonia that temporarily weakened her but her doctor said she should be good as new in no time."

I breathe a small sigh of relief.

"Anyway, because I'm heading up to the hospital, I won't be doing the post on Carla until later today. That's why I called Hurley. He said he wanted to be there for the autopsy so I wanted to let him know I'm not planning to start it until around eleven."

"Okay. Anything you need me to do in the meantime?" I've made my way to the kitchen to start the coffeepot up and both Rubbish and Hoover have followed. They are sitting patiently at my feet, looking up at me with beseeching eyes.

"Actually, there is," Izzy says. "We need more photos of the scene. I shot some yesterday in the room where Carla's body was but I didn't have time to finish because I got the call about my mother and had to head for the hospital."

"No problem. I'll run by first thing this morning and get the pictures for you."

"Thanks. The digital camera is in the office on my desk. I'll see you at eleven."

"Tell Sylvie hi for me."

"Will do."

I hang up, glad for the revised schedule since I overslept. After letting Hoover out to do his morning ablutions, I fill up the critters' respective food bowls and admire Hoover's restraint in not eating Rubbish's food after he snorts up his own. A shower, a cup of coffee, and a bowl of cereal later I head for the office.

I find the camera right where Izzy said it would be and sitting next to it is his digital recorder. Remembering that Hurley has mine, I grab Izzy's, figuring I can use it if I find anything at the scene I want to note. I tuck the recorder in my pocket, put the camera and a handful of gloves inside my purse, and then make my way to Nelson's office.

The place is locked and sealed up with crime scene tape, but Junior Feller is pulling guard duty in a squad car parked out front. I park a couple spaces away, grab a pair of gloves and the camera, toss my purse on the car floor, and get out, locking the car behind me.

Junior rolls his window down as I approach. He's sipping coffee and reading the morning paper. I see my face plastered across the front of it and realize that Alison did, indeed, use the last picture she shot of me.

"Morning, Junior."

"Hey, Mattie. Nice picture."

"I guess." He makes no big deal about my status as a headliner. In a town the size of Sorenson, just about everyone makes it into the paper at some point.

"You need in?" he says, gesturing toward the office door.

"I do. I need to snap some shots we didn't get yesterday."

"No problem." He balances his coffee cup on the dashboard and climbs out of the car. We walk up to the door together, managing to attract a crowd of curious onlookers in the process. After he slices through the evidence tape and opens the door for me, he says, "Holler if you need anything."

I thank him, don my gloves, and head inside. I take off my jacket and remove the recorder from its pocket, turning it to voice activation mode. I then slip it in its usual place, nestled between my breasts. I make a mental note to not tell Izzy where it was lest he worry it has girl cooties on it.

I snap some photos of the front room from as many angles as I can manage, making a verbal note when I shoot the corner where Luke Nelson was treated by the EMTs. Once I feel I've gotten what I need, I head into the office area.

The room is cold and dark; the blinds on the one window have been closed to keep people from peeking in. I flip the light switch and the first thing I notice is the files I was wading through yesterday still stacked atop Nelson's desk. I shoot a couple of pictures of the area, set the camera down, and then go about returning the files I looked through yesterday to the drawer. It takes two loads to get them all in and unbeknownst to me a hanger hook on a file in the second half catches on my sleeve. When I pull back, the hooked half of the folder comes with me and its contents spill out, some inside the drawer, some on the floor.

Cursing, I unhook the file and toss it on the desk. I round up the papers that spilled in the drawer and stuff them back inside. Then I kneel down to gather up the ones on the floor. A small slip of paper has slid far beneath the desk and I have to crawl underneath to get it. When I try to get back up, I miscalculate and bash my head on the underside of the desk's middle drawer, aggravating the area where my stitches are.

"Damn it," I mutter, wincing and rubbing my head gingerly. As I'm waiting for the pain to recede, I look at the paper that caused all my misery and see that it's a receipt from an Internet store. I start to toss it aside but the name of the store—Spies R Us—catches my eye. As I read further I see that the receipt is for a video camera, but not just any camera. This receipt is for a nanny cam.

Chapter
45

I stare at the receipt a moment, pondering its significance. Why would Nelson need a nanny cam?

I manage to crawl out from under the desk without incurring further injury, and I place the receipt on the blotter and snap a picture of it. Then I start examining the office with a new, more critical eye. The first place I look is the bookcase, but as I'm shuffling volumes around it dawns on me that this isn't the room Nelson would want to record in.

I grab my camera and head into the counseling room. Dried blood still covers the wall and couch, and the smell makes my breakfast churn threateningly. To distract myself, I focus on shooting as many pictures as I can. Even though Carla's body is no longer here, I keep seeing it in my mind's eye, lying on the sofa like a ragdoll, her hand on the floor filled with blood, the gun lying nearby.

And then it hits me: it was her right hand on the floor, the one affected by the stroke. Based on what I observed at her house, there is no way she could have used that hand to shoot herself. I make a verbal note of the fact for the recorder and a mental note to call Izzy when I'm done and fill him in.

I set the camera down on the table next to the stuffed chair and examine the rest of the room. I don't see anything obvious that looks like a camera, or anything that might be hiding a camera. But then I realize I'm not sure what a nanny cam looks like so I head back into the office and boot up the computer on Nelson's desk. I launch the Internet browser and type in the Web site that appears on the nanny cam receipt. Seconds later I'm looking at a page filled with cleverly designed mini-cameras.

I print the page off and carry it back into the counseling room with me. One by one I compare the items on the page with the items in the room. And it doesn't take me long to find what I'm looking for. I set the page aside and grab my camera again, this time shooting pictures of a part of the room I'd missed earlier: the ceiling.

I drag Nelson's chair across the room until it's positioned beneath the smoke detector. The cushion is too thickly stuffed to make for a solid foot base so I remove it and, in doing so, I find something crammed between it and the chair's side: an elastic leg stocking. Something about the stocking niggles at my brain and I hold it up and stare at it a moment. But I'm too distracted by the smoke detector, so I toss the stocking over the back of the chair for later consideration.

When I climb up and peer more closely at the smoke detector, I can now see the lens hiding inside it. I'm about to try to pry the outside portion loose to get a better view when I remember how I've mucked things up in this investigation already. I decide it would be better to go outside to get Junior as a witness, and my cell phone so I can call Hurley.

As I climb down from the chair, I nearly fall when a female voice startles me.

"You just had to meddle, didn't you?"

I jump onto the floor and spin around to find Jackie Nash standing in the doorway of the room. She is leaning against the doorjamb, one hand held behind her back, the other playing with her hair. Though her posturing is casual, the rest of her appearance is not. Her hair is mussed and wild looking, her eyes have an angry glint to them, and her mouth is pinched tight with fury. The scars on her face appear more vivid than usual and I can see that she's not wearing her usual make-up.

"Jackie? What are you doing here? This is a crime scene. You shouldn't be in here."

"And yet here I am," she says, flashing me a humorless smile.

That smile makes me cringe and the hairs on the back of my neck begin to crawl. "How did you get in? Where's Junior?"

She shrugs. "Last time I saw him he was hanging on the back bumper of his car flirting with a bunch of women. So typical," she chastises, shaking her head. "His type is always paying attention to the cute ones. They never notice me, unless it's to pretend they don't see my scars and aren't laughing behind my back."

"No one is laughing behind your back, Jackie." Even as I say the words, I can hear how false they ring to my own ears. I've been witness to what she's describing too many times.

"Sure they do," she says. "I've gotten used to it over the years. I'd pretty much resigned myself to a lifetime of lonely spinster-hood, working at Dairy Airs until I die. But then Luke came along and everything changed."

"I'm glad the counseling has helped you," I tell her, fearing it hasn't helped nearly enough.

She scoffs. "Counseling? Luke doesn't give me counseling. He loves me. Unlike the other cretins out there, he's able to see past all of this"—she thrusts the scarred side of her face toward me—"to the real me underneath it all."

"You're *dating* Luke Nelson?"

"Call it that if you want, but it's something much more. We're in love."

I wince, not relishing the revelations I'm about to make. "Oh, Jackie, you don't understand. Nelson was just leading you on." I move toward her, thinking that a sympathetic hand on her shoulder might soften the blow. "The man is . . . sick. He's got girl-friends in several different towns and—"

The hand behind Jackie's back shoots forward and I realize why she had it hidden. She's holding a knife, a really big knife. And it's now pointed straight at me. I stop where I am, afraid to move, afraid to breathe.

"He doesn't care about any of those other women," Jackie says irritably. "They came after him. He told me all about them, how

they hang all over him, begging him to sleep with them." Her lip
curls in disgust and she shakes her head sadly. "They are nothing
more to him than an outlet for his needs. I'm the only one he
truly loves. I'm the only one that really knows how to take care of
his needs."

Suddenly the relevance of the elastic stocking dawns on me.
It's the same type that Jackie would wear to help heal her wound
grafts and scar revisions. She must have taken it off during a dal-
liance here in the office with Nelson.

I stare at her, unsure of what to do or say next. Judging from
the crazed look in her eyes, a look I've seen plenty of times before on mental patients at the hospital, she is beyond reason. It
also means she is highly unpredictable and very dangerous. And
she's blocking my only exit from the room.

Deciding that a dose of shocking reality is my only hope, I
couch my next words carefully and try to keep my voice calm despite the fact that my insides are quaking. "You don't understand, Jackie. There's more to it than that. Luke Nelson is a
rapist and a very ill man. He needs help."

She shakes her head again, harder and faster. "*You* don't understand. Luke just has special needs, that's all. He explained it
to me, how his sexual drive is higher than most and he has to find
other outlets to get release. It's not an emotional thing with those
other women, only with me. I'm willing to let him get what he
needs physically, as long as he comes back to me in the end."

I stare at her, disbelieving. "He's raping women, Jackie."

"No, no, no. Those other women, they all slept with him of
their own free will."

"I'm not talking about the other women he was dating, Jackie.
I'm talking about his patients. He's been drugging them and
then raping them. I have proof. He needs to be stopped."

Jackie laughs, but it's a brittle, humorless, ugly sound. "Yeah,
that's what that bitch Shannon said, too, when she found out. She
said she had to report him because what he was doing was
wrong." She takes a few steps into the room, moving closer to
me. The knife now hangs at her side, but I harbor no illusions
about her ability to use it in a flash. "But I knew the real reason

Shannon wanted to report him," she goes on. "She was just jealous because she didn't have the kind of relationship with Luke that I have. She wanted to ruin it for me, to take away my one chance at happiness."

The significance of her words washes over me like an icy shower. Other facts crash together in my mind, suddenly making a horrifying sense. The blood type found in Shannon's kitchen was the very rare B negative and I now recall that Jackie's blood type is the same. We always had to make sure we had it on hand at the hospital whenever she came in for surgery. And I knew Jackie had mental and emotional problems because of all those times I cared for her in the ER during her breakdowns. I also recall Jackie's incessant questions about how the investigation was going every time I saw her, and how nervously she behaved. I remember the spilt glasses of milk and the slices of cheesecake we found on Shannon's kitchen table, which I now realize ruled Erik out. Per Jackie's own words—obviously not realizing she was clearing him in the process—Erik is lactose intolerant.

I'm afraid to ask my next question but have to. "Did you kill Shannon?"

I half expect her to deny it but instead she says, "Of course I did. I had to get rid of her to keep Luke safe. And it would have worked, too, if you hadn't gone and stuck your nose into things. It's all your fault that that other woman figured everything out and came here yesterday. She caught me and Luke making love and then she tried to kill him. Darned near did, too. If I hadn't wrestled the gun from her, she might have shot him a second time."

"You killed Carla, too?"

"I had to, don't you see? She came charging in here full of accusations that would have ruined everything. I had to shut her up for good. Luke and I decided we could pass it off as a suicide but you had to come back and keep on snooping. I knew you'd muck it all up. And now Luke is gone." The tenor of her voice has risen to just shy of hysteria. "Where is he?" she asks shrilly. "Where did you make him go?"

"I have no idea," I say, backpedaling. "He disappeared yesterday right after we questioned him."

She moves closer and raises the knife, waving it in front of her like a blind man's cane. "It's all your fault," she says, clearly angry. "Why couldn't you just leave him alone? Why couldn't you just leave *us* alone?"

I take another step back and feel the chair hit the back of my legs. My mind scrambles, trying to decide what to do next, trying to figure a way out of this mess. I remember the recorder nestled in my bra and decide I need to keep her talking. Junior Feller is parked right out front and if luck is on my side, he might come in to check on things. If not, at least I can record what Jackie says as evidence. Then my mind registers what the evidence will be used for—to help solve my murder—and I shudder.

"I don't believe you killed Shannon," I tell Jackie. "I don't see how you could have."

She smirks. "It was easy. She told me about the gun; in fact she asked me if I wanted to buy it. She said Erik had given it to her but it made her nervous having it around. At first I told her I wasn't interested, but when she told me what she'd discovered about Luke, I changed my mind. I went over there under the pretense of looking at the gun to see if I wanted to buy it. And then I shot her."

The flat tone of her voice as she admits this sends chills down my spine. How could I not have seen how disturbed she was before this?

Jackie says, "Since I knew Erik was the primary suspect, I took the gun with me when I went to the hospital with Mom for one of her radiation treatments. I had scheduled a mammogram for myself at the same time and it was easy to sneak the gun into a linen closet while I was in the X-ray department. I was careful to wipe it down so my fingerprints wouldn't be on it, and I knew someone would find it eventually and assume the inevitable . . . that Erik had hidden it there."

"That was very clever," I say, hoping a little ego stroking might buy me some time.

"Well, it would have been if you'd just minded your own damned *bus*iness."

She punctuates the sentence with a downward slash of her knife through the air. And then she starts toward me. Desperate and out of any other ideas, I decide to try a diversion. I purposefully shift my gaze over her shoulder toward the office door and look startled.

It works. Jackie whips around, wielding the knife in front of her, ready to strike at anyone or anything.

And then the most amazing thing happens. Hurley appears in the doorway, right in front of Jackie, right in front of the business end of that knife. Jackie shrieks like a harridan and lunges at him, plunging the knife into his chest.

Chapter
46

Jackie drives the knife home with a bloodcurdling scream and then pulls it out again.

"No!" I yell. "Jackie, for God's sake, no!"

Hurley lets out a little grunt, his eyes wide with surprise, and then slumps to the floor. I charge at Jackie's back with a guttural growl and when I'm only a foot or two away, she hears me and starts to turn.

I ram her on her left side and the two of us fall to the floor, landing hard. Her right arm, with the knife in her hand, hits a floor lamp and the knife clatters to the floor, leaving a splatter trail of Hurley's blood in its wake. I hear the breath leave Jackie's lungs with a *whoomph*. I push myself off of her, scramble across the floor on my hands and knees, grab the knife, and then quickly roll onto my back, the knife in front of me, ready for Jackie to come at me. But she's curled into a fetal position on the floor, crying.

I look beyond her to the doorway and my heart sinks. Hurley is sprawled in the doorway on his back, the left side of his shirt-front soaked with blood. I get up and hurry over to him, praying he's still alive. Setting the knife on the floor, I quickly assess him, see that he's breathing and conscious, and then rip his shirt open. The wound, an incision nearly an inch long and who knows how deep near his left shoulder, is oozing a steady flow of blood.

Hurley looks up at me and manages a weak smile. "I've fanta-sized about you ripping my shirt off, Winston, but I don't think I'm quite up to it right now." I smile despite how frightened I am for him. "What the hell happened?" he asks.

"Jackie stabbed you. She killed Shannon, Hurley. She's crazy and I should have seen it. I'm so sorry. This is all my fault."

His eyebrows arch. "How is it your fault?"

"She was coming toward me with the knife and I was trying to distract her. I made like there was someone behind her, hoping she would turn to look. And then suddenly you really were be-hind her. I didn't know you were here."

He coughs and the blood flow from his wound surges. I look around frantically for something to dampen it, and when I can't find anything I take my blouse off and wad it up.

Hurley blinks hard several times and shakes his head. "There you go again . . . taking your clothes off." He pauses and I notice his breathing is shallower. "Just . . . can't . . . help . . . yourself . . . with me . . . can you?"

The words come out in weak, gasping breaths, ramping up my panic. I glance back at Jackie and see with relief that she's still curled up and sobbing a few feet away. I push the wadded blouse harder against Hurley's chest wound, making him wince and moan.

"I'm sorry, I know it hurts but I have to do it," I tell him. "You're bleeding pretty heavily." He moans again and his eyes roll up in his head.

"Hurley, where is your cell phone?"

He doesn't answer me and as his head lolls to the side I realize he has passed out. I feel my panic rising and push it back down.

"Damn it, Hurley, don't you do this to me," I mutter as I push down harder on the wound with one hand and then start franti-cally searching his pockets with the other. It's not in his shirt or his pants. Finally I find it clipped to his belt behind his gun hol-ster. With a shaking hand I manage to unclip it and dial 911.

"911 operator, do you have an emergency?"

"Yes, this is Mattie Winston with the medical examiner's office. I need police and an ambulance right away. I'm with Detective Steve Hurley and he's been stabbed." Hurley's face looks horribly pale and a lump forms in my throat. "Please hurry," I plead, my voice cracking.

"Mattie? It's Jeannie," the operator says. Jeannie and I have a history; she's been on duty every time I've had to call 911. She didn't do very well the first time but that's because she was new to the job and I gave her a challenging case. "Where are you?" Jeannie asks, her voice calm and efficient. She's definitely gotten better.

My mind struggles to come up with the address but I can't think of it. "It's an office. Dr. Luke Nelson's office. I don't know the exact address but it's in the strip mall on the corner of South and Nesbitt. Junior Feller is parked out front."

"There's an officer there?" Jeannie asks, sounding confused.

"He's outside. I don't think he knows what's happened."

"Hold on," Jeannie says. She puts me on hold for a few seconds and then comes back on. "Junior's coming in," she says. "And I've dispatched an ambulance to your location."

"Thanks, Jeannie," I say and then suddenly Junior is there.

"Holy shit," Junior says, taking in the scene. "What the hell happened?"

I drop Hurley's phone and feel for a pulse. It's there, but it's fast and thready. I nod toward Jackie. "She stabbed Hurley. He needs an ambulance. She also killed Shannon Tolliver and Carla Andrusson."

Junior looks momentarily confused. "She killed Shannon and Carla?" he echoes, moving closer to Jackie.

"She did. She confessed to me. She was having an affair with Nelson and apparently Shannon discovered what Nelson was doing and threatened to expose him. So Jackie killed her to shut her up and protect him. Here," I say, pulling the recorder from between my breasts. "I think I got the whole thing on tape."

Junior takes the recorder and drops it in his shirt pocket, then he walks over and cuffs Jackie. She puts up no resistance and he leaves her sobbing on the floor so he can come back to Hurley.

He talks into his shoulder mike and then tells me, "The ambulance is almost here."

This information is unnecessary since I can hear the siren close by but it reassures me just the same. "Hang in there, Hurley," I whisper. "You're going to be okay."

"Is he?" Junior asks. "That looks bad." He eyes the bloody blouse I'm holding, then I see his gaze shift briefly toward my chest.

"My jacket is in the other room. Can you get it for me?"

He fetches the jacket and briefly takes over wound dampening duties while I put it on. By the time I button it up I hear the ambulance siren out front and seconds later the EMTs come rushing in. Within minutes they have taken over the wound management, started an IV, and loaded Hurley onto a stretcher.

"I'm riding with you," I tell the EMTs. Since my tone leaves no room for equivocation and the guys on the crew know me, they nod their assent. I follow them out to the rig and wait for them to load Hurley inside before I climb in.

We zip through town at a hefty pace with full lights and sirens. It's a bumpy, rocky ride that leaves me gripping the bench seat and watching as Hurley's IV sways back and forth.

"His blood pressure is pretty low," one of the EMTs announces. "Eighty systolic."

Panic rears its ugly head again and I struggle to keep it at bay. But it isn't easy. Hurley's color is nearly as white as the sheets and the amount of blood I can see on the chest dressing makes my throat tighten. Tears sting at my eyes and I swipe irritably at them. Then I take Hurley's hand in mine and lean over close to his ear. "You better not die on me, Hurley," I tell him as we hit another bump. "Because I think I'm falling in love with you."

Chapter
47

Our arrival at the ER is organized chaos. The staff on duty knew we were coming, thanks to the EMTs' radio report. But because the town is so small, the time span from when they heard we were coming to our actual arrival is only a couple of minutes, giving them little time to prepare.

I hop out of the ambulance and then back out of the way as the EMTs unload Hurley and wheel him into the ER. I follow close on their heels, checking out the staff on duty as we head for the trauma room. I'm relieved to see Dr. Cannady since I know she has an extensive trauma background and is an excellent doc. The nurses on duty are top-notch, too, an older, seasoned crew that has seen far worse and had their patients live to tell about it.

I stand in the doorway to the trauma room watching them dance their chaotic ballet, fighting an urge to jump in and help. My heart is telling me to get in there but my mind knows it would be best to stay on the sidelines. Even though the activity in the room looks frenzied and hectic, everyone in the room has their assigned tasks and knows what to do. Given the level of emotion I'm feeling, I'm not sure I'd be capable of thinking straight and would just be in the way. But I feel helpless standing here doing nothing.

Hurley is quickly stripped down to his skivvies and I can't

help but admire the brief glimpse I get of his physique. Within minutes the crew has blood drawn, a second IV line going, a heart monitor in place, and a set of vital signs. Hurley's blood pressure is still frighteningly low and his heart is beating much too fast. Dr. Cannady orders the IV fluids opened wide and a stat portable chest X-ray.

Hurley is responding some, mumbling and moving, but I'm not close enough to tell if his words are making any sense or not.

I hear a mechanical sound closing in behind me and step aside to let the radiology tech into the room with the portable X-ray machine. Right behind her, much to my surprise, is David. Then it hits me; the staff would have paged the surgeon on call the minute they knew they had a stab wound victim on the way. He sees me, frowns, and stops.

"Mattie? What are you doing here?" He peers past me into the trauma room. "Who is that in there?" He looks concerned but also confused, no doubt because his first thoughts are that it's my mother or sister in there, but one quick look makes it obvious the patient is a man.

"It's Steve Hurley," I tell him.

"That cop? What happened to him? Did he get shot?"

I shake my head. "Jackie Nash went nuts and stabbed him. She tried to stab me, too."

I see curiosity flit across his face and know he wants more of an explanation but he stays focused. "Are you okay?" he asks, eyeing me from head to toe.

"I'm fine," I say, glancing into the trauma room. "But Hurley is in bad shape." I look back at my husband, the man I once loved, the man I was married to for seven years, the man who just a few nights ago pleaded for another chance, and realize he may hold Hurley's life in his hands. "Please help him, David." The words barely get out before my throat closes with emotion. Tears sting behind my eyes; I make a brief but futile attempt to keep them at bay, then swipe irritably at them as they course down my cheeks.

David stares at me a moment, then sighs. "You have a thing for this guy, don't you?"

I don't answer; I just stare back at him, my eyes pleading. I'm afraid to say too much, afraid to admit too much. I hear the clicks of the portable X-ray machine and Dr. Cannady's voice follows.

"Dr. Winston? We could use your help in here."

With that, David disappears into the room. The flurry of activity continues and moments later the X-ray tech returns with film in hand. David puts it up on a wall-mounted light box and studies it for a few seconds. From where I'm standing I can see the X-ray clearly and note with relief that both of Hurley's lungs appear to be well aerated and expanded.

David confirms this. "The lungs look okay. I think the bleeding is our biggest problem. Let's get him upstairs so I can open him up."

As the nurses are making the final preparations for sending Hurley to the OR, David comes back out of the room and pulls me off to the side. "I can't say I'm happy about you moving on to someone else already but I know it's my own fault. And despite my feelings, you know I'll do my best."

I do. Despite his personal failings in the husband department, David is a dedicated and talented surgeon. Even if it's a bit awkward, I'm glad David is here because I know Hurley will be in good hands. "Thank you, David."

David takes off to get himself ready for surgery. I hear the nurses in the trauma room releasing the brakes on the stretcher and getting all the attached equipment ready for transfer. I turn to head back into the room to get one last look at Hurley, hoping to say some final words of encouragement even if I'm unsure he'll hear them. But before I reach the door, someone else rushes into the room. I blink hard, barely believing what I'm seeing. Alison Miller dashes to Hurley's bedside, grabs his hand, and leans over the railing to look at him.

"Oh, Stevie," she cries. "Are you okay?" She looks over at Dr. Cannady. "Is he okay?"

"He has some internal bleeding. We're taking him to the OR."

"Can I go with him?" Alison pleads.

Cannady defers to the nurses, one of whom nods and says,

"You can come with us as far as the doors to the surgical suite but then you'll have to go to the waiting room."

Alison nods. "Thank you," she says. Then she raises Hurley's hand to her mouth and kisses it. "He has to be okay," she says. "We're supposed to have dinner tonight."

What the hell? I'm not sure what surprises me most: the inanity of Alison's thought processes or the knowledge that she and Hurley had a dinner date planned. But then, what did I expect? Hurley clearly overheard me telling Alison that I had no romantic designs on him, that he was merely a toy to help me pass the time.

As the nurses whisk Hurley's stretcher out of the room and toward the elevator, I briefly consider trying to muscle Alison out of the way, or at the very least taking a spot on the other side of the stretcher and going with them. But then I catch a glimpse of Hurley's face and see that he's awake. He's looking up at Alison's face as if she is the angel of mercy herself, and then he smiles and says something to her.

My heart sinks. I realize what a huge mess I've made of things—romantically, personally, and professionally—and wish I could go back and undo some of what I've done. But I can't. My first thought is to head home and share my sorrows with Ben and Jerry and my fuzzy companions, but I don't want to leave the hospital until I know Hurley is okay. Nor do I want to share waiting room space with Alison. So I do the next best thing instead and head for the hospital cafeteria.

One Reuben sandwich and piece of peach pie later, Izzy walks into the cafeteria.

"Figured I'd find you here," he says. "I heard what happened when I was upstairs visiting Mom."

Typical. News always has traveled fast in this place.

"It was awful," I tell him. And then the whole story bursts out of me. "I went to take your pictures and I found this receipt Nelson had for a nanny cam and figured out that he had one mounted in the ceiling in his counseling room so I tried to take some pictures of it but then Jackie appeared out of nowhere and started waving this huge knife at me with this crazy look in her eyes and I didn't know what to do." I pause for a second to suck in a ragged breath and then continue. "Then Jackie tells me how she and Nelson have been dating and how Shannon found out about Nelson's little side activities with his patients and was going to report him, so Jackie killed her. She killed Carla, too," I add, telling him how I figured out Carla's death wasn't a suicide. "That car accident Jackie was in years ago scarred a lot more than her skin," I conclude. "She's crazy, Izzy, totally and completely crazy. I don't know how I never picked up on it before. And today she wanted to kill me. I tried to keep her calm by talking but then I ran out of things to say and she was coming at me so I tried distracting her by looking behind her as if someone was there, thinking maybe I could make a run for it. Except all of a sudden Hurley really *was* there and then Jackie just stabbed him." I lose it then, and start to sob. "She just stabbed him and now he might die and it's all my fault."

Izzy frowns and puts a reassuring hand on my shoulder. "It's not your fault, Mattie. You didn't stab him, Jackie did."

I dismiss his objection with an impatient wave of my hand and try to get myself under control, using my napkin to blow my nose. "You know what I mean, Izzy."

"The nurses upstairs said Hurley was in surgery," Izzy says, and I nod. "They said David was operating on him," he adds, and I nod again. "Interesting situation," he concludes.

"David won't let his personal feelings get in the way. And he's an excellent surgeon. Hurley is in good hands."

Izzy nods thoughtfully, then says, "I can have Arnie help me with the autopsy today so take the rest of the day off. After all you've been through you'll be pretty useless in the office anyway."

I smile at him. "I should probably be offended by that comment but I suspect you're right. And I would like to hang here until I know Hurley is okay. So I think I'll take you up on the offer. Thanks."

"No problem. If you don't mind, I'm going to hang until Hurley's out of surgery, too."

"Thanks, I'd like that."

"Want to head up to the surgical waiting room?"

"Not really. Alison's up there."

"So?"

I fill him in on what happened the other day when Hurley overheard me talking to Alison, and the scene that took place in the ER a little while ago. "I've totally destroyed my chances with Hurley," I conclude. "Alison clearly has her clutches in him at this point, and while I'm glad he has someone, I don't think I can stand to watch the two of them mooning over one another."

Izzy looks at me with a sad expression and shakes his head. "You are so clueless sometimes," he says.

"Tell me about it. If I'd known Hurley was standing there I never would have said those things about him."

"That's not what I mean. Come on." He stands, pushes his chair in under the table, and takes my tray of dirty dishes.

"Where are we going?"

"Upstairs."

I follow him to the elevator and from there to the third floor surgical waiting room. I expect to see Alison sitting there waiting, but there's no sign of her. One of the OR nurses, a young gal named Kate, appears.

"Mattie! Glad I found you. David wanted to let you know that Detective Hurley is doing very well. He's in recovery. The knife nicked an artery in his shoulder but we were able to suture it up and stabilize him. You can come in and see him if you want."

She's extending me a special privilege since I know that family members and visitors aren't typically allowed in the recovery area. I'm grateful but also wondering if the courtesy was extended to anyone else. "Is Alison Miller in there?" I ask.

Kate laughs. "Not hardly. She left right after we came up from the ER because Detective Hurley kept asking for you the whole way. He kept saying he wanted Mattie, and needed Mattie, and where the hell was Mattie, anyway. Alison was pretty ticked and lit out of here in a snit."

"He said all that?" I say, stunned.

"See," Izzy says. "I told you you were clueless."

I remember the stab of sadness and jealousy I felt when I saw Hurley looking up at Alison earlier as they were leaving the ER. I had no idea he was asking for me. "Wow," I say, still digesting it all.

"Yeah, wow," Kate agrees. "You are one lucky lady. And may I add that you have superb taste in men. That detective is one heck of a hottie. So come on." She turns toward the recovery area and motions for me to follow behind her. "It's not nice to keep a hottie waiting."

Chapter 48

It's been just over a week since Jackie Nash revealed that she's a few fries shy of a Happy Meal, and everything is right with the world. Well, almost everything. Jackie is locked away inside a mental institution up north and though it's now known for sure that she killed Shannon Tolliver and Carla Andrusson, it's unlikely she will ever stand trial. After the incident in Nelson's office, she withdrew into a babbling, incoherent puddle of scarred human flesh. Word has it she is catatonic and the few slim threads of reason that remained in her brain have finally snapped.

The blood DNA evidence we sent to Madison came back and proved a match for Jackie. When a cut was discovered on the bottom of her right foot—most likely incurred when she stepped on a piece of the broken glass we found in Shannon's kitchen—it became clear that she was at the scene at the time of the murder. During a search of Jackie's house, the cops found the blood-covered shoes she was wearing with a neat little hole sliced through the bottom of the right one. It also became clear to me why I thought something about Jackie was different whenever I saw her. The scarring from the fire left her with contractions that made her favor her left leg, but the cut on her foot, which was beginning to show signs of infection, had her favoring the other leg, too, giving her an awkward limp, different from her usual.

Erik Tolliver is now free and totally exonerated. I heard through the hospital grapevine that he resigned from his position there and has plans to move to Arizona where his mother lives. Carla's and Shannon's funerals were held within the last few days, both to stunning turnouts. Carla's death has left me with residual feelings of guilt I may never work through. The funerals were somber, sad affairs, but they also left me with a sense of closure and new beginnings.

And speaking of new beginnings, Bjorn Adamson and Irene Keller are the latest hot item in town. Rumor has it they plan to wed in a few days, a date that seems a bit rushed to me, but I suppose their respective ages has something to do with that. Bjorn's new catheter bags seem to be working well and now that Irene is in the picture, I feel confident that I will no longer have to worry about urine duties.

William-not-Bill and my mother have been on two dinner dates already, and judging from the fact that they were both reportedly banned from the Peking House restaurant after returning their plates five times each because they weren't clean enough, I'm guessing it's a match made in heaven. I won't be at all surprised to learn that William-not-Bill is going to become my next stepfather sometime in the near future.

Rubbish and Hoover have settled in nicely together and so far the lost-and-found ad I placed in the local paper a few days ago hasn't garnered any responses. I'm hoping that continues to be the case because the little furball has wormed his way into my heart. It's a bit frightening how fast he's growing however, gaining weight with more ease than I do, and that's without the benefits of ice cream.

David and I seem to have reached a détente in our relationship. He's still not happy about our breakup and doesn't want to talk divorce yet, preferring to "wait it out and see what happens." But his denial doesn't bother me as much as it once did because I think the reality of my growing feelings for Hurley is starting to sink in. Plus David's making an effort to be fair with our money situation. He handed over the check for my car and while I briefly considered using it to buy some wheels that were a little less conspicuous, the hearse is kind of growing on me and Hoover loves riding in the back of it. There are enough peculiar smells in there to keep any dog happy for a long, long time.

Despite all the good that's come out of the events of the past couple weeks, several downers remain. The nanny cam in Luke Nelson's office, and some password-protected files on his computer made it clear just how twisted the man is. Investigators found nearly two dozen videos of him drugging and sexually assaulting seven of his female patients. The resulting emotional backlash has been horrifying for the victims, a situation compounded by the fact that Luke Nelson has apparently disappeared from the face of the earth. Despite a nationwide APB and the involvement of the FBI since there is reason to suspect he engaged in similar activities when he was in Florida, there hasn't been a single sighting or report of him being seen anywhere. Though I suspect he's far away from Sorenson by now, the knowledge that he's still out there somewhere has me looking over my shoulder more often than I like.

I'm pretty easy to find right about now. Two days ago, a picture of my half-naked body standing beside the Heinriches' Caddy and Bitsy Conklin's rotting corpse appeared on the front page of a national tabloid. At first I blamed Alison, figuring she'd sold the pictures out of revenge. But then I remembered how Hurley made her turn over the memory card to me, which I had stuffed in the pocket of his jacket I figured out why the dry cleaning lady was so willing to give me a half-price deal. The dry cleaning store has been closed all week and the owners have disappeared. I don't know how much money they got for the pictures on that card, but it must have been enough for them to relocate.

Despite the front-page picture, the story inside the tabloid barely mentioned me and didn't include my name. Fortunately, the saga of the battling Heinrich-Conklin offspring and the startling revelations about Bitsy and Gerald's new wills were deemed more newsworthy than the underwear-clad deputy coroner standing next to the bodies. Of course, that hasn't stopped all the locals from commenting on it. The phone in the ME's office has been ringing off the hook since the paper appeared, and rumor has it Lucien was seen buying up an entire news rack of the paper the day it hit the stands.

One of the few good things to come out of all the events of the past couple of weeks is that Hurley recovered from his injuries. He was discharged from the hospital two days after his surgery and though he's still a little wan from the blood loss and limited on what he can do with his left arm thanks to some muscle damage there, he's back on the job and looking as hot as ever. Even better is the fact that Alison hasn't been sniffing around him of late. And the cherry on this sundae is my dinner date with Hurley tonight, payment on our wager regarding Erik Tolliver's guilt or innocence.

I'm very excited about it but also nervous as hell. Though I spent a lot of time visiting Hurley while he was in the hospital, so did a ton of other people. I was never alone with him and all of the conversations that took place were centered on the case. We never touched on anything personal and I'm still not sure if he heard my whispered words to him in the ambulance. The closest we have come so far to any sort of personal revelation was when I first appeared at his bedside in the recovery room. He looked up at me, smiled, and said, "It's about time you showed up." I told him I'd been there all along, just on the sidelines, and then his nurse gave him a shot of morphine through his IV and he was out until he was taken to his room.

Hoover and Rubbish are sitting on my bed watching curiously as I go through my usual attempts to find something suitable to wear. I try on a blue dress with a tight, low-cut bodice that gives me Grand Canyon cleavage. I add a V-shaped necklace that looks like a directional sign to the river bottom, and finish it off with a pair of navy blue pumps.

"What do you think of this one?" I ask the furballs, promenading for them both. Rubbish yawns, contorts himself into an impossible position, and starts to lick his butt. Hoover cocks his head to the side and whines.

"Yeah, you're right. Too slutty," I say, peeling the dress off.

Next I try a pair of beige slacks and a black, slightly see-through blouse that shows off some of my new lingerie.

"Better?" I ask the judges, posing again. Hoover just stares at me and sighs; Rubbish hocks up a hair ball.

Ditching that outfit, I next opt for something simpler; black slacks, a long, cream-colored blouse with a mandarin collar, and a low-heeled pump. Hoover, who has just lived up to his name by scarfing up the hairball Rubbish deposited on my comforter, licks his lips and barks his approval. And just in time. A second later I hear a knock on my door.

My heart is racing as I head out to the living room. Hoover follows on my heels, curious and wary since this is the first time anyone has come to the house since he's been here. I tell him to sit, which he does dutifully, and then I open the door.

There on my doorstop stands Hurley in all his long-legged, dark-haired, magnificently healed glory. He's wearing black slacks and a black sport coat with an azure-colored shirt that makes his eyes look like the color of the sky on a bright fall day.

He eyes me from head to toe and says, "You look great."

"Thanks. So do you."

He grins boyishly and says, "I figured the colors black and blue were appropriate, given the way I've spent the past week."

His words tweak my lingering guilt over what happened and I start to mutter an apology but Hoover, having exhausted his ability to remain patient, makes his presence known by running over to smell Hurley's feet.

"Who is this?" Hurley says, squatting down and giving Hoover a scratch behind both ears.

"Hoover." Hurley eyes me skeptically and I shrug. "Trust me. If you spent any time around him at all, you'd understand. I found him last week hanging out by the garbage Dumpster at the grocery store, starving and frightened."

"It's about time you came to your senses and got a real pet."

"Well, he isn't technically mine yet. He might belong to someone else. I ran an ad in the lost-and-found section the other day."

Hurley is stroking Hoover along his back and the dog's tail is wagging so hard he's thumping out a rhythm on the doorjamb.

Can't say I blame him. I'd wag my tail, too, if Hurley was stroking me.

"You have to keep him," Hurley says, giving Hoover a final pat on the head and then standing back up.

"I hope to." I summon Hoover back inside, grab my purse and coat, and shut my front door. "Ready?" I ask Hurley. He nods and takes my coat, holding it for me so I can slip it on. Then he walks over and opens his car's passenger door for me. I settle inside and fasten my seat belt. Hoover made for a handy distraction at the door, but now my nervousness has returned full force. I'm running dozens of conversational scenarios through my mind, wondering how the evening will play out, curious as to how our relationship might progress by night's end.

Hurley climbs in on his side and starts the engine. Before he slips the car into gear, he turns and looks at me with a curious smile.

"There's something I want to ask you," he says, and my heart does a flip-flop as I think, *Here it comes*. "That day that Jackie stabbed me, were you riding in the ambulance with me?"

"I was," I say, swallowing hard. Had he heard what I said? And if so, is he happy about it? Worried? Scared? "Why do you ask?"

And with that I hear my cell phone ring. A split second later, so does Hurley's. He pulls his from his jacket pocket while I take mine out of my purse, and we both look at the displays.

"Damn," Hurley mutters.

"Crap," I mumble at the same time. And then we each answer our respective calls.

Once again, the dead are putting my love life on hold.